PHIL LOVI

Phil Lovesey is the son of aw
Peter Lovesey. Born in Essex in 196
Boys School before taking a foundation course in art, leading to a degree in film and television studies, and a career as London's laziest copywriter at a succession of the capital's most desperate advertising agencies. He turned to 'proper' writing in 1994 with a series of short stories, and was runner-up in the prestigious MWA 50th Anniversary short-story competition in 1995. *The Screaming Tree* is his fourth novel.

He lives in South Shropshire with his wife and three children, dividing his time between writing, hill-walking and long evenings in country pubs.

By the same author

When the Ashes Burn
Ploughing Potter's Field
Death Duties

PHIL LOVESEY

THE SCREAMING TREE

HarperCollins*Publishers*

This novel is entirely a work of fiction. The names, characters and incidents portrayed in it are the work of the author's imagination. Any resemblance to actual persons, living or dead, events or localities is entirely coincidental.

HarperCollins*Publishers*
77–85 Fulham Palace Road, London W6 8JB

www.**fire**and**water**.com

Published by HarperCollins*Publishers* 2002

3 5 7 9 10 8 6 4 2

A catalogue record for this book is available from the British Library

ISBN 0 00 712736 7

Typeset in Meridien by Palimpsest Book Production Limited, Polmont, Stirlingshire

Printed and bound in Great Britain by Clays Ltd, St Ives plc

ACKNOWLEDGMENTS

Earnest thanks from the author go to the real heroes behind this book: my agents Lisanne and Jane for being tough in all the right places; Julia Wisdom at HarperCollins for keeping the faith; Dr John Walsh for proof-reading and essential psycho-babble corrections; Penny Isaac for the French Lazarus connection; friends, relatives and colleagues who've all known when to keep their distance, and (maybe more importantly) when to offer alcoholic support; Rosie Gittings for far too much.

And finally to you, Luc, for more reasons than there are pages in the world . . .

For Mum and Dad –
for providing me with nothing but
the finest memories.

PREFACE

Tonight, I made it to the red button.

Thank God.

I was in the woods again, fooling around, then running, way too fast, stumbling over dead branches and protruding roots. And shrinking. My hands were shrinking, hairs receding, changing into the soft, puffy skin of a child. Then, the footsteps behind – his – gathering pace, gaining on me.

Panic.

Where's the button? Where's my red button?

Finally, I see it, glimpse it between two trees, my button, set on a plinth held by a little boy with fair hair and oh-so angry eyes. Nothing else matters but getting to that button before I am caught, pressing it, being safe again.

A loud crash behind.

The monster's gaining, getting too close, an extending arm reaching for me, snaking horribly through the undergrowth to catch my ankles, bring me down.

My mouth opens, but no scream comes.

But I'm there. I've beaten him. I reach the boy, stab at the button, ignoring the pain in his eyes – he always looks this way – and wait for the forest to fade away . . .

. . . become my bedroom once more.

Slowly; always so agonizingly slowly.

It sits on my bedside table, a small custom-made box housing a tape-recorder operated by pressing the glowing red button. Pressing it initiates the calming voice of Dr Richard Carter. For the thousandth time his pre-recorded speech tells me of the reasons behind these 'necessary nightmares'. I know every word and nuance by heart. As his soothing tones fill the bedroom, my wife stirs a little, mumbles something inaudible and pulls the duvet up around her ears, used to the ritual, as tolerant as anyone could be. I always try to make it up to her in the morning.

Tonight was the worst yet – the closest call. Another moment longer, and the chasing beast would have caught me. He would have devoured me. And then what? I don't wake up?

I close my eyes and see the boy. So angry with me, teasing me, enjoying my terror. His tactics are changing. With each new nightmare he stands further back in the woods, changes location, makes it harder for me to find that goddamned red button. Most of his hair is now missing, pulled out in clumps. The accusing face is paler, lips bluer than I've noticed before. He's dying, a lost soul deep within my nightmare.

My name is William Dickson.

I'm thirty-eight years old, caught between a past I still can't reconcile, and a future that's often too difficult to face. What happened to me shattered every conception of who I was, and what I was to become.

Sometimes I feel as though I've been screaming all my life.

1

Remember how it started, William? Three knocks on the door.

We can't be blamed for that, can we? We didn't start it. Didn't start any of it. They did. Those knocks on the door . . .

Three knocks on an Essex door.

Strange how things begin, what we remember, what refuses to be shifted. Like those three knocks. A signature almost, rapped out by a friend on a Saturday afternoon more than thirty years ago. Rat-tat-tat. No need to wonder who that could be – only Fat Norris used to knock like that. Every Saturday, when he came calling for me, William Dickson, his best friend. But try as I might, I can't remember what happened in the minutes immediately after those three knocks: something's been obliterated, erased. There have been many times when I've wanted to track down those elusive mundane memories, wrap myself tight in their safety. Far from death, far from murder, far from all that happened.

If this were a film, then I guess the scene would cut outside; we would see the two boys leaving the house together, heading off down the road in the late afternoon sunshine, innocence framed. Maybe there'd be some heavy strings underneath, a musical foreboding that all wasn't well, something terrible was about to happen.

As it is, I'm left to fill those missing moments with guesswork. Mum would probably have answered the door, seen Fat Norris standing there, asked about his mother (her best friend, Margot), then called for me. Dad would probably have been watching the black-and-white, maybe had my little sister Nicola wriggling impatiently on his lap. And me? I'd have jumped at the chance to go out and play with my pal Fat from number ninety-eight – anything to escape the crushing boredom of another Saturday afternoon stuck inside. I expect

Mum would have told us to be back in an hour or so. Then we'd have gone, stepped out. Simple as that.

So there I am, seven, short black hair, pale legs poking from grey school shorts, white vest on my delicate chest, joking with my pal as we take our first steps on a journey straight to hell. Which for Fat Norris, at least, would be mercifully short . . .

Born Edward Paul Norris just three days after me, and weighing in at close to eleven and a half pounds at birth, Fat Norris never really stood a chance of enjoying his first name, especially amongst us kids. He was fat, so we called him 'Fat'. In normal circumstances I'd probably never have been friends with him, but because our mothers were friends we were pushed together. Other kids taunted us, and in revenge I guess I used to torture Fat sometimes, like those times in the woods just behind the rec. when I felt the thrill of sprinting away from him, my thin legs jumping effortlessly over dead-mossed logs as he puffed and spluttered behind, begging me to stop. I would wait, hide behind a tree, then leap out screaming and yelling, watching his face, the effort required to replace fear with nervous laughter.

More memories from that afternoon.

Thick smoke from garden bonfires clung to our throats as we ambled down the road towards the rec. One or two cars passed us, drivers not giving the familiar scene a second glance. Just two young boys, strolling along: one fat, one thin.

'Mum gave us a shilling for pop and that,' Fat said brightly.

It was a lot of money in those days, and we stopped – as we always did – at Mr Godwin's for provisions, judging it to the last penny, the owner shaking his head as he watched us calculate exactly the number of liquorice laces that we could afford. Then we would eat the lot in the thick woods that ran from the broken rec. fence to the beginnings of the bare grass slope leading onto the railway line. It was quiet in there, away from the playground with its bright swings and slides, the abandoned cricket pavilion, dog-walkers and snoggers, the periphery of the park at tea-time.

It was summer, but that day in the woods it was cold. I have clear memories of the cold.

I might have asked whether Fat had seen his dad lately.

Fat's dad had divorced his mum four years before, confining his visits to Sunday jaunts that I often went along on. It was fantastic – his dad had a Jag. We didn't have a car.

Great memories. The excellent places his dad took us to, sitting on brown leather upholstery, two young boys goggle-eyed at London's attractions, eating ice-creams along Brighton's heaving shore, or watching the oval ball spin triumphantly through the uprights at Twickenham, then dozing off on the return journey, serenaded by his dad croaking along to the latest eight-track. My dad used to take us to the docks occasionally to show us where he worked. It didn't really compare.

But that Saturday afternoon Fat Norris didn't answer my question. He stayed as still and silent as the airless forest, frowning.

'You seeing him tomorrow?' I prompted hopefully, though it would have been pronounced 'tomorrah'. 'He taking us anywhere?'

The flat round face turned. 'Can't,' Fat said. 'Mum's got this new bloke, and he says Dad's in prison.'

'Prison?' Wow! Now this was cool. Fat's dad in prison? 'What for?'

'Dunno.'

'Did he kill someone?'

'Told you. Dunno.'

'Bet he did.' My mind churned with exciting possibilities. If Fat's dad was a murderer – some kind of gun-toting gangster – then think of the benefits. My best mate's dad shot/stabbed/battered someone to death. I'd be feared, revered by implication. No one would dare tease us again. But I had to be sure.

'He's really in prison, your dad?'

'According to this new bloke.'

'And who's he, then?'

'Dave. Uncle Dave, me mum wants me to call him.'

'And what does your mum say?'

'About what?'

'Your dad an' that?'

Fat sniffed, looked away. 'Told me to shut up. Then tells me to get round yours for an hour because she and him were going to talk about stuff.'

All of which rang true. There always seemed to be an 'uncle' around in Fat's life. David this week, Stan the last, maybe Don the next. And, being seven, I accepted this as easily as Fat. It was simply how things were. The routine. Fat didn't have a dad at home watching the telly all the time, or any brothers or sisters. He just had a mum who wore too much make-up and smoked fags and drank coffee with my mum, and who had an endless stream of 'uncles' around. But now, this 'prison' thing. This was new, different, exciting.

And then it hit me: with Fat's dad behind bars, there'd be no more Sunday trips out in the Jag. What I'd be gaining in a tough new image, I'd be losing in freebies. 'Can't be true, can it?' I pressed, anxious for the truth. I wondered if Fat was about to cry. 'Probably just a joke.'

'Right.' A long pause. Fat looked all around, seemed to be straining to hear something, plump fingers scratching at the flat back of his puffed wrist.

A stick cracked somewhere nearby.

'They reckon I'm stupid,' he said, an audible petulance to his tone. 'Reckon I don't know what they're doing up there.'

'Who? Up where?'

'Upstairs. Him and Mum. Uncle Dave. You know . . . doing it.'

'Oh, sure,' I say, thinking – what? Doing what?

'Making babies an' that,' Fat supplied.

Another mystery. I was seven, what the hell did I know about sex? 'Haven't got any brothers or sisters, though, have you?' I countered, frowning.

'Don't matter,' said Fats, gaining confidence, enjoying the unexpected chance to show his superior knowledge. 'It's all just playing with their bits and stuff. S'how Mum gets her money.'

'Right,' I said, trying not to sound too unworldly.

'Saw it once.'

'Saw what?'

Fat began scratching at the other wrist. ''member Uncle Andy? Saw them together one afternoon. S'posed to come round yours one Saturday, but you was out. Went back. Heard stuff. No clothes on, or nothing. Both of them. And there's like, all this grunting.'

At which point I too began to grunt, out of embarrassment more than anything else, hoping he'd join in, that a game of apes among the trees would follow, anything to deflect us. Because I feared his expression, his tone, the look in his dark brown eyes. All pointers to the truth as he'd seen it, heard it. My world was a safe one. Dull, but safe. There were no grunts, no 'uncles', no prison. It was as if the more I listened to him, the more I'd somehow be dragged in.

'I'm watching through this crack in the door, and Mum's smoking.' He paused to remember, frowning. 'They both were. Then he gets out some money and gives it Mum. Notes, William, them green pounds. Least five, I reckon. Then they did all that kissing stuff again.'

'Yeah, they would've done.' Sure, William Dickson knew everything.

'Weird, ain't they, grown-ups?'

'Dead weird.'

Thankfully the conversation was over. The cool was settling fast, rising round our ankles, creeping higher as the sun began to redden and drop. Looking up, I glimpsed the crimson sky breaking through the black leaf canopy, and became suddenly and overwhelmingly consumed with the urge to climb, scale the hard trunk beside me, shimmy myself up through the gloom into the last of the setting sun's pin-pricks of warmth. Away from the conversation, from what frightened me within it.

I began to climb.

A minute or two later I reached the safest, highest point, heard leaves rustling in the evening breeze overhead, sounds of the town closer now, skimming over the top of the woods, then passing by, never drifting down to where Fat stood – alone, cold, shouting.

'William! Come down! We'd better be getting back!'

But I stayed, enjoying the feeling of being up and away from him, on top again. My feet stood weighted in the crook of a branch, hands on the one above. I was free from the trunk, moving away, inching out to look down at his balled body below.

'Come on, William!'

And then I had the notion of playing the kind of game

children love to play, venturing out on a trip-wire between fantasy and reality. 'Fat!' I called back. 'Come on up! Come on up here and it'll all be better!'

'Can't!'

'Come on!' I heard the grunts from below, knew he was trying to heave himself up. He was cursing, half-laughing as his plimsolls slipped on the dried bark, searching for suitable foot- and hand-holds.

More encouragement was needed. 'You join me up here,' I shouted down, 'and it'll all be rubbish about your dad, Fat.'

He mumbled something, then exhaled violently.

'Come up here with me, and he won't be in prison! He'll be waiting for you! He'll come to see you!'

OK, so it was a game, but with the game can come the belief, motoring the body on. I'm sure that's why he carried on climbing. Part of Fat Norris needed his dad to be there for him; he felt in some mysterious way that if he could only reach out and grab that branch above his head, he could somehow magic him out of prison . . .

But instead he fell . . .

. . . twenty-five feet to the ground. He died as I watched.

Silence after the fall.

Then I began to scream, praying for God to scoop me out, up through the rustling leaves, away from the lifeless mass that lay face-down on the cold, hard earth below. There was no way I was going down. Ever.

Three hours later they found me, voice shot from the effort, silently screaming at the top of that tree.

2

Remember the funeral, William? How scared you were? But there was nothing really to fear, was there? I was with you, all the time, watching all the way. Best friends don't leave each other, do they?

Another August morning, the following week. A group of us standing in the shadow of another tree, another oak, leaves dancing above the chipped gravestones and whispering grasses. About twenty of us. Margot Norris, the grieving mother; my own mum; Dad; sister Nicola (giggling); headmaster and form-teacher from the school; shocked relatives; solemn-faced priest; police officers and Fat's own pale-faced father, sprung from prison for the occasion, cuffed by each wrist to a pair of suitably maudlin-looking prison warders. And me.

Leaving just Edward Paul Norris, dead inside a three-quarter-sized coffin. There'd been a terrifying moment, as the grim-faced bearers had carried it towards the waiting hole, when one had slipped, causing the brown box to lurch, the front men to sway, the mourners to gasp. I was plagued with a vision of the coffin falling, its lid flying open and Fat erupting from the confines like a sponge from a matchbox, a pale fat finger pointing accusingly, singling me out. 'I curse you, William Dickson! I curse you from the depths of hell!' But after a horribly long moment the bearers recovered, moved towards the grave, set the coffin down, and the priest began the ceremony.

I shot a quick, nervous glance at Fat's sobbing dad, and knew then why Fat Norris didn't have to curse me – I was already cursed. Hadn't I been the one to promise him his father, now standing less than ten feet from the coffin? Just like I'd said – Climb the tree and your dad will be waiting for you! – and there he was. The laughing, chubby Jag-driver had turned up to see his son – only dead.

I was scared. Literally dumb with fear. I felt certain I'd be sent to prison. The policemen standing near the grave seemed to be looking at me all the time. I had lost my voice, and they'd tried talking to me for hours, telling me not to worry about trying to speak, that I could simply nod or shake my head to their questions. But sooner or later surely they'd catch on, come for me. Maybe they were only waiting for my voice to return before hauling me away somewhere unspeakable and trapping me with clever questions. It was like that Columbo man off the telly that Dad liked so much. I saw them in my mind's eye – all smiles one minute, then turning at the door to stop and ask that killer question: 'So, uh, William. You seem like a nice kid. But you know, I can't help wondering just why Fat Norris ever began to climb that tree? Doesn't make any sense, does it, William, a big fat kid like that? No sense at all.' And with that, I'd crumble, blurt it all out, be taken away for ever.

The priest droned on under the pale sky, as grey clouds loomed to smother a sun weakened by a long summer. It was early autumn – death was everywhere, especially in the trees. That's where He lived. I knew that now.

I'd stayed in the tree for three hours, frozen, clinging to the rough bark, damp from tears. I had screamed until no sound came any more, then kept on silently opening and closing my mouth, petrified. It wasn't the thought of climbing down and running past Fat's body that kept me there; rather it was the notion of what I'd be descending into. I remember that distinctly. What waited for me below? Everything had changed. I must have killed him. I must have encouraged Fat to climb up a tree that I knew wouldn't support his greater weight. I couldn't shake the feeling that a tiny part of me must have wanted that branch to snap, wanted him to die. It was like turning off a television programme that scared you. Fat's world scared me. The 'uncles', his mother, the sex-talk – it all felt wrong, black, involving. And the less I moved, the less I'd have to face it. So I stayed put and screamed.

3

And Christmas Eve, William? The party we had, just you, me, Mummy and Margot Norris? How could you ever forget that little bash? Well, maybe I've helped you there a little – but only as a best friend should. And I want you to remember how much I've helped you, William, all the things I've done for you. Because one day there might come a time when I need you to help me. And I really won't be happy if you let me down . . .

The months passed, and thankfully – incredibly – the Dickson family of 24 Ryder Avenue, Tilbury, Essex, drifted slowly and reasonably undramatically towards Christmas. My voice returned after six weeks and several visits to a speech therapist. It was a slow process, and a painful one, but eventually I was back to somewhere near normal.

Mercifully, Columbo never came knocking at the door for me. Visits from the police became less frequent, the questions easier to deal with. I stuck rigidly to the script that I'd rehearsed – Fat Norris had climbed that tree of his own free will, then simply fallen. Just an accident.

Often these visits would end with a long silence, before one of the officers would have hushed words with Mum or Dad, glancing across at me as they spoke. My feet would sweat, and I'd hold my breath, trying to look casual, innocent – heart pumping furiously inside, certain this was the moment they'd walk back over with handcuffs. But it never happened. After they'd left, Mum and Dad would give me cakes, sweets or ice-cream that I'd try to make a convincing show of enjoying.

Two months after Fat died, I returned to school to be treated as some kind of junior celebrity. It was bizarre, to say the least. Teachers were constantly asking if I was all right, did I want to go home? Classmates would beg for details of what had happened in the woods. I just fixed them with a look. I had the best seat in the dinner hall, and could simply walk out of the classroom whenever I wanted, whereupon Mum would receive a phone call to come and collect me.

It was too much. To gain all this freedom, this power, this status because I had killed a friend? But, as the weeks passed, I no longer felt quite so cursed, so afraid, but blessed instead. Invincible, forgiven – rewarded, even. Something was looking over me, protecting me – provided I kept my secret, provided no one ever knew. Because that's where it might all fall apart. One ill-judged remark to anyone, and I'd be done for. I might just get away with it if only I kept my mouth shut.

By night, I was a bed-wetter. But even then, I seemed excused. Mum went to great lengths to assure me that there was 'nothing wrong' as she changed the sheets, that it was just a phase that I'd grow out of. The doctor said the same thing. And the voice in my head.

Him.

I'd built an image of Him in my mind by now. Something I'd often seen on my grandmother's wall. She lived in Brentwood in a little flat that always smelt of burnt pork, and Mum used to take Nicola and me there every Sunday. She and Gran used to coo a lot over Nicola – most weeks Gran would have made her a new dress or something – while I read comics and wished the time away. There was one redeeming feature, however, in the shape of a small, framed picture in the hall. I used to look at it for ages, drawn to it, trying to put some kind of story to the pained silent face that stared back at me. In the picture, a figure stood on some sort of pier or boat decking. Face out, head in hands – screaming, to most people. Mum hated it, was always trying to get Gran to take it down, saying it was frightening Nicola and me. Maybe it used to – before the woods. But after Fat died, the expression on that thickly lined picture seemed to change. Now, whenever I looked at it, I saw a friend who stared back at me in open-mouthed surprise. A happy face, glad to see me again. As if it was saying, 'We know how good it feels to scream, don't we?'

Shortly before Christmas we went to Gran's and the picture was no longer there. A cheap colour print of a puppy in a basket had replaced it. But even this made a strange sort of sense at the time. I knew where the screaming man had gone. He lived in my head, now, and was happy there. Sometimes he even talked to me.

Gran died a few years ago. After the funeral, I went through some of her things. She had a small wooden chest in the bedroom, full of drawings and cards sent to her by her grandchildren, keepsakes treasured in her later years. At the bottom of the pile was an old brown envelope with 'William – Christmas 1970' written on it. Inside was the card I'd sent her that year – a near-perfect reproduction of Edvard Munch's *The Scream*, in coarse black crayon.

I sat silently on her bed for a while, picture in my hands, trying to find the 'me' in it, the memory of my input. Did I trace it, copy it, draw it from memory – what? Where did I do it – at home, school, in Gran's house, even? But the image just stared back, revealing nothing.

Inside, I'd written:

Dear Granny,
Happy Christmas.
Hope you like this. The man told me you would.
Love, William

I couldn't remember writing a single word of that, either.

My mum tried hard to restore the status quo with Margot Norris after Fat's death. The woman was almost a permanent visitor in our home. A permanent, scary visitor. Whenever I was around, I could sense Margot's resentment rising. A look perhaps, her eyes narrowing, glossy lips tightening around the near-permanent cigarette, then feeling the silent communication of nature's rawest anger – a mother denied her child. By me.

Margot Norris hated me.

Because she wanted you dead, William, not her son. Why didn't we die, not him?

The eyes, I remember her eyes. Black, piercing eyes. One look would terrify me. It was as if those eyes knew – they simply knew the truth about her son. I couldn't stay in the room while she was there, couldn't spend a moment alone with her. The police, parents, schoolteachers, I could deal with by silence. But not those eyes, boring themselves into my nightmares. Eyes that I knew wouldn't rest until they'd got the truth, searched out my part in her son's death. Such terrible dreams. And when I woke, the bed was soaked in the urine of my guilt.

Strange tales of 'Uncle Dave' began to emerge once my parents thought I was asleep. Hushed conversations I'd strain to overhear. Dad knew of the man's reputation. Dave Atkins was a broken-nosed docker, sitting high in the sky, king of the crane that lifted exotic produce from the dark rusting interiors of foreign ships. 'A nutter,' Dad said late one night, long after Margot had taken another black eye and hangover back to number ninety-eight. 'She's gone and got herself caught up with a right nutter this time.'

'I'm sure he hits her,' I heard my mum reply, her voice concerned, urgent. 'She comes out with all this stuff about falling downstairs, but I know it's lies.'

'It's her own bed, Theresa love. Dave Atkins is bad news.' This is how Dad dealt with issues, shutting them down with weary clichés as he watched the telly.

Mum probably chewed on her bottom lip a moment or two, sizing up what was to be lost or gained from taking it further. 'But she's my friend, Stan,' she eventually said.

A sigh from my dad. 'All I'm saying is, just be careful. That business in the woods was months ago. We've got over it, now it's her turn. Don't get me wrong, I feel for the woman – but that bloke Atkins is a head-case. It's her decision to live with him, so please, love, let it be, yeah?' Advice she seemed to silently accept, as I heard nothing more except the tedious commentary from the black-and-white.

I still sometimes wonder what drew my mother to Margot Norris. On the surface, you couldn't have met two more different women. Margot, always made up, dressed in caftans and headscarves; my mother, smaller, younger, slighter, her short fair hair the opposite of Margot's thick tousled black locks. Margot smoked; Mum didn't. Margot drank; Mum hardly touched a drop. Maybe it was simply the attraction of opposites that made them gel, the belief that both women could climb a little way from their extreme positions and tread warily into the no-man's-land of compromise. And this was, to an extent, an almost secret thing for Mum, something she kept from Dad, at any rate. I remember coming home early from school one day to find her sitting in the lounge in a caftan, smoking a Player's. Seeing me, she guiltily stubbed out the cigarette, opened the large french windows to air the room and disappeared upstairs. Five minutes later, she came back down in a clean print dress.

I suspect Mum gained things from Margot, insights into another life, one without kids and constant responsibilities; a life she could secretly aspire to when Dad wasn't around. Margot represented something different, fashionable – dangerous, perhaps.

And my dad? Well, he was certainly not dangerous. Except, maybe, dangerously dull. Not that he was a bad father. Dad, I now realize, worked damn hard to provide for us. He was always either working or watching the television. That bloody television: it took my father from me. He loved that little black-and-white box, tuning in and dropping off in front of the screen, knowing he'd done his bit, that he'd stood lashing cars onto the Tilbury ferry for ten hours, rain or shine, before coming home.

But he wasn't like Fat's dad. I never heard him suddenly break into a song, or tell daft jokes, or arrange crazy day-trips to amazing places. He went to work, then came home and watched the telly.

One day, Mum and I thought we'd play a trick on him. I was so excited. We found an old cardboard box, cut a screen-sized window out of the front, stuck some bottle-tops on the side for controls and made a crude painted television that I could wear on my head. It was fun, and really quite an elaborate prank, Mum going so far as to dress me in one of Dad's suits and whitening my face to look like a monochrome newsreader when Dad got home. As we heard him come through the front door, I went and crouched behind the living-room table, waiting to give my childish rendition of the day's news headlines. I'd only got about a third of the way through before Dad switched on the real television.

Mum told me not to cry, Dad was simply tired after a long day on the ferries.

Ah, but what about Christmas Eve, William? Enough of the childhood nonsense. You're drifting, searching, evading the blame only you yourself can take . . .

Christmas Eve, 1970. Dad's having a few beers with the other ferrymen, Nicola's tucked up in bed dreaming of Santa, and I'm sitting at the small table with my mother in the kitchen, watching as she stuffs Paxo into a dead turkey's rear.

A knock at the door, another signature rapped as distinctively as Fat Norris's used to be. But this time it's his mother, Margot, lurching into the hallway, split lip, crying, hair tousled. And my mum, accompanying her into the kitchen, from where I watched warily.

The two women hugged one another for a while, Margot moaning into my mother's hair, cursing Dave Atkins over and over, saying he'd gone too far this time, then calming slightly, spotting the bottle of Gordon's gin that Dad had won in the ferrymen's Christmas raffle, declaring she'd feel better if she had a little pick-me-up, which Mum duly poured, hands shaking slightly as she proffered Margot her glass.

And so, fortified, seated now, those all-knowing bloodshot eyes seeking me out, Margot began directing her hatred towards me. First came the frown, then a finger pointing, followed by the anger. The dam had finally broken.

I had no right to live, apparently. Should've been fucking dead, rotting in a hole, worms feasting on my eyes. Edward would still have been alive if I hadn't taken him to those fucking woods. I was evil, worse than the devil . . .

She stood, suddenly went for me. Mum, shocked, tried to intervene, stepped between us, pushed Margot back down onto the chair, inadvertently making matters far, far worse.

Margot was drunk, but quick and stronger. Mum was literally a pushover. I froze, horrified at the fight. It was like watching a young fawn up against a bad-tempered bear. In seconds, Margot had wrestled Mum to the floor with a hideous slap, then straddled her, showering her face in obscenities, calling out Fat's redundant name again and again. 'Edward! Edward! Edward! That bastard killed my Edward!'

Sounds. The awful noise of my mother's back sliding on the lino; her panicked grunts; the sudden scrape of a chair as a leg made contact; a shoe falling off, then skidding across the floor . . .

Got to do something, William. Got to do something now!

Somehow, I found the strength to move, leaden-legged, to the kitchen counter, side-stepping the thrashing bodies, my mind curiously disconnected, knowing I had the power to end this, His blessing . . .

'He killed my boy! My Edward! He killed my boy!'

And occasionally, in the worst nightmares, I still see my hand extending towards the knife-block, not choosing the steel blades, but emptying it, hearing the clatter of wooden handles on the worktop, choosing the block instead, turning, feeling the weight of it, eyes focusing on the back of Margot's head. My arm comes up – and I feel so calm, so good about this – then crashes down. The corner of the heavy block stops suddenly on the nearest head to mine. I scream at the burning pain shooting through my wrist. But I don't drop the block. Can't. Not until I see my mother's wide-eyed shock as the body above her falls heavily to one side . . .

Twenty minutes later, all is calm.

Mum had finally resumed stuffing the turkey, made up more Paxo, working frantically at the task as I made a lame job of scrubbing potatoes at the sink. Little is said, just the strained, shaking instructions she gives: where to put the skins, a little more salt in the water, cut out the eyes, William, cut out the eyes . . .

Three times Mum came to me, standing at my shoulder, then suddenly hugging me far too tight, watching me. Each time, stepping over the dead body at her feet, as if it were nothing more inconvenient than a large sleeping dog.

'Wrist all right, love?' she said. She had the beginnings of a large bruise on her cheekbone.

'Can I go to bed now, Mum? I don't feel well.'

'All in good time, William. Got to see to the meal first, haven't we, eh? Can't have Christmas without a good turkey roast, can we now?'

'No, Mum.'

'Such a big boy now, helping me like this. Such a grown-up William.'

I glanced down at the body, saw how the blood had now begun to darken and thicken, had the beginnings of a skin forming over the matted black hair and pink wound. Then realized I'd done that. I'd caused that damage. I'd killed again. Margot's slick red head was three-quarters turned towards me, the eyes I'd feared for so long now thankfully turned back inside the shattered skull. A potato slipped from my fingers, dropped to the floor, fell in the blood. Tutting, Mum picked it up, washed it in the sink, passed it back to me. 'There,' she said. 'Bit bruised, but none the worse. Cut the bad bit out, love. Can't waste a good potato, can we, eh?'

Once, Nicola began making her way downstairs, woken by the commotion, bewildered, clinging to her favourite stuffed rabbit. Mum moved quickly to hush her, and took her back to bed with a kiss and a cuddle. Then she returned to me, stepped back over the whitening corpse, wiped away a rogue tear with the back of her hand, leaving a smear of Paxo on her cheek.

'Very good, William. A fine job.'

I said nothing, swallowing hard, heart thumping. Couldn't she see it?

'The more we prepare tonight, the less we'll have to do tomorrow morning,' she said. 'Looking forward to Santa coming, are you? Have to go to bed soon. Can't have him seeing you up in your pyjamas.'

'No, Mum.' I wanted to bury my head in her bosom, but something else had taken her place in the kitchen, a robot woman who scared me almost as much as Margot's eyes once had.

'I'm so sorry, Mum,' I said, voice cracking with the effort of trying to stay composed. 'I'm really, really sorry.'

'For what?' she replied.

I pointed at the body.

She sighed, nodded slowly once or twice, then lots of times in quick succession. 'Well,' she said eventually, moving to the sink and taking out the mop and bucket. 'Perhaps the best thing is to pretend none of this ever happened.' She lifted the bucket and began filling it from the cold tap. 'Yes, I'm sure that's the best thing. Off you go to bed now, there's a good boy.'

She only began to cry once I'd reached the top stair.

There's no way I could ever condemn my mother for the way she reacted that night. Who knows how any of us would react in a crisis? I try to put myself in her head, try to imagine being a twenty-nine-year-old woman who has just seen her son kill her best friend – maybe seen the hatred in his eyes as he did it – and find myself thinking that she must have loved me so much. God only knows how much trauma she was going through – but she never once showed it to me. Instead she gave an Oscar-winning performance of maternal calm and control. And strangely, the longer the surreal pretence continued, the more the process worked. The body almost ceased to exist, became an inconvenience to be stepped over – a routine obstacle, as if there were any number of dead bodies in millions of steaming kitchens across the nation . . .

Inevitably, reality came crashing back as I heard my father's key, held by a happily drunken hand, finally negotiate the front door. From upstairs in my bed I heard him make his way unsteadily to the kitchen. I tried to imagine the scene in the long silence that followed. How much had Mum been able to clean up? Had she moved the body? (I doubted it, it looked much too heavy.) What did Dad's face look like when he caught sight of it? What would they do now? What was going on down there?

Nothing. No sounds, no raised voices – nothing. Just the silence of the house eventually sending me over to exhausted sleep.

4

A small plastic submarine. Two Matchbox cars. Cap-firing silver pistol. Marbles. Action Man. Spitfire Airfix kit. Glue. Enamel paints – blue, green and grey. Chocolate coins. Two shillings. Satsuma.

Not a bad Christmas stocking haul. Not bad at all. And the Action Man – well, he was the business, the one all boys dreamed of getting. 'Seeing-eyes' activated by a flesh-coloured lever in the back of his close-cropped head, moving joints, gripping hands – and, best of all, a pull-cord cueing a tinny voice from the middle of his khaki-clad back.

Happy Christmas, William.

Sitting up in bed as dawn slowly broke outside, I wondered what to call him, eventually settling on Clint, which I knew was some tough-guy cowboy my dad liked off the telly.

'Hello Clint,' I said, gently pulling back the drawstring. 'Happy Christmas.'

'Happy Christmas to you, William.' Which was a little shocking, but rather festive and proper of him, I thought. Exciting, too, to have an Action Man who knew your name.

'You OK?' I cautiously asked, pulling the plastic ring again.

'Fine. But I'm more worried about you.'

'Me?'

'They tell me you kill people.'

I threw the plastic figure down, watched it for a long moment. 'Who tells you that?'

'I know what you did last night.'

'Are you angry with me?'

The little head shook. 'I know what it looked like, too. The back of her skull. All black and wet with that little pink bony bit sticking out. Like mine, wasn't it? Feel it, William. Feel the little lever on my head.' I gingerly picked the khaki-clad plastic doll up again. 'That's the way. Just like the bone, isn't it?'

'S'pose.'

'Try it, William. Try moving the lever. See how it makes my black eyes move. Like hers, aren't they?'

I nodded – yes, his eyes did look like Margot's.

'William,' the irritated tinny voice said. 'You want to hear me talk, you have to pull my cord.'

'Right. Sorry, Clint.' I pulled the drawstring.

He smiled. 'That's better, Private Dickson. Much better. Now, I'm a soldier who's survived many a crisis, so here's how you're going to get through this. Just do nothing. Say nothing. Act like nothing happened.'

Sound advice, I thought. All the more impressive since it was coming from Action Man himself.

'Another pull, Private.'

'Sorry.' I pulled the ring again.

'Now, your mum and dad worked very hard last night making it all better. Should have seen your dad,' the small figure suddenly chuckled. 'He looked real funny carrying Margot's body back to number ninety-eight. Would have made a fine Special Forces man in his time.'

'The body's gone?' I pulled the ring again.

'Gone, Private Dickson. Your mum collected some of the blood in a jam-jar, got your dad to carry the body back, then they let themselves into the Norris abode with her spare . . .' I pulled the string again. '. . . key. Then she splashed the blood around the place, over the head wound, and poured a few drops on an old white shirt she found.'

'One of Uncle Dave's,' I whispered.

'Exactly. Smart woman, your mother. Then she got . . .' Another ring-pull. '. . . your dad to bury it in the garden. Mission accomplished, medals all round.'

'Wow.'

'So, nothing more to worry about. Happy Christmas, William.' The black eyes rolled one final time before settling back to their regulation white and blue. All Clint said for the rest of the day was – 'I am Action Man.'

And every day after that.

The police didn't discover Margot Norris's body for four days. Looking back, it must have been a godsend to my parents, each valuable day bringing more time to clean and scrub, swat up and agree on their story; perhaps most importantly, it meant the forensic evidence would decay even further.

A relative had alerted the boys in blue after Margot failed to show up for Boxing Day drinks in Colchester. More good fortune, as the young and hungover officer taking the call did not get anyone to act on it immediately. Maybe he felt it wasn't worth the effort to contact Tilbury police station and have them check out the missing woman; or perhaps he thought he'd leave it a while, guessing Mrs Norris was sleeping off a good time somewhere and had no intention of turning up at a dreary drinks do. Whatever the reason, a constable wasn't dispatched to number ninety-eight until mid-morning on the 27th.

The curtains were drawn downstairs, there was no answer to repeated knocking at the front door, the back door was locked. The constable tried speaking to neighbours, who reported nothing suspicious, except for the fact that there seemed to be a lot of gentlemen callers to the house, one in particular with whom Mrs Norris was forever arguing. No, they couldn't be certain of his name (too scared to rat on Atkins, perhaps?), but were well used to drawn curtains – the poor woman hadn't been the same since her son had tragically died earlier in the year.

A search warrant was applied for, but due to the Christmas break all judicial processes were still half stalled. It took two days before the officer and two plainclothes CID men kicked down the front door.

The rest is documented. Dave Atkins was arrested and charged with the murder of his sometime lover, one Margot Norris, with the trial scheduled to begin the following March.

Both Mum and Dad were called to testify, character witnesses for both the deceased and the accused respectively. Nicola and I stayed with my auntie Suzanne in Kent for the duration of the trial, and the visit was simply marvellous – fresh spring days, wet knee-length grass, and the resinous beginnings of bright green leaves unfurling all around. Plus no school for several weeks.

Back in Chelmsford Crown Court the jury deliberated for a little under an hour before returning a guilty verdict, persuaded by both forensic evidence (apparently investigating officers had discovered a hastily buried bloodstained shirt belonging to the protesting defendant), and by the host of witnesses who, along with my father, had testified against Atkins's character, a process that revealed that he had been a persistent blight on the community with a proven record for robbery, GBH and ABH. Neighbours also testified to the stormy, sometimes violent relationship he had with Margot Norris and, crucially, a local landlord reported overhearing Atkins over the Christmas break telling another villain that 'the dozy bitch was really going to get it soon'.

So it was that on 23 March 1971, Dave Atkins began a life sentence for the murder I committed in trying to protect my mother from the woman whose son I goaded to his death. Except, I wouldn't have called it a murder. More like self-defence by proxy. Like I've said before: it happens that way, sometimes.

You can see why, can't you? You can see how it happened, how it panned out this way? Or maybe not. Maybe you think it's just too extreme, too implausible. And I'm the first to admit that, with Margot Norris, I had a lot of luck on my side. Dead from just one blow from a wooden knife-block, well, that's a kind of murderous serendipity at work. Somehow, I hit the right spot with the right amount of force. The brain gave out. She died, Mum lived. It was enough. Please, take it from me, it happened that way. I had the memories to prove it.

It occurred to me that perhaps there was even a certain kind of justice in it. Granted Margot didn't deserve to die, but Tilbury was probably a safer place with Atkins behind bars. I often used to wonder if killing Margot offered a bizarre kind of relief in itself. Who knows how many more beatings she'd have had to endure, how many punters she would have taken to her bed under Atkins's threats and greedy instruction?

I found a lot of consolation in these thoughts – death made positive, fresh new beginnings from sudden endings. It was simply a matter of perspective. The screaming man in my head didn't use that precise word, though, opting for phrases like, 'It simply depends on how you look at things, William,' instead.

Well, he was talking to a seven-year-old, after all.

When Nicola and I returned to Tilbury after the trial, nothing further was said of Margot, Fat Norris or Atkins. I think Mum and Dad had had more than enough of the whole business by then. They looked haggard, beaten by it all. Once or twice I'd catch them giving me a funny look, but by and large life ground on, through the seasonal routine of school terms, birthdays, Easter, summer holidays and Christmases.

At school, I was treated to a harsh lesson in the frailty of playground fame. Within a few months any celebrity status I had been granted because of Fat's death withered away, as the spotlight shifted to other kids who had the latest bikes, or who played better football. I became a kind of junior 'has-been' – a boy who'd once witnessed something fairly interesting, but who wasn't really worth the effort of befriending to find out about it. Not that it bothered me too much. I was happier in my own company, fully aware that the more people I became involved with, the greater the chance that either I'd be found out – or maybe I'd end up killing them, too. It was a real possibility for me. Death, I'd quickly discovered, offered some kind of solution, a way of removing obstacles, changing life for the better, protecting myself and those I loved. And if pushed, I was fairly certain I'd kill again. And this wasn't born out of any psychotic bloodlust, just simple experience and practicality. Death worked for me.

So I was happy – mostly. A few nightmares now and then, occasional embarrassing bouts of bed-wetting, but mostly as content as I could be. The past, the Norrises, seemed forgotten – literally dead and buried. A new family moved into number ninety-eight. They whitewashed the front of the house and painted the front door and window frames sky-blue. Life moved on, for all of us.

However, events, I now realize, do catch up, springing sudden, unexpected surprises. Who could have imagined that Dave Atkins would serve his time as a model prisoner, impressing the parole board at his first application, shaving years off his sentence with one forty-minute encounter during which he faked and smiled his way to freedom?

Forty years ago, they would have hanged him. I don't support the death penalty as a rule; not many killers do. But given what he was about to do to my family, I would have made an exception in Atkins's case.

5

Look, I know it's tempting to become morose at this point, but, William, you must understand, you did the right thing. The woman was attacking Mummy, wasn't she? Had it coming to her, didn't she? Sometimes, William, sometimes I think that we have to do a bad thing to do the right thing. And didn't life settle down afterwards, after Mummy and Daddy had fixed things for us? Well, at least for a while . . . until the money arrived . . .

Five years on and, one Saturday lunchtime in January 1976, fortunes changed in the Dickson household. This time, it wasn't a knock on the front door, but something more internal, invasive – the shrill ringing of the phone. The phone still always made me jump. Something about that insistent ringing bell. In my mind I always had the image of a policeman calling from the station, asking me the questions that would finally nail me on two counts of murder. Despite only being a piece of black plastic, that phone made a damned good guilty conscience. As a result, I never answered it, even if I was just inches away. The Screaming Man always told me not to.

That Saturday Mum answered, then called Dad over, a look of bemusement on her face as she passed him the receiver. I watched warily as he took the call. Something about the way Mum still stood by his shoulder unnerved me further. I searched his expression for clues, watching as it changed from caution, to confusion, blinking recognition, before finally settling on something approaching elation. What was all this about? Next he slowly sat, listening, still nodding, occasionally saying, 'Yes, of course,' or, 'No, absolutely not.' To our astonishment, as he put the receiver down, he punched the air triumphantly.

Mum, Nicola and I waited as he milked the moment before the revelation that was to change our lives. 'Well,' he said eventually, unable to control the rapidly spreading grin. 'We've only gone and won on the bloody premium bonds, haven't we?'

The Dicksons were finally winners. ERNIE, the computer that picked winning premium bond numbers, had seen fit to throw up one of my father's bonds to make him the random recipient of its £150,000 prize. A hell of a lot of money. God only knows what it would be in today's terms, but suffice to say that the three-bedroom semi-detached house that we lived in was probably valued at a little over £2000 at the time. Maybe we were made millionaires by today's standards, I don't know, but – whatever – our win was sensational.

Later that day, we all sat round the radio and caught the announcer saying that 'this week's winner lives in the Tilbury area'. Which meant us. Us – the Dicksons of Ryder Avenue, the people least likely to. And yes, we all cheered.

That night the television stayed off as we sat down and made grandiose plans for the windfall. Mum and Dad shared a bottle of wine as they mentally spent the money on the fantastic new life that was suddenly achievable. There'd be a new house, new cars, new clothes, toys, new gadgets – new damned everything.

Three months later we moved to Kent, and settled into a converted oast-house three miles from Mum's sister Suzanne, who, incidentally, was the only family member who hadn't come knocking with a sob-story and an open hand once news of the win got out.

Kent – the village life. I suppose to most people it would have been a move made in heaven. Mum and Dad certainly seemed to adore their new home, especially its large cream and brown tapering kiln that had once roasted tons of Kent hops and now housed a converted circular lounge. But for me, a growing thirteen-year-old, it was dull, dark, old, a little scary and – above all else – boring. The rural quiet my parents had bought into offered me nothing.

The nearest lad my age lived on a farm two miles away, a boy called Tony. We'd idled around outside as our parents met for the first time, and quickly discovered that further friendship was pointless. We simply didn't click. I knew nothing about farming, he couldn't begin to feign an interest in my life – the rich kid from the oast-house with the Essex accent. I remember him trying to impress me with softly spoken tales of life on the farm – how many kittens he'd drowned, what it felt like the first time his father had held his hand as he'd drawn it trembling across a trusting ewe's throat. And I'll admit, a small part of me was tempted to air a few revelations of my own. But the voice told me not too; the Screaming Man put paid to any ill-advised confessions. All the same, I've often wondered what the expression on his face would have been if I'd described the sight of Margot's head cracking under the knife-block, or the sudden stark fear in her son's eyes as he fell through the branches onto the hard earth below. Drowning kittens in a bucket? I hate to say it, but Tony from the farm never even got close.

That September saw Mum and Dad waving me goodbye as they drove back in the new Rover along the gravel drive that marked the entrance to Chetwins Public School for Boys. I was thirteen, freshly scrubbed, uniformed, and alone. It was a world away from Tilbury and Ryder Avenue, but I tried to convince myself that this was my fresh start – here was a place where I could finally leave my past behind. I'd be safe here: no one would know me, no one would come to arrest me. The killer in me was simply a collection of my own secret memories. Tried, used, successful on two occasions, but now hopefully forgotten. Everything, I assured myself, would be OK from now on.

Eight weeks later, I'd taken another life.

6

Level with me, William: are you really so very surprised you killed again? Honestly, shocked by it? I wasn't. They shouldn't have put you in there. No friends – except me. And I never left you, William. Not for a minute. But we showed them a thing or two, didn't we, eh? We showed them what happens when you try and break us down. And it felt . . . it felt like coming home . . .

There are two types of public school. Those that recruit pupils from the landed gentry and send eights to compete at Henley Royal Regatta; and those that exist in flaking country halls, staffed by bored academics in moth-eaten robes and dust-encrusted mortar-boards. Eton, Westminster, Radley and Shrewsbury number amongst the former; Chetwins was among the worst of the latter.

I started at Chetwins as the oldest 'fresher' in the school. There were forty new-boys that year, thirty-nine confined to the horrors of the first year, and me, thirteen, leapfrogging the adolescent pile, catapulted straight into the third year, into a well-established class of thirty-six boys, fully bonded and grouped, all delighted at the entertaining possibilities I presented.

They were bored, back from the long summer hols sporting their Mediterranean tans, and I was precisely the fresh meat they'd wished for. Even better, I was an Essex boy, whose wince-making tone and clipped speech left him open to rigorous bullying, ignored by staff who seemed to leave all aspects of discipline to the prefects in the upper years.

Suffice to say, I soon began to hate every damned minute I spent in the place. Being tall for my age was no advantage in a fight, I was too skinny, unmuscular at that point, devoid of the techniques the others had learned from within a hundred headlocked rugby scrums. Violence is simply another sport in public school – tolerated, sometimes even covertly encouraged by staff. Perhaps it's considered part of the unspoken curriculum that boys learn to fend for themselves, a notion born out of a mixture of staff apathy and the wish to vent one's revenge on innocent boys whose only crime is to be the requisite year or two younger. You might once have been bottom of the bloody heap, but now your fists could be the ones cracking into young ribs and skulls.

The one redeeming factor was the trees. I loved the trees, specifically the 200-year-old cedar alley, for me Chetwins' most notable feature. Forget the overrated oak: it's too dense, its leaves are laughably small; a badly proportioned tree unfairly collecting the nation's greatest accolade. My mental arboretum is devoid of oaks and acorns, but livid with cedars instead, dappling the ground, gripping the soil with roots that are tighter than a hawk's claw.

Thankfully, I wasn't totally alone. There were two of us in my class who bore the brunt of the bullying. A stunted, squinting blond boy called Cooper (inside Chetwins' gates first names were always dispatched in favour of surnames and nicknames), and myself, the late arrival, a fortuitous event for Cooper, as he now had someone with whom he could share the burden of his pain.

And let's not forget Webster, shall we, William?

Most of the rough stuff was dealt out by a crop-haired butcher's son called Jonathan Webster. His father had a shop and slaughterhouse, and his son the face of a young bull, great dark eyes, enlarged head sitting on the thickest neck I'd seen. A freak, to all intents and purposes, the one individual in the school who really merited consistent cruel teasing and, but for the bastard's size, would have received it. It had taken him the best part of two years to secure his well-earned reputation as school psychopath, and now, secure in the third year, surrounded by spineless flunkies, he set about dispensing random acts of violence.

I feel certain that Webster would have been expelled from any other school, but there was no question of him leaving Chetwins. Not when his father gave free beef to the school's miserably under-funded canteen. As a result, Cooper's complaints were ignored, crucial thumpings 'missed' by patrolling staff, the occasional broken limb blamed on falls down the rickety stairways (of which there were plenty), or on sporting accidents or general misadventures. At which point, I suspect, the majority of fathers would nod understandingly, maybe even return the headmaster's wink. Former public school boys themselves, they were used to the form, and were now bullying any number of employees as a result.

Strangely enough, the concept of buying into a better education was one of my father's rare ideas. I sincerely believe he thought that packing Nicola and me away to separate schools for ten weeks at a time was a sure-fire ticket to advancing our future prospects. And with little knowledge of the horrible truth behind the ivy facade, Chetwins must have seemed truly exotic to the former ferryman, a fabulous opportunity for me. I can't blame him – he simply didn't know. I often used to wonder why Mum had let us go so easily, though. It just didn't seem like her at all.

I sent her three letters within the first fortnight. She never answered once.

By the end of the first month the darkness was returning. Bad, black thoughts, the past I couldn't escape. I wouldn't tolerate Webster for much longer. He had discovered the provident source of my funding, and had redoubled his efforts to make my life a misery. Kicking, punching, sneaking into our dormitory, and once even urinating over me as I slept. The staff response? Simply to tell me to stop telling lies about the benevolent butcher's son. I persisted, but when the showdown came and Webster was summoned to answer my charges, witnesses disappeared, and sighing masters reported that I wasn't working on settling in, that I had to grow up, stop telling fibs. Which narrowed my options somewhat.

Half-term arrived, and I spent the best part of a week trying to convince my parents not to send me back. The pleas fell on deaf ears. Nicola, to my dismay, was deliriously happy at her school, had made new friends, couldn't wait for Sunday afternoon when she could return to the Sussex Downs. As a result, Mum and Dad, their consciences soothed by my sister's enthusiasm, assumed I was making a mountain out of a mole-hill. Only five weeks and my speech had improved immeasurably, they said. To their way of thinking Chetwins was obviously doing a good job. Dad, in a rare moment of paternal affection, took me quietly to one side and told me I would simply have to learn to fend for myself, buckle down, take the knocks and seize the opportunities such a wonderful education offered. It would be the making of me; something he was sure I'd want for my own son in later years.

In the second week back, nursing new bruises, I sat down and began to consider the reality of the situation. I was bright; I knew so from the ease with which I absorbed the new subjects. There had to be a way round this Webster predicament, besides the murderously obvious. The school itself, once I had acquainted myself with the various rituals, should have been a breeze. In a strange way, Dad was right. If I applied myself to my full abilities, chances were I would fly from Chetwins to university, then on to a safe, secure career. The library, surprisingly, was well stocked with classic works shunned by the majority of pupils, but holding a fantastic allure for me. While fellow pupils did their things with bats and balls, I read voraciously, wrapped in old fiction: Dickens, Hardy, Lewis, Austen and others. I read and re-read them, loved every page, the language, pacing, painstaking descriptive detail, even the names of their characters. Those long-dead authors rescued me, drowned me in their stories.

But still Webster made his frequent calls to punish me. Webster was the sticking point. Webster made the difference between a potentially easy time and the bruising nightmare that Chetwins had become. Without Webster, Cooper pointed out to me one night after a particularly ugly encounter, it could all be so different . . . And, reluctant as I was to kill Webster, Cooper's words, spoken painfully from behind loose teeth and split lips, carried more than a degree of truth.

Cooper and I talked long into the night, hushed voices fantasizing over ways and means. Speared by a rogue javelin, perhaps, the still jerking body puking crimson blood over the wobbling spear. Ground glass in his food, poison from the chemistry lab, stabbed with a kitchen knife – each hushed suggestion bonding the two of us further, yet taking us dangerously nearer to the inevitable. For talking about Webster's death made it worryingly closer to happening . . .

But there were always flaws. Killing someone, I'd unfortunately discovered, was dangerously easy. It was getting away with it that taxed our brains. Cooper was a born pessimist in this respect, and every suggested scenario ended in the pair of us serving life for the crime, no matter how devious the means. I began to realize that I'd misjudged him. He was too afraid to kill, too afraid of everything, faced a lifetime cringing in a mental dark alley surrounded by any number of 'what ifs?'. And I knew then that, if the deed was to be done, then I was the one to do it, the one with experience.

Not that death was an automatic result of the plan I had in store, simply a potential outcome. I hoped it wouldn't come to the pine box; it might just involve a lengthy stay in the local hospital, a broken neck, perhaps, Webster wheelchair-bound for life, paralysed from the eyebrows down. Honestly, I'd have been far happier with a serious accident.

For the record, it happened like this. Chetwins' first XV was a mediocre rugby side, bolstered almost solely by Webster's insatiable appetite for violence, given full legal vent and encouragement as tighthead prop. Indeed, such was the monster's ferocity that he played with and against boys three years his senior, executing legendary and bone-crunching tackles that went some way to restoring a little credibility when set against the inevitable dismal scoreline.

It would be an exaggeration to suggest Mr Barrington (pint-sized, broken-nosed Scotsman employed as Chetwins' games-master) actively encouraged Webster to lay into the shocked opposition with such violent enthusiasm, but he certainly did not do anything to stop him. These carnivals of physical destruction had an upside as far as we softies excluded from the team were concerned. Saturday afternoons were devoted to matches: home games required us to file onto the games field and yell chilled, lacklustre support; while away fixtures ensured that the school was free from Webster and his mob for a few precious hours.

Rumour had it that Barrington had befriended most of the landlords in Kent; certainly he seemed to be able to persuade many of them to let the entire rugby team knock back a few pints in sub-zero beer gardens on their way back to Chetwins. Every other Saturday night it was the same story: we would lie awake in our dorms, ears straining for the familiar crunch of worn tyres on the gravel outside, then hear the droning coach vomiting forth a drunken rabble that noisily staggered up to bed. Webster, youngest and loudest of them all, would make his way straight to our dorm, six boys pretending to sleep, eyes screwed tightly shut, all hoping he'd pick Cooper. God knows what Cooper hoped for, just that the ugly freak get it over quickly, I suppose. Twice it had happened in the first half of the term, Webster stumbling in, naked, burping, muttering, playing with himself before climbing in to my short, blond friend's bed.

I asked Cooper why he hadn't resisted. He countered by showing a livid red scar on the back of his neck, a bite-mark from his inebriated seducer. Since then, he'd simply tried to concentrate on relaxing, mind struggling to mentally fly him to faraway lands while Webster pumped at his rear with short, sharp slaps.

That fourth Saturday marked my eighth week in Chetwins. Enough, I'd decided, was enough. During the afternoon I secured a capful of cooking oil from the abandoned kitchens. I told Cooper to hide under my bed soon after lights-out, without disturbing the four others in the dorm. He didn't ask any questions, seemed to sense I was to be obeyed. The eyes were curious but compliant.

Around half past ten, the coach returned and the commotion began. My heart-rate rose a little, dark-adapted eyes stung from focusing on the doorknob. Cooper used the fracas as cover to slide under my bed. I waited, totally calm, completely prepared.

Ten minutes later, as the noise begun to subside, the door opened. Webster stumbled in, nude, stood swaying for a moment, fumbling his half-hard cock, the moonlight blue on his horribly muscled torso. 'Come and get it, Cooper,' he mumbled, walking towards the empty bed, throwing back the sheets. Then he stopped, looked round, his huge head bewildered.

My cue. 'He's not here,' I whispered.

It took a moment to register. 'Where the fuck is he, then?'

'Downstairs. Hiding in the laundry room. I saw him earlier. He said . . .' I paused.

'He said what?'

'. . . that you were a revolting queer with a stinking prick. Hoped you'd rot in hell.'

More confusion, more hesitation. Still he swayed. Then suddenly bent low to my face, hot beery breath all around. 'Cooper said that?'

I calmly repeated the charge, watching the expression change from cruel tormentor to outraged maniac.

'The . . . fucking laundry room, right?'

Just a nod from me this time, watching as he straightened, made for the door, pace increasing, obscenities slipping from the cavernous mouth. 'When I'm done with him, Dickson, I'll be back for you. You fucking mark my words.'

The door opened, and he was gone. I pictured him making his way to the far stairway, a tightly winding set of spiral stone steps leading to the utility section of the sleeping school. What thoughts would be passing through that neanderthal mind? Vengeance, a spot of rape and battery? Or something worse? For surely, I consoled myself, if anyone was capable of cold-blooded murder, it was Webster, not me.

Then it came, hard to identify at first. A sudden distant intake of breath. Then a muted bump. A short pained cry, more of a squeak. Then another bump . . . another . . . another . . . a moan this time, cut short . . . more bumps – then silence.

I waited a full minute, calmly counting each second before taking three deep breaths and slowly levering myself from the creaking bed. I dropped to my knee, whispered to Cooper, still cowering, ordered him back into his own bed, then stood, turned to the rest of the room, heard nothing but heavy breathing, deep sleep. Were they really asleep? I couldn't stop to consider. I had work to do. It was time to see for myself the results of a little oil, a well-oiled thug and a dangerously dark stairwell.

I carefully made my way silently along the corridor to the top step, took out a previously pilfered paper tissue from my dressing-gown pocket and quickly wiped what remained of the oil from the cold stone floor. Someone coughed nearby and I froze, waited for an agonizing count of twenty before steeling myself and beginning the descent into darkness, step by faltering step . . .

A moan. I froze, then heard it again, ears pitched to the slightest sound. A low moan, but not human, just the chill winter wind coursing through a cracked window. A final step, and I was on the wet tiling floor. To my left a short corridor housed a vast tumbling washing machine, labouring to remove grass, mud and bloodstains from the recently used rugby kit.

Where the hell was he?

I looked around, but couldn't see for looking; had to force myself to shut both eyes, count again, taking deep breaths throughout, knowing he must be there somewhere. Then opened both eyes once more.

There!

Six feet from me, a heap lying against the far wall. Indistinct, but definitely the same pale blue moonlit mass from the dormitory. Naked flesh host to strangely twisted limbs. Is that a foot? Or an arm? Hand? Elbow?

I moved closer, ears ringing in the quiet. I see the head – then smile.

Webster. Dead.

Stooping, I pulled on the thin rubber surgical gloves stolen from the biology lab. Gingerly locating and lifting a cold ankle, I wiped the remaining oil from the sole of the foot with another tissue from my dressing-gown pocket. It occurred to me that this was the first time I'd touched a dead body. Bizarre. Perhaps this was how Mum and Dad felt when disposing of Margot Norris's corpse: excited; certain that nothing else exists – matters – but that the very essence, the self survives. As I wiped the oil from the sole of Webster's dead foot, the world disintegrated around me and I sucked it in. Then ate it, became better than it, conquered it.

I repeated the exercise with the other foot, careful lest a single incriminating drop of my sweat fall to the floor. Then stood, took one last look at the body, turned, and wheeled straight round into a staring face.

Cooper. Silent. Eyes rooted to his former tormentor.

'Jesus Christ!' I gasped. 'You nearly gave me a . . .'

And then the strangest thing. He turned to me, offered a hand, which for some reason I took. 'It's Alan,' he said. 'My name's Alan Cooper.'

Just a first name, unexceptional in a world populated with thousands of Alans, yet sadly the most precious thing he had to give by way of thanks, the possession he valued above all others.

7

Problem was, it was different with Webster, wasn't it, William? We went and killed the boy. Deliberately. Murdered, some might say. Those who weren't there. Those who never knew what the animal did to us. Murder. No excuses to hide behind. No child's game. No protecting Mummy. But did it really feel so bad? Surely he deserved it? You rid the world of a total bastard. Like in war, no one gets uppity when a few enemy troops are killed, do they? Pop, pop – bang! Give the man a medal . . .

Attending the funeral was obligatory. One hundred and ninety-three boys, thirty-four teaching staff, six technicians, twenty-eight house staff and sixty-three parents, all turned out for the big event to stare solemnly at the coffin – a shiny wooden affair adorned with two photos and a brave attempt to create a rugby ball from lilies.

I know this because I counted them all – bored, if anything, by the hypocritical show of respect for a pig like Webster. For most of us there the boy had been little more than an animal. If I'd had my way, his body would have been tipped in with the weekly swill and sent straight to the pork farm – a pig delivered to pigs. Instead we all had to endure this ridiculous charade. Still, it got us off double physics and German.

Standing with my classmates, I wondered if Webster was perhaps a killing too far. I'd taken some pretty dangerous risks, and someone, a dorm-mate perhaps, was surely bound to pipe up, finger me as the culprit, end my run of luck. Yet, looking at their fearful faces, I somehow doubted it. They were all silent, shocked, worried – the bravest of them occasionally shooting me a nervous glance before quickly averting their eyes. And in that moment I knew I was safe. I'd done it again – killed and got away with it. Any theories or whispered gossip they had regarding Webster's death were going to be kept to themselves. Maybe fellow pupils now saw me as their protecting avenger. Or perhaps I'd become a far more terrifying option than the obvious bully Webster ever was. Webster only beat you up, but Dickson, well, he kills. Either way, those lips were sealed, the eyes were scared. I was safe – for now.

The parental turn-out was heavy, which was explained after the service when we all returned to Chetwins for tea and scones, and nervous, fee-paying mums and dads began begging the head to assure them that nothing as tragic would ever happen again at the school. Most seemed to go away satisfied. However, I did spy Cooper, perhaps in tears, in deep conversation with his worried-looking parents; his mother suddenly choking scone into his father's dutifully supplied handkerchief. Watching from the shadows of the cedars, I understood Cooper's desire to spill the beans. While Webster had still been alive, so were the threats. Once the last shovel-full of Kentish earth had surrendered him to the worms, it could all come out in safety. I wondered just how much Cooper told them; if he had mentioned the Saturday sodomy, or opted for one or two of Webster's more standard violent practices instead.

Either way, I never found out. As the last of the parents drove away waving tearful farewells, the Coopers walked quickly behind the head's back into the main building. Fifteen minutes later Alan was packing in the dorm. Another ten minutes and he was gone. No goodbyes, just a glance. The eyes said it all. He simply couldn't stay, sleep in the same bed another night. I worried then that he'd spend a lifetime cringing under the bedclothes at the slightest interruption. After all, Alan Cooper had been the closest thing to a friend I'd had in a while. Perhaps I was too late, the real, long-lasting damage had already been done, his life permanently cursed by the freshly buried bully-boy. In a moment of optimism, I constructed another scenario, whereby Alan Cooper settled comfortably into another private school, made new friends, blossomed. I hoped that perhaps he'd write to me one day to tell me about it. He never did.

More strange events a month or so later, when a second-year boy called Harris was swiftly withdrawn. Rumour spread round the decrepit school like a forest fire on a hot summer's evening. Harris's father was a local police superintendent, disturbed by the autopsy findings on Webster's broken body. Blood samples pointed to a tremendous amount of alcohol in the under-age boy, enough to warrant Harris senior pulling his son from school.

Sports-master Barrington was made sacrificial lamb, given his cards a few days later in order to avoid a scandal. However, any euphoria at his leaving was quickly smothered with the arrival of Mr Castle, a brick-shithouse of a man, hideously well trained in brutalizing any pupil unable to run a try in from thirty yards, climb a rope with hands only, knock a competent fifty in the face of the fastest bowler, or complete the three-mile cross-country course.

However, Castle aside, Chetwins, as my parents had predicted it would, was getting easier. The years sped by, choreographed by vivid changes of season bringing leafy buds of glistening growth to the trees, cladding hard branches with soft sappy petals, until autumn claimed them. It hooked me, the cycle of death and regeneration, and confirmed my standpoint – that secret thing – I had with trees. For as the branches died back, new buds, new leaves took their place. Death as a liberator, a natural force of inevitable change.

My friend Death.

Then the school holidays. Strange to say it, but holidays back at the oast-house with Mum, Dad and Nicola became exercises in domestic harmony that merely had to be endured, safe in the knowledge that within a short while I would be returning to Chetwins' comforting neutrality. For as the years wore on, I'd come to realize that Chetwins didn't really demand anything from me, other than that I simply exist within its confines, obey a few rules, complete the required workload and keep my nose clean. By now, I had the necessary physical skills to deflect anyone foolish enough to have a go at me. All without killing another soul. I'd filled out, put on muscle, and still starred in an underground rumour as the boy who'd fatally ended Jonathan Webster's deviant ways several years earlier. Believe me, whilst not to everyone's taste, being a possible killer is one great way to be left alone and get the most out of life in a public school.

It was a long way from life at the oast-house. Here I was

expected to perform. No comforting neutrality to be had back at home. Mum, now driving to work as a PA at a legal firm in Tunbridge Wells in order to boost our income, began making me her dinner-party turn, regaling politely interested local nobodies with tales of my academic prowess, glowing as she heard me blandly recite sonnet after sonnet, my Essex accent largely obliterated now. OK, it was a pain, but I couldn't mind too much for the simple reason that it pleased her. And there was no better reason than her smile.

It was different for Dad. Times had changed for him in ways he couldn't have imagined when he first took the call from the premium bonds people. Put simply, the money wasn't enough to last a lifetime. He'd invested heavily in a local printing business that had gone under. The house, although fully paid for, was now in need of repairs he couldn't afford. Worse, he couldn't find a local job suitable for a former ferryman. Each time I came home he was progressively more withdrawn, depressed, tired of life. Mum told me he drank a lot at the Partridge, our local pub, where he still insisted on playing the rich winner with the deepest pockets, buying rounds for the locals, desperate they shouldn't know how broke he was becoming.

At home I was too young to make a difference, too old to feel unaffected. At school I had status; at home I could only watch my parents' dream collapsing. Sure, I had height, strength, intelligence and enthusiasm – but not the money to make it better for them. If there had been a way to rob the money they needed, I'd gladly have done it. Killed if it had been necessary – after all, they'd helped me with Margot Norris. But try as I might, I had no practical plans, no magical murderous solution for their problems. Death deserted me this time.

It was the summer of 1978, I was fifteen, and tensions in the house were high. A deadly stillness prevailed, which seemed to swallow every ounce of surrounding energy, absorbing it into the cold stone walls. The sun seemed to stop in the garden, its rays too timid to pour through the flaking window frames. Nicola had a friend over to stay, and the pair of them made themselves as scarce as possible. With Mum at work in

Tunbridge, I was left alone with Dad, the loaded silence heavy and horrible between us.

One afternoon, he came to my room, sighed wearily and sat on the edge of my bed. 'OK, son?'

'Fine.' I was trying to finish some sort of dissertation.

'We need to talk.'

I put down my pen, turned to him, saw the embarrassment in his eyes.

'It's about Chetwins.'

'Dad, I know what you're going to say.' Because I did. I'd expected this conversation for some time. Maybe dreaded it initially, but now that the moment had finally arrived, it wasn't so bad. 'I'm not going back, am I? To Chetwins. We can't afford it.'

He slowly nodded, looked at his hands. 'Pretty much like that, William, yeah.'

I turned back to the essay, tapped my pen on the close-written lines, thought for a moment or two. Then, on impulse, tore it up, tossed the pieces in the bin. 'Just wish you'd told me before I starting writing all this shit, Dad.'

He looked up, shocked. I saw his mouth moving to form some kind of words, then stop, unable to find them. 'It's OK, Dad. Really.'

'William, I'm sorry.'

'Don't be.' In a strange way, I finally felt I was contributing. By not going back to Chetwins I would be saving thousands on future fees. I'd be an asset, not a drain. 'What about Nicola?' I asked.

'I've talked it over with your mum and . . . we can only afford for one of you to . . . you know . . .'

I nodded.

'She's . . . less able to cope than you, William. She's younger. You . . . well, you have this way of coping, son. Getting by.'

I stood, walked to the window, looked out over the overgrown garden, suddenly taken with its tumbledown stone wall. Now that's a job I could do, I thought. A few bags of concrete, some new stones . . . A wonderful image of the wall stuffed with the crushed skulls of all those who had ripped off and failed my dad came to me. Senders of begging letters, local businessmen who'd been keen for his initial investment and now refused him work, the parasites at the Partridge who swallowed his dwindling generosity without ever once enquiring about his welfare – all dead, walled up, killed by me. Or better still, father and son, working, hacking, chopping, together. A bloody labour of love, Death's new beginning sealing us into a safer world.

'Sure,' I said eventually. 'I'll cope.'

September of the same year saw me starting as a final year 'O'-level student in Maidstone sixth-form college, a run-down redbrick affair housing more pupils in one year than Chetwins had altogether. I was, of course, an utter snob, unhealthily programmed by my years at Chetwins, swamped by the assortment of green-haired punks, long-haired hippies and anorak-wearing students who inhabited the place. Ironically, I guess I was the one student who really stuck out from the multi-coloured crowd – all clean cut, Oxford English, the ultimate square. Not that it bothered me. I had ambitions rather than friends. My aim was simply to complete the full set of requirements, then slide into a reputable university somewhere.

There was one notable difference, though: Maidstone sixth-form college was full of girls. Before this, my only real experience with girls had been the occasional visits from my sister's friends. Yet suddenly I was in and amongst girls my own age. Hurled in. Within a few weeks I'd been shown the rudiments of sex by a girl called Naomi – short, slim, with a blonde bobbed haircut and full lips. Her parents were 'something in the City'. She came from a seven-bedroomed house somewhere near Tunbridge Wells, and spoke with the same plummy accent as I did, which perhaps explained why we found mutual solace in a building populated by leather-jacketed heavy rockers, dope-smoking Rastafarians and wannabe punks with badly silk-screened T-shirts.

After we first made love (in bedroom four of her parents' home, a pink affair reserved for guests), she asked me what was wrong. Nothing, I replied, forcing myself to hold her closer, unable to tell her of the physical disappointment I'd felt even before the first waves of impending orgasm had washed over me. Sex, I'd quickly concluded, was largely overrated and a little unreal, the point being that I had the ultimate comparison.

Death was a real experience. Wiping cooking oil from the dead Webster's foot had been a real experience. Sex was fun, a physical distraction – but, for me, simply rhythmical gyrating responding to inbuilt impulses. One up from masturbation, I supposed, but far from the mysterious experience it had promised to be. Where was the intimacy that death provided? Where were the real thrills? Chances were, I thought, that you could make love to hundreds of human beings in a lifetime if you really set your mind to it, but how many could you kill? Death won out every time, sex paling by comparison. Shocking to say, but true: at the time I'd far rather have killed Naomi than made love to her.

Pushing my private theory further, the next time we had sex I closed my eyes and imagined I was killing her instead. A simple strangulation. And while the fantasy moderately heightened the experience, Naomi wasn't overly pleased with the thumbprints on her neck. Tiny bruises, barely visible, a world of vivid difference between them and the ugly, toothy weals she'd possessively left on my neck, yet she couldn't see it, couldn't wait to cool it between us. Three weeks later, she began hanging around with a tall punk called Ash, got her nose pierced, started dropping her aitches and dyed her hair green. She seemed happy, which was fine by me.

I cycled the twelve-mile round-trip to college each weekday, strength and endurance increasing all the while. Then, four evenings a week, I worked as a cash-in-hand potman at the Partridge, collecting empties in the sombre village local, a job my dad had managed to secure for me. Although I was legally underage, the work secured me fifteen pounds a week, which I was able to put on the table at home on a Friday as my contribution to household expenses.

The pub was owned by Bob and Sally Squires, an amiable enough old couple, who maybe had enough pity in them to realize that Dad's generosity had almost come to an end, but that employing his son as a skivvy would ensure that a fair proportion of my wages would eventually return to their till. Dad still drank there, but largely alone, sitting in a corner, no longer the popular Mr Dickson who bought the motley crew of regulars their evening's drinks.

At the weekends I'd turn my attention to their garden, initially mowing the lawn and tending the weed-infested beds, digging up thistles and dandelions to make space for the suffocated bulbs and primroses beneath. After a while, the Squires saw that I had an ability with the work, and saw also that the area I'd cleared could be developed as a summer beer garden. Word began to get round the small village that 'the Dickson boy' had green fingers. Other offers for gardening work gradually came in. As I had little difficulty with the academic burden of the sixth-form college, I had enough time on my hands to do the pub job, and be gardener to four other local residents. In three months I'd doubled my wages, and began thinking about a possible career in landscape gardening. It was the happiest I'd been for a long while.

Then, in mid-October of the same year, the Squires died. Honestly, this one had nothing to do with me! Faulty foreign wiring was responsible, as both of them roasted to their deaths in a Spanish hotel fire whilst on a 'dream' holiday. It seemed the whole thing was merely bad luck. I felt quite sad for them in a way – they were nice enough people, really. But I had a hell of a job getting the thirty pounds they still owed me from the relief landlord.

A week later I attended their funeral. It made a pleasant change not to be the only mourner worried about being arrested. And there was a curious kind of comfort in that, a feeling that I could participate as a fully paid-up innocent bystander, taking in the ritual, languishing in the pomp of it all. I'd read about the paid mourners in Greece, old women who could effortlessly turn on the waterworks when required. Seemed like a good job to me – a safe career. After all, the work was hardly likely to run dry, was it? And if it did, then an enterprising young man of my experience could surely ensure a few 'accidents' to bolster the local funeral registers.

In fact, I enjoyed the Squireses' funeral so much that, having managed to convince the elderly vicar that the churchyard could do with some mowing and tidying, I was able to 'attend' seven more guilt-free funerals that year.

I only lost the job when someone complained.

8

Summer, 1980.

Over a year had passed since the embarrassing incident in the churchyard – and yes, I did think long and hard about killing the old goat who blabbed to the vicar, but by and large life drifted on without too many murderous incidents. However, if you came to the house looking for Stan Dickson around this time, you'd be in the wrong place. Dad had left home last October, unable to cope with the situation any longer. One day he went to see a friend back in Tilbury and never came back. We didn't ever get to build our wall of the dead.

For the next six weeks Mum would take days off work to go and see him, leaving me behind, saying it was all strictly between Dad and her. Fair enough. They needed 'space to work things out', apparently; although personally I felt another premium bonds win would have done the trick. With money Dad had been happy; without it, he suffered.

I was always waiting for Mum when she returned after seeing him, and generally had some kind of supper prepared, watching as she tried her best to eat without crying. She confided in me very little, and I respected her need for silence. I was there for her if and when she needed me. Sometimes she'd come and hug me, saying everything would work out, and that she'd tell me everything one day, but mostly she kept herself to herself – still working days, worrying nights.

Did I miss him? Initially, yes. But as the weeks wore on, a certain inevitability worked its way in. Eventually Mum told me that Dad wasn't coming home for a while, but that he still loved us all, and thought of his boy often.

'Where is he then?' I asked her.

'London.'

'Can I see him?'

'One day.'

'Saturday?'

She shook her head. 'No, love. Not Saturday. Not for a while.'

Strange situations, I've come to realize, are only strange if you can't accept them. Acceptance is the key, the vital card. Once played, life becomes easier, a process of adaptation, conforming to the new needs thrown up by the situation. Adapt or die, the business gurus are always telling us.

So I adapted, became a sort of junior man of the house. Now studying for three 'A'-levels at the dreaded sixth-form college, I set out to do what I could to help Mum. Basically, we needed money. Mum and I talked it over: if she could secure some sort of bank loan, we could do up the oast-house and sell it, realize a little of its value. It seemed like a good plan. Chances were I'd be heading off to college or university soon, and Mum wouldn't need a huge place. A flat was what she had in mind, somewhere closer to her work, a place Dad and she could perhaps share together in future years without the financial worries that had driven him away. It seemed hopeful. Mum had it all sorted. And with the money from the sale of the oast-house, she reckoned she could buy a flat outright and still have money for Nicola's final two years' school fees.

Which would have been fine if it had all turned out like that.

I was gardening for a lady called Edith Fitzroy. She lived at the end of the village, in a small seventeenth-century cottage set in two acres, about a quarter of which was overgrown garden. She was sixty-two, a retired schoolteacher with an imposing manner gleaned from years in the classroom. After the churchyard debacle, I was grateful for any work I could get. Ugly rumours, gross representations of my intentions had circulated on the village grapevine. The old guy who worked in the local post office and store even refused to serve me any longer (it had been his wife's funeral, apparently), implying I was some sort of deviant, which really angered me. I thought about killing him too, but the Screaming Man told me it wasn't the answer. Impulsive kills, he assured me, were often the messiest and the most risky. And frankly, did I really have the inclination to plan an elaborate dispatch for such an ignorant old fool? Of course not. Instead I satisfied myself with a routine dismemberment fantasy that I could play in my mind whenever I wished. He died a lot, that guy from the post office.

I'm fairly certain Edith Fitzroy gave me the gardening work because, despite her imposing demeanour, the ex-teacher felt a little sorry for me. She always took the time to enquire after my well-being. I used to show her the weekly letters from my dad; after reading them she always wanted to know about my college studies, what plans I had for potential careers. What did I intend to do with the rest of my life, how did I 'see' myself in ten years' time? All questions, she confidently assured me, that a young man of my age should be addressing. She looked quite disappointed when I told her I had absolutely no idea.

I also knew the job was largely a charitable gesture, as she had very little interest in the overgrown garden. Just as I had no plans for my future, she had no plans for her garden, no instructions, no favourite beds or potting ideas – she simply let me do what I wanted. If anything, it was becoming more my garden than hers. If I went to her with a suggestion for a new bed or rockery, she'd almost immediately say yes, then minutes later return with some money so that I could buy whatever was necessary. It was great, really. I gardened there on Tuesday and Thursday evenings, often staying on to study in a deckchair in the summer evening twilight as she pottered around inside the cottage.

One evening, as I was putting the last of the garden tools back into her shed, she called me inside.

'William,' she said, motioning me to sit opposite her at the kitchen table. 'There's something I want to do for you.' She pushed an envelope across the smooth oaken surface. 'It's a gesture, nothing more.'

Frowning slightly, I took it, opened it, felt my heart miss a beat as I drew out the bundle of notes inside.

'You're a nice young man,' she said firmly. 'Just a little misunderstood. Do you know why I let you loose on my garden?'

'Because it was a tip?' I replied.

She smiled. 'To give you some real responsibility, William. Most of the time that's all it takes. Especially with boys like you.'

'Boys like me?' I asked, not knowing what she meant by that.

She held my eyes for a long moment, then said, 'The money's yours to do what you like with, you understand?'

I nodded, still frowning, trying to put a figure on the notes I held in slightly trembling hands. All tens. Dozens of them. Unbelievable. Five hundred pounds, six, a thousand? The side of the envelope had torn, it had been so full of the stuff. I didn't know what to do, what she wanted from me. Because it couldn't be a gift, not that much money. No one gave you that much money.

'Mrs Fitzroy,' I said, clearing my throat, 'it's very kind, but really, I can't. It's too much, way too much.'

'Nonsense,' she replied. 'Prices of things these days are downright ludicrous.' She poured herself an apple brandy. 'I'm comfortable, have no need of the stuff. Put it to good use, William. You've done hearty work on my garden, transformed it. This is a just reward for your efforts.' She took a sip of the pale green spirit. Then smiled. 'Something to write and tell your father about, eh?'

I was still reeling. 'Well, maybe. But . . . listen, you've already paid me for the gardening . . .'

'He'll be proud, I think, to know his son is applying himself so well without him.'

I found myself nodding, still in shock. Her hands gently prised the money from mine, put it into the envelope again before passing it back to me. 'Just don't fritter it, William.'

I turned the envelope over a few times. 'Are you sure?'

'Absolutely certain.'

'Well . . . thank you. Thank you very much, Mrs Fitzroy.'

'Your mother sold the house yet? The sign's been up for weeks.'

I shrugged, putting the envelope into my pocket, trying to

do it as casually as possible, as if I always relieved elderly widows of vast amounts of cash while small-talking about my mum. The damn thing dropped onto the floor. I blushed as I picked it up. 'We just can't seem to find any buyers for it,' I said eventually.

'It is rather run-down,' Mrs Fitzroy agreed. 'Garden looks wonderful, of course, but the structure, well, I daresay it's one of the few properties to have lost some value recently.'

'Dad couldn't really afford to do it up. He lost a lot of money in business. Mum wanted to get a loan out to help, but the bank refused her.'

She finished the apple brandy, poured herself another, looked out of the small recessed kitchen window for a few seconds. It was almost dark outside. 'Bloody awful stuff, money,' she said softly.

I never went back to the cottage again – she didn't want me to. Two weeks later I bought a course of driving lessons and a beaten-up Fiat 127. Mum never asked where I got the money.

It took another seven months before we finally made the move to Maidstone. Dad never returned home – frankly, I think even Mum was beginning to give up hope by now – and his letters changed from weekly to monthly bulletins. Mum and I got on as best we could.

She ended up selling the oast-house to an American couple shrewd enough to see the desperation in her eyes and make an offer woefully short of the asking price. The result was that, although we could make the move to a three-bedroom flat in Maidstone, it wasn't exactly the worry-free fresh start Mum had planned for. It wasn't Tunbridge Wells for a start. The kitchen was cramped and damp, the third bedroom was little more than a box room, while my window looked out onto the less-than-scenic breezeblock wall of the motor-works next door. But it was home, cheaper than before and, as Mum kept telling me, at least we'd had a few years of the good life – plenty of others wouldn't ever know the pleasure.

I started casual evening work in a local chippy, sending hundreds of potatoes through the peeling and chopping machine and throwing thousands of raw chips into black, water-filled plastic dustbins, ready for frying. I returned home late each night with wrinkled hands and my hair stinking of batter. On Friday nights, Mr Jeffries, the owner, would let me take two wrapped portions of haddock and chips home for Mum and me. Eating the things after spending five hours in a steaming chip-shop was more of an ordeal than a meal for me, but Mum always seemed pleased, so it was worth it.

Our domestic harmony, though, was suddenly shattered. One April evening in 1981, Dave Phillips, seventeen, drunk, and looking for a bag of chips on the way home, walked into Maidstone's Silver Hake Fish Bar. I guess it made his night to glimpse me working in the back. 'Oi, Dickson,' I heard him slurring. 'Get us some chips right now, you frrrreak!'

Mr Jeffries, frying meals in four gallons of bubbling oil while his wife wrapped and served, politely asked Phillips to leave. Then again, not so politely, after the inebriated sixth-form-college student told him to fuck off. Phillips, although obviously drunk, was still large enough to be threatening, but Mr Jeffries, though fifty-five years old, was stone-cold sober, an ex-Royal Marine commando, and had a look on his coldly enraged face that seemed to be begging the young chancer to try his luck.

Mrs Jeffries, a large jovial sort in a white nylon housecoat, tried her best to soothe the situation, but to no avail.

'Bollocks to ya,' Phillips sneered, then added, 'Fucking wouldn't eat anything out of this shit-pit, anyway.' He pointed back across the counter to me. 'Fuck knows what the pervert's been doing with all the food back there, anyway.'

'Out! Now!' Jeffries barked, opening the counter hatch. 'While you've still got legs to walk on, son!'

Phillips hesitated, shot me one final look, mouthed, 'Later, cunt,' then turned and walked from the shop.

Mrs Jeffries came to me as her husband watched him walk away. 'You all right, William?'

'Fine.'

'Someone from your college, is he?'

'Yeah.'

'Got a bad mouth on him that lad.'

'Sorry about that.'

She smiled. 'Not your fault, is it, William? Stupid types everywhere.'

Her husband joined us. 'All bloody mouth and no trousers that lad,' he announced, voice shaking slightly. 'See how he bolted when I came out from the counter? Tail between his bloody legs, he was. No-good young piss-artist.'

'Language,' Mrs Jeffries chided.

The ex-commando kissed her on the cheek then, mumbling, went back to the fryer.

For the next twenty minutes I concentrated on feeding peeled, desiccated parts of Dave Phillips into the chipper.

Forty minutes later, I said my goodnights to Mr and Mrs Jeffries, leaving the clammy wet heat of the shop and stepping out into the cool of the night. A slight breeze was blowing as I made my way quickly down the street, cooling the sweat on my forehead, making me pull my coat tighter . . .

'Hello, freak,' was all he said.

A man moaned, then a woman screamed – distant, unreal voices I seemed almost to recognize. Then a terrible smash of glass, so much louder, heavier than I'd have imagined. I saw the pavement rise up towards me, then felt the world explode round me. Such brief, cold, incredible pain.

Phillips had waited for me, found me, then damn near killed me.

9

I'm told I was in a coma for twenty-seven days. I say 'told' because, as you'll appreciate, one of the primary disadvantages of emerging from the ethers of near-death is that you are reliant on other people's testimony. Time past, time future – who you are, even – initially means nothing. Newspapers have a certain date on them, medical staff, relatives and friends tell you that a certain period of time has elapsed. As far as I was concerned, I felt as if I'd been out for about an hour. To be told it was the best part of a month was extraordinarily confusing.

For the first few hours after coming round I felt like a newborn baby. Everything hurt. The pain of light in my eyes was intense, my body cramped at the slightest impulse to move. Simply lying on a bed and trying to lift my forearm a few inches off the hospital mattress was an almost Herculean task.

Later people asked me what it felt like to be technically dead for so long, a corpse sustained by machines. Could I hear anything? Only occasionally. Did I ever have an out-of-body experience? Never. Was there much pain? Only when I came round. Was it peaceful, or frightening? Neither. Was I aware of who I was? No. Not in that plane. I remember only two events during those twenty-seven days. Visions, perhaps, unconscious dreaming. Both equally surreal. The first involved the Squires, landlords of the Partridge – a couple I knew to be long dead in their Spanish hotel fire – now restored, sitting somewhere close, simply staring at me. Her eyes blazed accusingly, while he wore some kind of neck-brace, his face sullen, sad. I felt an inexplicable sense of shame – guilt almost – and tried to talk to them, but no words came.

The second vision was my father. This time at night. Again, sitting, glimpsed between racks of strange beeping machines, trying to be brave, trying not to cry. And next to him a police officer, bored, reading a magazine. So many questions came to me but, frustratingly, I had no voice to air them.

They pay a lot of attention to memory when you first come out of a coma. Apparently, it's a primary indicator with severe brain injury. Traumatic amnesia, they call it. The longer you're under, the more you tend to forget. It's as if memories themselves are like the solid body tissue that's atrophying around them. They can't be sustained, aren't permanent, are almost desperate to escape. And the moment the system goes down, the instant the skull cracks, then the memories are released, fleeing God knows where.

Mum was at the bedside when I finally came round. It was around four in the afternoon, and I remember making out her blurred, white, shocked face as I felt my eyes and jaw fractionally – painfully – begin to open. Next I heard her muffled, panicked voice, rising to a scream, calling frantically for doctors, nurses, over and over.

Seconds later, the bed is surrounded by medical staff, urgently switching machines, changing drips, injecting me. Their shoes squeak on the polished ward floor, and I find the noise too loud, a jet screaming three feet above the bed. Something grips my hand, fingers that feel like hot coals press my wrist to take my pulse. Every sensation is huge, hurtful, frightening. I want to cry out, scream, but can't. My throat is blocked. I'm suffocating, choking on the intrusion. It's the worst kind of helplessness, absolute fear mixed with sudden confusion and aching dread. Smells seem to tear into my nose like boiling acid, and the feeding tube in my throat now burns the length of my gullet.

'Get it out, get it out,' a distant doctor urgently commands, as a figure on my left begins pulling at some kind of constriction in my nose. I feel the thin plastic tubing rise out of my stomach and want to heave, vomit the whole of my life back into the comforting nothing of minutes before.

I want to be dead, dead, dead . . .

I spent a further week in the Brain Injuries Unit before being transferred to another ward. Mum came to visit me every day, and gradually, through initially painful conversation (my throat still felt as if I'd been trying to swallow razor blades for the last month), I began to fill in some of the gaps.

I'd spent five hours in surgery on admittance, and needed twelve pints of blood. Together with the fifty-two stitches in my shaved head, I also had a dislocated shoulder, broken collar-bone, a shattered ankle, a fractured left femur and extensive internal bruising. Dave Phillips had certainly gone to town on me as I lay unconscious on the cold pavement. Fortunately all internal organs were now beginning to function more or less normally, and although I was still on heavy pain-killing medication, it was generally assumed that I'd make a good recovery.

I was assigned a personal physiotherapist, and twice each day would have to do various draconian exercises on the bed. After another week, the cast on my leg came off, and I was finally able to use the overhead bed-hoist to pull myself up into a sitting position, then gradually move my lower body round in stages until, with support on either side, I could stand on the floor. After just a few vertical seconds, however, I felt myself blacking out. Too much too soon, I was later told.

I had other visitors, most notably the police. They wanted to know more about my injuries, specifically if I had any memories of how I'd sustained them. Which, of course, I did, but I was damned if I was going to tell them. Two plain-clothes officers visited me three times in the first fortnight after I came round. Each time I feigned amnesia, told them I had no idea what had happened. One moment I was walking home, the next – nothing. At which point they'd look at each other, maybe have a hushed conversation with Dr Collins, the consultant overseeing my mental recovery. Then they'd leave, leaving me to wonder how much they already knew. Surely Mr and Mrs Jeffries had mentioned Dave Phillips's threatening behaviour in the shop less than an hour before my injuries? Or maybe not. A chippy like the Silver Hake acted as a magnet to young, hungry drunks. And Phillips had been careful not to carry out his cowardly attack too near the place, choosing a darker, quieter venue with no witnesses. Perhaps, I began to convince myself, no one but Phillips and I knew the truth of what had happened that night. And if that's how it was, then it was more than fine by me. I'd deal with him in my own way – when the time was right and I was ready.

My appetite began to improve, too. And whilst the food was typically dreadful lukewarm mush delivered from a trolley, I began to hold it down for longer, until, one triumphant day, three weeks after coming out from the coma, I passed my first solid stool on a yellow plastic bedpan. To my embarrassment at the time, the nurse, a pretty young girl called Charlotte, even congratulated me.

By now, I was in an open recovery ward, looking forward to being discharged in the near future. The physiotherapy became easier, I began putting on weight again. The night cramps abated as my atrophied muscles grew back. The medication stabilized to just three painkillers a day, all oral, no more injections. Nurse Charlotte called me in from the television lounge one afternoon with a silver kidney dish and some scissors in her hand. That evening when Mum came to visit, those fifty-two stitches were out. I was allowed off the ward for limited periods of time, so that night we took a short stroll down the long linoleum corridors and ate in the refectory.

Mum ran her fingers through the stubble on my head, lightly brushing the scar which ran from the back of my left ear, up and over my head. 'Bet that feels better, now those stitches are out,' she said, smiling.

'Mum, I look like a skinhead who's been in a machete war – and lost.'

'The hair will grow back, William.'

'Not over the scar, it won't.'

'Bit of clever combing will disguise it. Besides,' she leant forward, lowered her voice and raised her eyebrows mischievously, 'some women prefer a man with scars.'

'Mum!'

'Just saying there's always a bright side to everything. How's the studying going?'

'OK.' I paused. 'Mum, I want to leave, get out of here. I feel fine. I'm tired of writing essays on my lap in the television lounge wearing sodding pyjamas. I want to wear shoes, not slippers. I want to talk to people who aren't ill for once. When are they going to let me go? No one's telling me anything.'

She looked at me, chewed on her bottom lip, then looked

away. Behind her, a steady stream of doctors, nurses, relatives and the occasional patient queued for their supper. 'Dr Collins,' she said eventually, 'still wants to run some more tests.'

Dr Collins – my bête noire in that hospital. A short, sandy-haired man in his thirties, who always wore the same light-brown suit, cream shirt and a range of thin bow-ties. A man who asked me the same psychometric questions four times a week, then simply smiled at both my answers and my subsequent questions. I had the growing feeling that, if it were up to the irritating Dr Collins, I'd be staying in that wretched hospital for months.

'The man's an arse, Mum.'

'He just wants to be sure, William. He's very well thought of.'

'Sure of what?'

She laid down her knife and fork, picked up a spoon and began pushing thick custard around her slice of apple pie. 'That . . . that everything's OK.'

She wasn't looking at me, knew more than she was letting on.

'Mum,' I stressed. 'Everything is OK. I feel fine, really.'

She nodded, eyes still on the pudding bowl. 'I'm sure you do, William. But coming out of a coma like you did . . . well, they just have to be sure, that's all.'

I reached out for her wrist. 'Mum, you're beginning to sound like the rest of them.'

Her tired eyes met mine. They seemed suddenly so much greyer, older than I remembered. Worry had taken the life from my mother's eyes. 'Sometimes we just have to leave these things to the experts,' she said diplomatically. 'I know it's hard on you, but –'

'But what?'

'William, there're some areas, some things, that Dr Collins is still concerned about.'

Finally, we were getting somewhere. 'Such as?'

'I can't tell you. It would ruin the tests.'

One step forward, two steps back. 'Mum, please.'

'William, I'm not allowed to.'

'Am I doing something wrong?'

'No. Nothing wrong, exactly.'

'What then?' I was having trouble controlling my voice. I watched as she slowly put down her spoon and wiped her mouth with the paper napkin.

She looked around, then back at me. 'Not here,' she said simply.

We found a small storage room a little distance away. I watched confused as she quietly closed the door.

'It's your memory, love,' she said quietly.

'My memory?'

'It's nothing to worry about, it's quite common in cases like yours. But . . . well, the upshot is that some of the things you've been telling Dr Collins, you know about things that have happened . . . well, you've been getting them a bit muddled up.'

She was trying so hard not to upset me, eyes flicking intently over mine, as if searching for any sign of anger or confusion. 'Oh,' I said, wanting suddenly to sit. I knew then exactly what the problem was. Ever since my first session with Dr Collins, he'd pried into my past – not just the memories I had concerning the night of my assault, but further back into my childhood. And frankly, here he was treading on dangerous ground. Of course I had to hide certain events, lie a little. How could I possibly tell him I'd killed three people to date? Chances were he'd run straight to the two policemen who'd come to see me three times already. Then the lid would really be off.

Standing alone in the cramped storage room with my mother, I immediately understood her concern, too. We'd never really talked about Margot Norris – never really had to. Up until that point I believed we'd both put the incident behind us. But the truth still stood. I'd killed her, then Mum and Dad had framed an 'innocent' man for the murder. But now the past had reared its ugly, blood-covered head.

I exhaled heavily, feeling giddy from the weight of it all. 'What do you want me to say?' I asked.

'I shouldn't be telling you any of this.'

'But you have, Mum.'

She took one hand, held it between both of hers. 'William,' she said, voice urgent. 'Has Collins asked you about Dr Tremaine?'

I frowned. 'Tremaine?'

'You do remember Dr Tremaine, don't you?'

I shook my head, completely confused, unable to follow any of it.

'Just tell Collins you remember Dr Tremaine. That you think something might have happened. And that you're sorry . . .'

'Mum –'

'Listen to me!' The sharp rebuke shocked me. I felt the warm, angry puff of her breath on my face. 'Next time you see Collins, mention Dr Tremaine. It might be enough to get you out of here.'

'What are you talking about?'

But she was turning around in the confined space. 'God knows, I shouldn't have told you this much. Let's get back to the ward.'

We left the room, made our way back to the ward without another word passing between us. I followed half a pace behind, utterly confused, and more worried than I'd been in a long while.

'Thing is, Doctor,' I said to Collins in his cramped hospital office the following morning. 'I asked to see you because something's come up, and it's really playing on my mind.'

'Oh?' The bow-tie was red today, his manner as unfathomable as ever.

'I keep getting flashes of this name, and I'm sure it means something to me. I just don't know what.'

He made a note of that, which encouraged me on. Acting, I was quickly discovering, wasn't as complex as the Hollywood elite made out. It was simply lying with a few frowns, a couple of pauses and a good smattering of conviction. Despite the confusions of the previous day, I was enjoying myself.

'What is this name, William?' Collins asked.

'Tremaine.' Another note on the clipboard.

'Tremaine?'

'Yeah.' I looked him full in the eyes. 'I know it means something, I just . . .' (see how the pause adds authenticity?) '. . . I don't know, it seems to, kind of, bring up feelings. As if . . . as if I say the name and feel really sorry for something.'

He nodded, took his time. 'And what might that be?'

'That's the confusing thing, Doctor. I have no idea.' I leant forward, aped great concentration by covering my face with both hands and moaning slightly. 'Is he –' I suddenly withdrew the hands, sat upright in the chair, '– a doctor of some sort?'

Collins was trying not to look excited, but the eyes were the tell. Specifically the pupils, enlarging with interest. He crossed his legs too, for no particular reason, then followed this up with a pointless clearing of the throat. I'd read enough amateur psychology in American teach-yourself body-language books to know that Collins was hooked.

Whatever I'd said, I'd hit home, and it was all down to Mum – though I still hadn't the slightest clue who this Dr Tremaine character was. But I figured I'd have a whole lifetime to make sense of that one. What mattered now was getting out of the hospital before Collins began probing too deeply into my past. Those two police officers were never very far from my thoughts. If I wasn't careful, I'd be spending a long time in another institution, only this one would have higher walls and bars on its windows.

In retrospect, perhaps I should have questioned what I came to call 'the Tremaine defence' a little harder in my mind. There I was, merrily spouting some complete stranger's name, implying he had had some kind of impact on my life, and I'd never even heard of the man. But at the time, all I could feel was a growing sense of being reeled in by the authorities. I felt cornered, and Tremaine was my lifeline. In circumstances such as mine, the instinct is to bolt first, ask questions later.

Tremaine was a key that unlocked the doors of the hospital, allowing me to be discharged. That night, when Mum came to visit me, she told me I'd be leaving the following day.

I spent the best part of a sleepless night planning how I'd kill Dave Phillips.

Tremaine never entered my mind for an instant.

10

Nine weeks and three days from the date of my attack, I walked back into Maidstone sixth-form college. Limping, perhaps, but only slightly. In many ways, it was a re-run of my return to school after Fat Norris's unscheduled plunge into eternity. People stared, they wanted to know how I'd got the scar, the crazy haircut. Within minutes of walking into the neon-lit refectory I was surrounded by at least a dozen intrigued inquisitors, wide-eyed and desperate for details. One or two of the girls wanted to touch my scar, squealing and giggling as their fingers traced the angry red line just beneath my close-cropped hair. Naomi, my one-time amour, even went so far as to confide that she thought the new look suited me, and as things with Ash were apparently on the slide, she was not averse to picking things up where we left off. With reservations, obviously, she whispered into my ear as he loitered and glowered nearby. None of the strangling stuff. In the traditions of the best Sunday tabloid journalists, I made my excuses and declined. Naomi and I had nowhere left to go.

Experts will tell you that one of the most common after-effects of being in a coma is that sufferers undergo a dramatic reappraisal of life itself. The patient comes round and is forced to admit that, barring modern medical technology, they would be dead. Some take this very badly indeed, and are completely unwilling or unable to step back into the life they once had. They leave partners and families behind, and never fully come to terms with their medically powered second chance. Post-traumatic survivor syndrome is an extreme example of this – where the sole survivor of a plane crash may spend much of his or her life racked with terrible guilt that they somehow lived while all the others died. Strange how the dice land sometimes, and weirder still how the mind struggles to cope with it.

Maybe I was fortunate, or made of stronger stuff, but I had none of these symptoms. I had no desire to re-evaluate my life, or live every brand-new day as my last. It didn't make any great philosophical difference to me that, by rights, I should be dead; what mattered more was dealing death back out to someone else. I was consumed with one burning ambition: to kill the bastard that scarred me. I'd been spared, I concluded, in order that he should die. Simple, really.

More fortunate still was that Dave Phillips – unimaginative thug that he was – was entirely predictable. The creature of habit, I've heard it said, is the easiest to kill.

He owned a car, or at least drove his father's old one, a red Triumph Spitfire that he'd bastardized with various drilled exhausts to emit the loudest noise possible. People couldn't fail to notice when Dave Phillips pulled into the car park which, of course, was the transparently obvious intention. He'd arrive around ten o'clock, when the bulk of us had already sat down to lectures, a deafening throaty roar heralding the great man's arrival, then slump moodily at the back of the lecture room until lunchtime, whereupon, with a gang of his mates, he would saunter off to the local pub for a few 'liveners'. Phillips rarely made the afternoon lectures, preferring instead to fire up the Spitfire around three o'clock and roar back out of the narrow car park as fast as his drunken reactions would let him. A narrow car park with a thick red-brick wall and an extremely sharp right-hand turn onto the main road.

Get the picture? It wasn't exactly going to be the stuff of murderous genius to kill the guy. The Screaming Man and I had already whipped up an obvious plan.

On the day in question, Phillips never made the right turn. Instead he hit the wall at around thirty-five m.p.h. with a distinct crump. Apparently, some ne'er-do-well had tampered with his brakes and steering column earlier in the day. Shocking what goes on when all you want to do is sink a few beers with your mates. And although I was quite eagerly awaiting Phillips's last yet most spectacular exit – I'd positioned myself right by the window in the first-floor humanities block – the ironic thing was that none of the others paid too much attention to the crunching din initially. It was only when the red sports car burst into flames with a growling 'whump' that people realized something was wrong. A window shattered with the pressure of the sudden explosion. Glass showered over us. Burning air rushed inside. The girl in front of me screamed. Others joined in. It was really rather chaotic for a while.

Fire and ambulance services had to put up a tent round the still-smoking shell in order to pull pieces of his corpse out.

Quite a 'triumph', all in all.

My release from the hospital, I learnt from my mother, was conditional. Apparently there were 'areas' of my recovery that the boffins were still concerned about. Confusing to me, for barring a few aches and pains, occasional bad headaches, and the niggling limp from my freshly fused leg, I'd never felt better. Mentally, I felt on top of the world, as if the coma had refreshed every brain-cell, hosed it clean from the past, left it sparkling fresh for the future.

They called it an 'outpatient care programme', but essentially I was on some sort of probation. Once a fortnight I had to go to a clinic in Richmond and see a Dr Danally, a tall, thin-lipped blonde in her forties. It was a nice old building, set up on the hill and overlooking the river below, but her office was at the back. There were bars on the windows, and the sun rarely made it onto the small concreted courtyard outside.

Here, conversations would go round and round in endless bloody circles. She sat in one corner, I sat in another, both in the type of upright easy chairs found in too many old people's homes. Everything in the room was dour, uncomfortable, from the bland magnolia walls with their predictable Athena woodland prints, to the look of deep professional contemplation she always gave me. Dr Danally never took her eyes off me.

A typical conversation might go: 'So, William, how have you felt the last two weeks?'

'Fine.'

'Any incidents?'

'Incidents?'

'Faints. Nightmares. Any strange visions entering your head?' By 'visions' she meant memories, but, as she'd gone to great and endless lengths to explain to me, while my memory recovered from the effects of post-traumatic amnesia, any suppressed or buried memories would appear in the form of visions – points of surreal reference that my conscious mind would initially refuse to accept as memories. Psycho-babble, all of it.

'No, no visions,' I'd respond.

'Any more on Dr Tremaine?'

'Nothing.'

'But you still have . . . a feeling about him?'

'The name means something.' I had to say this, didn't I? After all, the mysterious Dr Tremaine had been my pass out of the hospital. 'Perhaps if you'd show me a photograph?'

She'd shake her head. 'The memory has to be kick-started by you, William. From the inside. To give you a photo of him would be cheating. Once you think you have a vision of him in your mind, we'll begin to look at photographs.'

'Fair enough.'

One afternoon, shortly after I had dispensed with Phillips, she said, 'A boy died at your college the other day, didn't he?'

'S'right.'

'I saw it on the news.'

'I saw it in real life.'

'What was it like, William?'

'Like?'

'How did it affect you?' She was making notes all the time.

'The rest of the lecture was cancelled.'

'Did you feel sad, angry, frightened?'

'Why should I be angry?'

'Death affects us all in different ways.'

'I wasn't angry.'

'How does death affect you, William?'

'Ask me when I'm dead.'

And so on, and so on. Dr Danally, probing, me giving nothing save assurances that I was coping excellently well with college studies, and – barring the Dr Tremaine lie – that

I had no 'visions' of any kind. I tolerated these sessions mainly because my mother asked me to. They weren't compulsory, yet I had the feeling from her intense expression that if I failed to keep an appointment, then something else would weigh in for me instead. And, frankly, with my record to date, I preferred to be going round in circles with Dr Danally once a fortnight than to be grilled by CID officers linking me now with four suspicious deaths.

There was a fish-tank in the reception of the Richmond clinic, a large affair, standing by a wall, home to about fifty fish. By this time I'd read enough on memory (Dr Danally had given me a reading-list) to know that your average gold-fish has a memory of approximately four seconds. One day I bought a plastic galleon in. I'd made it from an Airfix kit of the *Golden Hind*. As I waited for my appointment, I rolled up my sleeves and gently lowered the galleon into the light green water, watching as the fish swam for safety to either end of the tank.

'What on earth are you doing?' the alarmed-looking receptionist asked.

'Making it more exciting for them,' I replied, water up to my bare elbows, weighting down the boat with two large stones.

Moments later Dr Danally appeared and stood by my side. 'William,' she said, 'they're only fish. They don't remember anything. Each time they turn a corner, it's as if for the first time.'

'Sure,' I said, watching as the first fish began swimming towards the sunken ship. 'But imagine the pleasure of seeing the *Golden Hind* afresh, every day, for ever.'

I learnt a lot about memory after my coma. Memory, Dr Danally's books told me, is the very essence of us. We are ourselves because of a series of stacked, interconnecting memories. The memory of a mother's heartbeat brings us feelings of calming, womblike safety. Mother's eyes – two blurred black dots – seen for the first time by a wet, bloodied newborn, form the cornerstone of the most powerful human bond.

Memory is us. Hoover a man clean of memories, and he

has no idea of who he is, where he is, what he is. Memory and madness are intimately linked.

Memories push us forward. The past governs our future. We take decisions based on experience gleaned from thousands of memories. Our models of the world are jigsaws of millions of memories. Preferences are born from pleasant ones, while, more importantly, bad memories slot themselves into a mental survival manual. And while some say that instinct is the overriding factor determining choice, psychologists argue that instinct itself is merely a subconscious collective human memory system. We cross the road to avoid the stranger with the wild staring eyes because the memories of our long-dead forefathers ring alarm bells in our minds. Memories passed from one generation to another.

Occasionally – as in all things – there are glitches. I didn't know it yet, but I was one. Not that it bothered me at the time, why should it? Life was OK. I'd evened the score with Phillips, and was getting on.

That summer I passed all three 'A'-levels with average grades. In September, I'd be starting at Manchester Polytechnic.

11

September 1981, a Sunday evening, and my mother and I sit in the kitchen of the Maidstone flat over a couple of bottles of red wine. I'm not normally a drinker, but as it's my last night before I leave for Manchester, and as I suspect Mum needs the drink more than I do, I join her in draining the bottles.

My one time 'little' sister Nicola is out with a bunch of friends, leaving just Mum and me, the wine and long silences, the future heavy on both our minds.

'She seems to be adapting to normality quite well,' I said, referring to Nicola, who had finished at her private school the previous July, and now looked set to follow the same sixth-form college avenue I'd just finished.

Mum put on something approaching a weary smile. 'Dickson family trait that, love. Adapting.' She reached across the table, patted the back of my hand. 'My God, we've done some adapting.'

'She was telling me she wants to take four "A"-levels,' I said, glad we were finally talking, and especially glad that the subject wasn't me. 'I think she'll go far. Really. Her head seems screwed on the right way. Strange, I hardly know her, really. I mean, she's my sister, blood and all that, but . . . well, I've hardly seen her over the last few years.'

Mum finished her wine, poured herself another glass. 'It'll be nice to have her around. Especially as you won't be here.'

Guilt. I'm sure none was intended, but nevertheless I felt a slight pang as she said it. 'Mum, you're going to be OK, aren't you?'

She smiled. 'I'm old enough to look after myself, William.'

'Any news from Dad? Is he . . . ?'

She shook her head. A foolish question, really, one we both knew the answer to before I even asked it. Dad hadn't written to me in months. The man was starting to fade from my life. Secretly, I wondered if he'd found another woman, set up home with her, a new, uncomplicated life away from us. Glimpsing the sudden sorry look in my mother's eyes, I wondered if she knew that perhaps he already had, and was living there now, curled up on the sofa in front of his beloved television, my mother unable to come to terms with telling Nicola and me. Because I'd understand that, the simple psychological expedient of making the truth real by voicing it. Put it off, and the possibility ceases to exist.

I refilled my own glass. 'Can't believe I'm actually going,' I said, watching her.

'No.'

'Hardly reading law at Oxford, but –'

'Don't, William.'

'What?'

'Put yourself down.'

'Humanities at Manchester Poly? I just don't want to be a disappointment, I suppose.'

She took my hand again. 'I'm very proud, William. You've done so well, in spite of . . . don't spoil it by being cynical.'

'I'm going to miss you. You and Nicola.'

'Have you spoken to Dr Danally?'

'I always speak to Dr Danally,' I sighed. 'Though quite what the point is, I'm not really sure.'

'And?'

'She told me I'd be seeing someone called Dr Carter in Manchester. Crazy. I feel like I'm being passed from one dodgy quack to another for everyone's entertainment. Or maybe worse. Maybe it's simply that these people earn their livings persuading people like me that we need to see them. Like – I don't know – some sort of mental emperor's new clothes. I lie awake waiting for some kid in the crowd to point at me and say, "Look at him! He's just as sane as the rest of us!"'

'William,' she said earnestly. 'There's nothing more important right now than your recovery.'

'But I feel fine,' I protested. 'Really.'

'I know you do, love. But seeing Dr Carter is one of the admission requirements from the polytechnic. If you don't keep those appointments, they'll be entitled to –'

'What, chuck me off a sodding humanities course that I could do standing on my bloody head?'

'Don't get angry, William.'

'Christ's sake, Mum, it's a joke! How many other students will have to see a fucking shrink as part of their coursework?'

The 'f'-word shocked her. Immediately I'd said it, I wished I hadn't. She waited a while, then slowly, deliberately, said, 'William, how many other students have possible post-traumatic amnesia?'

'It just makes me feel like a freak,' I explained.

'I know. But Dr Tremaine says Carter is a real expert. If anyone can help you –'

'Here we go.'

'What?'

'Dr Tremaine again.'

'What about him?'

As if I had to explain. 'Mum, the man dogs my life. First you tell me to mention the guy to get out of hospital . . .'

'And I shouldn't have done that. That was the wrong thing to do.'

Despite myself, the anger was coming. '. . . then Danally wants to know what I remember about him. Which is bugger-all . . .'

'William, please –'

'Now you say he's fully endorsing this Carter guy I've got to see in order to be allowed to stay at some crummy, second-rate polytechnic, for Christ's sake! Just who is this bloody Dr Tremaine? Time and time again the name crops up, and no one's giving me any answers! You try it, Mum – go on, you try "remembering" someone you've never met in your life!'

She looked straight at me, her tired eyes pleading with mine for some sort of base understanding. 'William, you know very well that I can't tell you who he is. It's up to you to remember. It's part of the treatment, your recovery.'

'Unbelievable!'

'It's just how it is, love.'

And if I could have, I would have killed my mother at that moment. Such was my anger, the unstoppable rising force of the black within me, that if I could have been completely sure of getting clean away with it, I would have done for her, right there and then. Instant retribution, Dickson style. What in God's name did I have to lose? Answer: a mother who was clearly acting with them, who sat making ludicrous excuses while I wallowed in oceans of confusion. She had answers to my questions, but still she rattled out the same worn excuses. All bollocks in my book. All pointers to another truth, one she was too terrified to tell me. Why? Why wouldn't she tell me about Tremaine?

But I didn't kill my mother. I had a sip of wine instead, perhaps gripping the stem of the glass too tightly, covering the venom as best I could. Then I said, 'Fine, you can't tell me about Tremaine. I respect that. So let me see him. You're obviously still in contact with him. Take me to him. Then maybe whatever wire's loose in my head will reconnect. We'll turn up on his doorstep, and who knows? There could be some miracle cure for whatever it is I'm supposed to be suffering from.'

'I can't do that.'

'Oh, for God's sake! Do you see, can you begin to understand how frustrating this is for me? I get snippets of things I can't see. No one tells me anything, but everyone wants to know everything about me.' I stood, the chair grating harshly on the kitchen floor. 'Most of the time, I can cope. Most of the time I can get on with my life and say bollocks to the lot of you. Especially Dr Tremaine, if he even exists. But sometimes . . . Jesus wept, Mum, you really don't want to know what I sometimes think about.'

'William, listen . . .'

'What's the problem with me seeing him? Everyone tells me he exists. Where is he? I want to see him.'

'Two problems, if you really want to know.'

'Of course I do!'

She closed her eyes for a moment, composing herself. 'Firstly, it's against the medical advice for people with your particular diagnosis . . .'

'And the second reason?'

'He doesn't want to see you.'

'Doesn't want to?'

She nodded.

'Can I ask why not? Or aren't you allowed to answer that, either?'

'William. Sit down, love. Come on. Sit back down. Please.'

I reluctantly sat, heels bouncing furiously on the floor.
'He's frightened of you,' she said.

It took a while to sink in, to make any sort of sense. Then it made me want to giggle. A man who I'd never met, who seemed intricately connected to my life, whose name alone was enough to get me discharged from the hospital, was now scared to see me? 'Why?' I asked.

'Something happened. Between you and him.'

It was my turn to reach out and grab her hand. 'Mum,' I said smiling, trying not to laugh, frantically trying to place some of this – any of this – in a semblance of order. 'I can honestly assure you that nothing has ever happened between Dr Tremaine and me. Nothing. I've never met the man, ever. You have to believe me. The first I heard of him was when you told me to mention him at the hospital.'

'I believe that you believe that, William, yes.' I wondered if she was about to cry. Maybe she was, but somehow managed to blink back the tears before they came, saving them for later. 'There are things, William.'

'Things?'

'Things you still can't remember. Things in your mind. Connections that aren't working very well.'

'I'm not a mental patient, Mum.'

'I know, love. But it's going to take time to sort out what's going on in that head of yours. They all say that, the people in the hospital, everyone – it takes time. Your . . . accident didn't help. The coma made things worse.' She let go of my hand and turned away. This time, it was to cry. Shit. I saw her shoulders bob, heard the small whimpers, then rose and walked to her, sank to my knees, held her, moved her head onto my shoulders, let her weep into me for what seemed like an age.

Later, she came to me as I was packing the last of my stuff in my room. I had a suitcase full of clothes, and a hold-all with books and bits. She opened the case, looked at the crumpled clothes inside and tutted. Then, while I sat on the bed and watched, she emptied the suitcase and began repacking it, this time carefully folding each item before placing it inside.

'You don't have to do that,' I said, yet sensed somewhere that she did, that this was her way of coming to terms with the imminent loss of me.

'William Dickson,' she muttered. 'Always so independent.'

'Best way to be.'

She turned to me, smiled. It was nice to see her smile again. 'Look at you. I can hardly believe it. My son. Handsome, clever, capable. And once all this . . . this business is sorted out . . . well, you're going to be quite a catch for the right girl.'

I probably blushed puce. 'Sure.'

'You'll make so many new friends in Manchester.' A look of sudden concern crossed her face. 'You will make friends, won't you?'

'Maybe.'

'You've always been such a loner.'

'Just never really felt the need for loads of friends, I suppose.'

She put two jumpers into the suitcase and began closing the lid, fingers trembling slightly with the metal fastenings. 'So different from your sister.'

'Thank God for that, eh?'

'I suppose so.'

'Besides,' I continued, feeling a tiny bit irked by the suggestion that I was somehow made deficient by a lack of friends. 'Remember Alan Cooper at Chetwins. Got on like a house on fire, we did.'

'Alan Cooper?' she whispered.

'Yeah. Little guy. Blond hair.' What was the problem?

'At Chetwins?'

'Mum, are you feeling OK?' I thought she was about to throw up from too much wine. Her face was ashen, her mouth agape in shock.

'How much?' she suddenly asked. 'How much can you remember about the tree, William?'

I stared back, confused. The tree? What the hell was she talking about?

'Come on, William. The woods. Tilbury. You and Edward Norris. Please,' she begged. 'Please try to remember.'

'But this is later, Mum,' I insisted, frowning, unable to

follow her sudden manic thread. 'After all that. This has nothing to do with the woods. This is about schoolfriends. Chetwins. I was thirteen when I first met Alan Cooper . . .'

This time when she gripped my hand, it hurt. 'William, you've had a serious head injury. It's messing with your memory . . .'

'Mum, please. Listen –'

'No! You listen, William!'

I jumped at the outburst.

She took a massive breath, stared straight into my startled eyes. 'There was no Alan Cooper at Chetwins, William, ever . . .'

'No, Mum, you're wrong,' I replied, feeling increasingly uncomfortable. Her intensity unnerved me, was beginning to scare me. 'He was there, honest. We were best friends.'

'He never went to Chetwins, William. Alan Cooper's dead.'

Which hit me like the hand of Satan.

Then, in the shocked silence, another revelation rose from somewhere deep inside, an inner voice trying desperately to make sense out of the chaos, to explain the ravings of the wild-eyed woman in front of me. Something I should perhaps have been more attentive to earlier, but now could no longer avoid. My mother was disturbed, traumatized. Mad, maybe . . .

I had goose-pimples on my arm. An image flooded my mind: Mum calmly instructing me to peel vegetables as Margot Norris's corpse wept thick black blood at my feet. This was a mother who calmly allowed her son to prepare Christmas lunch over a slaughtered neighbour. My mother . . .

I saw my father, drinking at the Partridge, unable to cope. With what – Mum's madness? Is this how it had really been all along? Had he known how ill she was, and finally lost the will to stay with her any longer?

The bank, refusing us money to spend on the oast-house. Why? Because she wasn't stable enough? Then other thoughts and images, briefly flashed memories. Edith Fitzroy, pushing the envelope of money across the table towards me. Because she felt sorry for me, was that the reason? She felt sorry for a boy who lived largely at home with a mother who was clearly disturbed?

I began to sweat, beads breaking out over my close-cropped head, running the length of the pink raised scar. I felt giddy. The room, the outside world faded into nothing, a world beyond memories and all their boundless complications. Had I missed something vital? In all these years, had I missed my mother's madness?

The grip on my wrist was becoming unbearable. I felt fingernails tearing into my flesh. I couldn't move, couldn't breathe, couldn't cry out. I was paralysed.

Another long pause.

'There were three of you that day, William,' my mother eventually said. 'Three of you went into those woods that afternoon . . .'

I struggled, but she held me closer.

'Three of you . . . Edward Norris, Alan Cooper and you. Three went in, William. And only you came out.'

12

Calm down, William. Deep, deep, breaths. You've had a shock – and what a shock. Mummy's a loon. Still, is it really such a surprise? There are times when it's just plain bad manners to say 'I told you so', but I've always had reservations about that woman. And, William, you hit it right on the head, my boy, when you hit Fat's mum smack on the napper. Yes, it was horrible; yes, you were only trying to protect Mum – but really, what kind of mother would have you peeling spuds in your pyjamas with a body at your feet? Clearly this mother Theresa has a little to learn from her more charitable namesake. OK, let's get serious again. It's going to be hard, William, but I guess it's time we faced up to the facts. It's just you and me now. And that's not such a bad thing, is it? The old team, partners, bestest friends in the world, for ever. Listen, the way things are panning out right now, who else can we trust?

With daylight came a semblance of sanity.

The following morning I was up early, breakfasting while Mum slept off what I presumed would be the mother of all hangovers. Both wine bottles were empty, sitting on the same table as the milk and cereal, a potent reminder of just how much she'd drunk the previous evening. The radio churned out nonsense behind me. Cars raced along the road below. The sounds of the starting day gradually filtered up into the kitchen, obliterating – rationalizing – the night before.

God, what a load of twaddle Mother had come out with. Clearly it was the effect of the best part of two litres of Spanish red on a mind unused to heavy drink and stretched to breaking point by stress. Simple really. It had been the drink talking, not her. And what she'd said had been too damn ludicrous to contemplate. Alan Cooper, not at Chetwins – impossible! Yet despite the fact that the outburst was clearly absurd, it seemed to be an indicator, a powerful pointer, that maybe my mother wasn't too far from breaking down completely.

I found myself thinking what a very dangerous thing that would be. How well would she cope if nosy shrinks and police started probing around in her past – specifically her connection to the former Margot Norris? I knew what these people were like, knew full well how mental health professionals worked. One visit to her GP for sleeping pills could light a short fuse to the dynamite of my destruction, could bring a host of unwelcome inquisitors to our doorstep. And then things would be looked into, dates and names cross-referenced, records checked . . . Yet how could I possibly prevent it, 200 miles away?

I tried not to think too hard about that one.

Some time later Nicola wandered in wearing pyjamas and dressing gown and yawning. She plonked herself down at the table.

'Good night, was it?' I asked, watching as she poured too much milk on a bowl already overflowing with Sugar Puffs.

'How do you know when it's time to wash the curtains?'

'No idea,' I replied. This was my sister now, a store of the latest jokes on the street.

'Look in your pants. If you see a penis, it's not time.'

'Sounds like a great night.'

She chewed on a mouthful of cereal, eyeing the two empty bottles. 'You and Mum finish those off?'

'Mum, mostly.'

'Shit. No wonder she's sleeping it off.'

'Nicola, listen to me.' She rolled her eyes. 'I'm worried about her.'

'Such as?'

'I just think she's under a lot of stress at the moment.'

Another spoonful of cereal quickly followed the first. 'And?'

'I want you to call me – if there's a problem.'

'What sort of problem?'

'Christ's sake, any kind of problem.'

'All right, keep your hair on. Or what's left of it.'

I did my best to hide my smile.

So – and I sincerely hope this is the case – I was the only student ever to enrol at Manchester Polytechnic with a body count of four. Not that this was anything to be particularly proud of, simply a thought that occurred as I queued with fellow first-years to register on my first day.

Strange, in hindsight, how death can help you cope – specifically, I suppose, if you have become used to dispensing it. The truth is that, after you've killed, very little else holds any real excitement, tension or fear. Sure, there're the underlying worries of getting caught but, by and large, to be a murderer at liberty is a liberating thing. Anxieties lessen. You have an invisible rank that places you higher on the secret pile. The other freshers who started that September may have had heads crammed with concerns, but not William Dickson. His mind was blinkered, absolutely focused on getting by, getting ahead. He didn't go out of his way to rush round making too many friends; he didn't spend half his term's grant in the first week in the union bar; he didn't spend nights crying or writing long letters home – he simply got on with it, walked tall.

You walk a lot taller if you've killed.

My uncle Trevor had managed to sort me a room in a three-bedroomed student terrace in Fallowfield, three miles south of the main All Saints polytechnic campus. An investor he brokered for had interests in a Mancunian property-leasing company, and he was able to slide me into decent digs at half the price of the student halls-of-residence. Which was all well and good, because money was still an issue. I knew I'd have to find some kind of temporary work to support myself in the near future – but there was plenty of night work around.

I shared with two others: a second-year maths student called Kris Jordan, and a first-year architect called Ian Bailey. I had the smallest room, overlooking the backyard, but had no real complaints. Most times the others kept themselves to themselves, which I was glad about. Kris was a maternal girl, the self-appointed matriarch of the household. She'd lived in the place during the previous year and now took on the role of oracle, dispenser of all student knowledge. She told Ian and me which were the places to go for the best bargains, times of buses, places to avoid. Small, a little overweight with short brown hair and thick glasses, I suppose she matched the clichéd view of how a maths undergrad. might look. Kris divided things, worked out rotas, applied various mathematical formulae to ordering our lives in the house. She left notices on a cork board in the kitchen: reminders about the rent, splits on fuel bills, shopping rotas. One morning I came downstairs to discover a page of the *Radio Times* pinned to the board. Underneath were three coloured pens. A note on the kitchen table told me I was now the 'red pen', and that this new system had been devised to 'avoid any possible TV viewing conflicts'. We had to put a star beside the programme we wanted to watch, apparently. When Ian came down he told me that this was entirely reasonable, a system to avoid possible confrontation, and that really I oughtn't be taking the piss out of Kris.

'I think she had some troubles last year,' he said, taking a green pen and optimistically ticking off the European Cup quarter-final. Kris, I suspected, would never allow that. He, too, was small and a little overweight, and wore thick dark pullovers with stretched sleeves that seemed permanently to hide his hands. It had often struck me what a good match he and Kris were. If only Cupid would fire his little arrow their way, what a great scheduled life of red-pen rotas they might lead.

'Troubles?'

'I think, you know, the sharing thing might have got out of hand. She doesn't want that this year.'

'Ian, she's a control freak. It's getting ridiculous. Next we know we'll both have set times for a crap each day.'

He didn't answer, merely clenched his jaw a fraction.

At the sixth-form college, after my experience with Naomi, I'd never really bothered much with girls. Whilst I had found plenty of girls desirable, I had never experienced a real pull, a yearning to share, a need to embark on any relationship beyond a semi-drunken snogging session during the last hour of a party. It didn't bother me and, as far as I could make out, that's how it was for most of us. We were too young for any serious business. In my case there was an added reluctance to let anyone get too close. What would happen if I suddenly started to talk in my sleep, and the girl at my side discovered some of my darker secrets? I might have to kill her, too.

But now, at the poly, it seemed that everyone was chasing the rainbow of a steady relationship. Casual sexual affairs soon settled down into long-term coupling. Students who were strangers just a few weeks before were now seen strolling around campus as 'an item', the guys looking vaguely worried, the girls relieved that this part of their emotional curriculum had got off to such a flying start.

I sensed that Ian was keen to join them, dive headlong into a relationship as soon as possible. His defence of Kris's increasingly irritating domestic schedules led me to suspect the object of his unfulfilled expectations was none other than Kris herself. In his first term, he was required to produce drawings and sketches for an imaginary new library building in Salford. One night he called me into his room and showed me the project so far – about a dozen drawings from different elevations and perspectives. Each one had been entitled, 'Preliminary sketch for the Kris Jordan Library building'.

'Wouldn't it have been better if you'd chosen a local literary figure?' I asked him.

'Everyone's going to do that,' he replied.

'You shown Kris?'

He blushed, squirmed a little on his tall swivel chair. He also had a full-size drawing board in his room, complete with cables and weights. 'Not yet.'

'You going to?'

'Don't think Danny'd be too pleased about it.'

'Faint heart never won fair mathematician.'

He began quickly packing the sketches into a portfolio. In some ways his earnest frailty reminded me of Alan Cooper. 'And unfair drug-dealer always pulverizes nine-stone weakling,' he quietly replied.

'Danny's not a drug-dealer,' I tried.

'He tried to sell me some resin the other day.'

'What, an eighth of blow? Pablo Escobar must be quaking in his Columbian boots.'

'Drugs are drugs, Will.'

I nodded, left the room, went back to my essay on eighteenth-century social reform.

Thing was, I quite liked Danny Black – if that was really his name. And this attraction was, ironically, the only thing Kris and I shared. I met him for the first time about a week into that first term. He wandered into the kitchen on Sunday morning in just his underpants, yawned, scratched his arse, and put the kettle on. Then spotted me.

'You're the humanities bloke, aren't you?' he said, collapsing into a chair opposite, totally unbothered that he was virtually naked. 'Spotted you from the scar.'

'William,' I said warily, wondering who the hell the tall unshaven stranger was.

'Dan. Danny Black,' he supplied, reaching over with an outstretched arm. 'Mate of Kris's.'

Which really surprised me.

He stood, rifled through an old greatcoat hanging on the back of the kitchen door, took out a small brown suede bag, then sat back down and began rolling a joint. 'How are you finding it, then, student life?'

I was trying to age him. Late twenties, early thirties? There were wrinkles round his eyes, but they looked like laughter lines. The grey eyes, too, twinkled with mischief, hinted at a life devoted to scamming and scheming. But no malice there, just interest in who I was, what benefit I could be to him.

'It's OK,' I said, watching as he lit the corner of the brown Lebanese cube, quickly blew it out, then crumbled the charred sides onto the waiting tobacco.

'Depends what you're after, I suppose,' he said. 'I did all this student shit years ago. Got myself a crap degree, no job afterwards. Me own fault.' He winked at me. 'Didn't apply myself enough. S'how it happens with geezers like me.'

'So what do you do now?' I asked, knowing full well what he was going to say before he said it.

'Bit of this, bit of that.' He lit the joint, inhaled, held it in for a long time. 'S'not all bad though. I'll settle down one day. Just waiting for . . .'

'What?'

He giggled. 'Fuck knows, Willie-boy. Fuck knows what I'm waiting for. Regular bloody Estragon and Vladimir rolled into one, I am.'

He offered me a toke, which I refused. Like sex, I'd tried dope, but it gave me no real sensation. Danny shrugged, not offended, then fiddled around with the kettle, eventually making three cups of tea – one for him, one for me, and – apparently – one for Kris.

'Only one thing she likes more than a cup of char in the morning,' he said by the doorway. 'And after the night I had, there's no way I could cope with any of that, I tell you. See you around.'

'Yeah. See you.'

Later that same Sunday, towards evening and after Danny had left, Kris came to my room. The lingering smell of the roast dinner she'd cooked for her amour wafted in with her. I'd eaten out at a greasy-spoon earlier, then studied at the Central Library until four. When I'd got home, Danny had gone. Ian was away for the weekend seeing his parents in the Home Counties, and wouldn't be back until the next day. Kris and I were alone.

'Listen,' she said, sitting awkwardly on my bed. 'I just don't want you to get the wrong impression about . . .'

'You and Danny?' I said, putting down my pen, shuffling my chair round to face her. She was blushing, eyes avoiding mine, looking out into the gloom of evening behind me.

'He's just a friend, that's all.'

'Sure,' I said.

'I mean, I wouldn't want you to think . . .'

'I don't. I try and avoid thinking altogether.'

A tiny trace of a smile crossed her face. She looked up at me. 'You avoid a lot of things, don't you, William?'

'Especially answers to questions like that.'

'Listen to him, so cryptic. What have you got to hide?'

I realized she was looking at my scar, still slightly visible through my short hair. 'We've all got things to hide.'

'Sounds mysterious. I like mysterious men.'

'Like Danny?' I wondered if perhaps she was drunk, feeling the after-effects of a few too many glasses of cheap wine over the roast dinner. Her demeanour, the way she looked at me, unsettled me.

She frowned. 'I told you, it's not like that between him and me.'

'Kris, it really doesn't bother me what it's like, as long as I can get on with my life.'

She thought for a moment, shifted slightly on the bed. Another thought occurred to me as I watched her slowly smooth out the creases on her skirt – maybe she was coming on to me. Jesus, I hoped not. I was fairly happy in the house, the last thing I wanted was any complications. Yet still the thought persisted.

'We met last year,' she said, referring to Danny. 'We had a thing going for a time, but then . . . you know, some blokes find it hard to accept the truth.'

'Truth?'

'That it's over between him and me.'

'Right.' This was from a woman who'd cooked the man a full English roast before kicking him out? 'Maybe you're not sending him the right signals.'

Instantly the expression changed, her brows narrowed, she cocked her head to one side. I wondered if we were still in the same time zone. 'How old are you, William?'

'Nineteen.'

'I'm twenty-two,' she said, quickly rising from the bed. 'And I think if anyone knows about signals, it's me, not you.'

'Fair enough.' What the hell had I said to upset her so much?

'I've left the washing up. It's your turn on the rota.'

'But it was your meal.'

'And it's your turn.' She opened the door, stood there for a moment, then turned back to me, still smiling, yet emanating a cold disdain. 'Don't ever try to tell me my business, William,' she said. 'You're vulnerable here. I can change things. Very quickly.'

As she said the word 'vulnerable', she slowly drew a hand over her head, mirroring the path of my scar. Then she left, leaving me in stunned silence to wonder whether it might be worth my while to look for some new digs.

As it happened, nothing more was said about the conversation. But the atmosphere in the house had changed. When

Ian came back he took me to one side and wanted to know what he'd missed. I shrugged off the enquiry, but it was clear he knew something had changed.

The following weekend he met Danny himself, and couldn't wait to moan to me about the injustice of it all. 'The bloke's an arsehole,' he said as we watched an old movie late at night. Fortunately, I'd 'red-penned' it, and Kris had gone to bed early.

'She seems to like him,' I said.

'Unbelievable. He even insists on calling me "geezer", while she cooks him breakfast like some sort of fawning robotic Stepford wife.'

'Takes all sorts.'

'And I'm sure he smokes dope in their bedroom: I could smell it. That's illegal, isn't it, William?'

'Absolutely.'

'I can't believe what she sees in a freeloading prick like that.'

'Ours isn't to question why, I guess,' I replied, not knowing whether to enjoy or commiserate with his melancholy.

'He's a tosser of the highest bloody order.'

'Well, you know what to do, Ian.'

He stared blankly back.

'Stop shaving, walk around in your pants and start smoking ganja.'

'Ha bloody ha.'

I would ring my mother twice a week from the coin-operated phone in the hallway. Eight o'clock on a Wednesday evening; six o'clock on a Saturday. Strained conversations every time, as we both probed sensitively for updates on the other. She wanted to know if I was still taking my painkillers (I was); I needed to know if she was coping OK without me. Each call would end with a chasm of unsaid things. Neither of us ever mentioned the bizarre conversation we'd had the night before I left, yet in the often heavy silences I could sense that it still weighed as heavily on her mind as it did on mine.

'You made an appointment to see Dr Carter?' she asked me one Wednesday night in mid-October.

'Seeing him Saturday.' I'd made the call an hour earlier.

'That's good, love, very good. And he's excellent, too. The best.'

'Right.'

'You'll tell me how it goes?'

'Sure.'

'I'll be thinking of you. I always do – you know that, don't you?'

'I know that, Mum.'

'And your dad. He thinks of you, too.'

'Right.'

'He says he's proud of you, love. We both are.'

'You OK?'

'Don't you worry about me. Lord knows what you said to Nicola, but your sister's become some sort of blooming nurse. I can barely move without her fussing over me.'

'Just asked her to keep an eye on you.'

'Well, she does that. She really does. You tell me, you hear?'

'What?'

'How it goes on Saturday with Dr Carter.'

'OK.'

'Bye for now, then. Love you.'

'Yeah. Ta-ra, Mum.'

Three days later, I would go to Dr Carter for the first time.

Strange to think about it now, but that one meeting would embark me on a path that would eventually change every aspect of my life, for ever.

If I'd known what was about to happen, I would never have even made the appointment.

13

The thing that most surprised me about Manchester was its contrasts. Yes, it rained a lot; yes, its buildings were blackened from the grime of its industrial past; but beyond that, twenty miles south, it was possible to step from a train into some of the most beautifully rugged country imaginable. The Derbyshire Peak District, an awesome sight for someone whose previous encounters with hills of any description was the annual Chetwins day trip to Box Hill. But here there were mountains, silent giants of black, purple and green forming the first majestic vertebrae of the Pennines, backbone of all England. I loved it all, from the moment I stepped from the train at Edale Station to see mountains looming up on all sides.

It was a Saturday morning, the weather bright and clear, and consequently the small two-carriage train disgorged a mass of backpacking hikers onto the platform with me. I felt quite out of place, the only person not wearing nylon waterproofs and hiking boots. I slowly followed the chattering climbers out of the station into the village of Edale itself.

Dr Carter had given me precise directions from the station to his house (which suggested to me that here was yet another frustrated control-freak shrink) but, as I was a few minutes early, I sat on a moss-flecked dry-stone wall and watched the endless parade of backpackers in their swishing anoraks. Their loud chattering ripped through the quiet village; maybe the silent Peaks scared them a little. There was hardly a house that didn't have a 'Bed and Breakfast' sign in the window – Edale obviously relied on hill-walkers for the success of its economy – but something about the place made me wonder about the relationship. I suspected that if I lived here, it wouldn't be too long before one or two hikers went 'missing' on the tops, bringing peace and harmony to this quiet little village once more. Further thought put paid to this idea. No doubt the press would arrive in droves, gore-seekers would follow, the tabloids would re-christen Edale 'The Village of Blood', or somesuch. One instance, I reasoned, where death might not provide a quick-fix solution. Shame, I'd have been glad to help out where I could.

I began thinking about Carter, the reason I was here at all. I might be sitting on a wall, but in effect I was roped over a damn barrel. The frustrating thing was that I really had to keep the appointment. I'd been lucky in putting it off for as long as I had, but eventually my personal tutor caught up with me. She reminded me of my conditions of entry, that I must see the campus doctors once every fortnight for medication (I'd been doing that), and must continue my psychoanalysis with Dr Carter. If I didn't go, I would be dropped.

'You do think that's fair, don't you, William?' She was horribly sincere, middle-aged, and Australian, the accent only coming out during our one-to-one chats.

'Fair dinkum.'

A tight smile. 'You know what I mean. The polytechnic has to protect its reputation. It's the same for everyone. Anyone who's suffered a severe mental or physical injury has to undergo continuing treatment.' She squirmed a bit in the silence. 'You know, just in case . . .'

'In case, what?'

'Anything happens.'

'That screws the poly's immaculate reputation, I suppose.'

A small sigh. 'William, we're looking after you as much as anything else. You've been in a coma, and from what I've been told, you may have one or two kinks to sort out . . .'

Kinks? I sounded like a twisted hose. She caught my expression.

'. . . that is, problems with your long-term *mimory,*' she twanged. 'This Dr Carter guy can help you put it right, then you can go on and get your first-class honours with it all behind you. You know what I'm saying, don't you?'

A long pause.

'William?'

'Sorry? Bugger me if it hasn't shot straight out of my head.'

Yes, I know, games. Infantile games I played for my own amusement. I knew deep down she was only the messenger, but in truth, if I'd had a loaded Magnum in my pocket right there and then, I would have gained a fair degree of satisfaction from shooting the bitch.

I checked my watch and headed towards Shallice House, finding it easily: it was virtually the only house in the village without the obligatory 'Bed and Breakfast' sign. Obviously the nutter-restoration business paid bigger bucks than bacon-buttie-eating backpackers. It was a nice-enough-looking place, set back from the road by a small, well-maintained front garden. Clematis grew over the wooden front door. I found a bell, pushed it. Waited.

Well, William, here we go again. Another appointment with some over-qualified bore determined to unravel our secrets. Two things strike me from where I'm watching the action: firstly, won't these people ever give up? Answer – probably not, best be on our guard all the time. And secondly? I guess it's a little more personal. Best friend to best friend. Sometimes, William, especially lately, I've begun to wonder about the relevance of our little chats. Very occasionally, I've caught myself wondering if you can even hear me at all. Maybe you choose not to, but that would be such a bad thing, such a foolish thing, that I can't believe a fine loyal friend like you would stoop to it. No, perhaps it's because the connection's wrong. Faulty wiring, another 'kink'. And you heard me that time, didn't you? Heard me describing the arc of her blood and brains as it splattered the wall behind her empty Aussie bonce. No problem with the connection that time. No, actually it's the Kris woman I'm concerned about. She's the biggest threat. Way I see it, if she keeps flashing her knees and pushing her flat little tits at us, then we've only one of two options. Fuck her or kill her. And I keep telling you this, but like I say, the message doesn't seem to be coming over so well any more. I'll fiddle around a little inside and see if I can fix things up for us.

'You must be William.'

It was a girl, about my age, standing behind the half-open door. Short brown hair, Yale University sweatshirt and faded denims. Quite striking: slim yet curved, high cheekbones, sparkling green eyes.

'Come in,' she said, standing aside to let me pass. 'Dad's

faffing about upstairs ringing some buddy in the States. He'll be down in a minute.'

'Thanks,' I said. It seemed appropriate.

'I'm Karen. You fancy a cup of tea while you're waiting?'

'Be nice, yeah.'

Karen Carter led me into the kitchen, made me tea, sat me in a creaking wicker chair. 'Just got fired today,' she said, sitting opposite me, challenging me with a smile. 'That is to say, I'm not normally here, you know, when Dad sees –'

'People like me,' I said, wondering if it was the warmth from the Aga or the conversation that was making me blush slightly. I didn't want her to make excuses for herself, didn't want to appear 'not normal', someone you apologized to if you bumped into them in your own house. 'I don't mind,' I said. 'It's nice to meet you. How did you get fired?'

Another smile. 'Dozy old cow who owned the little fashion joint I worked for said I was too pushy.'

'That's a sacking offence?'

'It is if all you're selling is Korean import dresses and tops, and you've got a highly talented fashion designer constantly showing you her portfolio ideas.'

I took a sip of tea, tried not to slurp it. 'You rocked the boat, huh?'

She shrugged. 'It's no big deal. There are other oceans.'

'And it's about time you set about finding them,' came a voice from behind me. Turning, I faced a tall man, about forty, casually dressed, slightly thinning short brown curly hair, rugged face, and an arm outstretched to mine. Here he was then, Dr Richard Carter. I shook his hand.

'Dad,' Karen protested, 'I've only been laid off for three hours.'

'Strike while the iron's hot,' her father replied.

'On a Saturday afternoon? What do you suggest I do? Ring Armani long distance and set up a flight and an interview for Monday morning?'

'Local papers, try those.' He turned to me. 'William, I'm Dr Carter. Let's leave Karen here to her teenage angst while we go upstairs, eh?' It was more of an order than a suggestion.

He led me into a small box room painted a sickly shade of

sky-blue. Two table lamps placed discreetly at floor level lit the place, the tiny window looked out onto the dark Peaks beyond. All in all it was a pretty dull, claustrophobic sort of room. He offered me a seat.

A muffled cry came from downstairs, followed by the heavy crump of the front door. Karen had apparently stormed out.

'Problems?' I asked, watching as he took his time settling opposite me.

'She's eighteen, just lost her first job and thinks her father's an uncaring arsehole. I'd say a quick door-slamming tantrum proves she's fairly well-adjusted.'

'And are you,' I said, unable to stop myself, 'an uncaring arsehole?'

He put on some reading glasses, expensive-looking with flashy frames, then pulled out a file and set it on the small table between us. 'It doesn't matter what I am. It's what she thinks I am. She'd really much rather be talking to her mother. She'll go for a walk, blow off steam.'

Now isn't he the cool customer, eh? Not a hint of embarrassment. Did you hear it, William, just now? Did you hear her calling darling daddy a wanker? I did and I laughed. He did, too, only he's trying to look unfazed. Dr Rugged and his icy-cool demeanour. Lives with his daughter and the mother's God knows where. Probably off fucking someone with a tad more humanity. Because this guy, William, is a very slippery fish. Go carefully now . . . very, very carefully . . .

Carter flicked through a series of papers from the files as I watched in silence. Finally he took off his glasses and sighed. 'William Dickson,' he slowly said. 'You're a mess, aren't you?'

'Beg your pardon?'

'Thing is, I'm what's called a specialist. Up till now, you've been seen by psychiatrists at the hospital and suchlike. But as they have failed so spectacularly, you've now been sent to me so that I can clean up the mess.'

OK, if that's the way he wanted to play it. 'Strange, I don't feel like a mess at all.'

He stood, pointed out of the small window. 'Want to tell me what colour the sky is, William?'

'Blue.'

'I see green.'

'Well then, I reckon you're in more of a mess than I am.'

'I see purple clouds floating in a green sky. You see them?'

'Strangely enough, no.'

He sat back down. 'Memory, perception and the self – one of the greatest philosophical conundrums. What are we if not the products of our own memories? You say you see blue, because your memory files the recognition into your consciousness, cross-referencing every other time you've glanced up on a sunny day. But what happens if that process is skewed? Then it becomes a perception problem, compounded by failing memory–synaptical connections. Your brain still continues to tell you you're right, while everyone else knows you're a bloody mess.'

'That's what makes you a specialist, is it? Seeing purple clouds in a green sky?'

'Hard study made me an expert.'

'In what?'

'Post-traumatic amnesia. PTA. Reconnecting people with reality, dislocating them from corrupted memories, putting them back in touch with lost ones.' He looked me straight in the eye. 'Any questions?'

I nodded towards the small table. 'That stuff to do with me?'

His turn to nod, still watching me.

'How did you get it?'

'From the polytechnic admissions people. That worry you? You look concerned.'

'They've blackmailed me into coming here.'

'Not been too bad so far, has it?' he replied. 'Apart from you getting increasingly nervous about whether I'm some kind of nutter or not.' He nodded towards my hands. 'Your palms are sweating. And you're swallowing too hard. You've scratched your head three times since you sat down. All signs you don't know what the hell's going on.'

'Maybe I've just got an itchy head.'

He ignored it. 'I'm forty-seven years old. I worked for twelve years as a hospital shrink before meeting up with Dr John Tremaine. There's a name you probably won't want to hear, eh?'

I sat back in the small chair, tried to appear more relaxed than I felt, made a conscious effort to separate my hands, keep them from wandering to the side of my head. Had I scratched my head three times? I wasn't even aware of doing it once. Or was he bluffing? Trying out some well-worn routine, the shock approach to establish who was boss of the session. I had no idea, save that Dr Richard Carter was unlike any other shrink I'd ever met – which did little to ease any lurking consternation.

'The name Tremaine doesn't bother me in the least,' I said, sitting straighter.

'Listen to the formality of the answer, William,' he replied. '"Doesn't bother me in the least." Not "I've never met the guy" or "not bothered, really", but "doesn't bother me in the least". You see how uptight that sounds?'

'Put it down to the green and purple sky thing,' I said.

'So I'm making you uptight?'

'I guess you are.'

'Good.'

'Good?'

'William, listen to me. There're two schools of thought in psychoanalysis. The first is that client and shrink establish a buddy–buddy bond. Become pals, then begin wading through the crap together. But it's false, because more often than not the client is the last person you'd want to have a few beers with if you bumped into them in a pub.

'The second route is based simply on analysis. In counselling terms it's coined as "professional boundaries", ethical-speak for maintaining distance in order to proceed with the work. In my case, I call it being honest. We're both here for a reason, why pretend we're great friends from the off?' He flicked the report. 'I've read this a couple of times, and basically can see you've been given a lot of rope, William. The psychoanalysts you've dealt with so far have all tried the first approach. You're a smart kid, I guess it was easy to give them the run-around. But it doesn't work that way with me. You come here once a fortnight, and we work at sorting you out. I couldn't give a stuff whether you think that's a "good" thing or not. It's simply how it is.

'I'm going to tell you things that make green skies and

purple clouds look utterly normal. And gradually you're going to have to accept them, as well as a few things about yourself that you're not going to be too happy about.'

'Such as?' Outside, below, a group of laughing hikers passed by.

'Your relationship with Dr Tremaine.'

'Which never was. Ever.'

He looked at me once more, held the stare, won the contest as I eventually looked away. 'Purple clouds, William,' he said slowly, 'in green, green skies.'

'OK,' he said after I'd returned from having a pee. 'Let's start again. My name is Dr Richard Carter. I'm forty-seven years old, enjoy outdoor pursuits, the occasional cigar and a bottle of red wine with my daughter when the time allows. I'm a widower, my wife June died three years ago. I worked as a psychological therapist in several London hospitals and mental health practices before studying in America for another three years at the Boston Associated Institute of Psychiatric and Cognitive Studies, and at Yale University. I then returned to England with my family, moved to Derbyshire and set up practice here. I'm considered to be one of the foremost experts in PTA, but professionally my reputation sucks as I'm often too busy throwing rocks at the glass houses of conventional psychotherapy. I'm harangued on lecture tours, articles I've written for professional medical journals are frequently attacked by so-called establishment shrinks. This I largely put down to petty jealousy as I make a good deal more money than most of them, and have far more success treating clients in the field. Ninety per cent of my patients are private referrals, though I'm just as willing to take on National Health clients.

'I have been close friends with John Tremaine for many years, and know him to be a sound, highly qualified analyst working in a similar field. Three months ago, he sent me some additional papers referring to you concerning a series of sessions you had with him prior to receiving your head-injury.'

The dry delivery, humid room, coupled with the confusing

absurdity of the situation was making me sweat again. I felt myself scratching my head again but simply couldn't stop my-self. 'Listen,' I said quickly. 'You must believe me, I've never even heard of this Tremaine man before my mother men-tioned him to me one day at the hospital.'

He nodded, referred to the file. 'But on meeting the hos-pital psychiatrist, you claimed that you knew him, didn't you?'

'Because my mother told me it was the best chance I had of getting out of there.' Why was I telling him all this, giving away tit-bits so easily? It was seeing the file, the evidence against me, knowing he'd been through it, analysed it with his 'expert' brain. I felt as if I was being cross-examined. Carter, if he ever felt the need to change profession, had the natural demeanour to be a damned effective QC.

'So you lied?'

'Maybe, yeah.'

'What was so bad about being in the hospital?'

'It bored me. It was going nowhere.'

'But if you'd stayed, sorted it all out properly, you wouldn't be here now, would you?'

'Chances are I wouldn't have been anywhere,' I replied. 'I'd have missed my studies, exams, the chance to get to the poly, everything.'

'So it was a white lie, is that what you're saying?'

I paused. Then said, 'Purple. Definitely purple.'

Carter opened the beige file, took out a small photograph, held it a while, then passed it to me. 'Perhaps it might jog your memory if I show you a photo of Dr Tremaine and his wife.'

'Who knows?'

'It was in the package he sent to me. I believe your mother gave the shot to them shortly after a garden party. They were good friends with your mum and dad.'

'Crap.'

'Take a look.'

'Pointless,' I said. 'I won't be able to recog—'

'Humour me.' He handed me the print, and I took it, keen to end the whole Tremaine nonsense.

As I held the photograph, I distinctly felt something cold and hard churn away inside me. I braced myself to take a look, scanned the glossy paper. There were four figures in the picture. I assumed my father must have taken the snap before he fled the marital home for his new life elsewhere. He'd lined us up in the back garden, the familiar low privet hedge obscuring the white rounded bottom of the oast-house. Mum, me, and two others, the mysterious Dr and Mrs Tremaine . . .

I glanced quickly at my own image first; I must have been in my early teens, still boarding at Chetwins. Then, as my eyes moved onto the Tremaines, I wanted to laugh. It wasn't frightening any more; there was no mystery to unravel, simply a colossal balls-up. Another look confirmed it: standing beside my mother and myself were none other than Bob and Sally Squires, village landlord and landlady of the Partridge, burnt to death in Spain two and a half years previously.

The churning stopped almost immediately. Not a Tremaine to be seen.

14

'No,' I said firmly, placing the photograph back down onto the neatly ordered table. 'There's been a mistake. There's no one called Tremaine in this photo.'

To his credit, Carter didn't seem too worried 'OK,' he said, making notes. 'Is it anyone you recognize?'

'It's the local landlady and his wife. The Squireses. More friends of my dad than anyone else. Or used to be.'

Another note rendered. 'Do you remember the photograph being taken?'

'No. Mum's sent you the wrong picture.'

'She often get these sort of things wrong?'

'She gets confused sometimes. This photo proves it. Believe me, I know – these people aren't Tremaine and his wife. No way.'

'Confused? Your say your mother gets confused?'

'Like I said, sometimes.'

He pointed the pen at me. 'I expected so much more from you, William. This blaming your mother thing, it's such a cliché. The old "it's someone else who has the problem, not me" routine. Tiresomely predictable.'

'Because,' I said through gritted teeth, 'she's made a mistake. She's been through a lot lately, it's taken its toll.'

'And of course you haven't been through anything at all, have you?'

'You don't understand.'

'Who would be more likely, in your opinion, William, to be confused about this? A middle-aged woman who's "been through a lot", or a young man recovering from a severe head injury and subsequent memory loss following a coma?'

'My memory's fine.'

'Care to turn the photo over, William?' he said. 'Read out what you see?'

Sensing the beginnings of a trap, I cautiously did as he asked.

The writing was unmistakably my mother's. 'William and I,' I read aloud slowly. 'Carole and John Tremaine. August 1977.'

'Your mother seems to agree with me,' Carter said, watching me all the time. 'No mention of the Squireses there, is there?'

I was frowning. 'Like I say, she gets confused.'

He rose. 'Wait a minute, will you?' Then he left, leaving the door slightly ajar. Evidently Karen had returned. From downstairs came the sound of a television, canned laughter from an American sit-com echoing in the old stone cottage. As if somehow the joke was on me, and the whole damn world was in on it.

William! Now's not the time to brood. We've got to act. Leave before this phoney gets me any more worked up! We've done what we came to do. He's a fraud. A dangerous fraud. It can't go on like this. You're too exposed. Too nice to be dealing with con-men like Carter. This is not a nice man, William. This is someone who could really harm us. Why don't you see it, William? Why do you still sit there? We've got to go before he – shit . . . !

Carter returned clutching a photo-album, opened it, passed it across. Reluctant as I was, the bright colours drew me towards the mounted images, pictures of Carter, a younger Karen, the tall familiar figure of Bob Squires, his laughing roly-poly wife. In a foreign restaurant, red-eyed from the evening flash. On the beach. Standing in a hotel lobby, ready for another night out. Spain? Had to be. The ill-fated holiday from which the Squireses never returned.

I turned the page. Variations on the same four principal characters: duos, threesomes, and the occasional shot of the happy foursome taken by an obliging stranger. All marked, Kos, 1980.

Pictures taken in 1980? No chance – the Squireses had burnt to death in 1979. So what was this latest nonsense all about? And as far as I knew Kos was in Greece, not Spain.

Too much to consider. Too much to take in. A pulsing throb began under my left eyebrow. I felt as if I was standing over a deep, dark well. One slip and I'd be swallowed by the inky blackness for ever.

Carter's voice shocked me back to a Saturday afternoon in Derbyshire. 'We took a holiday with John and Carole Tremaine just last year, William,' he said. 'You see, the same people you claim were friends of your father's from the pub?'

Logic fought and failed to unscramble the mess, throwing fantastic coincidence into the ring. 'Doubles,' I heard myself saying. 'They're the doubles of Bob and Sally Squires. Doppelgängers.'

He nodded. 'And just think, to be living so close to each other in Kent?'

'But that's what it is, though – coincidence,' I insisted. 'Can't be anything else. These pictures were taken after the Squireses died.'

'I called this place Shallice House, William,' he said calmly, 'after T. Shallice, a psychiatric pioneer who in 1970 was first to develop the theory that short-term memory works in parallel with long-term memory, and is best viewed as a series of separate processing modules. He revolutionized the way in which we think about the way we all think.'

'Good for him.'

'I think he would have liked you.'

An alarm rang close by, startling me.

Carter smiled. 'That's it. Time's up for today.' He took back the photo-album. 'Time for you to go.'

I sat quite still, fighting an urge just to get up and leave, knowing I had to ask the question. 'Why do I see them as other people?' Something inside me screamed as I said it.

Carter opened the door. 'I haven't got the foggiest.'

'I want to know. I mean, if it's true, I want to know what's happening.'

'Keep looking at the sky,' he told me. 'When you see blue, think green.'

'What the fuck's that going to do?'

'Start shaking some things loose, hopefully. These things take time.'

'But what happens if –'

'If what, William? You're the one saying there isn't a problem. That you're fine, there's nothing wrong with your memory. If that's really true, then there won't be a problem, will there? I'll see you in a fortnight.'

Ninety minutes later, I was back in Fallowfield, lying on my bed, wondering why I wasn't hungry. I hadn't eaten since the previous night, yet could not face the thought of forcing even a mouthful of food down my throat.

15

Nine o'clock that night and, quite suddenly, I began to laugh. I hadn't moved from the bed in three hours; I'd dozed off fitfully for a while, and then awoke laughing. Hysterical laughter, the kind you can't check or stop, the kind you can only surrender to, feeling the pain in your ribs as you gasp for breath between each racking spasm.

I laughed for the absurdity of green skies made suddenly real. The photo-album I'd seen at Carter's – that couldn't have been faked. I'd seen the thing with my own eyes, pictures of two dead people alive and enjoying themselves in Greece. But they had different names. No longer the Squireses, they were now the Tremaines: people who apparently didn't want to speak to me any more. Why? I had no answers. Maybe I'd got blind drunk one night and thrown a brick through their living-room window. Or goosed the woman in the street before running off laughing like a madman. God only knows. I had no memory of any of it, and no one seemed willing to tell me. I felt impotent, made useless by that photo-album, adrift. Here I was, unflappable killer, turned into a gibbering fool by a few holiday snaps.

It was true what Carter had said, eventually you have to choose what to believe in: the memory of a blue sky, or the seen evidence of a green one. And I'd have to start choosing, I knew that now. Carter obviously had more on me in that damned file. But how much? How deeply had he probed events in my life? How much more would I 'give away' in his formidable company?

And I laughed too because I felt scared, worse than I had in a long while. As scared as I'd been as a child, seven years old and surrounded by police asking me about Fat Norris in the woods. Dumbstruck and terrified, the taste of metal filling my broken throat.

Christ's sake, William, pull yourself together! Laughing like some banshee – do you know how close we're sailing to the wind? Too damn close. So now's the time to be cool, try and work one step ahead of them. They're only out to confuse us, that's all. We know the truth of everything, William. It doesn't matter what they say. They can't hurt us if we stay together, stay calm, stay ahead. I can forgive you lots of things, William. But now isn't the time to be taken in. It really won't do. One of us has to ensure that won't happen. Don't make me do things that could be bad. We're strong. We've killed. We've survived, the others didn't. We're stronger, so much stronger than anyone else. If anyone can survive this, it's us, William. Come to me, and I'll show you the bluest skies. From up here I can almost reach out and touch them. I'll colour them any shade you like, any hue. But for now we have to be on our guard. Carter's good – a weasel – but we're better. We have history to battle his knowledge. Experience versus books. We'll win. We'll go on. And if we don't, then we'll kill him. Think how easy it would be, alone up on the hills. Just pick up a rock, and bingo, another Margot Norris number . . . Then no one would bother us again, would they?

At half-nine, I tried calling home. Mum and Nicola were both out. My mother's pre-recorded voice asked me to leave a message after the tone. And how would that go, I wondered? 'Mum, I don't want to worry you, but there's some really strange shit going on up here, and I'm concerned for your mental health, too. Hope everything's fine with you, love William'?

I replaced the phone without speaking.

Come the thin grey light of another Manchester Sunday morning, I took stock, wrote it all down, began sifting through what I knew for certain, what I suspected, and what I could only guess at. Twenty minutes later I'd filled half the page with questions to which I had no possible answers. Yes, I now suspected that there was something amiss in my head, but how dangerous would it be to put it right? What if Carter probed too deeply into the past? Where would his loyalties lie if he discovered something unsavoury about his latest client – to me or to the police? What would happen if he suggested hypnosis? Should I refuse, pretend to be in a trance, what?

For almost the first time in my life I wished I had a friend, a close confidant. Sure, being a killer at large is all very liberating, but when it comes to personal problems, the loner's lot comes up a little short. I guess the choice is: have friends and don't kill people, or do the deed and run with the consequences. Problem is, once you've killed someone, you don't really have the choice any more: it's you against the world, for ever.

Strangely, before that Sunday, I'd felt absolutely no need for close companionship with anyone. Any problems I had, I could manage by myself. OK, so there was the Screaming Man of my youth, but one look at any basic psychology textbook will tell you that most kids have imaginary friends. Mine just went a little deeper and lasted a little longer than most. Since coming out of my coma, though, I'd hardly thought about him at all. Maybe I didn't need him any more. Perhaps I needed to develop real friends to fill the vacuum. If so, who?

But inviting someone into my life meant I might have to suffer the consequences of discovery. Maybe I should try to find another person like me, someone else who'd killed and would understand the life I led. I spent a minute or two imagining the possibilities: an ad in the *Manchester Evening News*, 'Wanted: Serial-killer, pref. female for friendship, understanding and possible relationship'; a killers-at-liberty singles club offering fondue evenings and masked balls. But it would all have to wait, all surreal and ridiculous plans put on hold. For the moment I had no choice but to go on alone, the same as always, forever careful, never carefree.

I went and made a cup of tea, took my medication, filled in the chart measuring frequency and severity of headaches (there'd been a fair few of those lately), then popped an extra three Paracetamols for good measure. Fortified by chemicals, I wandered into the backyard where Danny Black was nonchalantly burning an old easy chair. Bizarre. Thick black fumes billowed into surrounding yards and gardens.

''Lo Dan,' I said, sitting on the back step, hoping the wind wouldn't suddenly change direction. 'Practising for bonfire night?'

He turned, grinned, a roll-up dangling from his bottom lip. 'Goes up like a bastard, doesn't it?'

'Hope the neighbours haven't put their washing out.'

'What a fucking deal that'd be! All those white-shirted execs turning up on Monday stinking like they've spent all weekend in an oil refinery.' He shot a fist into the air. 'Freedom for foam-burners! Oppress the white-collar wankers!'

It really was too early on a Sunday morning for any of this. I expected to hear approaching sirens any minute. 'Why are you burning it?'

He came and sat beside me, barefoot, in what looked like a pair of Kris's tracksuit bottoms and a faded T-shirt. 'Thing was, Billy-boy, I had a bit of an accident last night. Had too many jars, went and fell asleep in front of the telly. Only pissed meself, hadn't I?'

I quite admired the uninhibited way he told me all this. For a wild moment I thought Dan might be the friend I'd been looking for. Then I thought again. Subtlety wasn't the guy's strong point. Chances were if I ever got round to telling him any details, he'd salute and shout, 'Freedom for misunderstood, mentally confused PTA serial-killers!'

He took another drag on his miniature roll-up. ''Course,' he continued, 'I was all for soaking it up, like. But Norman Bates's psycho-sister up there insists I torch it forthwith.'

He jerked a thumb complacently behind him, and I twisted to see Kris standing in her nightie at the window, observing proceedings.

'Good night, though,' he mused, chuckling softly to himself. 'Get this, right. We all go out, me, Kris and Richard Rogers Jr up there, and have a few jars. Get a takeaway, that kind of thing. All the time I'm watching the little prick, and it's like, well, obvious he's got a thing for Kris. Can't keep his eyes off her. And Kris, well, she's a woman, ain't she? So she plays it, you know, teasing him like a little puppy, trying to make me jealous and shit.'

'Sounds like a great night.'

'Hang on, Billy-boy, it gets better. When I come round after pissing the chair, guess what I see?'

'About three of everything?'

'Only Kris and RR Jr having a snog on the settee.'

'She was kissing Ian?' All the while as I'd been sleeping.

'Only looking straight at me, you know, giving me the dirty eyeball.'

I could well imagine the scene.

He laughed. 'Should have seen the look on the poor cunt's face as I sort of stood, held out my hand, then took her upstairs for a seeing-to. All in me piss-soaked jeans. Honestly Billy-boy, there was one fucked-off kiddy. See the things you miss with your off-to-bed-early routine?'

'It's hardly a recommendation for staying up, Dan.'

'Suit yourself.' He went and prodded the disintegrating chair, dancing as he did so. Drips of molten foam splashed onto the warmed concrete, each with a thin black pluming tail. I looked briefly at the sky – it wasn't blue or green, simply dark grey with billowing smoke.

A minute later he joined me again. 'Know why I like you, Billy-boy?'

I shrugged.

''Cause of that,' he said. 'You don't ask all these stupid shit questions. You're a thinker, a private kind of a guy. Bit like meself, really. See, a lot of them I know, they're always asking me why I stay with Kris, you know, what I see in her. But you already know, don't you?'

He was waiting for a reply. 'An occasional bed, quick shag, night out and breakfast to follow.'

'Proves my point. You already know. Now for the hard one. What the fuck does a girl like her see in a geezer like me?'

'I've no idea – and neither have you.'

He slapped me on the shoulder. 'Fucking psychic, you are! Bang on the money, son. I have no bleedin' idea. Can't be the bit of rough stuff, can it, eh? I'm worse than rough.'

'Rougher than a dog's backside,' I agreed.

'And I'm crap in bed.'

'Inevitably.'

'Unreliable. Unfaithful.'

He nodded, then scratched at his short stubbled head. 'What the bleedin' hell is it, then?'

I made a pretence of looking suitably studious. 'I think,' I slowly theorized, 'that Kris is riddled by sexual guilt. And the only way she can handle it is if she sleeps with old tramps like you. It's sort of punishing herself for taking her pleasure at the same time.'

'This is so deep.' Danny grinned, enjoying the game. 'And

something I fear we must explore fully over a cocktail of mind-expanding substances one night.'

'Not me, I'm looking for night-work as of this week.'

'Capitalist bastard.'

'I prefer the term skint student.'

'What about love?' he asked, back to the Kris topic again. 'What happens if she ever falls in love with a geezer?'

'Couldn't possibly sleep with him, no way.'

'Unless he pissed himself first, right?'

'There's always that.' I finished my tea in one long gulp, stood and headed back inside. 'Good talking to you, Dan.'

'Yeah,' he said returning to the chair. 'I know it was.'

I rang Carter from the pay-phone. Karen answered.

'Your dad about?'

'He's walking on the hills. Always does on a Sunday.'

'You OK?'

'Fine. You?'

'OK. Just burning chairs. The usual for a Sunday morning in Fallowfield. Listen, can you give him a message?'

'I'll try.'

'Just tell him I saw a glimpse of green sky this morning.'

'That's it?'

'That's it.'

At eleven o'clock Mum rang the house. Ian picks it up, comes and calls me from my room whispering that 'we need to talk'. I have a feeling that after talking to Danny I know exactly what it's going to be about.

I wander down, pick up the receiver. 'Mum?'

'Hello, love. Did you go and see Dr Carter yesterday?'

'Yeah. I went. I called, you were out.'

She sounded relieved. 'I know. Nicola took me for a pizza.'

'Lucky for some.'

'You sound annoyed. It was just a pizza.'

'Mum, I couldn't give an arse about the pizza. I'm glad you had one.'

'Did Carter upset you? Is that it?'

'No. Sorry. I'm just feeling a little tetchy right now. Green bloody skies, really.'

'What, love?'

'Doesn't matter.'

'Listen, William, I know it's all a bit strange, but this is how it has to be done. Dr Tremaine says . . .'

'Oh, I'm sure he does.'

'. . . that Dr Carter's one of the best. You're in good hands.'

'But this mysterious Tremaine bloke still won't talk to me himself, right?'

'William, it's difficult.'

'Bloody stupid is what it is.'

'You have to have faith.'

'I mean, you know stuff that I'm "not allowed" to know.'

There was a slight pause. 'Well, I think the reason for that was amply illustrated the night before you went away. There are some things that you're simply not ready for. It all has to be taken step by step. I had a little too much to drink and said some things that –'

But I didn't want to hear her say it. Not then. Not ever. Instead I cut her off quickly by saying, 'I saw photos of him. Tremaine and his wife.'

'And?'

'He looks just like Bob Squires.'

Another pause. 'What, from the Partridge?'

The frustration rose. 'Only it can't be him because he's already dead, isn't he?'

'William, don't get angry. You just have to trust Dr Carter.'

'Because he's the best, blah, blah, blah . . .'

'You want to come home next weekend?'

'No. I'll be fine.'

'I could send you the money for the coach.'

'Thanks, but no thanks. Keep it. Buy yourself something with it. Have another ruddy pizza.'

We small-talked for another few minutes before hanging up. I managed to calm down a little, end the conversation as best as I could. Afterwards, I wondered why I was so insistent about not going back to Maidstone for the weekend, and knew my mother would be thinking the same. And perhaps coming to the same uneasy conclusion that I had – that after our last night together, the wine and the drunken conversation about Alan Cooper, going home to more of the same was simply more than I could cope with at the moment. Life, I was discovering, was already complicated enough.

Around four the phone rang. Kris called up to me that a 'Mr Green' wanted to talk to me. She gave me an enquiring look as she passed me the receiver.

'Hello,' I said, knowing exactly who was on the other end. 'Enjoy your walk?'

'It rained,' Carter replied.

'Can't have everything.'

'I like the rain.'

'Thought you might.'

'I want you to tell me something.'

'Go on.' Kris was still standing close by, watching me, blatantly eavesdropping. 'Hang on,' I said to Carter, cupping a hand over the mouthpiece. Then said to her, 'Kris, bugger off, will you?'

She pulled a mock-offended face, turned, then left me alone.

'Sorry about that,' I told Carter. 'Walls have ears and stuff. What did you want to know?'

'Who's your favourite band?'

'My favourite?' I thought for a moment. 'No idea. Kind of like it all. That is, apart from country.'

'What about films?' he went on. 'Name your favourite movie.'

Again, I thought for a second or two, during which no obvious contenders sprung to mind. 'Cowboy films,' I said, more to give an answer than anything.

'Which one, then? *Shane*, *The Searchers*, Clint Eastwood stuff, what?'

'Yeah, all of those. Especially the Clint stuff.'

'So which is your favourite?'

But try as I might, I really couldn't recall the title of one single spaghetti Western.

Carter thankfully broke the silence. 'Makes you wonder, doesn't it? There you are, nineteen-year-old young man, world at his feet, reasonable academic brain, yet I'm willing to bet that you don't have any real favourite things, any real opinions at all right now. A person without opinions – rather like a robot, isn't it?'

'Is this part of the treatment?' I asked, taken aback. 'Insulting your clients on the phone? Or do you just get some sick little kick out of it?'

'I'm right, though, aren't I?'

'I can't remember them, that's all. You're putting me on the spot.'

'I'm willing to bet two things,' he said. 'Firstly, if I phoned you up tomorrow, you'd still be none the wiser; and secondly, right now, you're scratching at the side of your head again.'

He was right on both counts.

Ian finally managed to collar me on the following Wednesday evening. I had a new night-job to go to, and was already late for the bus connection to the McVitie's biscuit factory in Longsite.

'Not now, Ian,' I said as he stood eagerly knocking on my already open bedroom door.

'It can't wait,' he replied, all wide-eyed excitement. 'Just can't wait.'

'It's going to have to, mate. I'm off.'

He stepped inside, practically barred my way out onto the landing. I was forced to take a step backwards, he stood so close. 'Just now,' he quickly whispered. 'In the bath. Me and Kris. Unbelievable.'

'What? You and her, you . . . in the bath?' He didn't look wet enough.

'No, no,' he said, moving further into my room and shutting the door quietly behind him. 'We didn't do it, but as good as.'

'Fine, Ian. I'm very happy for the pair of you, but if you'll excuse me, I've got to –'

His words came in quick light breaths. 'I'm passing the door, OK, and she calls out, tells me we need to talk about things. You know, after what happened on Saturday night?'

'I had heard.'

'So I go in, and she's only lying there, in the water, naked. Just a flannel covering, you know . . . the area.'

'Look, Ian . . .'

'She tells me to close the loo-seat and sit down, then starts talking, calm as you like, about what happened.' The excited eyes darted everywhere. 'And she's naked, William. All I can do is stare at her . . . her . . . breasts, and sort of drink her all in.'

A fairly repugnant image in my opinion, but I felt obliged to feign some interest. 'And what did she say?' I asked, wondering if I could just about squeeze a taxi-fare together to get to work.

'That she thought we had potential.'

'There's romance.'

'But don't you see?' he keenly insisted. 'She showed herself to me. She wants me, not that hippy dollop of shit who's always using her. Me, she wants me.'

'I think you'll find, Ian,' I replied, trying to be diplomatic, 'that they both get off on using each other.'

'No, it's not like that. She's had enough. He's disgusting. He weed himself last Saturday night, right there in front of us. Like some sort of wrecked old wino. She's going to chuck him really soon.'

'Ian,' I said, almost having to shove him physically out of the way to get to the door, 'I think you'll find that if Danny loses his bed, board, sex-and-eggs ticket to you, then he's most likely to batter you senseless.'

'I'll be ready for him.'

'What are you going to do, whack him with your T-square?'

His chin jutted defiantly. 'Whatever's necessary . . .'

'How about finding a girl who doesn't come with these physical and domestic complications?'

He looked at me as if I was mad. 'William, she showed me her breasts in the bath, for God's sake! How many other girls do you know who'd do that? And all I've done is to kiss her!'

'Just be careful,' I warned, walking from the room. 'Dan looks as though he'd be pretty handy in a scrap. And take it from me, life in a coma isn't the holiday camp it might appear.'

He gave me a thumbs-up, puffed out his chest, and struck a badly co-ordinated boxer's pose to prove his willingness to fight for his love. I reckoned Danny Black would have broken his jaw before Ian threw the first punch.

16

Over the next week and a half I tried as best as I could to simply get on, fight the feeling that a part of me was merely counting down the days until my next trip out to Edale. I dreaded it, yet also felt intrigued. Carter obviously had some kind of planned agenda, a measured, softly-softly approach to revealing the contents of that all-important beige file. I wanted to know just what he had on me, where the gaps were, how many more 'kinks' I had.

I was working three night-shifts a week at McVitie's, standing alongside other broke students, Asian women and rough-looking Irishmen overlooking production lines belching forth a variety of warm biscuits. The actual 'job' was to weed out the broken ones, quite the dullest task ever. But it gave me plenty of time to think. Maybe too much time. Thinking, I was learning, was a rather dangerous pastime. They all came back to me, my deficiencies, and occasionally something else would trip into place: my head would fill with murderous thoughts and killing schemes – Kris Jordan, Ian, Richard Carter, my errant father, Nicola, the Australian tutor; all were routinely butchered and buried to pass the time.

After a couple of nights it became automatic, my eyes subconsciously scanning the thick rubber belt for cracked biscuits, my mind on other things. Despite my hygienic hat, it didn't take too long for our line supervisor Paul 'Double' Decker to spot the scar angrily protruding from under my short dark hair.

''Kin 'ell, kid, how the fuck did ya get that basta'd?' he delicately asked me during one fifteen-minute break.

'Got jumped on in my last job,' I replied, knowing I had to tell the truth, as he was a mate of Danny's, who'd got me the job in the first place. A favour that made more sense when I was told that I could take home bags of the 'bad 'uns', and I realized that Danny was going to make it his business to relieve me of these as a kind of 'agent's fee', as he described it. But they paid OK, which meant that I had a few pounds left over after rent and food, so really, I wasn't too bothered. Besides, after standing over the production line for seven hours, the last thing I wanted to do was to eat another sodding broken biscuit.

''Kin 'ell, kid,' Double Decker replied, eyes still fixed on my scar. 'They did yas over right good an' proper, din' they, eh?'

'It was just the one of them.'

He gave a low whistle. He was mid-forties, bloated, and looked ten years older. Always unshaven, with fat fingers topped by yellowed chewed nails, he carried at least two extra sagging chins fortified by years of excessive biscuit eating.

'You get the basta'd back?' he asked.

'When I got out, yeah.'

He gave a short admiring nod. 'Dark horse, ain't yers?'

'The darkest.'

He beckoned me in with a stubby forefinger, then whispered, 'Dan got anything for me?'

I nodded, fully prepared, then reached into my pocket, passed over the quarter of black.

The fat hand struck quickly, snatching the cling-filmed cube and thrusting it into his white nylon pocket. 'Tell 'im I'm good for the money next Friday.' Then he clapped his hands, turned to the dozen others in the windowless refectory. 'OK, you lazy basta'ds, tea-break over. Back on yer 'eads.'

And if some of you think that I should have raised some moral objection to soft drugs-dealing, kindly remember I was already a multiple murderer.

A week and a half later, an early October Saturday, and I was back in Edale. In the intervening fortnight winter had arrived. Temperatures had dropped by close to ten degrees. It was darker, too, overcast with grey clouds threatening snowfalls for the highest Peaks. Yet still the little village was buzzing with backpackers. I wondered what it would take to keep them away. Granted it was a lovely area, fantastic to marvel at the nearby mountains, but to set out for a day's climbing in this weather? I suspected that, come the Armageddon, it wouldn't only be cockroaches that survived . . .

In the warm confines of Shallice House Carter took me straight to the blue box room, a man in a hurry, with no time for small-talk or pleasantries. Karen was nowhere to be seen, and I briefly wondered if they'd had another row. He seemed to have his mind on other things, avoiding eye-contact, irritated, as if he were simply going through the motions with me. Part of me felt a slight twinge of disappointment, though I didn't really want to work out why. He was just another shrink: why was I so keen to have his full and undivided attention?

He was dressed in a suit, the tie unbuttoned, and had obviously been out somewhere important. I wondered whether to ask him what was wrong, but his mood prevented it. From what I'd already seen, I knew he could be a cantankerous shit if he wanted. Instead I followed him silently upstairs to the box room, where I sat and waited in the heavy silence. He sat opposite, took off the jacket, loosened the tie some more, then suddenly almost tore it off, flinging it on the carpet. Next he put on his glasses, took up a pen and paper, read a little and made one or two notes before finally looking up. 'You OK with William?' he asked.

'As opposed to what?'

A frown crossed his face. 'I really don't have time for games today.'

'You asked a question, I tried to answer it.'

'No. You tried to get smart. Different thing entirely.'

'OK. What about you? Are you happy with Carter, or would you prefer I called you Dr Stroppy Git?'

He shot me a look. 'It's not about me. None of this is about me.' Then we held a long stare. His eyes were cold, made bland by some deeply hidden pain that I instinctively knew he'd never share. But there was something, a definite spark to him that I found more than intriguing. I wondered briefly if it was the father thing – this rugged intellectual, pioneering maverick in his field was everything my own father wasn't. Perhaps in seeing him with his daughter, I'd glimpsed something I'd been denied and maybe longed for. Perhaps.

'You seem really pissed-off,' I said.

'What I am, how I seem, is of no consequence,' he replied. 'Let's get on. Let's talk about you.' He shuffled through some papers in my beige manila file. 'Care to tell me about the scar, William?'

Uh, uh. No way, José. Now listen very carefully, William. You don't tell the bastard one word about our scar. He's not giving you anything, why the fuck should we tell him about our lives, eh? And be careful, very careful . . .

Something stung inside. 'No. I don't think I want to, actually.'

'Why not?'

'Because you're not being straight with me.'

'So you're going to be difficult with me, right? How wearily pathetic.'

'You tell me what's up with you, I'll tell you about the scar.'

He took off the glasses, rubbed at his face. 'OK, I've just been giving evidence at a coroner's inquest. A client of mine hanged herself three months ago.'

'Well, doesn't that just give me all the confidence in the world.'

'Bye, William. You know the way out.'

'That's it? It's over?'

'I think so.'

'Based on what? A cheap crack about my own well-being? Pardon me for being sarcastic, but I think I have the right to be a little worried if stringing yourself up is the standard outcome for all your doctor–patient relationships.'

'Just get out.'

'No.'

'Don't test me, William. Not today.'

'I've travelled a long way to be here.'

'Well maybe you shouldn't have bothered.'

My turn to get surly. 'And maybe,' I replied, voice level, yet oozing obvious annoyance, 'you could have had the common fucking courtesy to ring me up during the week and warn me that today was most likely to be off, as you'd be in a right arsehole after the coroner's meeting. Maybe it's you that's at fault, Dr Richard fucking Carter.'

He looked up at the ceiling, exhaled twice. Then let out a brief smile, half-laughing at some sort of private mental joke. Finally, after a long pause, he looked at me and said, 'The scar. I've told you about my morning, tell me about your scar. How do you think you got it?'

'It's all in the notes. You already know what happened.'

'But I want to hear it from you.'

I shrugged. 'I got done over. Beaten up.'

'Who by?'

'Just some lad.'

'No other explanation?'

'Should there be?'

He pulled out a typewritten page from the beige file. 'This is a medical report written by the admissions officer of the hospital you spent the following five weeks in.'

I stared blankly back.

'Take a look.' His finger pointed to the top left-hand corner of the page. Five handwritten words, next to a pre-printed entry.

CAUSE OF TRAUMA - Self-inflicted. SSA.

My eyes begged the question. SSA?

'Suspected Suicide Attempt,' Carter supplied.

A pounding began somewhere deep in the back of my head.

'There was no lad, William. There was no attack. It says so right here. The reason you were admitted to Maidstone Hospital was because you'd tried and failed to kill yourself.'

17

Well, this is just fine and dandy, isn't it? The prick asks you to stay the night and, despite all my warnings, you agree? Are you out of your tiny mind? And look at the track record of the idiot – the last person he 'treated' went and hung herself! And to cap it all, you sit there like some sort of zombie as he calmly tells you we're supposed to have tried suicide, too? Christ's sake, William! Forget the friendship, I've a good mind to leave you to it, let this madman eat you up and spit you to the pigs. But, hey, whoever said I was unsporting? You want to give this guy his best shot – fine. Let the bastard fire away. Only don't come bleating back to me when he prises something lose that we'd both rather keep somewhere safe inside . . .

A crash of glass.

Perhaps it was a cocktail of things that made me agree to stay the night in Shallice House, but one thing above all others proved the most definitive. That hideous, overwhelming crash of glass.

For moments after Carter had said the words 'suspected suicide attempt', something totally terrifying had happened. I'd heard the crash – not outside, but inside, from within my mind, a memory reawakened, crashing through.

It's a strange and dreadful thing to audio-hallucinate for the first time – I've got used to it now – but on the first occasion, it blows you away. And this isn't like an acid trip, where you get a warning, a warm-up period as the drug takes a hold, begins to bend reality slowly at the edges. A hallucination simply charges in, does its stuff, arrives screaming without warning, like a suddenly backfiring car passing by on a quiet country lane. Worse than the noise, though, were the flashed images. I saw the glass pane shattering before my outstretched hands, felt the pain of razor-shards as they slashed at my flesh then flew past my head.

All completely, terrifyingly real.

Nothing could have prepared me for it, yet somehow, in some deep and base place, I knew it to be a part of me. This had happened to me. In that one fleeting hallucinatory moment I no longer had control. Conscious thought obliterated, senses blocked, all reason vanquished.

A nightmare moment.

Carter watched my terrified face as I slowly re-entered his world. 'OK?' he asked.

'No,' I somehow managed to reply. 'I'm fucking not.'

To be fair, I didn't immediately agree to stay the night in Edale. Carter had to spend the best part of an hour persuading me to. Eventually, maybe through some kind of guilt at his earlier treatment of me, he broke me down. I wanted to go straight back to Fallowfield, never to see the man, his daughter, or the damned house again; but after listening to him I eventually agreed to stay.

He confirmed that the hallucination was merely a resurfacing memory, and that I'd have to get used to the experience, as there were doubtless others waiting in line. It was, he explained, a very positive experience, proof that whatever was suppressing these memories was losing its grip. He described the workings of my brain like a battleground. It didn't really help, but I stayed anyway.

Later we ate lamb casserole. The three of us: Karen, Carter and I. I watched as they shared jokes, anecdotes, poured more red wine. Their intimacy detached me, thankfully alienated me from their lives. I began counting plates on their shelves, books, the red and grey quarry tiles on the floor. At one point I began thinking about Mum, how much she would have liked to be there, sitting at the table, laughing, joking, watching the candles die. She would have joined in regardless, ever the social animal.

Carter was talking to me. I made an effort to listen, turn my thoughts to his voice. '. . . and they pulled her from the wreckage unconscious. She was out cold for close on three weeks. Afterwards, this perfectly reasonable American housewife, married with three kids, had no recollection of her previous life, the accident, or just what she was running from.

In the space of those three weeks, her mind had somehow totally reinvented her past. She was convinced a man who worked at a local convenience store was her husband, that their kids had died, and that her name was Didi, not Janice. It took most of a year before she could be "rebalanced".'

He was looking at me, expecting some sort of reply. I nodded back, unsure. 'And that's me, is it?'

'Her first retrieved memories came in the form of a powerful hallucination.'

'So I'm not the only one, is that what you're saying?'

'We're all unique in varying degrees,' he replied, pouring more red. Karen glanced across at me, raised her eyes as if to say, 'Here goes Dad on another one of his work theories.' I smiled back, hoping he wouldn't spot it. 'But basically ninety-nine per cent of us on this planet fall into easily recognizable traits and personalities. Some are simply a little more extreme than others. With you and Janice, yes – yes, there could be some similarities. Both cases involve head trauma, a subsequent confusion over past events, memory distortion . . .'

'I know who I am, Doctor, what I've done . . .'

'So did she.'

'Until you "rebalanced" her, right?'

He nodded.

'But I know my life,' I pressed. 'Events to date. Things that happened to me. It all makes sense. There's no confusion there.'

'But when I show you proof that it could have been otherwise . . .'

'Dad.' It was Karen, gently admonishing her father. 'Maybe now's not the time, eh?'

He looked across at her, nodded, made a grudging apology. 'Sure. Sorry, William. Guess sometimes it's hard to stop working.'

She turned to me, raised her eyebrows again. 'Tell you what. Let's let Dr Freud here wash the dishes, while I take you for an exhaustive tour of Edale's throbbing night-life.'

'Edale on a Saturday night, eh?' Carter said, polishing off the last of his wine with a well-practised flourish. 'See you back here in half an hour, then.'

* * *

'Dad's OK,' Karen said as we settled at a corner table in a quiet village pub. 'He just gets a bit too involved at times. Doesn't know when to stop. A sort of terrier attitude.'

'He was more like a bad-tempered Alsatian earlier.'

'It's this coroner's enquiry thing,' she said. 'It's stressing him out. He blames himself, when in reality he was onto a loser from the start.'

'Oh?'

'I met her once at the house. Came back from work early. They were in the kitchen, and Dad was desperately trying to stop her baking scones. There was flour everywhere, and she was singing, screaming almost at the top of her voice. Typical manic. I wasn't too surprised when he told me she'd killed herself.'

I sipped at my pint of orange squash, wishing it could have been a local bitter, but knowing that with the red wine I'd already had, coupled with the medication I was still taking for my injury, any more alcohol would have been extremely unwise. I did get a few looks from beer-drinking locals, but happily, Karen didn't seem too bothered to be seen out with a squash drinker. In fact, the more I got to know about her, the less she seemed particularly bothered about anything. Not that she didn't care, she just didn't appear to feel the need to conform, even down to her choice of clothes – a brightly dyed top and tight green crushed-velvet trousers – which stood out in the small smoky pub like a party balloon in a funeral parlour.

'Thing about Dad,' she continued, taking a large slug of cider, 'is that professionally other shrinks either loathe him or secretly admire him. This stupid woman's suicide will give his opponents all the ammunition they need.'

'Were they nice?'

'What?'

'The scones.'

She smiled, flicked back her hair. 'Terrible. Burnt to bloody cinders. I'm surprised she didn't burn the place down, really.'

Our eyes met, and I found myself wondering at how quickly life was turning itself around these days. A few hours ago, I was terrified at hearing the sound of crashing glass. Now I was sitting by a fire enjoying this charming girl's company. Yeah – it hadn't been such a duff decision to stay, after all.

She opened a bag of peanuts, then poured some into her palm, began eating them one by one. Then she looked at me for what seemed like an eternity.

'What is it?' I asked, rather nervously.

'You're embarrassed, aren't you?'

'Erm . . .'

'You're embarrassed because you think I reckon you're a loony, right?'

Did I blush? 'I'll try and keep off the midnight scone-baking exercises.'

'Lighten up, William. Look at you, all uptight.'

That surprised me. I thought I was doing a fair impression of 'casual end to a surreal day'.

'You're a client of my dad's. Without clients, we don't eat.' She began crunching on the nuts, then turned in her seat to wave at another customer. I tried to avert my gaze from the unexpected glimpse of bare midriff underneath her T-shirt. She turned back to me. 'Besides, Dad's such a stodge he wouldn't let me within five hundred miles of anyone he thought was genuinely bonkers.'

'Comforting.'

'Besides,' she whispered, eyes teasing me mercilessly, 'I've always had this thing for good-looking mixed-up young men with scars.'

Now I was certain I was blushing. 'You should get out more often. Another drink?'

Her eyes twinkled a response.

Sunday morning, and Carter and I began our ascent of the worn muddy path rising two miles to the top of Kinder Scout. I wore borrowed hiking boots, two sizes too big, which chafed my ankles and rubbed my heels. My heavy overcoat was useless at preventing winds at altitude. My head ached. I felt like a German army infantryman on the retreat back from Moscow. It really was bitterly cold, and I briefly wondered if I wasn't about to puke my cooked breakfast.

Carter seemed untroubled by my slow progress, sometimes marching on silently ahead, mind on other things, stopping at various strategic viewpoints, waiting for me to catch up, to pass other walkers, all seemingly amused at my wheezing lungs struggling to fill with thin cold air. One guy was even bold enough to suggest I use oxygen tanks, and the others in his group chuckled; somehow I managed to prevent myself from punching his smug bearded face. Some people, honestly, they walk around almost begging you to end their lives.

Karen, Carter told me, had left the house early – to go riding, apparently. Game girl. The thought of bouncing around on a damp horse's back was even worse than struggling in badly fitted boots up a mountain. I liked her, a lot. We'd had fun in the pub the night before. She was larger than life in many ways, with a wicked streak that surfaced through boredom. Last night she'd introduced me to friends and locals as 'William – the session guitarist who gave the Smiths their best licks'. And while most of them probably thought the Smiths were the people responsible for salt'n'shake crisps, it was fun to be in on our secret joke. If I'd needed a diversion the previous night, Karen Carter had more than provided it. As a result, I slept soundly for the first time in a long while, without a single dream of crashing glass or tall trees and falling friends to sully it.

After forty minutes, Carter and I stopped, letting a group of determined ramblers by. The fellow with the beard was amongst them: I was pleased to see even he was puffing a bit. The brisk pace had warmed me a little, and the sun had come out. It wasn't warm, but tolerable. We sat on a waterproof Carter had spread on the soaking mossy turf. For a long while it was all I could manage just to take in the view, drink in the slope of the dark heavy ground gently giving way to a distant white horizon.

'Tell me more about Tremaine,' I said eventually, watching smoke trails rise from the chimney-pots of distant cottages.

'John Tremaine? He's my mentor, I suppose. I studied under him years ago. We've kept in contact ever since.'

I pressed on. 'If I'm going to . . . believe in all this stuff you're saying, then I've got to know more. Because right now, this is very pleasant, sitting up on the hill, but the rest of it, all you've been saying . . .'

'Doesn't mean a damn thing, right?'

I nodded.

'So what do you want to know?'

I pulled some moss from the underside of a limestone boulder, threw it at my boots. 'Why doesn't he want to speak to me?'

Carter waited a moment. 'Your case is . . . potentially beyond his area of specialization, William. He got part of the way with you. It took a long time. Years. Then came the suicide attempt . . .'

Here, I had to interrupt. 'Which is still crazy.'

He nodded.

'I'm just not the type to try and kill myself.'

'The type being?'

'God, I don't know,' I replied, picking another piece of moss and launching it into the wind, praying I wouldn't hear the sudden explosion of crashing glass, see the shards again. 'Insane singing female scone-bakers?'

Bravo. Too true. Ending the lives of others, not our own, is our style. Killing ourselves? – never, never in a billion lifetimes . . .

He looked across at me. 'And the hospital records, William? What do they tell you?'

'A mistake? Forgeries?'

'It was a perfectly standard document, William,' Carter replied. 'You'll have trust me on that.'

'But I was beaten up. Beaten senseless. Put in a coma by some drunken yob . . .'

'Tell me about him, William.'

'Nothing to say, really. Just some lad my age, thought he'd end his night by picking on me.'

'Why?'

'Why does anyone pick on anyone else?' I said. 'It just happens. I was working in a chip-shop. He was pissed, knew me from college. Probably reckoned I was some sort of weirdo because of the way I spoke. Decided to have a go at me. Next thing I know, Mum's at the bedside.' Another memory popped into my head. 'No. Wait. Dad was there. I think my dad visited first.' I paused, struggling with the memory. Did he come to the hospital?

Carter took off his backpack. 'You first met Dr John

Tremaine at Chetwins, William,' he said, bringing out a flask and plastic cups.

I watched him pour two coffees, steaming invitingly in the cutting chill. Then the words sunk in. Tremaine, at Chetwins?

He passed me a coffee, took a sip of his own, perfectly calm. 'He was seconded to the school. Part of the outside psychiatric team that worked with some of the boys there. You included.'

'No chance.' And I really was trying to remember, place the name, the face I knew to be Bob Squires, but all I saw were Alan Cooper's grateful smile and the trees, the cedar avenue that had watched over me as I read voraciously on long autumn afternoons.

'It was nineteen seventy-six. You were thirteen.'

'I don't disagree about how old I was,' I said, the coffee burning a warming trickle down my throat. 'But there was no Tremaine and certainly no psychiatric team at Chetwins! Christ, it was just a regular crappy little third-division boarding school.'

He nodded once or twice, taking his time, seemingly timing his moment. 'Be a little odd, wouldn't it,' he slowly replied, 'for a special-needs school to have inadequate psychiatric provision?'

I shook my head. 'Bollocks.'

'Chetwins provided specialist teaching and resources for children with a variety of learning difficulties. You included.'

This one was even easier to dispute. 'Sorry, Doc, but I never had any learning difficulties. I passed all my GCSEs. Top grades, mostly.' I couldn't help the beginnings of nervous laughter now. If it wasn't so absurd, it would almost have been entertaining. 'Listen, Chetwins wasn't exactly Eton, but it sure as hell wasn't Rampton Juniors, either.'

But he was quite still, simply looking, assessing me in that detached academic style that was really beginning to wind me up.

'But then again,' I said coldly, 'you've got it all right, and I don't know my own mind, eh?'

'Your subconscious, William. You don't know your subconscious mind.'

I watched as he refilled both cups with the last of the coffee. 'You saw Dr John Tremaine for a period of four years, on and off. He became good friends with your family. I used to stop by and see him in Kent on occasions, catch up, exchange opinions. So I knew a little about you, his treatment with you, long before I ever met you. He used to speak about you with great excitement, great affection.'

'Crap.'

'He was treating you for a variety of behavioural problems and disorders that he believed were symptoms of a previous traumatic incident. Specifically, the deaths in the woods. He began using various regression techniques to try to unlock your subconscious memories of that time. Mild hypnosis amongst them.'

A cloud had appeared, just above my eye-line, laden with threatening rain. Something was happening to my eyes. The world was slipping at the edges. I couldn't focus on the distant cottages. My hands trembled, spilling warm coffee over my fingers. The moment he'd said 'woods', the sudden overwhelming instinct was to stand, run, race back down the hill, far away into wherever.

'Dr Tremaine was getting close,' he continued. 'The hypnotherapy was yielding results. Each session was bringing you closer and closer to the original incident . . .'

'I have to go,' I said quickly. Then heard my mother's voice, the evening before I'd gone to Manchester. The woman I loved more than anyone, spouting gibberish, claiming that three of us went into the woods that day. Three. Someone else besides Fat Norris and me. Alan Cooper, the sodomized boy I'd saved from further abuse at Chetwins. I saw his face, the quietly ashamed look in his eyes as he'd told me – given me – his first name. I began to feel dizzy, slightly nauseous.

Carter's voice, again, drifting on the wind. 'There was to be one final session, William. Dr Tremaine was convinced he could regress you safely back to the afternoon you were found in the woods. You family was consulted, and agreed. You agreed. The police were informed . . .'

'Police?' My head swam.

William, we leave now! Right now!

'They were as keen to know what happened in the woods as anyone. The case is still listed as unsolved.'

Maybe he'd drugged the coffee. I was coming out in hot and cold flushes. 'Nothing happened,' I managed to say. 'Nothing happened in the woods. Just an accident. Fat fell. The branch broke. He was too heavy –'

'William. Listen to me.'

No, William, listen to me! We're going, now! Otherwise things are going to start getting very messy, very quickly!

I had to go, couldn't bear any more of it. I stood, uncertain on trembling legs, all instincts urging me to run from this man – or end it for him right then and there. Leave, or kill him. Find a stone, bring it crashing down. I'd killed before, what would be so difficult about taking out this man? He was a whispering conman, a greedy liar, parasite. Who would know? We were alone now, just Carter and us. Kill him, dump the body. It would be a while before he was discovered.

We'd be miles away, William, just you and I, back down the hill . . . on the train . . . escaping . . .

'And during that session, William, you tried to kill yourself.'

'No.'

Carter persisted. 'I have a theory.'

'I don't want to know.'

'I suspect your subconscious couldn't cope with Tremaine getting at its most precious secret.'

'I said,' I stressed, struggling to stay calm, fight a plethora of murderous urges, 'I didn't want to know.'

'And it would rather kill you than have you face what happened in those woods.'

Something flashed – exploded – white before my eyes.

'Perhaps your own subconscious sees you as the enemy, a weak link in its defences. Someone who can't be trusted not to spill the beans. So it has to take certain steps to protect itself, steps you're not even aware of –'

'No!' I shouted, choking back red-hot bile.

Kill him, William! Do it. Kill the smug piece of shit right now!

Carter stood, suddenly grabbed me, spun me round to face him. 'You saw something in the woods that afternoon that scarred your mind. Up till now, you've buried it deep inside . . .'

'Fine! Let me go and fucking leave it where it is!'

His face was too close, inches from mine, blocking everything. He was too intense, too threatening, too strong. 'Even now, it resists any effort to uncover it. But believe me, William, it won't go away. It can't go away. All your life, you're going to be dogged by it –'

I tried twisting from his grasp, madly searching for anyone on the misty path. 'Get off me!' I shouted. 'I'm warning you . . . !'

Do it, William! Kill him! Find a rock. Bang! – on the head, and he's history!

Carter held me firm, shocking me with the strength of his grip, the determination in his eyes. 'I know what it's like to deny the truth,' he hissed. 'And it's a very dangerous path. I did exactly what you're doing when my wife died. Simply denied it. All of it. Pretended none of it had ever happened.' His sudden laugh was as chilling as the mountain air. 'I still cooked for three of us, still took phone calls from friends saying she had just popped out. And believing it, William. Really damn well believing it . . .'

Use your head, William! Butt this crazy loser in the face, then drop rocks on him!

'. . . until I had to face it, William. Deal with it. Find out who I really was. I mean, picture me,' he said, finally slackening his grip. Was this my chance to do it, kill him? I frantically scanned the ground for a large stone. 'Dr William Carter, the memory man, sitting in the world's biggest bubble of self-denial. Until I burst it with a bit of reality, William,' he said. 'The hardest thing I've ever done. But if I hadn't, I would've been certifiable, years ago. And you're the same . . .'

'No. Fucking. Way.'

He moved back in close. 'Your eyes. I can see it in your eyes. Sure, your face is trying to be hard. But your eyes tell it different. You're frightened, William, shit-scared, just like I was.' He tapped the side of my head. 'Know what you've got in there? A time-bomb. Ticking away. A subconscious safety device that's so well constructed, it's prepared to kill you rather than let the truth out.'

'Only after I've seen to you first!'

'What?'

The voice was mine, but the words came from somewhere else, a place I instantly recognized. The woods. The words came from the woods . . .

Atta boy, William! Now I'm through! Let's let the bastard have it!

I reached down, grabbed hold of a small rock, held it tightly in my bunched fist above my head. 'Just get back,' I warned. 'Keep away from me!'

Carter paused, eyed the rock, my shaking fist, then slowly took a cautious step towards me. 'William,' he said, voice utterly level. 'It's OK. Everything's fine.'

'Don't try me. I've done it before.'

'When?' he asked, moving another step closer. 'In the tree, William? Did you kill them, did you? Both your friends? That was you, was it, William – the killer?'

No! No! No . . . !

'No!' I screamed, rushing at him, tripping, falling, the rock rolling away as a sharp pain exploded in my knee, and then . . .

. . . a long forgotten sound – a rush receding, crashing through dry branches as the body fell. The smell of cool musty bark, pressed against my cheek. The horrendous wait for impact, my dust-dried eyes screwed tightly shut. A screaming second that stretches for a gut-wrenching eternity. Until it ends with a horrible winding, rib-breaking thump . . . Fat Norris's grand, spine-shattering finale. He's down, dead, smashed . . .

Then I'm coming to, back on the mountainside, Carter somewhere close, turning me, making me sit, moving my knees slowly, pushing my head between them. I see blood under the torn denim.

I felt my own anger gradually and finally begin to wane, pushed aside by shaking adrenergic embarrassment.

For a long time he said nothing, simply sat by me, slowly rubbing my back.

'I wanted to kill you just now,' I finally managed.

He nodded, then stepped away, began folding the waterproof. 'Maybe now's not the right time to deal with this,' he said. 'Maybe you're simply not ready to face up to it. There's a lot that can go wrong. Memories are perhaps the most dangerous aspect of ourselves.'

'I think I'm going to throw up.'

He walked back over, began rubbing my back again. 'I'm guessing at this stage,' he quietly explained, 'but I'd say your subconscious is one step ahead of me already. Take Chetwins. You honestly had no idea it was a special-needs school, did you?'

'No,' I truthfully answered. 'And I don't really want to know, either. Can I go home, now?'

He offered a hand, which I took, then slowly helped me to my feet. I still shook, but it was from nerves rather than cold. I was warmer than I'd ever been; sweat streaming down my back under the heavy greatcoat.

'You're going to have to accept that there are whole areas of your early life that you have no recollection of, William. It's all been changed around, reconstructed. Just as with Janice, the American woman in the car-crash. Once you accept this, then begins the fun part. We can begin to find out why.'

'That simple, huh?'

'Don't underestimate your mind, William. It's strong. Maybe it's a lousy cliché, but you're going to have to climb a lot higher mountains than this one before we're through.'

Moments later, we began making our way slowly back down the pathway. He led me past another group of gawping hikers. 'You're right,' I said, envying them their easy, uncomplicated lives. 'It was a lousy cliché.'

18

My mood didn't improve on the journey back into Manchester. Tired, confused, nervous, even a little scared, I probably looked like some smouldering psychopath to other passengers.

It had been an extraordinary weekend, one that had filled my mind with unanswerable questions, then drained it with seemingly inescapable facts that I could no longer ignore. Except that I had to ignore them, find some way to hide from the first dark waves of paranoia that were beginning to lap at my exhausted mind.

So, as the train pulled back into Manchester Piccadilly around seven that evening, I headed straight for the nearest, cheapest pub, sat at a quiet corner table and proceeded to drink my way methodically into oblivion. Crazy, when you consider the medication I was taking, but at least alcohol offered the promise of a few hours' escape from the insanity of the past few weeks and months. I wished Karen was with me.

An hour and three pints of bitter later and it no longer mattered that I shouldn't be drinking. What were the drugs doing to me, anyway? Probably adding to the delusions, I figured; powering them, perhaps. Maybe I'd be fine if I simply binned them, got on with my life without tablets, confident, assured of my own indestructibility as I had been before.

Alcohol therapy – pint by pint, watching the large bar begin to fill with others, then list and bend at the edges, knowing speech was becoming harder by the sip, yet feeling strangely OK, warmed, divorced by the beer from anything and everything.

I took out some more money from my wage-packet, made my way unsteadily back to the bar, bought another pint, returned to my corner table, watching as groups of standing drinkers parted obligingly for me as they sensed my drunken unpredictability. Which satisfied me, restored me in some way. Some briefly glanced my way, whispered something to their friends about me. They were scared. This is how it should be all the time, I thought. This is when William Dickson felt best – when the world shied away.

Outrageous thoughts began fighting their way to the top. I felt like standing, shouting, 'Hey, arseholes! Free beer to anyone who can guess how many people I've killed!' Then watching their stunned silence and shocked faces – because surely they'd know I wasn't bluffing.

Oh, they'd know, William. Just one look into our eyes would freeze their bastard hearts! You're the one, William. The one they all have to fear . . .

How I wanted to spill the beans, wallow in their fear of me, grab a little reward for all those years of terrified silence. Eleven years, four bodies. How much longer could I keep those achievements a secret? Didn't I deserve some recognition for my guile, coolness under pressure?

Back to the bar, for a whisky this time, as my mind fleshed out the fantasy. I imagined the papers, banner headlines, 'Student Killer Confesses to Four Murders!'

And we could have had five if you'd only listened to me and ended it for that smug shithead Carter! Should have done it, William. He deserved a little taste of our unusual talents more than any of the others . . .

'Billy-boy! What the 'kin 'ell are you doing here?'

I glanced up, saw the tall familiar figure of Danny Black standing over me. And just behind, taking more interest in the others around her, a young girl, chewing gum, blonde, overweight, wearing far too much make-up.

'Getting pissed,' I replied, watching as he and the girl settled opposite. She gave me a small smile, then began chewing on highly glossed lips.

'Who's she?' I asked rudely.

'This?' he replied, all innocence. 'Sandra. Family. Cousin of mine. Right, San?'

She nodded vacantly, took a sip of her drink.

He lowered his voice. 'No need to tell Kris, know what I mean? She's a bit . . . well, she can get the wrong idea. Big possession kick in her, needs to chill out a little.'

'Shouldn't you be there now?' I asked. 'Back at the house sleeping off a roast dinner or something?'

He tapped the side of his nose confidentially. 'Doesn't do birds any harm to know you ain't at their beck an' call, Billy-boy. I'll pop round tomorrow. She always uses Monday as some sort of fuckin' study day or something. Get me grub then, when she's all coy and grateful.'

'Move over Casanova,' I said. Then asked 'What about Ian? Aren't you worried he might be helping himself to your portion, so to speak?'

'Nah. Prick's away for the weekend, seeing Mummy and Daddy somewhere down south. Besides, he's too shit-scared. If I caught him doing any of that, I'd kill the cunt.' Danny nudged the girl. 'Billy-boy here does the old McVitie's night-shift.'

'Really?' She couldn't have looked more bored if she'd spent three years at RADA perfecting it.

'Guess you could say he takes the biscuit, eh?'

'Yeah. Sure.'

He paused, looked around, then back at me. 'You here on your own?'

'Twiggy's just gone to powder her nose.'

'Rough weekend?'

'Was up till now. Things have got decidedly better in the last couple of hours.'

He looked at the collection of empty pint glasses. 'Should you be, you know, drinking that stuff? What with your head, an' all?' Again, he nudged the girl. 'Billy-boy here's a right dark horse. Only gone and been in a bleedin' coma, ain't he? Ask him yourself if you don't believe us.'

She scanned my short hair and scar. 'What's it like then,' she asked, 'being in a coma?'

I shook my head. 'How the hell am I supposed to know? You're out cold, aren't you?'

The girl relapsed into sullen silence while Danny began work on a roll-up, his long tongue flicking out suggestively before licking the gummed Rizla. 'How about it, Billy-boy?'

'How about what?'

'Some ale. Jesus, fella could die of thirst before you got your bleedin' hand in your wallet? Wassamatter, you carryin' an endangered species of moth in there?'

I took out a tenner, passed it across to him. He passed it straight to the girl. 'Look sharp then,' he told her. 'Mine's a pint, he's on Scotch, then get yourself something, eh?'

She stood, walked away to the bar.

'Honestly,' he said, lighting the roll-up. 'You really have to spell it out to some folk, don't you?'

I watched his mouth forming speech, but heard nothing, as if some generous entity had suddenly turned the volume of the entire pub down. I saw heads rock back with laughter, groups engaged in earnest conversation, orders taken at the crowded bar; yet none of it reached my ears. It was if I was suddenly locked out, neutralized. If I'd have been sober, the sudden silence would have worried me, but drunk as I was, it felt heavenly.

Then just as suddenly, it all dropped into place, a lone, mad thought into the silence. If I killed Danny, it went, then I'd know for sure what was right and what was wrong. If I ended his life, I'd know what the truth was, who I was. I'd be William Dickson, a killer of five, with no problems about memories, special schools, Alan Cooper, suicide attempts, nothing. All order would be restored.

I'm right with you on this one, William. Every damned step of the way. Forget this afternoon – forget Carter. Maybe we'll have a pop at him some other time. Besides, if you want to bed his daughter, it's probably politic not to kill her father first. But this Danny creep? Pissed as we are – good call, William. Very good call . . .

The girl returned, and with her the sounds of the pub, filling the space that the murderous thought had vacated. Over the next couple of hours we proceeded to drink the end of my wages. I was largely silent, letting Danny chatter on, wondering two things: firstly, did he deserve to die? (answer: we all do, and at least I could promise him a sympathetic exit); and secondly, how was I going to do it? A more complicated one this, made more difficult by the alcohol. The Scotch was serving a deadly cross-purpose: on the one hand it was strengthening my resolve to kill the man; on the other it made executing the plan harder by the mouthful.

I found myself looking at the girl as Danny wittered on, her head turned away, bored by both of us. Boy, I mused, running with the evening's theme, how her life was about to change. After I'd seen to Danny, she'd become known as 'the girl who survived', the one 'Dickson spared'. Maybe get guest appearances on daytime television, local radio spots. And simply for strolling innocently into the same pub as me! Life turns too fast. And Death. Jesus, can't that turn fast? Like your friend coming to your house for another afternoon in the woods. Just three knocks on a door and suddenly you're screaming from the treetops . . .

Steady now, William. You're too drunk to be making these connections. Forget the woods, focus on tonight – the hippy. Let's do the hippy. Oh, please let's do the hippy . . .

Now that the decision had effectively been made, I spent the remaining time devising plans for Danny's death, trying to sober up, weighing one method against the other. Broken bottle on the head? Not certain enough. Smashed glass pushed straight into his chest? I doubted I had the strength. The neck, maybe, right into the soft, fleshy part . . .

It was only as we stepped outside that the perfect opportunity presented itself. It was raining. We began slowly, walking and stumbling towards the bus stop, still fifty yards away. He was mumbling something about it being a 'top-night, good scene, Billy-boy', before preparing to see his 'cousin' home. She was in better spirits now, half-pissed herself, laughing at his every word. They stood by the road, intending to cross, looking both ways as I swayed dangerously close behind them.

The bus was barely thirty yards away, coming towards us, accelerating, speeding away from the stop.

Oh, this is perfect, William! Simply divine!

We all waited for the orange and brown double-decker to

pass. I tried to judge it as best I could. Knew I'd have to separate them before shoving him out into the road.

Only a split-second to do it.

Now, William!

Bursting between them, I broke his grip on her arm, then pushed with all my might . . .

. . . then watched, as his shocked, confused head twisted briefly to face me before slamming into the front of the bus . . .

Bye-bye, Danny, you free-loading shit!

The girl screamed. Brakes screeched, horns hooted.

I watched his broken body tossed before the braking bus, then smacking loudly onto the road, the driver's shocked face clearly visible through the rain-flecked windscreen.

Too late. The bus stopped fifteen feet too late. In turning sharply, it compounded the previous hideous injury by running over Danny's prone body with its huge kerbside tyre.

Then, silence. Nothing save the rain on the road, the bus, bystanders. The girl puked. I could see passengers inside picking themselves up, piling forward to see. Others nearby stood frozen in the eerie quiet.

And me? I felt grounded, content, re-monstered. Safe from Carter's speculations about invented pasts, welded back into what I knew was real – William Dickson, killer. And I'd just killed again, exactly as I'd seen to the yob who had beaten me into a coma. There never was a suicide attempt. Alan Cooper never went into the woods that day; he was a pupil at Chetwins whom I'd saved from horrendous bullying. No one could deny any of it now. Everybody would know what I was from now on . . .

'Jesus, man!' The voice came suddenly, shockingly from my left. 'What are you trying to do? Kill yourself?'

The black roared angrily inside my head. I turned, half-screamed, as Danny's concerned face peered into mine. 'Calm down, Billy-boy!' he said.

'What the –?'

'Don't piss about walking in front of buses, no matter how smashed you are. Fucking lucky I caught you!'

Another angry voice, this time to my right. I turned to see

the driver, face contorted with rage. 'Twat!' he cursed. 'You want to kill us all?'

He was saying more, but already he was fading, becoming softer, smaller, as hands and arms I could only assume belonged to the dead Danny Black led me quickly away.

But I'd seen him die. So how could he?

19

Physically, I remember waking up the following day; mentally, I couldn't tell you where the hell I was. Maybe it *was* Hell, caught between conflicting memories of the night before, and the worst hangover in world drinking history. Me, lying in bed, not daring even to move, throat ripped, head exploding, stomach churning, eyes seared by creeping daylight, trying to decipher what had happened. Had I killed again? Jesus, what was I even thinking the previous night? Please don't say I've killed another one.

'Fraid so, William. Wakey, wakey, rise and shine. You pushed him, remember? Then saw the loathsome Danny smack right into that lovely, obliging bus. Remember the crunch of his rib cage under that big wheel? Sounded like it was running over a cheap wardrobe. We did it, William. Number five . . .

Somehow I made it to the bathroom, retched thin, whisky-smelling puke into the toilet, then clung on, stomach sore and still convulsing at the stench. My next thought was of my medication. I had to take my pills. What an effort that took. Maybe ten minutes, sitting on the side of the bath in the same stinking clothes, unable to raise my head to swallow. Then finally throwing up again, a horrible stomach-churning effort expelling a mere spoonful.

Thoughts – the previous night – the bus – Danny – the girl. Christ Almighty, what had I done?

But then, seconds later, Danny'd reappeared, stood at my side, berated me for my stupidity. Another hallucination? More mind games from the brain that had apparently already tried to kill me?

Quietly moaning, unable to cope with any of it, I stumbled back into my room, gingerly lay down on the creaking bed, and tried to find the impossible road back to sleep.

Some time later I finally made it downstairs, finding Kris earnestly toiling over lunch in the small kitchen. The sticky smell of roasting pork made me heave.

She turned, smiled sweetly. 'You look like you had a night of it.'

I nodded, needed to sit, knew that both legs would give way without a chair. I managed to pull one from under the table and slowly collapse onto it, a cold sweat forming on my upper lip. She bought me a pint of cold water in a straight glass that had been stolen from one of Danny's many trips to the union bar.

'Rehydration,' she said, grabbing a tea towel and opening the oven door to poke around at the roasting contents inside. 'Always helps. Try and have it before you go to bed next time.'

Her cold kitchen efficiency did little for my condition. 'There won't be a next time,' I croaked, feeling the cool liquid trickle down into my tender stomach.

'And I'm Princess Anne's secret love child.'

'Congratulations, Your Highness. I never realized.' I gave up to a painful coughing fit.

I felt her eyes on me, calmly assessing me with the unemotional manner of a biochemist gassing a lab rat. 'Food. That'll help. Why don't you join us? I expect Dan'll be coming over for lunch. I've cooked plenty.'

Shit. Double shit! I'd clean forgotten Danny's conversation the night before. How he intended to 'keep Kris keen' by missing his Sunday meal and dropping over today instead. But if I'd killed him, how could he?

'No. It's all right. I mean, thanks. But . . .' My mind battled with two surreal scenarios. In the first I saw Danny Black's body flying towards oblivion; in the second I jumped in horror as seconds later his arm grabbed my shoulder . . .

'There's more than enough to eat,' she added.

'Thanks. Just not hungry, you know.'

She nodded, smiled again, then returned to the roast, leaving me to the inescapable thought that all I could do now was wait. If Dan arrived, then clearly I couldn't believe my own senses. If he failed to show, then I'd killed him. Which meant that I was in serious trouble. I couldn't believe the stupid drunken risks I'd taken, the ludicrous plan that had overtaken me. What the bloody hell was I thinking? That by killing him I'd seriously be able to get some kind of grip on who I really was? Jesus, what an idiot! A weird weekend in Edale, followed by too much drink on an empty stomach, and suddenly I'm transformed into a mentally retarded psycho. Sure, I'd done a few things in my life that might or might not be perceived as a little out of the ordinary, but to sink to last night's depths?

And worse, what if I'd succeeded, killed him? Surely there must have been witnesses? And after, how did I get home? Did I sprint like a lunatic, evade the police sirens? I honestly had no idea. All I could do was wait and see. Both Danny and my fates were held in the all-telling hands of time.

William, a word in your shell-like. First off, give us both a break, will you? Believe me, this hangover's doing me in as well. The point is, you were pissed, just like the bad man who hurt your head outside the chippy. And when we're drunk . . . well, we do silly things. And stop worrying about the police, too. If they had any clue about us, they would've been banging on the door at two o'clock this morning. Yet, look around you, William. Any sign of Plod and his dim-witted associates on this fine morning? I don't think so. Believe me, we're safe. We've done it again, made life a little more tolerable, we know who we are now, what we've always been . . .

Kris and I waited another forty unbearable minutes, and Danny never showed. Another ten minutes and she reluctantly began serving out overdone meat and vegetables onto two cracked plates. All the time, as I watched her, I couldn't believe she knew nothing about the previous night. Surely she'd have heard something?

'Do you know what time I got in?' I tried to ask nonchalantly, playing with a forkful of food I hadn't the will or the stomach to eat.

She looked up. 'No. No idea at all. I was out.'

'On the town?'

'Out cold, stupid. Fast asleep. Beauty sleep.' She paused, frowned. 'You're supposed to say something.'

'What?'

'That I don't need any.'

'Oh.'

'You OK?'

'Not really.'

She painstakingly piled up a forkful of food: roast potato, a carrot, some peas, and a neat cube of pork. 'Could be the sign of a good night,' she said. 'The fact that you don't remember getting in.'

'Maybe.'

'Not like you, though. All this drinking stuff. Very disappointing.' She slowly chewed on the forkful, making me wait. 'I thought you were so much more sensible than that. I mean, it can't help your head, can it?'

I didn't bother replying, so she changed the subject, now wondering where her admirer Ian had got to, then assuming he'd decided to stay an extra day in the bosom of his loving family. 'Not like him to miss his lectures,' she said. 'Very conscientious is Ian. Unlike some of you.'

'Perhaps something's come up,' I offered, not knowing how I'd react if Danny walked through the front door at any moment. Would I be relieved? Probably. Scared I was really losing my mind? Definitely.

'Like what?' Kris suddenly asked.

'Sorry? I was miles away.'

'You said something might have come up. For Ian. Like what? I mean, what are you saying?' The meat fell from the end of her next immaculately prepared forkful.

'I dunno,' I replied, a little taken aback. 'Something, you know. Anything.'

'Right. Like his parents were both eaten by a runaway lion, I suppose? Jesus, William, I'm not that bloody stupid.'

'Fine.' What the hell was she talking about?

'Thing is,' she said. 'Neither of us knows, so it doesn't do us any good to speculate.'

'Right.'

She ate in silence for while. Then suddenly said, 'Know why I like maths, William?' She was smiling brightly. 'It's logical, follows laws and idioms. Problem-solving without emotion. I think people would be far happier if they were more like equations.'

'Just about sums it up.'

She missed the gag, or pretended not to hear it. 'It's all about balance. Equations teach you that. One side has to balance the other. It's the key to solving the problem. You start by knowing both sides are equal.'

'Both sides?' I asked, foraging for some hidden agenda. 'You mean men and women?'

'No,' she teased, leaning across and patting the back of my hand. 'I mean the real human divide. The used, and the users.'

'Oh, sure.' Still no sign of Danny. Had I used him?

'Come on, William, you may have been in a coma, but you're not as thick as you make out. It's how the world divides itself. A few people on top, the rest on the bottom. Take Danny, a user. Then me, what would you say I was?'

'A pretty good chef when it comes to roast pork?' On balance, I could have been far more insulting.

She withdrew her hand, placed her knife and fork carefully on her unfinished meal, then pushed the plate slowly, deliberately to one side. 'I used to be used. Not any more. From now on, I'm going to be a user. I'm going to sit on the other side of the equation.'

'Hurrah for you.'

'No more fucking roast dinners and a quickie upstairs afterwards if the idle bastard doesn't have the sodding good grace to phone up and tell me he's not coming!'

'Maybe he got delayed?' I offered, a little nervous of the sudden change in her.

'Delayed, my arse,' she spat, taking her plate to the sink and loudly scraping the remains into the bin. 'He's dead meat when he gets here, William.' She almost sang it. 'Mark my words – dead meat.'

Another half-hour had passed and there was still no sign of Danny.

We went and sat in the lounge, watching an old black-and-white movie. The television picture rolled and broke up with each passing lorry, making following the plot near impossible.

Kris tried banging it increasingly heavily, to no avail. 'Fucked,' she said simply, sitting back down, simmering with a rage I knew Danny would stroll headlong into if he ever showed.

Maybe it would be better for him if he was already dead. At least I'd been quick with him. Kris looked as if she had the means to mathematically prolong proceedings for quite a while.

There was, of course, another explanation for his absence, which had occurred to me as I struggled to eat 'his' lunch. And although this option again involved the rather unsettling possibility that my own mental state was far more serious than I realized, it was brighter news for Danny. Quite simply, it could well be the case that he simply hadn't bothered to tell her that he wasn't coming over, and at that very moment was lying in his rotund little 'cousin's' bed, doing whatever they fancied.

As time passed, and the film finished, I clung to this possibility more and more, then tried not to think too hard about the consequences for myself. OK, maybe I was the unwitting victim of some surreal self-hallucination, but at least I wouldn't have to worry about the police knocking on the door.

Later that night it was time to go back to the biscuit factory. There was still no sign of Danny before I left. Or Ian, either.

I was just walking out of the front door when Kris appeared at the top of the stairs, chewing at her bottom lip. 'I'm going to call round the hospitals,' she said, full of purpose. 'It's just not like him to be late. I mean, not this late.'

'Well Kris,' I flustered, still anxious about what the hell I'd been up to the night before. 'Maybe it's a little too early for that . . .'

'Or the police,' she persisted. 'Maybe they know something. I just feel . . .'

'What?'

'There's something wrong.'

'Oh, I doubt it,' I answered, trying to sound casual. 'He'll have some excuse. Probably bowl up here the moment I'm gone.'

'You think so?'

'Certain of it,' I said, looking away. 'Maybe he's simply sick, or something.'

'But he would've phoned, let me know, wouldn't he?'

I sought sanctuary in the morning's conversation. 'Comes back to the old equation thing, eh? The guy's just a user. Give him a bit more time before you start ringing the authorities up.'

But I couldn't trust just leaving it there. What if the neurotic woman phoned the police five minutes after I'd left? I needed a concrete reason to keep her away from the damned phone. My mind raced. Then arrived.

'Anyway,' I said, opting for worldly wise and sensitive, 'I'm not sure Dan would want the police involved in . . . certain aspects of his life, Kris. Not that I'm saying anything bad about him, but . . .' I mimed the man taking a deep draw on a spliff.

'Oh,' she said quietly, chewing at the lip again. 'I see. Maybe you're right.'

'Risky, you know?'

She thought it over. 'Yeah. Perhaps I'll leave it.'

'I think it's best. For now.'

I stepped out into the black winter's night, closed the front door behind me, looked to the heavens and blew out a long breath of relief. Then offered up a prayer that if she so much as even thought about trying the phone, she'd break her neck falling down the stairs on the way.

Though I'm not sure God answers those.

At work I managed to ask Double Decker, my line supervisor, if he'd seen or heard anything of Danny during the day. He shot me a wide-eyed look, asked me if I thought he was the guy's father or something. I tried shrugging casually, then turned my fairly minimal attention back to a chugging line of raspberry creams. No crumbs for me at that particular table.

I got back to the house at around six on the Tuesday morning, trying to shift my weary brain into college-lecture mode, aware that the distractions of the weekend had made me late with two assignments. However, all plans to work doubly hard to catch up disappeared the second I opened the front door. Strange voices came from the lounge. I froze, hoping to hear one belonging to Danny. A head suddenly appeared from the doorway, female, blonde. Uniformed.

'Mr Dickson?' she asked officiously. 'Would you mind?'

I stood open-mouthed in the hallway, staring at the WPC, hearing my own short breaths and Kris's muffled crying somewhere beyond.

This was it. Danny was dead.

They'd come for me.

Maybe I was, too.

20

'And then what happened, William?' Dr Carter asked.

'I just . . . went into the room.'

'The lounge? The one Kris was in?'

'Yeah.'

'And?'

I stared at the micro-cassette, watching the small white wheels turn slowly behind the clear plastic window. Previously I'd have been loath to give my name, age and star-sign into a tape-recorder, but since I was now so spectacularly in such deep shit, well, there seemed little point in hiding anything any more. Lies would only have made the situation worse. 'There were two other policemen in there with her,' I said. 'Plainclothes. CID.'

Carter nodded, waiting for more.

'Kris was crying, looking at me accusingly.'

'Accusingly?'

I struggled with the memory of her face. 'As if . . . as if I was the one, you know? The person who'd killed him.'

The chair creaked as Carter shifted his weight. 'But you didn't know if you'd killed him, did you, William? You said just now you couldn't remember what you'd done.' He looked back briefly through his notes. 'You had two conflicting memories of what happened outside the pub.'

I looked up, searched for some kind of empathy on his hard lined face. Found none. 'All I could see was him dead under the wheels of that bloody bus. It's all I could think of.'

'What was your motive?'

I closed my eyes, mumbled something.

'Louder, William.'

I took a deep breath. 'Something stupid about needing to prove who I was. It made some kind of sense at the time.' I rubbed my face with both hands. 'I was drunk. Didn't really know what I was doing.'

Another note, another silent nod from Carter. It had been one of the longest twenty minutes of my life, spent in that claustrophobic blue box room, falteringly divulging every detail of the previous forty-eight hours to a man I was just coming to realize was perhaps the only person I could really trust. Possibly.

What had happened? Quite simply, when the brown stuff hit the fan, I'd panicked, run, come back to Carter, the sanctuary of Shallice House, not knowing whether I was a murderer who could kill on little more than a drunken whim – or someone else entirely. And it was close-run thing, which was beginning to scare me more.

'Then what?' Carter prompted.

'They asked me if I'd come with them . . .'

'They were arresting you?' An edge of concern in his voice.

'No. To help Kris.'

'Help her?'

'The woman constable led me outside, explained that they'd found a body. Stabbed. Left in some back alley somewhere in the city. No identification, save for a kind of key-ring thing. Seemed whoever had killed him had missed it, been through all the other pockets, cleaned out his wallet, everything. But left the key-ring.' I looked up at the ceiling, sighed.

'And the significance of this key-ring?' Carter asked.

'It was the one Kris had given Danny. She'd had her name engraved on it, telephone number. They used to make a joke about it, him not knowing her phone number. She gave it to him to remind him. Anyway, the police found it, rang the number, found Kris while I was at work. Now they needed her to identify the body, and wondered if I'd go with her as a friend.'

'So they didn't suspect you at this point?'

'I don't know,' I quietly replied. 'Could have been a game, couldn't it?'

'A game?'

'I mean, if they ran a few checks on me, then . . .'

'What, William?'

Silence as I considered the response, knowing each precious second he waited would arouse his suspicions even further.

'What might they discover, William,' he pressed, 'if they

ran a few checks on you? That you have a history of pushing people under buses?'

'Of course not.'

'So?'

'Christ's sake, isn't it obvious? They'd find out about you and Tremaine. My head injury. Make me out to be a loony, a psycho. It wouldn't do my case any favours, would it? Danny dies, and then they discover his girlfriend's sharing digs with a nutter.'

He looked at me, and my heart sank as I knew I hadn't convinced him. He was too good at the honesty business, rigorously trained to spot the poorly told lie, the dismal excuse. I wondered if that's how the police would be, if that's how easily they'd demolish my alibis and untruths.

'But you don't believe that you're a nutter, do you, William?'

'Listen,' I said, trying not to sound belligerent. 'You're the guy with all the fancy certificates on the wall, telling me all sorts of stuff about my life, my school, my family and friends that's screwing me up daily. I think that in the eyes of the law I would probably qualify as mentally confused, yes.'

He frowned, made yet another note. 'You're . . . accepting it, then? That certain events you remember might not have actually taken place?'

My head dropped. 'Maybe.'

You fool, William! Watch what you're saying! You think you can mess with people like Carter and come out ahead? Jesus H. Christ! The man's set his pathetic heart on trying to make us swallow a load of psycho-babble crap. But we've got to get a grip, William. Re-root ourselves in what we know is real – our truth, our secret truth. Nothing else matters, William, nothing . . .

'So you agreed, did you?' Carter went on, the tape still turning. 'Agreed to go with your flatmate with the police to identify this corpse?'

I nodded, swallowed hard, the stuck body still all too fresh in my mind.

'And it was this Danny Black, was it? The man you said you pushed under the bus on Sunday night?'

I closed my eyes, scarcely believing my own words. 'No. It wasn't Danny. It was Ian. Ian Bailey. My other flatmate.'

What decides what any of us remembers? How is it that some things simply refuse to be retrieved, stubbornly resisting all attempts at recall, whilst other cranial snapshots can linger for years, unmovable, un-erasable? Like the image of Ian's dead body, three-quarters covered by a cream wax-paper sheet, crammed into a human filing cabinet, being rolled towards Kris, myself, and the other officers.

This is where even I get confused. Really threw me to see the boy laid out like that. Ian? It can't have been Ian! Black was the dead one, the one we put away. The hippy was number five. Not Ian. We had no gripes with sad, deluded Ian. Something's going on here, William. Some wicked shit's afoot, and we've got to tread very carefully not to step right in it . . .

Bleach – that's what sets it off, even today. Just one whiff of the stuff, and suddenly I'm back in the Manchester morgue, nineteen, staring shocked at the pale grey damp head, hearing Kris's gasp of horror, feeling police eyes on me, waiting for a name, a clue to the unlucky cadaver's identity.

Bleach – a dead body. So much more horrible than I could have imagined, more so for being so empty, abandoned by the life and soul that had previously filled it. Suddenly it's like looking at your own mortality, seeing what's in store for you, the inevitable indignity of it all. One day, you'll look like this, it says to you. Ain't nothing you can do to stop it.

'You told the police it was Ian?' Carter asked.

I nodded.

'You must have been very confused.'

Another nod.

'Then what happened?'

I cleared my throat, still trying to shake the image. 'They took us to another room, asked us some questions about him. Where he said he was going that weekend, that sort of thing. Then they drove us home, Kris and me. We just couldn't believe it, were in shock. We hardly said a word. The police were informing his parents. They told us not to tell anyone at college, that they'd do it. Then asked us to think about him.'

'Think about him?'

I took a deep breath. 'They wanted us to make lists and stuff. Anything and everything we knew about him, his habits. They took us back to the house, stayed with us for about half an hour, then more CID people arrived. Began searching through his room, the whole house, going through all our stuff. Kris was crying. Talking about harassment, saying we were in shock, they had no right.'

Carter stroked his chin. 'And what did you do?'

Spent the time completely paralysed with fear, waiting for one of them to turn to me, nod to his colleagues, push me into the back of the squad car. But I couldn't tell Carter that, couldn't tell anyone. 'Just stood about,' I said. 'Got in their way. Answered a few more questions. Then –'

'What?'

Now came the worst bit, the moment I'd dreaded all the way out on the train from Manchester Piccadilly. But I was going to have to tell him, couldn't put it off, no matter how hard my instincts told me to.

I swallowed hard. 'They said they needed to do a proper search on the place. We'd have to spend the night somewhere else.'

'And?'

'Kris said a mate of hers would put her up. She gave the police the address and phone number, then they took her over there.'

I could sense he already knew what was coming. The body-language had changed, he'd stiffened, drawn back in his chair. 'And you, William? Where did you say you were staying?'

I closed both eyes. 'A friend's place. Two streets away.'

He slowly took off his glasses, pinched the bridge of his nose. 'And this would be . . . a lie, would it, William?'

I gave a small nod.

'You fool.'

'I'm sorry.'

His eyes blazed. 'For God's sake, William!'

'I said, I'm sorry.'

'Oh, and that makes it all fine, doesn't it?' He stood, went to the small window, looked out at the cloud-shrouded peaks beyond. Then turned back to me. 'Why, William? You lied to the police? What the hell were you thinking?'

The pressure kept building all the time. 'I don't know, I just . . . panicked . . . and then . . . shit, I don't know . . .'

'Why did you panic?'

I looked up, searching for some kind of understanding, a hint of forgiveness on his angry face. 'Because I had no one else to come to, because you've always said . . .'

'No!' he barked, causing me to jump. 'Why didn't you tell them you were staying with me in the first place?'

I hung my head. 'Jesus, I wish I had.'

He sat. 'Don't you see how bad this looks? For God's sake, if anything looks suspicious, it's giving the police false information about where the hell you're staying.'

'I know.'

'You've really ballsed up, William. Seriously ballsed up!' He practically spat the words out. 'Why, for God's sake?'

More intolerable pressure from within. I felt torn, ripped from the urge to blurt it all out, frozen from a fear of doing so. My throat burnt from the effort of simply sitting in silence.

'For God's sake help me to understand!'

Then, inevitably, eruption. 'Because I'm a bloody murderer, all right! That what you wanted to hear? I'm a fucking murderer who's already killed four people! The police get wind of that, and I'm a dead, man, Dr Richard-bloody-Carter! A fucking dead man!'

So I told him. Had to. No going back from an outburst like that. Out it all came, two hours of murderous cathartic detail, starting with Fat Norris in the woods; moving on to his mother in the kitchen; Webster, the sodomizing bully at Chetwins; and finally my psychopathic assailant from the sixth-form college. All four. I was at the end of my run, mind crumbling, police on my back and, perhaps most tellingly, had no one else to turn to.

At times, Carter would hold up a hand, silence me, change the tape over, make a brief interjection, then wave me on. The rest of the time he simply listened.

It was mid-afternoon by the time we finished. I'd never felt so exhausted, yet strangely, colossally unburdened. I imagined marathon runners felt the same way – spent, but somehow triumphant. There was nothing else I could do now. No more lies to concoct, no more barriers to be rigorously maintained. The truth was out. I'd thrown myself on his mercy. It was up to him now.

He said nothing at its end, but I could feel his mind churning, weighed down by a thousand decisions, innumerable options.

We went downstairs, had soup and fresh bread, just the two of us, eating like monks, nothing to say, heads bent over thick broth, tired hands tearing at wholemeal rolls.

Carter said we'd talk about 'things' later. He said I needed sleep. I didn't argue.

It was morning when I came to. I had to check my watch to be sure, confused, then amazed that the tiny date window had moved on another digit. But as the room came slowly into focus, so did the previous day's conversation, then the escape to Edale, and finally the unshakable image of Ian's dead head lying on the mortuary trolley. A day played out in reverse, with each moment worse than the previous one.

I made my way slowly downstairs. A radio played. Occasionally cars passed by the front of the house. I'd never felt more alone, detached or vulnerable.

Well, you've gone and bollocksed this right up, haven't you? Screwed us good and proper. Sung like a bloody canary. Hope you're feeling just as pleased with yourself this morning, William. See, the point is, it doesn't matter to me where we end our days. You surprised at that? You thought I'd be horrified at your damn stupid runaway mouth? Uh, uh, no way. I was only trying to warn you off Dr Dickhead for your sake, William. Me, I couldn't give a toss. Not any more – you're just too much of a loose cannon, William. Besides, I'm beginning to wonder if you're really cut out for the great things I had in store for you. So, you've decided to up the stakes – fair enough, I'll rise to the challenge. You've only got this far because I let you anyway . . .

Carter was on a phone call. I saw a long list on the kitchen table beside him. Some items had lines drawn through them – jobs already done, calls already made.

I sat opposite as he talked. He glanced up, then quickly looked away, finished the call.

'I had to tell them,' he said after replacing the receiver.

The police. I simply nodded, had been expecting it. 'About all four?'

'No, William,' he replied. 'I'm not about to turn you in as a student mass-murderer. I think I'd benefit more by going to the tabloids with that story.' He glanced at my pale face. 'It's a joke.'

'Oh, right.'

'Psychiatrists, we're just not very funny.'

I wasn't going to disagree. 'So what did you tell them?'

'Where you're staying. They already knew the information you gave them was false. I told them you were safe with me.'

'And what did they make of that?'

'Don't know, really. They don't give a lot away on the phone.' He poured me a fresh coffee. 'How did you get away with it, anyway?'

I took a sip, remembering the police squad car pulling away from the phoney address. Me waving to them from the front-garden gate. Opening it, heart pounding, walking slowly down the small path towards the front door until the squad car turned out of sight. Then turning quickly back onto the street, gathering speed, heading for the railway station, Edale. 'I just ran,' I said.

He nodded. 'They want to speak to you this morning. I've vouched for you, but . . .'

'Looks bad, doesn't it?'

'Like I say, I've no idea.'

'I'm really sorry.'

He swatted the apology aside with a flick of his wrist. 'Whatever, William. Now, on to the important stuff. I've got a solicitor coming over this morning who's going to go to Stockport police station with us. We're going to need someone who knows the legal side of things. French.'

'But I don't speak a word of it, I –'

A small smile flitted briefly across his face. 'No. Brian

French. Lancashire man through and through. He's good. Knows his stuff. He reckons we can put . . . this lie of yours down to a panicked mistake made when in shock, and that your co-operation today will indicate a willingness to help with their enquiry. He'll paint you as naive rather than suspicious.'

'But . . .' I tailed off, unwilling to face it.

'What?'

I had another slug of warm coffee. 'Suppose it was me?' I asked. 'Suppose I somehow met up with Ian, killed him, but just can't remember a damned thing about it?'

He studied me for a long moment. 'Don't suppose you brought a shirt and tie with you, did you?'

We drove in French's silver Mercedes to Stockport police station, where officers waited to interview me. Outside, it rained. Inside I sat in the rear in Carter's clothes, trying to remember the last time I'd worn any kind of shirt and tie. Chetwins, I reckoned, and remembering Carter's previous remarks about the place, only felt more uncomfortable with the whole situation. I tried also to make some sense of my options, the madness of the last twenty-four hours. To be fair, there was very little I could do about the current situation – I'd more or less thrown myself on Carter's mercy the moment I'd run for Edale. For now, I'd simply have to abide by his moves, trust to his experience.

But the rest of it? There I was completely lost. Who'd want to murder Ian Bailey? – a first-year architect student whose most vicious act was probably to snap a few HB pencils on his way to designing the perfect library memorial for Kris. I spent a couple of minutes thinking about him, then wondered why I didn't feel as sad as I reckoned I ought to. Had I murdered him, was that the reason? Had that telling key-ring somehow found its way into my pocket on Sunday night as I sat in the pub with Danny and his latest squeeze? Was I the one who had somehow bumped into Ian later, taken him into a dark alley, then coolly dispatched him with a knife?

As I'd recently come to realize, anything was now possible.

What about Danny? Drunk, half-stoned, perhaps dumped

for the night by his bored 'cousin'; had he stumbled across Ian making his way back across town to the house, then seen red, attacked him for trying it on with Kris? Maybe. After all, I didn't really know him at all. Perhaps he was the type to do just that. Maybe he had a prison record longer than my arm; I'd warned Ian he looked as if he could handle himself in a fight. But trying to rationalize it was pointless: anyone could have killed Ian; there were any number of madmen around.

French, the solicitor, drove the smooth German car at a steady speed. He was a rotund, good-humoured, balding guy, early fifties. During the twenty-minute journey he interrupted my brooding with an almost constant stream of terrible jokes, then pointed out local places of interest or made cutting observations on the driving skills of other road-users. Passing the Davenport Theatre, he began on a scandalous character assassination of virtually every cast member of the pantomime shortly to be playing there. I'm sure he intended to put me at my ease, but he was attempting the impossible.

Before long all three of us were standing in Stockport police station before a large bearded custody sergeant. After a phone call, we were led to a much smaller room in the back of the old stone building. My first experience of a police interview room. French and I went in, whilst Carter was led back to the reception area. He didn't even look back.

Inside, two plainclothes CID officers already sat behind one half of an old table, home to two files and a battered blue tin ashtray. The room stank of bodies and old cigarette ash, mingling with the fetid stench of numerous past interrogations. I tried my best to appear unconcerned, sensing it did little to convince the two men opposite me. Then we sat, French by my side, bringing out a notepad and pen from an expensive-looking green leather folder, an action that seemed carefully choreographed to take as much time as possible. He finished by giving me a quick, reassuring smile that I tried to return, leg bouncing nervously under the table.

Brief introductions were made. The larger of the two men had a close-cropped bullet-head and announced himself as DCI Shrimp. Don't be fooled by the name, he told me, he'd caught some pretty big fish. The other, thinner officer had high, pockmarked cheekbones and wore a stained brown suit. He answered to the name of DS Harris, Shrimp told me. Harris inserted two cassette tapes into a machine by the wall and let the senior man make the necessary legal identifications.

And we were off. Or rather, French was. Gone was the jovial chauffeur, giving way to the consummate professional.

'Can I ask why my client hasn't been given the chance to make a formal statement, Detective Chief Inspector?'

Shrimp leaned back in the creaking chair. 'At the present stage, Mr Dickson is merely –'

'Assisting you with your enquiries?'

'Correct.'

'Just so we're all clear on that one,' French smiled, clicking his silver ballpoint pen. 'Fire away.'

'Right, William,' Shrimp announced, frowning slightly, 'guess you know why you're here. Can you tell us why you misled my officers about where you were staying?'

French spoke firmly. 'I think you'll find my client made a simple error of judgement under what would have been very difficult emotional circumstances. A mistake was made, but whether this indicates a conscious desire to mislead is a different matter entirely.'

I hadn't uttered a word.

'And I think,' Shrimp replied, failing to disguise his annoyance, 'that Sergeant Harris and me would like to hear a little more from your client, Mr French, and a lot less from you.'

'That's I, Detective,' French shot back. 'Sergeant Harris and I.' He offered a small grin. 'I'm afraid I'm a stickler for correct usage.' He lowered his voice and leant across the table. 'Thing is, Inspector, you'd be surprised how often my clients' fates can hang on the balance of one little word.'

Shrimp sighed. 'William?' he finally said, fixing me with a deadpan stare. 'Care to tell us what happened?'

I tried to work some saliva over my dry tongue. 'Well . . . it was all so shocking. Like Mr French said, I was confused . . . I'd been working all night. Then I had to go and see Ian's body . . .'

'Why did you lie to us, William?'

'I wasn't thinking straight, got the wrong address. That's all. I'm sorry. I didn't mean to –'

'Why?' Shrimp quickly interrupted. 'Why weren't you "thinking straight", William?'

French – to my rescue. 'I think my client's been quite specific about that already, Inspector . . .'

'Could it be,' Shrimp steamrollered, flicking his fingers and being passed a yellow file, 'something to do with a certain incident concerning a . . . Well, where do we start with you, William, eh? How about,' he ran a finger down the page, 'Mrs Edith Fitzroy? Ring any bells, William?'

Edith Fitzroy?

'For the benefit of the tape, William Dickson has just shrugged his shoulders in response to the last question,' Harris said quickly.

'Care to tell us about Mrs Fitzroy, William?'

I shot a nervous glance at French, completely ambushed by the question. Why the hell had they brought up Edith Fitzroy's name? I wondered how well French had been briefed by Carter. How much did he know? The full story, every last detail as confessed the previous night?

'Inspector,' French almost casually announced, 'I fail to see the relevance of this line of questioning. Unless you can provide specific evidence as to why it is pertinent, then I'm legally obliged to inform Mr Dickson that, once again, he does not have to answer.'

Shrimp smiled, then fixed me with a look which seemed to bore right down into my boots. He flipped through the file. 'Makes interesting reading, some of this, William. Very interesting.'

I tried to crane my head as inconspicuously as possible, to see just how much of my life he had written down in front of him. He caught me doing so, then slowly passed the file back to Harris with a smile.

'But it's early days,' he said.

'Sorry?'

'Lot of sniffing around to do in a murder enquiry. Lot of avenues to be explored. Let's just say that Sergeant Harris and me – sorry, I – will be spending quite a time delving down yours.' He stood, scraping the chair on the hard floor. 'You might well regret the fact that you gave us a false address, William. But somehow, I don't think I will.'

French stood, gathered up his papers. 'Have we finished, Inspector? Or do you wish to really put your foot in it by arresting my client on suspicion of murder?'

My heart missed a beat.

Shrimp walked to the door, gesturing for Harris to take up the reins. 'You'll be required to report to the duty sergeant of this police station every morning before ten. You'll stay with . . .' a brief pause while he consulted another file, '. . . a Dr Richard Carter at Shallice House, Edale, Derbyshire, until such time as we say otherwise.'

'Sounds rather like house-arrest, Detective,' French said.

'Your client has already given false and misleading information to officers conducting a murder enquiry,' Harris answered coldly. 'Plus, his name already appears on our records. Strangely enough, in connection with another murder enquiry – that of a Mrs Edith Fitzroy. I don't think we're being overly cautious in wanting to know where he is, Mr French, do you? Interview ended at . . . ten thirty-one a.m.' He switched off the dual tape-recorder.

French nodded at me, which was my signal to stand. I took two paces towards the door, hesitated, unwilling to pass by the grinning bulk of DCI Shrimp.

'This Dr Carter,' he said slowly, 'ain't no GP, is he, William, eh? Psychiatrist, isn't he? By the way, nice scar you've got there.' He winked, tapped the side of his head, as French's arm on my shoulder gently urged me through the door.

21

'He knows,' I said quietly. 'They both do. Know everything there is to know about me.'

There was silence from Carter and French, nothing of the jovial atmosphere of the journey in.

'I'm going to prison for life.'

French spoke, his tone quiet, considered. 'Tell me about Edith Fitzroy, William.'

Carter shot him an enquiring look, then glanced back to me, nodded.

'She was just some woman I gardened for,' I said, 'back in Kent.'

French's eyes met mine in the rear-view mirror. 'So why the police's interest?'

'I've no idea.'

'You heard what they said, that she was murdered?'

'Yeah.'

I saw Carter raise his eyebrows.

'Well?' French asked.

'I just don't know.'

'Not good enough, William,' he replied grimly. 'Not nearly good enough.'

I'd told Carter all I knew about Edith Fitzroy when I'd given him the two-hour taped confession of my life to date. That she was a kindly woman who'd seen fit to offer me a job tending her cottage garden when the rest of the village turned its back on me for the churchyard episode – when I got fired by the vicar for attending other people's funerals. Carter hadn't dwelt on the episode at all, merely allowed me to move on to the attack outside the Maidstone chip-shop. In truth, I hadn't given Edith Fitzroy a thought in years. Why should I? She gave me some money, then we'd both agreed I didn't have to garden for her any more. Months later, Mum, Nicola and I had moved to the Maidstone flat. I never saw her after our last meeting, never gave her another thought. Until now.

'They seem to have records connecting you to that enquiry,' French continued. 'How would they have those, William?'

'No idea.'

'You knew she'd been murdered?'

'No,' I replied, recalling chatting with the kindly ex-schoolmistress, the look of concern in her face as she warned me not to fritter the money away. 'First I've heard of it.'

'You say you worked for her?'

'Yeah.'

'And you had no idea she'd been killed?'

'None,' I replied.

'You live in a small village, garden for one of its residents, and have no recollection of her murder?'

I shook my head. 'We moved soon after I finished working for her. It must have happened after I left.'

French clicked his tongue, seemed to want to say something, but didn't.

We continued in heavy silence for while. Twice I noticed French and Carter exchanging further glances, but didn't stand a hope of making out their silent communication. Part of me wanted to say more, to mention the money Mrs Fitzroy had given me – I hadn't felt the need to tell Carter any of that – but something stronger warned me to stay silent, to try and work things out before shooting my mouth off again. After all, it didn't seem to have done me too many favours so far.

'Where are we going?' I asked, trying to change the subject as we turned into familiar streets.

'Got to stop off at your house and pick up some clothes and stuff,' French replied, popping a stick of gum into his mouth and glancing briefly at me in Carter's suit and tie. 'That is, unless you want to spend the next few days looking like a badly dressed Burton's window-dummy.'

'I'll have you know those threads are mine,' Carter said, a little hurt.

French chuckled, turned to Carter. 'Thought you said you liked him?'

A uniformed officer waited outside the Fallowfield house,

bored, cold. It was surreal, seeing a policeman standing there, somehow made the whole situation so much worse, more real, unavoidable.

I suppose the three of us provided the bored officer with something to do, a welcome diversion to simply standing around, and he duly took his time, radioing back to various unseen offices, checking who we were, what permission we had, before finally allowing us through the front door.

Inside, it was a suburban terraced *Marie Celeste*. Monday night's thorough search had changed the entire look of the place, given it a dark, abandoned feel, a cruel museum of a life I felt I'd left a long time ago. The policeman kept a close watch as we went to my bedroom, and I began throwing an assortment of clothes into an old holdall. It was a painfully slow process. Each item had to be noted down, then permission granted via the radio. It took twenty minutes to fill one bag. Next a CID team arrived to go through the items again. And all the while Carter just stood around, his expression blank, saying nothing, hands deep in his overcoat. Once or twice I managed to catch his eye, keen for some kind of supportive gesture, but got nothing.

Afterwards, as we left in the smoothly upholstered Mercedes, I spied neighbours who I'd never spoken to before watching from behind twitching lace curtains, and knew that everything would change from now on. Chances were I'd never return to that house, perhaps never even set foot in the poly again. I was a suspect in a murder case, the irony being that, in all four previous instances, I'd got away with it, slipped through the net. Yet now, when I was fairly sure I had nothing to do with Ian Bailey's death, I was increasingly looking like the main contender for the guilty verdict.

What would happen if it all came to court? I thought of Mum, and wondered if she'd be spared newspaper photographs of her son bent under a blanket, being ushered into a packed courthouse. Exactly how much would come to light? Would it roll right the way back to Fat Norris and me, our games in the woods? And if so, surely my parents' disposal of Margot Norris's body would also be discovered. What then? Would Mum be beside me in the dock? Meet the Dicksons, Tilbury's most notorious criminal family.

I needed to talk. 'Do you think I did it?' I asked French.

'Did what?' he asked.

'Any of it? Ian Bailey, Edith Fitzroy, the others . . . I know you've been speaking to Dr Carter. I don't suppose he's spared you any of the details.'

'It's not my job to think about guilt or innocence,' he replied, slowing for traffic lights. 'Simply to see you're afforded your rights under the law.'

'But if you had to bet on it?'

'I'd stick to horses, William. They're a lot more dependable than folk.'

Carter and French were still outside, talking, swaying slightly in the gusting wind. I watched from the warm front room, trying – failing – to lip-read their conversation.

Footsteps behind. I turned to see Karen, in a dressing gown, slippers, yawning, nursing a coffee, slumping into an armchair.

'Hi.'

'Hello,' I answered.

'You OK?'

'I've been better.' I sat on the edge of an expensive leather sofa, body forward, tight, leg beginning to bounce again. 'Your father told you?'

She nodded. 'Yesterday evening, when you were asleep.'

I sighed. 'So much for client confidentiality.'

'He doesn't work like that. I live here too. Having a . . .' she tried to find the most diplomatic term, '. . . client staying over at any therapist's house is breaking professional boundaries, big time. I deserved some sort of explanation.'

'Maybe.'

'He could really cop for this, William,' she said, glancing briefly outside. 'He's already got the coroner's case hanging over him. Now you turn up on the run. He's not had a good week.'

I couldn't stop the sarcasm. 'Well, I'm sorry to be such an "inconvenience" in your happy hillside lifestyle.'

She put the coffee down, shot me a filthy look. 'Oh, grow up,' she said, flouncing from the room.

I was still silently cursing the stupidity of my outburst when I heard the distinctive sound of French driving away, followed by Carter making his way back into the house. After hanging up his coat, he joined me in the lounge.

'I think I've just upset Karen,' I said. 'No – scrub that, I *know* I've just upset her.'

'Congratulations, William. You join an exclusive club. I manage to do the same at least ten times a week.'

'Do you think I should, you know . . . ?' I pointed upstairs.

'Not right now. Maybe later. She blows, then needs a little time to get over it. Listen, is there anyone you want to call? Family, your mother?'

'And tell them what, exactly? "Hello, Mum, it's William. I'm at Dr Carter's house because I'm a murder suspect"?'

'She deserves an explanation,' he said. 'In case she rings Fallowfield and can't get through to you.'

'Maybe later,' I replied. 'She'll be at work at the moment.'

He took a sip of the coffee that Karen had left on the low table, then rubbed the side of his neck.

'What were you and French talking about outside?' I asked.

'An ethical issue.'

'Meaning what?'

'Meaning, how would it affect my professional status to have a client of mine staying on the premises?'

'And?'

He paused for a few moments, seemed to be warming his hands from the cup. 'It's not exactly in the rules but, then again, I've never really gone a bundle on rules in the first place.'

'You're sticking your neck out for me, aren't you?'

He seemed uncomfortable with the idea. 'William, why don't we put our time to more productive use by talking about you?'

'OK.'

He placed the cup carefully back on the table. 'You're going to have to trust me, here. Brian has gone back to his office to find out all he can on what the police may or may not have on you in their files. Specifically, about the Edith Fitzroy woman.'

'Like I said, I don't know anything about that.'

'That might not be the case.'

'What?'

'There's a difference, William, between what you know and what you remember. Or in your case, seem to have selectively forgotten.'

It hurt. I felt angry, deficient, still unwilling finally to voice the fact that – yes – I did have some kind of mental problem. And when you feel that way, attack is sometimes the best form of defence.

I fought for a level voice. 'I told you everything about myself yesterday afternoon. Stuff I've told no one else! The truth –'

'Why the anger?'

'Because I feel betrayed,' I answered. 'You've no idea how hard it was for me to –'

'Crap, William!'

'What?'

'The truth? You told me the truth?'

'Yes, I –'

'Have you any idea how serious this is?' he barked, suddenly standing and throwing his arms out wide. 'You couldn't even remember your own suicide attempt! How's that going to look in court, eh? How long are you going to last, William, if the police decide to finger you for this murder? What happens once a half-decent barrister gets his teeth into you? How long is it going to take before you start coming out with fairy-stories about lads attacking you outside a chip-shop? Ten minutes, twenty?'

'I was attacked!'

'Didn't happen like that, William.'

'And you're the oracle, of course!'

'You jumped. You jumped from the first floor of John Tremaine's house.'

His eyes held mine for a long moment. This time he looked away first. But there was no sense of victory, just an icy feeling clawing its way up from my stomach.

That crash of glass had come back to haunt me.

'He was asking you about a very specific event in your past.'

It was ten minutes later, and we'd moved into the kitchen. I sat listening as Carter leant against the sink. 'The tree. Remember the tree?'

I nodded.

'You were in a light trance, regressed to the age of seven. Two-thirds of the way through the session, you suddenly sat upright, came right out of it. John tried to put you back, moved over to you, wanted to know what was wrong. Then,' he let out a breath, 'then you tried to strangle him. Damn near succeeded. He blacked out. Last thing he remembers is seeing you rush for the window. You crashed right through. Fell fifteen feet onto his patio.'

I said nothing, fighting it.

'That's how it was, William. There was no laughing lad outside the chip-shop. Just you and John Tremaine in his study.'

'And that's why he's too terrified to see me, I suppose?'

'You damn near killed him. Do you blame him?'

A simple enough question, but no answer came.

'I've got something I want you to listen to,' Carter said, walking to the door. 'I think the time's right.'

He led me back upstairs into the blue box room, made me sit, then reached into a drawer and bought out a cassette recorder. Next he took out a tape from a brown A4 envelope, checked the label, inserted it, pressed 'Play'.

A stranger's voice drifted from the machine. '. . . so what happened next, William, after you'd had your sweets?'

Then another voice – mine. But younger, somehow, higher, fearful. 'We went further in.'

'Into the woods?'

'Yes.'

'Are you there now?'

'Yes.'

'What can you see, William?'

'The trees. Paths. Branches. It's cold.'

'The others, are they still there?'

'Yes.'

'What are they doing?'

'Fat is just sort of sitting. Alan's running ahead. Wants me to chase him.'

'Are you going to chase him?'

'I want to . . .'

'But?'

'Fat wants me to stay. Says it'll all go wrong if I do. We'll be in trouble if we run off.'

'What sort of trouble, William?'

'Big trouble . . . bad trouble.'

'Why?'

'Because he won't be able to find us.'

'Who's "he", William?'

'That's a secret. Can't tell.'

'Is it a man, William? A man who comes to the woods?'

There's a long silence on the tape before Tremaine asks the question again. This time, the voice I now know to be my own begins to groan, emitting some sort of dreadful animal sound, a wolf's call of insane chaos. There's a few seconds of this before a solid thump. Tremaine calls out my name, panicked. Then again, coming in muffled, choked stages this time. Two more thumps, then a crash of something falling. Tremaine begins to moan. Then my voice again, cold, vicious, swearing at him. One last burbled moan from Tremaine, before I scream. A solid thump. Fast footsteps. Then that same terrible crash of glass, followed by an audio blur the recorder cannot accurately reproduce. Silence.

Carter turned off the recorder. 'That last bit's you, barging through the glass. You shattered the frame, smashed the window. The ambulance crew reckoned you must have virtually taken a running leap at it.'

I tried to collect my thoughts, make some sense of my unknown parallel life. 'What happened next?'

Carter turned the player back on.

This time I heard a woman's voice, curious at first, muffled, distant, then becoming anxious, calling 'John' and 'William' over and over. Her voice got louder, then the sound of a door opening. Three footfalls, during which I can hear her short, shallow breaths. Then she cried out.

Carter switched off the machine. 'Carole Tremaine discovers her husband's unconscious body,' he explained.

I shook my head. 'It just can't be me. It can't. I don't remember any of it. I mean, it sounds like me, but –'

Carter held up a hand. 'The point is that your subconscious

won't let you remember, William. When Dr Tremaine tried to get to the truth, something inside you took over, tried to kill him.'

'This is insane . . .'

'And then,' he continued, 'it tried to kill you. And maybe, just maybe, it tried again on Sunday night, William.'

'Christ, what are you saying now? That I'm a permanent suicide case?'

'Maybe you really did try to step in front of that bus. Maybe the man you thought you wanted to kill actually saved your life. William, I'll level with you. Things don't look that good for you right now. We need to explain to the police what's going on inside that head of yours. At the very least to give them a plausible psychological reason why you lied to them. Get them off your case. Clear you from their possible suspect list.'

'I didn't kill Ian,' I moaned. 'I'm sure I didn't do that.'

'Because at the time, you were very drunk, and uncertain whether you were trying to murder Danny Black or not, yes?'

I saw the point. He wasn't trying to trap me, merely showing me how it looked from the police's perspective. 'I'm in the shit, aren't I?'

'You have absolutely no recollection of jumping through that window?'

'I don't know, I –'

'The hallucination you said you had when you were with me the other weekend?' he pressed. 'Wasn't that this same smash of glass?'

'A crash is a crash, isn't it?' I took a deep breath. 'What's happening to me?'

'If I had to stake my professional opinion on it, then I'd say your buddy Danny probably saved your life on Sunday night. Think about it: if you'd killed him as you described, it would have been all over the papers by now.'

I slowly nodded.

'I think something in your mind tried to kill you that night. The same part that made you want to kill John Tremaine and then jump through the window.'

There were goosebumps on my forearms. 'Why?' was all I could quietly ask.

'Because we're getting close to unlocking its secrets, William.'

'My own brain wants me dead?'

'Bitch, isn't it?'

I smiled back, suddenly caught in the hysterical absurdity of the moment. Maybe the room was too small, our proximity too close, the revelations too startling, but suddenly I was caught by a rising giggling fit. 'What about you?' I asked, unable to control it. 'Aren't you a little worried that I'm going to do away with you in the night?'

'Kitchen knives are all hidden away,' he replied, the mood catching, beginning to crack as well.

'Weedkiller hidden?'

'Duelling pistols in the safe.'

We both surrendered to the laughter, a release perhaps from the intensity of the last few days.

Later, back in the house after lunch and a walk on the hills, we tried, more seriously, to recap.

'So basically,' I said, 'my mind's trying to kill me? And I don't know when?'

'It looks that way.'

'Because it's trying to keep something secret?'

He nodded. We were in the kitchen, Carter making tea.

'And it would rather I died than let this information out? Doesn't that go against all the logic of survival and self-preservation?'

He passed me a steaming cup. 'What logic? It is trying to preserve something, a secret. And for that part of your mind, that secret is more important than its survival. You heard the expression "I died of shame" – well, it could be true in your case.'

'You really have a way with words.'

He sat. 'Listen, I'll level with you. When you left here on Sunday, I'd more or less put you down as a standard PTA case. With a few sessions I'd be able to reroute you into reality, and there it would all end. Sure, I knew about the suicide attempt, but what really shocked me was just how quickly your mind tried again. I'm pretty certain that if your friend

Danny hadn't been there to catch you, you'd have been dead under that bus.'

'When I laughed before, it was only because I felt frightened, you know?'

'I know. Me too, in a way. The mind can be an objectionable bastard if it feels threatened. It has protection mechanisms that we're only just beginning to understand. It has ways of bending reality, justifying any number of horrors as standard occurrences. And for you, your own mind could well be your very worst enemy.'

He went and fetched the tape-recorder and padded envelope from upstairs, then pulled out more cassettes. 'This is the rest of the stuff John Tremaine sent me. They're recordings of the last twelve sessions you had with him, all done under a light hypnotic trance. I want us to listen to them, but –'

'What?'

He shifted a little, frowned slightly. 'William, I want you to imagine that there are three of us in this room. You, me, and your subconscious. Treat it as another being entirely. The good news is that there's two of us, and only one of it.'

'And the bad news?'

'It's probably already tried to kill you twice. If we go too deep too fast . . .'

'It'll try again?'

Carter ejected the previous tape before pushing another into the machine.

22

How many times have you flicked back through an old photo-album and had trouble making the connections? How many times have you stared befuddled at an old snap of yourself and found that – initially, anyway – no real memories attach themselves to the shot? Like a photo taken from childhood, perhaps: you see yourself as a grinning youngster, but have no recollection of the time, event or place. Maybe there's some pretty powerful clues there, too, indisputable evidence – younger versions of your parents holding you, for instance, so now there's no way you can deny the episode. It is you, but a dead part, taken from a time in your life now lost.

That was how it was for me as I listened to those tapes. The voice was undoubtedly mine, but the content – hell, the content threw me completely.

Carter was in and out of the room all afternoon, making or answering phone calls, then reappearing to stop the tape dozens of times to ask questions, to which I always answered 'No'.

As in: 'Do you recall this conversation?'

'No.'

'Can you tell me anything about Dr Tremaine's house?'

'No.'

'His room?'

'No.'

Each tape was a recorded counselling session with Dr Tremaine, the man I now tried, but still failed, to picture as Mr Squires from the Partridge. He'd used a lot of techniques on me, including hypnotic regression, and it was those tapes, complete with my cautious juvenile responses, that disturbed me the most.

One particular tape concerned the so-called 'memory' I had of events on that fateful Christmas Eve: Margot Norris lying slain and bloodied on the kitchen floor as Mum and I prepared vegetables. But even here, I was confused. My younger voice hadn't remembered it that way. Worse, I seemed uncertain of the obvious truth – that I'd murdered her – and seemed far more concerned with what she'd said to me, doing a hideous impression of her drunken ranting, how she'd wanted me dead, not her bloated beloved Edward. All in that eerie voice.

I deserved to die, she'd said, over and over, as Mum had tried to calm her. All stuff I remembered vividly well. But then – nothing. No mention of her terminal encounter with the heavy wooden knife-block – no mention of that at all. Why? Surely I wouldn't have forgotten that I'd killed the woman? It was basic, the entire bloody point to the encounter. So why wasn't it on the tape?

Carter merely shrugged in a way I was beginning to recognize signalled that he knew far more than he was prepared to let on at that stage. It was as if his strategy relied on me answering the questions themselves, that one day the faulty memory circuits would suddenly kick back in, make the necessary connections. The problem I had, however, was that if I trusted to his experience and continued with such agonizing progress, then I also had to accept other things besides. The worst being that he was also right about both suicide attempts. And further, that whatever mechanism was impeding my mental progress was liable to try again at any given moment. I began to wonder if this wasn't the main reason why he had agreed to my staying at Shallice House. From here, he could keep an eye on me. One thing was certain, though: being alone was the last thing I wanted. It felt a little too close to walking around with an unexploded bomb in my head. One false move, one clumsy prod, and boom . . . !

Over supper that night, I asked him about Karen. I'd been slightly disappointed not to see her since my crass remarks earlier in the morning.

He paused while I sensed him choose the words. 'She's staying over with friends for a few days.'

I tried to hide the disappointment with a glib reply. 'Because of me, right? Just in case I land on her head after throwing myself from the stairs, I suppose?'

'William, she's my daughter. My responsibility. We

discussed it, she said she'd feel comfortable somewhere else in the village for a few days.'

'Another ethical dilemma.'

'More of a practical one.'

'What about you?'

'Me?'

'That's why she's gone, isn't it? Because I'm a danger, right? A murder suspect, can't be trusted. Aren't you worried? Especially after what I am supposed to have done to Tremaine. What if this crazy bit in my head takes over and I come after you in the dead of night?'

He smiled. 'I think you're more a danger to yourself than you are to me, William.' He watched me with a familiar stare that I'd initially mistaken for arrogance – the good and great Dr Richard Carter, playing the part of the all-seeing wise one, as if the assembled at his feet had somehow to wait in awed silence for his every utterance. However as time passed, and I'd got to know the guy better, I began to see these pauses in a different light, accept them for what they were: simply the process of editing out irrelevancies in order to be clear, concise, empathetic. Looking back, I now realize Carter was one of the least ego-driven individuals I've ever met.

Finally he said, 'Remember when we spoke about the "three" of us?'

'Sure.'

'I was wondering,' he slowly said, 'if it wouldn't help to give our unseen guest an identity. A name, perhaps.'

I frowned. 'I don't know. It just sounds stupid.'

'But if we name it – him – then he becomes real. Less "stupid" as time goes on.'

'Are you trying to turn me into a paranoid schizo?'

He shook his head. 'They're a very different bunch, believe me.'

'So what am I then?'

'You're you.' He raised his glass to me. 'William Dickson. And, as far as I can make out, an exception in psychological therapeutic research. A landmark in hysterical amnesia. An enigma.'

'Great.'

'How about Bill?'

'What?'

'The other you,' he answered. 'Bill – the one that makes you think he pushed Daniel under the bus. The one that makes you think you were beaten up outside the chip-shop. Bill – the one who's in your head, messing around with William's perceptions.'

I blew out my breath, shrugged. What the hell? It had been that sort of day. In my state, I was more or less prepared to accept anything. 'Maybe. But it still sounds –'

'Odd?'

'Very.'

'Scary?'

'Definitely.'

'Good. It's a perfectly normal healthy psychological reaction.' He stood, and began collecting plates. 'I'd be terrified if I were you.'

Later, I dried while he washed up.

'I'm confused,' I said.

'Fire away.'

'OK, about that tape,' I began. 'The second one. Christmas, after Fat Norris had died in the tree.'

'You want to know why there's no mention of you killing his mother?'

I nodded as he passed me another plate.

Another long silence as he considered his reply. 'I suspect, William, that it might be one of Bill's games.'

'This "Bill" thing's here to stay, isn't it?'

'You want a different name? Choose one.'

'Bill'll do. Go on.'

He stopped washing up, both hands still in the warm soapy water. 'I think Bill might have been very busy in those few days after you leapt from Dr Tremaine's room. I think the reason you didn't mention the murder on the tape was because you had no memory of it at that time.'

'You're saying it never happened?'

'I'm saying, William, that I believe that while you were in your coma, our friend Bill was hard at work reshaping things, remoulding you.'

'Turning me into a killer?'

He looked across. 'No. Making you think you were. Supplying you with an immaculate set of totally false memories. Tweaking reality, making it real for you.'

I was becoming agitated, fighting rising feelings and deep dark urges. 'Why?' I asked, almost dropping a saucer. 'What's his gain? What does this "Bill" get out of it?'

'I don't know yet, William.' He was watching me closely, studying every reaction.

'It's getting serious, isn't it?' I said, voice cracking slightly. 'You're serious, aren't you, about this whole Bill business?'

He passed me the last of the cutlery, let the water drain away, then dried his hands. 'You'd be amazed, William, at the amount of brain activity in some coma-victims. Incredible. On the one hand, there's a prone body, all vital physical functions merely sustained by external medical equipment. To any observer, little more than a vegetable kept alive by the miracles of modern technology. But inside . . .'

'What?'

'Wait.' He left the kitchen, returned a minute later with a long thin roll of paper, spread it on the kitchen table. 'This is your scan, William.'

I stared at the paper, then at him. It meant nothing.

'It's a copy of the record of your brain activity while you were unconscious. Another gift from Tremaine via the hospital.' He began tracing a finger along a thin black line that ran along the middle of the roll, occasionally dipping and rising slightly. 'This is the first twelve hours after your admission onto the critical ward. It's absolutely consistent with what we'd expect. Minimal activity, but a bit none the less.'

'I'm not going to like the next bit, am I?'

He unrolled the scan another metre or so. 'See what happens on the second day.' His finger pointed to a gradually fluctuating line. 'Your brain activity increases dramatically. Tremaine was called to the hospital. Said he couldn't understand how you weren't conscious at this point. The level was far higher than you'd expect in the average REM dream-sleep by a normal subject.' He looked straight at me. 'Or an abnormal subject, for that matter.'

I sat, watched him reveal more of the scan. The black line

now dipped and rose so violently that it looked like a toddler's first effort at crayoning.

'Days three and four,' Carter continued. 'Unprecedented levels of synaptic activity. Four independent hospital specialists had been to see you at this point. All baffled.'

'Perhaps the machine was duff,' I weakly offered, feeling both legs begin to twitch and jump.

'The monitor had been changed, twice. No one knew what was going on inside your mind, William. No one.'

'Bill?' I heard myself asking. 'Was he . . . doing that?'

'Look at this,' Carter quickly unrolled the final section showing the mad scrawl giving way to a virtually flat line. 'An hour before you came round, it all reverts back to normal. It's as if . . .'

But I filled in the pause. '. . . On the final day, he rested.'

Carter didn't reply. He simply rolled the scan back up as I stared into empty space.

23

Eleven o'clock the following morning – Wednesday – and I sit in the glass, chrome and leather-upholstered premises of 'French, Mailer and Associates – Solicitors'. We're in the inner sanctum, Brian French and Carter chatting earnestly in his office as I look out of the third-floor window at central Manchester's distant street-life making its way hazardously through sleeting winter rain fifty feet below.

My mind wanders, obscures all conversation, torn back to the tape of the suicide attempt – me jumping from another window. Jumping? The thought chills me. Why would I even have considered it? Yet the ferocity, the energy of the recorded crack of my supposed body against the window frame, the explosion of wood and glass, meant that if the jumper were me, then clearly I'd been sincerely committed to the project.

Too frightening even to contemplate. As was 'Bill'. When would he strike again? How about right now? Rear up from somewhere deep inside and command that my legs rush for French's smoked-glass window? Be a better bet from his perspective than Tremaine's, I guessed; another two storeys higher at least . . .

Somehow, I'd managed to sleep the previous evening, emotionally shattered, comatose. It was only in the morning that I wondered if Carter had slipped something in my juice, a powdered insurance policy, perhaps, preventing me from committing any nefarious deed in the night. After all, he was a shrink: chances were he had access to all kinds of antidepressants, uppers, downers and sleeping tablets.

After a quiet breakfast, we'd kept our rendezvous with the duty sergeant at Stockport police station, and thankfully were out of the place in moments, without being pounced on by Shrimp and Harris. But I knew they were burrowing away somewhere, delving as they'd promised, winkling me from my shell. It was only a matter of time before they came knocking again. They had to – after all, I was such a quality suspect, wasn't I?

Then from the police station to the solicitor's, no further comment between us as Carter and I sat enclosed in the BMW, all thoughts turned towards our individual problems.

French and Carter prattled on, tossing legal jargon and psycho-babble to and fro. Most of it didn't mean a damn thing to me, yet I knew it was about me. I began to feel annoyed. Why weren't they talking to me?

Brian French shot me a look, sussing my mood, held up a polite hand to halt Carter's monologue.

He beamed warmly. 'Load of old tosh, this, isn't it, William?'

I turned from the window, tried to unlock my cramping jaw.

'It has to be run through, I'm afraid. Dick here knows about all the therapeutic stuff; I shove my two pennies'-worth in on the legal side.'

I couldn't help the smile. Dick – I'd never thought of Carter as Dick. His Dick to my Bill. How many of us were there in the room?

'Something amusing you, William?' Carter asked.

'It's nothing. Dick.'

He raised both eyebrows a fraction.

French continued, 'I've had some people look into a bit of background. Specifically the Fitzroy woman the police mentioned yesterday.' He took out a file from a desk drawer. Another file. I was beginning to weary of the sight of them, bits of my life stashed away inside brown, yellow, red and blue cardboard envelopes, each seemingly containing some damning new revelation, fresh conundrums.

'Makes interesting reading,' he said, pausing to light a cigar.

'Like I say, I barely knew her.'

He nodded, blowing out a large plume of smoke. 'A neighbour found her at the bottom of her stairs, William. Quite a shock, but it could have been an accidental death.' He took another drag. 'She had cancer, very brittle bones. Wouldn't have taken a lot to break them. Curious thing was, her bedroom was downstairs. And the bathroom, toilet, the lot. Upstairs there were just two virtually empty rooms. So what, the police wondered, was she doing upstairs?'

'I've no idea,' I replied, feeling suddenly obliged to answer.

'You may also be wondering, William, what damning piece of evidence pointed out to our friends the Kentish plod that Mrs Fitzroy's death had been – how shall we put this? – assisted.' Another drag as he threw his head back to exhale in a dramatic flourish. He may have been balding and stout, but the whole world was very much Brian French's stage.

'First off were the marks on her wrists,' he announced. 'She'd struggled before she'd fallen. Large thumb-sized bruises on either arm, which could be said to belong either to a large man with thin gloves, or to a smaller chap with thicker ones. Gardening gloves, perhaps.'

They were both watching me now – Carter and French.

'You did say you gardened for the poor woman, didn't you, William?'

'Sure, but –'

'Then,' French cut in, 'there was the matter of the envelope.'

My stomach turned.

'Or missing envelope, as it happened.'

A trickle of sweat ran down my back.

'See,' French continued after yet another puff, 'our friends the police are very thorough when it comes to this kind of thing. They discover a sweet old dear dead at the bottom of some stairs that she really had no earthly reason to go up in the first place, and they get to work as fast as their little bonces will let them. They're checking everything, taking statements, dusting for prints, looking into the victim's background with gusto. Makes you feel safe to have them on your side, doesn't it?'

'Sure,' I said, clearing my throat.

'And in the course of all this fanatical detection, they unearth that most coveted thing – a lead. Mrs Fitzroy's bank statements. Strange how little bits of paper can tell the most intriguing stories, and these statements did just that. Once a fortnight the deceased had drawn out substantial sums in cash. Very substantial. More than simple living expenses for a single woman.'

'Maybe she had a gambling habit,' I said, cursing myself at

the same time. What was I doing? Keep quiet, William, for Christ's sake!

'And popped up to the West End every Friday for a night at the casinos?' French replied. 'Come on, William, this was a woman who could barely make it to the toilet.'

'She made it to the bank all right,' I said, trying to disguise the rising panic.

Thankfully Carter broke in, and I turned to him like a drowning man offered a lifebelt in an increasingly stormy sea. 'William, is this how you remember her? Virtually bed-ridden, dying?'

'I don't know, I . . . she was old, but . . .'

French: 'Someone else used to run her to the bank, William. Someone the police finally arrested on suspicion of murder. A man called Holloway. Jimmy Holloway. A widely known Kentish scumbag with plenty of previous. A silver-tongued chancer who'd made his reputation with any number of immoral money-making schemes. Apparently he'd been fleecing the old girl for hundreds of pounds. He'd been posing as an alternative therapist who could offer her some kind of cancer cure. He sold her chunks of herbs in plastic bags. Charged her hundreds.' He took a contemplative puff. 'Strange what people will believe, how deluded they'll allow themselves to be when faced with certain death.'

'William?' Carter asked. 'Did you ever meet this man?'

'Total parasite,' French sniffed. And for a moment I thought he was talking about me. Something in the way he said it, the look he gave me, made me even more uncomfortable. French was turning out to be a man of many faces: jovial chauffeur; consummate police-baiter under pressure; and now an unnerving inquisitor. I didn't know if he practised in court, but I wouldn't have liked to face him from the witness box.

'No,' I said in answer to Carter's question. 'I can't remember ever meeting him.' I turned to French. 'But he killed her, did he?' I asked. 'This Holloway bloke killed Mrs Fitzroy for her money?'

'That's what the prosecution alleged,' French replied, giving me another unsettling look. 'A straightforward con. He gets the victim to draw out large sums, then takes his cut of the cash.'

Carter shifted slightly, perplexed. 'Why the envelopes?'

French nodded. 'I was coming to those.'

I wondered if I wasn't about to puke. All I could see in my mind's eye was Edith Fitzroy pressing that damned envelope full of money into my hand.

'Each conman has his own method, Dick. It's a sort of warped professional pride. Others defer to their stings. And Holloway's "tell" was the envelope gag.'

'Wouldn't it have been easier to put it straight into his back pocket after they left the bank together?' Carter pressed.

'Certainly,' French agreed. 'But don't forget the name of the game. Confidence trickery. The secret is to gain the confidence of your intended mark. The smoothest operators con their victims into willingly giving them the money. In Holloway's case, it was in an envelope. He used to get her to count it all out while he wasn't there, stuff it into an envelope for when he next came round with more cancer-curing weeds. She probably felt in total control throughout, trusting him with not just her life, but her life-savings also.'

'Sad,' Carter sympathized.

'But as true as it's all written down here.' French leafed through the file, found the appropriate page and scanned it quickly. 'Basically, when the police got a tip-off about Holloway, they raided his caravan. In it, they found a stack of envelopes, all empty, all with handwriting matching the late Mrs Fitzroy's on the front. All dated and detailing the amounts inside, which incidentally were getting progressively larger in fortnightly intervals.'

Carter was rubbing his chin. 'He was keeping them,' he said. 'Mementoes. Trophies to show his conmen colleagues.'

French rewarded him with a nod. 'One of whom was jealous enough of Holloway's success to put two and two together about the old lady's death and tip the police off as to his whereabouts.'

'Professional jealousy?' Carter wondered.

'Maybe,' French conceded. 'More likely blackmail. These people are the ultimate opportunists. The informer probably threatens Holloway with the police, Holloway calls his bluff, but fails miserably. Next he knows, a ten-strong team of police and dogs are breaking down the caravan door.' French took two quick drags to refire the tip of his fading cigar. 'Interestingly enough, though, the one thing they didn't find was the envelope relating to the last time he visited Mrs Fitzroy.'

My stomach turned again.

'Kind of strange for an avid collector, don't you think?' French teased.

'Certainly not within the pattern, no,' Carter replied.

'Which is exactly,' French said, extinguishing his cigar with a flourish, 'what the defence for Mr Holloway pointed out to the jury. Together with another glaring inconsistency.' He turned to me. 'William, you're a bright lad. Plenty of experience in the killing game, I'm led to believe. Any ideas?'

Although I didn't care for the sarcastic tone, I knew exactly where he was heading. 'He was a conman, not a killer. Hardly likely to kill someone he could still con, was he?'

French performed a slow handclap. The man was annoying me as much as he was unnerving me. Whose side was he on, anyway?

'Plus, at the eleventh hour, Holloway's defence team pulled an irrefutable alibi. The prosecution eventually conceded, and the judge ruled the charges to be dropped and changed to lesser ones of obtaining monies by deception. Holloway got four years, was out in less than half of it, and was last seen hanging around outside hospitals in the Devon area.'

'Looking for the next victim, no doubt,' Carter sighed.

'Leopards, spots and all that.' French shrugged, turning back to me. 'So you see, William, the police had something of a problem on their hands. Their number one suspect had bounced, and pressure from Mrs Fitzroy's irate immediate family more or less forced them to reopen the case.' He timed the moment. 'So they came to you.'

I shook my head as he rifled through the file once more.

'You were living in Maidstone with your mother and sister by this time, attending the local sixth-form college.'

'What's that?' I asked, pointing to the paper in his hands.

'A copy of the statement you gave Maidstone police,' he simply answered, moving it round to show me. 'See, there's your signature on the bottom. I'm pretty sure Shrimp and his grinning chimp Harris have the original.'

I looked. No doubting it. My signature. Worryingly, indisputably mine.

'I suppose you have no recollection of this, either?'

'No.'

He shot a quick look at Carter, turned the statement back, scanned it quickly, tutting throughout.

'So what's it say?' I asked.

'Essentially, it's a question of timing.'

'And?'

'The police worked out you were probably the last person to see her alive.' He was looking directly at me again, expecting something. I gave him nothing. 'The body was found on the Sunday – you last visited the cottage to garden on the Thursday. The pathologist put the time of death as sometime during the Saturday.'

I stood. 'What are you saying?' I asked angrily. 'That I killed her now? That it? There's no way I killed her, no way! I liked the woman. She was kind, gentle.'

I felt Carter's arm on my mine. 'William, Brian's just taking you through what he knows. Come on, sit down.'

I sat. Reluctantly.

French continued, 'Think of it from plod's sometimes limited point of view,' he said. 'A few checks, and suddenly they unearth all sorts of stuff about you.'

'Such as?'

He looked surprised. 'You have to ask?'

'I want to know.'

'Well, there's the graveyard dramatics for starters.'

'I was only gardening there,' I protested. 'It was just a job to earn some more money.'

'Not according to the local vicar. He implied you were . . .' he flicked through the paperwork, '. . . here we are, "little more than a local nuisance".'

'Not true,' I said.

'Apparently you used to turn up to funerals and disrupt proceedings. During the burial of a Mrs Salt, formally the postmaster's wife, you apparently climbed into a tree and began screaming obscenities at the top of your voice.'

'Untrue,' I quietly replied.

'You sure?' Carter asked. 'You've already told me on the

tapes that you liked to go to other people's funerals.'

'It was peaceful,' I replied. 'No one objected. Except Salt. That old bastard was the only one to get the hump. But it had nothing to do with climbing into trees.'

French watched the pair of us, jutting out his lower lip and nodding slowly. 'And then, of course,' he continued, holding up yet another piece of paper from the file, 'Maidstone police ran a check on you and found you had a connection with the Tilbury Woods murders. Plus they get the connection with Chetwins, made suddenly more relevant by the fact that Mrs Fitzroy in her later years did occasional supply-teaching at the – well, it was hardly a conventional school, was it? Let's just call it an "establishment for young men with behavioural disorders".'

'She taught there?' I asked, shocked.

French nodded. 'The police do a little further research and discover you're currently undergoing psychiatric treatment with one Dr John Tremaine. When they interview him, he tells them that it was his idea to send you to garden at Mrs Fitzroy's. She had experience with juveniles like you, and he thought the experience would be very beneficial.'

'This is absurd,' I said, shaking my head.

'So,' French finally concluded, 'I have to say in all honesty that, if it were me on the CID team, you'd have made a damn fine suspect.'

'I didn't kill her.'

Carter, to my left. 'Did they arrest him?' I could tell by the tone that he was annoyed. I'd missed too much out when I'd initially told him about Edith Fitzroy, and something inside me knew he knew that.

'He was lucky,' French replied, leaning back. 'William escaped any further investigation by two things: firstly, a lack of any real evidence, no prints, witnesses, et cetera; and secondly, the unfortunate arrival of the railway-rapist. Six attacks and one murder in less than four months. Kent police were under massive public pressure to bring him in, so the spotlight swung off young William for a while. The investigation tailed off. Mrs Fitzroy's death is still listed as unsolved.'

'I never killed her,' I insisted.

'Come on, William,' French said, beginning to raise his

voice. 'This is from a young man who happily confesses to my good friend Dr Carter here that he's already done away with four other people?'

'I didn't happily confess to anything,' I growled.

'What happened to the envelope, William?' he pressed. 'Did you see it there, lying on the table, waiting for Holloway, then think, "Hey, I fancy a bit of that?" Was that how it was?'

'No!'

Carter shifted uneasily. 'Brian, do you think this is really necessary?'

French waved the objection aside, still fully focused on me. 'You bought a car, didn't you? Less than two weeks after she died.'

I felt faint.

'Didn't you?'

I nodded, couldn't face even glancing across at Carter's frowning face.

'I had one of my juniors make a call to the DVLA. Just on the off-chance. I mean, what if it had been you, William? What if you had taken the money, then killed her? What's a young man going to do with the loot, I wondered? Take a holiday, perhaps? Get out of the country for a while?' He shook his head. 'Too obvious. So how about some wheels, I thought? Maybe. We look into it, and guess what? Your registration documents for the new ownership of a Fiat 127 drop straight into our lap.'

'William?' Carter asked.

I took a deep breath, held it a while before replying. Outside, the rain increased, gusting against the smoked glass. 'She gave me the money,' I whispered.

'She what?' Carter said.

'The last time I saw her, she gave me the money.'

'In the envelope?'

I nodded. Carter looked away, shaking his head.

French: 'Because old ladies do that kind of thing, don't they, William?'

'It's the truth.'

'Bollocks!' His large fist suddenly crashed onto the desk. 'You wouldn't know the truth, lad, if it came up and bit you on the arse!'

'Why didn't you tell me this the other day, William?' Carter asked.

I shrugged, hopelessly trapped. 'Just didn't think it was relevant, that's all.'

His face twisted into incredulous anger. 'Christ's sake! You go out gaily spending an old woman's money two weeks after she was probably murdered, and you didn't think that it's relevant?'

'But I didn't know she was murdered until the police told me yesterday!' I protested. 'She gave me that money. I never really thought too much about it up till now, and I certainly didn't kill her!'

Silence descended. Just the rain drumming relentlessly against the windows.

'Thing is, William,' French said eventually, 'our friends Shrimp and Harris are going to be ploughing through this sort of stuff right now. To be frank, the more I discover about you, the worse it looks. You just better hope, and I mean really hope, that they find Ian Bailey's killer soon. Because if they don't, son, they're gonna have a field day with you.'

24

The rain had stopped when we finally left the office.

French led us to his silver Mercedes in the office underground car park two paces ahead, whistling, unfazed. Carter and I followed, the atmosphere between us heavy and strained. I had so much I wanted to say, so much to apologize for, but didn't know where to start. He did not trust me now, I knew that. But I hadn't meant to mislead him deliberately, I simply hadn't told him about things I didn't consider relevant. Then again, he must already have known about Edith Fitzroy if Tremaine had indeed fixed up the job with her, yet he hadn't mentioned the fact to me at the time, either. Maybe, I thought, as we walked in the concrete gloom towards French's car, neither Carter nor I still fully trusted the other.

'In we get, happy campers,' said French, who'd once again morphed back into his jovial alter ego.

We pulled out onto the drizzling streets. French tapped the side of his nose. 'A little bird at Stockport nick tells me they're rather keen to trace the whereabouts of one Daniel Black.'

'Kris's boyfriend,' I replied. 'Sort of.'

'Owner of the key-ring found on Ian Bailey's body?'

I nodded.

'Seems he's gone to ground. Upped sticks and offed. Which is good news for you, William. Shrimp and Harris will be doubling their efforts to find him, and hopefully might not be as far ahead in the game as we are.'

'He didn't kill Ian,' I said. 'It's not his style.'

'Ah, but maybe,' French replied, 'he knows a man who did.'

Ten minutes later, we pulled up outside a garage in Salford, French quickly stepping from the car and enthusiastically shaking the hand of the proprietor. I looked a question at Carter, searched his face for a reason as to why we were there. He offered the smallest of reassuring smiles by return, then with a tilt of his head and a raised eyebrow he gestured to me to follow the others inside.

We stepped into the workshop, empty except for one car up on a rack. I guessed any other mechanics were out at lunch. Piccadilly Radio fuzzed from a corner. French, immaculate in a navy lamb's-wool coat, walked back to me and took me to one side while Carter and the boss had words by the raised car.

'As you've probably guessed, Dick gave me the tapes you made at his place on Monday night,' he told me quietly. 'Interesting listening. Four deaths to date. Proper little serial-killer, aren't you?'

'I've made a fair stab at it.'

He smiled at that one. 'There's a few grey areas I want to go through. I've asked Dick's permission, now I'm asking yours.'

'Fine.'

He draped an arm over my shoulder, urged me gently towards and underneath the raised car, until I was standing in its oily shadow, staring up at the dirty pipes and underseal above my head. French nodded to the proprietor, who turned and walked back to a small office, out of earshot.

'It's a Triumph Spitfire,' he said. 'Just like the one belonging to victim number four – Dave Phillips.'

My heart began beating a little faster.

'Mr Phillips was the lad you claim beat you up outside the chip-shop, right? The same lad who put you into a coma?'

I nodded, throat beginning to tighten.

'Who you then killed by messing with the brakes on his car.'

'Right.'

'So show me,' French calmly insisted, 'show me how you did that, William. We've got an equivalent car. Show me how you messed with his brakes.'

I felt trapped, as if the oppressive weight of the car inches above my head was about to fall, crush me flat on the damp concrete floor. I looked at the worn wheels without seeing, unable to place them in any other context apart from Dave Phillips's death – a black twisting shape screaming in the fiery interior, filthy smoke billowing from a slightly opened window, a burning hand trying to engineer an escape . . .

Carter joined us. 'William,' he encouraged. 'You've said you took tools from your car, then tampered with the brakes. Can you show us how?'

I tried, really tried to remember. It was pointless. Nothing came. The underside of the car was simply an alien surface completely without register. I passed a hand over its grimy surface, yet felt nothing. 'I just . . . I . . . I can't . . .'

'Remember?'

'No. Yes . . . no.'

'And it wouldn't have been made as easy as this, William,' French went on. 'His car was on the ground, in full view, in a college car park. Don't you think someone would have seen you sprawling underneath, tampering away?'

'But I know I did,' I insisted. 'Nobody saw me. I just did it, OK!'

'So show us how.'

'I don't know how! I can't bloody remember!' I turned to Carter for some kind of explanation, a reason. 'Look, you're always going on about how the memory plays tricks. That stuff we've been talking about, the "Bill" in my head? This is him, isn't it? Muddling me up while I was in the coma, taking away skills I had.'

'But, William,' Carter quietly replied, 'this was supposed to have happened after your head injury, wasn't it? It was revenge, wasn't it? You getting back at the lad who'd beaten you up? After your coma, William, not before. You'd still have the same mechanical knowledge – if you'd actually done what you believe you did.'

It was too much to get what parts of my sane mind remained around. I felt like crying, felt suddenly totally alone – abandoned by a past that seemed to enjoy tormenting me at every turn.

'I've had about as much of this as I can stand,' I said. 'This whole thing is fucking me up, big-time.'

'Listen,' Carter soothed, 'this is about the most important thing you're going to hear today. It's vital you take it on board, William. Crucial. Both Brian and I absolutely accept that you believe every word you told me the other day. And that you have the only real proof: a set of memories that justifies everything. Except that in your case they aren't the real truth. They're Bill's, William. You didn't kill that boy – you couldn't have done. Tampering with the brakes as you described – it's impossible. Sure, he died. There was a report in the local paper about it. The car caught fire because of a leaking fuel line. But it was an accident. You weren't responsible. You have to at least try to understand that, even if you can't believe it. You didn't kill him.'

French: 'Just take it as a possibility, William. Accept there's a chance that you had no more idea about cutting brake cables than I do. You never have had, have you? And, while we're on the subject, who the hell's Bill, anyway?'

'Ask Dr Dick. He's the expert on nutters like me.'

'A terrified part of William's subconscious,' Carter explained.

'And you've given him a name, a flipping personality?' French shook his head. 'I'll live to a hundred, and I'll never get the hang of how you buggers work.'

'Bill made William think he'd killed Dave Phillips because it was a chance thing, an unhappy coincidence. William went to college, heard about the tragic accident in the car park, then Bill slotted it into a different scenario entirely.'

'And made him the murderer?'

He nodded. 'It was a way of mentally backing up the chip-shop mugging story, disguising what really happened at John Tremaine's.'

'The suicide attempt?'

'Right.'

French thought for a moment, turned back to me. 'Sounds like you've got a rather tricky lodger in that head of yours.'

'Apparently he's already tried to kill me twice.'

'And I thought I had problems.'

'Bill's strong,' Carter interjected. 'And fear is by far the most powerful emotion. William doesn't remember a lot of what happened, because his subconscious isn't letting him.' He looked back up at the underside of the Spitfire. 'It's only when he actually sees evidence like this that the doubts can creep in, that reality can begin to undermine the hold Bill has on him.'

There was a long silence before French finally spoke. 'Tell you what, though,' he said brightly, 'I've just remembered something deliciously vital.'

'What's that?' I nervously asked.

He rubbed both hands together. 'There's a damn good fish restaurant just down the road. It's lunchtime, and I'm starving.'

25

Hello, William. How are you? Confused? Yeah, I bet you are. Maybe you're wondering where I've been? Biding my time, William, simply biding my time. Oh, and having a damn good laugh as well! Hasn't it been an entertaining couple of days, eh? Just sit back, relax, and let these clowns put on a show. So now I'm called 'Bill', am I? Oh, and I'm supposed to be scared, right? Wrong. But you can call me Bill, if you like. See, the truth is, William, maybe I have been fiddling around with your grey matter a little, but only to save you from – how shall I put this? – certain distasteful details. You're a lucky killer, William, believe me. See, what I do for you, no one else can do. I edit stuff, William. Paint a slightly rosier picture; reassemble events; make them more palatable. I mean, do you really think it only took one blow from a knife-block for us to kill that foul-mouthed bitch Margot Norris? You think we didn't nearly puke as that bright pink stuff shot from her nose? Because we did, William.

And then there's Webster, another one I cleaned up for the files. You still believe he died instantly? That we didn't have to get our rubber-gloved hands good and dirty on his broken, rasping neck? I was going to leave you the memory of his eyeball popping as he realized it was us – but I decided not. Knew you to be a sensitive lad underneath; thought I'd spare you that one. See, that's the kind of friend I am, William. A good and proper caring chum, spring-cleaning the memory of all that's distasteful. No mystery there, is there? But there's only so much a chap can take. Sorry to come the heavy, but frankly Laurel and Hardy's delving is beginning to annoy. I bore of their theories and patronizing intellectualizing. French and Carter have become a tad too dull. We're better, so much better than them. OK, they have some tin-pot theory that you couldn't have messed with the Triumph. But what they forget, William, is that I'm the guy sitting in the driving seat. You want to see those memories, fine. I'll show them to you. But only when I'm ready. I'm calling the shots, not them. And they've got to be careful. All this delving and speculation is only going to be funny for so long. If I get too bored – well, we both know what we're capable of, don't we, eh . . . ?

The following lunchtime – Thursday – Carter and I sit in a pub somewhere out on the A6, delicately trying to restore some trust to our relationship. The previous day's events had cast a long shadow over any rapport we might initially have had. He did not trust me. I felt it. He had given me looks the previous evening that had encouraged me to go to bed early, to try to find what peace I could from occasional sleep.

He drinks bitter-shandy, while I do my best with my inevitable pint of orange squash. We are alone in the back bar.

'So,' he says quietly. 'How does it feel to know that you've murdered people?'

I shrug.

'I only ask because it's such an extraordinary thing,' he persists. 'I mean how many of us can lay claim to having ended the life of another?'

'It's no big deal,' I say, mind returning to the duty sergeant at Stockport police station earlier that morning, and the look he'd given me. How much had been told about the young man with the scar? What did he know that I didn't?

'Tell me about Edward Norris.'

'Fat? You know all there is to know. We climbed a tree. He fell, died. Alan Cooper's supposed to come into the equation somewhere, but I'm buggered if I know how.'

'But how do you feel about Fat's death?'

I thought for a moment, tried to picture his face as he fell. 'Sad.'

'And?'

'Guilty.'

'Responsible in some way?'

'Maybe.' A longer pause, during which my memory held me high in that cold canopy, as far as possible from the broken body underneath. 'Because of the game, I suppose. The dare. Stupid kids' game. I'd told him his dad would be out of prison if he made it to the top. Wasn't meant to end like it did.'

'And Margot Norris, his mother? How do you feel about killing her?'

'Very little.'

'Any remorse?'

'Why should there be?' I whispered. 'She was drunk, attacking my mother. Before I knew it, I'd picked up the knife-block and hit her with it.' An image shot into my mind – something crude and pink flying from Margot's broken nose. I felt revolted. Then a sound, difficult to identify at first, but gradually fusing into a muted echo of distant childish giggling.

'William? Something bothering you?'

'No.' Chances were it was just some kid laughing outside.

Carter drummed his fingers gently on the table-top. Then said: 'Do you not think your parents were very lucky, William?'

'Lucky?'

'Not to be caught. Arrested as accessories to Margot Norris's murder. They took a massive risk in covering up for you that Christmas, didn't they?'

'Sure.'

'You see what I'm saying?'

'Not really, no.'

'How many other parents would have done what they did . . . ?'

I had no idea.

'. . . when all they really needed to do was ring the police the moment it happened. Your mother could have explained what had gone on; they'd have sorted it out. Yet, instead –'

'What?' There it was again! Still faint, but growing, definitely a young boy's laugh.

Carter continued, 'Instead they concocted this very elaborate scheme.'

'Which you don't believe a word of.'

'The point is, William, do you believe it?'

'Stranger things have happened,' I said, trying to concentrate on Carter's voice alone. 'That's how it was. My parents wanted to save me.'

'From what?'

'Being taken away. You know, by the police.'

'That simple, huh?'

'That simple,' I replied, holding his stare. 'Listen, I know what you're thinking, but you have to believe me, Margot Norris wasn't another Triumph Spitfire job. I can remember every detail. The technical side wasn't exactly the stuff of rocket scientists, either. Unfortunately it doesn't take much to hit someone over the head with a blunt instrument.'

'Child's play?'

I nodded.

He finished his pint. 'Think about it anyway, will you?'

I looked away, drinking down the last of the squash.

We separated outside the pub, Carter heading back to Edale, while I took the bus back into Manchester, ostensibly to meet my personal tutor and give her an update on the situation. In reality, I got off in Longsight, outside the McVitie's factory, plans formulating all the time.

'Hello,' I beamed to the bored receptionist once I'd stepped inside. 'Wonder if you could help me? Me name's John Decker. I'm looking for my uncle Paul.'

She gave me the visual once-over. 'Paul Decker?'

'Double Decker, they call him.'

'Hang on.' She answered a call as I waited, taking an age. I tried to look as anonymous as possible, hoping no one from the production line would wander through and recognize me.

Finally, she hung up, consulted a staff list. 'Paul Decker, you say?'

I nodded.

Her finger traced the index, stopped on the D's. 'Here we are. Decker, P. Line supervisor.'

'That's the one. Fat bloke, eats too much of the profits.'

'He don't do days. Nights, he's on.'

'Shit.'

'He'll be in about six.'

I took a step forward, leant against the desk and lowered my voice. 'Thing is, it's supposed to be a surprise. I'm just back from the forces in Germany for the weekend. Wanted to look him up.'

At this, she brightened, looking at my scar surrounded by its close-cropped hair. In retrospect, I probably made a fair impression of a squaddy on leave. 'Army, are you?'

'Fifth Ordnance,' I bullshitted. 'Based in Bremen. Do a lot of stuff with mines an' that.'

The heavily made-up eyes widened a little further.

'So, you know, time's precious, and I'd be dead chuffed if you could tell me where he is.'

She seemed lost. 'Who?'

'Me uncle Paul. A home address?'

'Oh, right.' She lowered her voice. 'Strictly speaking, I'm not supposed to . . . you know, give them out to strangers.'

'But I'm family,' I gently insisted, sensing victory.

'So you must already know where he lives then?'

'I've been out the country for a while. Haven't set eyes on the bastard for a couple of years. Knocked round his old address and he weren't in. So I come here.'

She spent a moment or two considering her options before finally looking over her shoulder and furtively slipping the list over the counter.

'You're a beauty,' I said, wondering whether to top it off with an all-purpose army wink. No, it'd be going too far. Quit while you're winning.

'Chances are your uncle's kipping, anyway.'

'I know,' I said, finding Decker's name and memorizing the address before passing the list back over. 'Isn't he in for a surprise, eh?'

Decker's place was a 1930s semi in Heaton Chapel, normally a fifteen-minute walk from the factory. I made it in a little under eight. I reckoned the place was rented, evidenced by the overgrown front garden and the drawn brown and orange curtains held up by clothes pegs in the front windows. The house stood out like the proverbial sore thumb from its neighbours, which were all far better maintained and looked somehow ashamed to share the street with Decker's abode. Whatever else a career as line supervisor in a biscuit factory had given him – a very obvious weight problem being one thing – obviously it wasn't wages that were high enough to cover a mortgage.

It took close to three minutes before a shambling figure I eventually recognized as Paul Decker opened the door. He was dressed in a striped towelling dressing gown and peeling slippers, his hair stood on one side, and his lips were flecked with dry white spittle. An advert for biscuit hygiene he certainly wasn't.

'Hello, Double.'

He squinted, eyes still puffy with disturbed sleep. 'Will?'

'Can I come in?' I asked, marching straight past the bewildered figure.

'I was fast a-kip, lad.'

'Where is he?' I said wandering through to the space that in most houses would have qualified as a kitchen. 'Shit,' I said, opening the back door to let in some much-needed fresh air. 'You live like a pig.'

He wandered through, eyes still squinting. 'What the fucking hell do you want?' He pronounced it 'fokin'.

'I fokin' want to know where Dan is.'

'Dan?'

'Come on, Dan-the-man, Danny Blow, Daniel Black.'

'Oh.' He was watching me now, his voice a little nervous as I opened cupboards and drawers.

'So?'

'No fokin' idea, pal.'

'You're going to have to do better than that, Double.' I reached behind some tea bags, pulled out an Old Virginia tobacco tin and popped the lid. Inside were Rizlas, tobacco and three lumps of resin of various sizes wrapped in clingfilm.

'You want some gear or something?' he asked. 'Take one.'

'I might just do that,' I replied. 'In fact I might just take the lot down to personnel at McVitie's, show them what their line supervisor gets up to during the night-shift.'

He shot me a puzzled look, slowly sat down in a chair that creaked under his partially clothed bulk. 'What the fok's up wi' you?'

'Danny. Where is he?'

He shook his head slightly, chins wobbling. 'Around, I guess. Over at your place, maybe. Shacked up with that bird of his – wossername – Kris, or something?'

'Try again,' I said, closing the tin and waving it inches from his face. I didn't enjoy terrorizing him, but sometimes needs must. 'And make it better this time. Or I walk with this little lot. And so does your job at McVitie's.'

He looked from the tin to the determination in my eyes. 'You're serious, aren't you?'

'Deadly, Double. Deadly.'

The Henry Royce pub was a bus ride and another ten-minute walk away. I strolled through the battered doors less than forty minutes after leaving Double's sty.

He'd given me the tip without any further trouble, and I had no reason to doubt the information. Apparently he'd met Danny in 'the Royce' on a few occasions, but lately had been able to get his gear via me. It was the only place he could think of to find Danny. I gave him no hint as to why I needed to track him down. Before I left, he asked why I hadn't been in for my shift, and I told him I was done with biscuits for a while. The big man looked a touch forlorn, perhaps a bit concerned about how he would get his stash in future. It surprised me a little that he hadn't made the connection between my appearance and Ian Bailey's murder, since the case was no doubt getting plenty of local coverage, but given how he lived, it wasn't too difficult to imagine Decker eating chips out of a newspaper rather than reading it.

The Henry Royce looked like a run-down social club for the mentally scarred, physically wrecked and emotionally depressed. So, on looks alone, I probably fitted in a lot better than most.

It was quarter to three, five minutes from 'last orders' in most normal pubs, but then the Royce hardly fitted into any conventional mould. It stank of stale booze, disinfectant and body-odour. Around a dozen punters turned my way as I walked in. People came here to score rather than drink. Twenty-four eyes assessed me in the instantly suspicious way that only those who live in a tight-knit community can. It felt like a scene out of a second-rate Western. A stranger had wandered into their saloon. If there'd been a piano player, he'd have frozen mid-note. But if I felt in the least bit intimidated, I was determined not to show it. Besides, the way my life was shaping up, what did I have to lose? The overwhelming need to take some control crushed any fear I might have had.

I ordered a pineapple juice from a silent barman, then went

and sat at a table on the far side of the room. It took about ten minutes before I was approached by a tall black guy in a long leather jacket, designer jeans, and shoes that must have cost the equivalent of Paul Decker's wages for a month.

He slid into the next seat, made a pretence of watching a card game nearby. 'Shoppin'?' he quietly asked.

I nodded, then followed him outside as he led me away from the pub to a concrete stairwell at the foot of one of the depressingly imposing curved blocks of flats. Welcome to the Crescents, Hulme. The stench of urine was almost overpowering. Three hypodermics lay casually abandoned on the floor. It was hard to imagine the serenity of Edale was just twenty-five miles away.

'Wha' y'afta?' he asked, hands in pockets, looking everywhere but me. 'Weed, H, whizz, acid, Charlie?'

My new friend – a mobile junk emporium. 'Danny Black,' I said.

He smiled. 'Now, there's a lotta fellas lookin' for 'im.'

'I'm not the police.'

'Don' say? I 'ad yas figured for that fella off "The Sweeney" when ya's walked in just now.'

Dealer by day, piss-poor comic by night. 'Where is he?'

He shrugged.

'Listen. I know he's gone to ground, and potentially he's in a lot of shit. So am I. But I've got some information he's going to want to hear. You tell him Billy-boy needs to talk.'

The look was one of amused outrage. He spoke, the deep voice calm, unfazed. 'You thin' I'm some erran' boy, that it?'

'I'll be here for half an hour. After that, I'm gone. So's the information.'

'Fair 'nough. You wan' waste your time standin' round in alleys, bro, you do that.'

I watched as he ambled back towards the pub, head bowed against the sleeting winter rain.

And then I waited. Watched as up to a dozen people passed me during the next twenty minutes, none of them sparing me a second glance. Loitering strangers, it seemed, were nothing unusual in the Crescents. Occasionally a door would slam somewhere above, there'd be a scuffle of footsteps, young voices shouting, or elderly ones objecting. But by and large it was quiet.

A kid arrived. A boy – eight, maybe nine years old, wrapped inside an old parka, his trainers torn, trousers thin, wet and at least three sizes too short. He ambled over, then pointed back over his damp shoulder with his thumb.

'Five minutes,' was all he said.

If I thought he was going to lead me somewhere, I was wrong. We both stood side by side in the silence. After a while he rolled back his frayed sleeve and checked an expensive-looking watch.

'Four,' he announced. Then pointed into the distance once again.

I started to walk from my shelter, turning back to the boy. He nodded, waved me on. Thirty seconds later, pushing the driving rain from my stinging face, I spotted the phone-booth, a lone sentry on a large, moon-shaped area of grassland overlooked by the huge block above.

A minute after I arrived, it rang.

'Billy-boy!' came the familiar voice.

'Very James Bond,' I said, wringing wet in the cold booth. 'What do I do now, meet you in the lifts with a rolled-up copy of yesterday's *Express*?'

'Can't be too careful,' Danny replied. 'Lot of heat coming down on me.'

'Where are you?' I asked, peering through the grimy glass, trying to make out a tall figure with a phone standing at any of the distant windows.

'Nowhere near where you think I am, Billy-boy, that's for certain.' He coughed loudly, and I pictured him toking on an enormous spliff. 'How did you get to Sharkey, anyway?'

Sharkey? Had to be the black guy in the long leather coat. 'Decker told me you sometimes hang around in the Royce.'

Danny sighed. 'Useless fat bastard. Mouth's too fuckin' big from stuffing biscuits all day long. Tell you this, though, you were lucky it was Sharkey you bumped into. Mention my name to half the dead weights in the Royce, and they'd have taken you outside and booked you a one-way trip to the Royal Infirmary, old son.'

'That's me,' I said, still scanning windows. 'Lucky William Dickson. Pity the same can't be said for Ian, eh?'

There was a slight pause while I heard him exhale.

'Why did you do it, Dan?'

'Funny, I was going to ask you the same thing, Mr Constant-Bloody-Suicide-Bid. Kris told me, you know, about the real reason you got that scar, had the coma thing. Jumping out of shrink's windows, weren't ya?'

Which really stunned me. How in God's name did she know? Not that I was about to confirm anything to Danny. In this game, I was fast learning not to trust anyone.

'If anyone's up for Ian's death, Billy-boy, it's you, not me.'

'You're so wrong.'

'Convince me.'

'No motive, for starters. I mean, why the hell would I want to kill him? It was your girlfriend he was mooning over.'

'Folk do some seriously weird shit when they're wired, Billy-boy. And that night, you were really gone. Jumping under flamin' buses an' such. Shit, if I hadn't grabbed you, you'd have been a dead man.' A short silence. 'Then again, maybe if you'd have died, Richard Rogers Junior might've lived.' He paused to take another toke. 'A mental night, Billy-boy, a really mental night.'

'Did you get me home?' I asked, mind still turning frantic circles as to how Kris knew so much about me. Perhaps she had inside information from the polytechnic admissions board, but that was supposed to be completely confidential.

'Stuffed you in a cab, didn't we? Then me and the lass are off for a couple of nightcaps at Richie's.' He laughed, but it became a bubbling cough. 'We'd only been there about an hour, and in walks Kris with lover-boy.'

'What?'

'Straight as you're there and I'm here. They both stroll in round midnight.'

'Kris and Ian?'

'Too weird, eh?'

'Richie's? Some sort of night-club, isn't it?'

'Let's just say it's an establishment that permits the consumption of various intoxicants after hours.'

A drinking den. The name was familiar. I remembered Dan inviting me out to the place a couple of times. 'What happened?'

'Fuck-all, really. They stood about, him trying to look hard, her giving me the filthy looks 'cause I'm with me cousin, like. Then that's it.'

'They go?'

'Just up and off. Only she gives him this big tonguey number right in front of me and squeezes his arse, like. Poor kid, he blushed that much I reckon he shot his wad right there and then. A while later, I goes and crashes at me cousin's. Sofa stuff, you know. No jollies or nothin'.'

'Sure,' I replied, as the rain finally began to ease. 'And I'm ringing you from the front lobby of the Acapulco Hilton right now.' All the time I was being drawn back to the Monday morning, as Kris and I had waited for Danny to show for lunch, discussing Ian, whether he'd stayed another day with his parents – when all the time she must have known he'd already come back and spent part of the evening with her at the club.

'When did you find out about him?' I asked.

'Tuesday afternoon. Kris gives me a bell from her mate's, tells me Ian's dead, and to get the hell out as the old bill are coming over to shake the place. Apparently the poxy fuckin' key-ring she gave me was found on him. Kind of makes me the prime fuckin' suspect, don't it? 'Cept I never did nothin' to the twat. Stabbing him in an alley, for Christ's sake? Just not my style, man. Not my fuckin' style.'

I said nothing, knowing this was true. 'So why don't you go to the police?' I asked instead. 'Tell them you were with this woman, get an alibi from your mates in the club?'

A short sarcastic laugh. 'Listen to 'im! If only life were that fuckin' easy. She's married, you twat. Got hitched at sixteen to some Greek pillock. A local hard-arse, pocket Mafia. He'd have given her a right spanking if he knew she'd been playing around. Then he'd have put me on a liquid diet for six months. And as for the club – get a grip, Billy-boy. How many of those heads in there do you reckon are law-abiding enough to turn up in a suit and take the Bible in their right hand to give me an alibi in court?'

He had a point.

'So that's me fucked,' he continued. 'Until the heat dies down, anyway. Way Kris tells it, the Old Bill'll get their man sooner or later, and I can pop me head above the parapet again.'

Another young kid was loitering outside the phone-booth, making faces. 'So what did she say happened? After Ian and she left the club?'

'Not a lot, really. They walked around, looking for a cab. Then he decides he needs a piss. Disappears up some alley. Never comes out. She thinks he's playing some kind of prank, and doesn't want to go up there. A cab comes, she flags the bastard down, gives him one last chance to come out, then goes. Next she knows about it, the filth are knocking on the door on Tuesday saying they've gone and found the poor sod.'

In which case, why hadn't she told the police any of this? Why hadn't she told me any of it? Why had she spent most of Monday apparently unconcerned about Ian?

'You've not spoken to her since?' I asked.

'Even phones have ears, Billy-boy. The old bill'll have put a tap on her mate's place by now. Oh, and I wouldn't hang around where you are now for too long if I were you. Sharkey says my place has been dusted down three times already. Plus there's been a lot of long blue macs and size ten shoes hanging around the estate trying to look inconspicuous.'

'I didn't kill him, you know.'

Another long pause. 'All I know is that the last time I saw you, Billy-boy, you seemed pretty keen to kill yourself. Ain't the actions of the sanest geezer alive, is it? Ta-ra.'

'Yeah, but . . .' The phone went dead.

Outside, the young boy had run off. The sky was brightening. Too much information fought to be processed inside my head. I knew Danny wouldn't have killed Ian. Intuition told me he was a scally – but no murderer.

But what about me?

I had form. I'd taken lives before. Did I kill Ian? Did I find some drunken excuse to leave the cab, then set off back to the city centre, run into Kris and Ian, then conspire in some way to murder him?

Maybe. After all, it was pointless relying on my memory for denial.

Then again, why would I kill someone who had done me no damage whatsoever? Previously I'd killed in revenge or to protect. Ian Bailey represented no such threat. Therefore I couldn't have . . .

An image suddenly burnt itself into the front of my mind. A face, familiar, but changed. No longer smiling as I'd known her – but horrified, utterly fearful.

Edith Fitzroy, falling away, her fingers finally giving up on the crisp white envelope in my hand . . .

26

'Jonathan Webster?'

'Got what he deserved,' I said.

I was back in the safer confines of the kitchen at Shallice House, Carter resuming his lunchtime topic: how I felt about those I'd already killed. I found the conversation irritating and distracting. There was only one person I wanted to talk to – Kris Jordan. If anyone was hiding things about Ian Bailey's death, it was her. The girl's behaviour was unbelievably suspicious. That is, if I'd remembered it correctly. Plus, I couldn't for the life of me work out how she'd managed to find out so much about my past.

'No guilt?' Carter asked.

'No.'

'Why? It's another life ended.'

'He was a bullying prick,' I said. 'He terrorized people, abused them, messed with them. I did the world a favour in killing him.'

'OK,' Carter conceded, shifting slightly. 'Let's assume Jonathan Webster, for whatever reasons –'

'Very legitimate reasons.'

'– was your first premeditated murder, Edward Norris being the victim of a childhood accident, and his mother dying as you tried to protect your mum. But with this murder, you really planned it from start to finish, didn't you?'

'Like I say, he had it coming.'

'Olive oil, rubber gloves, tissues to mop up after; Alan Cooper complicit in it. It was quite different from the other two, wasn't it?'

'Save the fact that he wound up dead, yes.'

'So I ask you again, how did it make you feel afterwards?'

I reluctantly thought back to the funeral, the whole school listening to the head extolling the dead rugby player's mythical values. 'Relieved,' I said. 'A little nervous in case I was discovered. But mostly invincible.'

'Invincible?' He made a note about that one.

'Strong. Stronger than the rest of them.'

'Death empowered you?'

'Perhaps.'

'What about pleasure?'

'Pleasure?'

'Were there any pleasurable sensations associated with the killings?'

The question shocked me a little. 'I never killed for fun.'

He spent a moment or two searching through yet another blasted file, red this time, then withdrew a photo, held it away from me, slightly against his chest. 'Jonathan. You have any clear physical memories of him?'

'Bull-headed, short cropped hair. Real thug, piggy eyes . . .'

Carter placed the photo on the low table between us, turning it towards me. A head-and-shoulders shot. 'Yes,' I said, studying the face. 'Very like that. Very like that indeed.'

'But is this him?'

I looked again at the black-and-white image, and noticed a hand on the shoulder, as if the grinning figure was being pushed by some unseen assailant. 'Could be,' I replied. 'It's sort of how I'd imagine Webster to be if he'd grown up. But this guy looks about thirty or so. Like Webster's older brother; his dad or something.'

Carter consulted another set of notes. 'He was thirty-three at the time.'

I looked up. 'Thank God for that.'

'Thank God?'

'I thought for a moment you were going to say it was another Triumph Spitfire situation. That I hadn't killed him and he was alive and well somewhere.' My eyes returned to the astonishing likeness. 'So who is it?'

Carter was already on to his next prop, reaching beneath the table to bring out a small white tube. He began unfurling it on the kitchen table. It was a school photograph. Three rows of monochromed boys stared out from in front of a vaguely gothic-looking ivy-clad building. Chetwins, taken during my time there.

He placed a mug at either end to flatten it. 'Brings back a few memories, I bet,' he said quietly. 'Now, let's start with you. Care to find one William Dickson for me?'

That was easy: my finger went more or less directly to the small squinting boy with the foppish black hair.

'How about Jonathan Webster? Where's he lurking in this ragamuffin bunch?'

My finger moved, began tracing the rows, moving up to the older boys. But no Webster. Very odd. 'Exactly when was this taken?' I asked.

'You can't find him?'

'I only knew him for eight weeks. Chances are he was already dead.'

'Want to read what it says at the bottom, William?'

My eyes fell to the small copperplate text. 'Chetwins School for Boys – October, 1976.'

'And you killed Webster when?'

'Mid-November.'

'So where is he?'

I searched the faces once more. 'Maybe he was sick that day,' I tried, 'or truanting. Kept inside for bad behaviour. There could be any number of reasons.' I looked straight into Carter's sceptical face. 'But you don't believe any of them, right?'

Carter singled out a thin-looking blond-haired boy in the row above me. 'Jonathan Webster,' was all he said.

I looked at the unknown boy. 'No. No way. No.'

'And you're right, William. Seven weeks after this photo was taken, he was dead.'

'That's not Webster.'

'He died in a freak sporting accident,' Carter continued, reaching into the file and pulling out a faded newspaper cutting before passing it to me. 'A genuine tragedy. Scrum collapsed on top of him, broke his neck. Made the papers.'

I began to read. 'Enquiry into Rugby Death at Chetwins' announced the bold headline; and, further down, inset into the text, was another grainy shot of the same boy, blown up from the school photo with a caption underneath; 'Jonathan Webster, 15. Died while playing the game he loved most.'

There were quotes from Barrington, the sports master,

Webster's parents and one or two boys. It concluded: 'Critics of the school have often argued against letting boys with psychological difficulties play contact sports. However, even in the light of the tragedy, Headmaster Norman Guthrie disagrees. "To deny any of my pupils access to team-building sports would merely serve to exacerbate their sense of isolation from the rest of society. I don't run a prison here. I'm headmaster to three hundred boys with varying special needs. As far as possible we combine many individual therapies with the routines found in the majority of mainstream schools. This terrible accident will not change my belief that successfully reintegrating these boys into society means allowing them the same privileges afforded to the rest of the nation's pupils. Indeed, I believe Jonathan Webster's distressing death could have occurred at any number of conventional schools in the land. Chetwins intends to carry on playing rugby, and we will be hosting a special memorial rugby-sevens championship in Jonathan's honour."'

I closed my eyes, massaged the lids with tired fingertips.

'It was a good school, William. Guthrie was well respected, admired for his stance.'

'So you say.'

'Not just me. The papers, too.'

'Newspapers have always lied.'

'Why resist the truth? Black and white, it's staring you in the face.'

I had no answer, felt too tired, confused by it all.

'Alan Cooper?' Carter asked.

My skin prickled at the name.

'He in the picture anywhere?'

'Probably not,' I said, unwilling to search the photo for the small fair-haired friend I'd saved from Webster's horrible drunken bullying.

'Want to look for him?'

'Not really.'

'Why?'

'Because of what my mother said about him.'

'And what was that?'

God, I was tired, worn down with it all. 'The stuff about him going into the woods with me the day Fat died. The stuff about there being three of us.'

'Impossible, right?'
'I thought so at the time.'
'And now?'
I sighed. 'I don't know what to think. I dread looking for him in the picture, because if he's not there . . .'
'What?'
But I couldn't answer him. To have acknowledged that Cooper had joined us in the woods that afternoon would have been too much. The memories were too strong. Just Fat Norris and me, the trees, the conversation, the game, the fall – no one else. Not Cooper, never.
I tried changing the subject. 'The photograph you showed me earlier,' I said, 'the one I thought was Webster's dad. Who is he?'
'You mean, who was he? He's dead now.'
Out came the picture once more. Again, I was struck by the undeniable resemblance to the only Webster I knew. The man's grin was almost triumphant, just like the teenage bully who burst into the dorm and drunkenly demanded the physical compliance of his younger victim. The hairs on the back of my neck stood up a little under his dead gaze.
Carter's voice was barely above a whisper. 'The man's name was Atkins . . .'

No way, William! The man's screwing with us! No way is it ever Atkins! Ever!

'Dave Atkins?' I asked.
'Margot Norris's sometime boyfriend.' Carter held up the photo once again. 'This is him in February 1971, being led into Chelmsford Crown Court.'
I felt dizzy with it all. 'For the murder of Fat's mum?'
'Partly, William, yes.'
'Partly?'
'Initially he pleaded guilty to two murders. Margot Norris, and your little friend from the woods, Alan Cooper.'
At which point, I threw up.

27

An emerald-eyed eighteen-year-old surprise arrived at the house an hour later. Karen Carter. I'd just finished a long bath, letting the warm water take me elsewhere, slipping into mental neutral, lying neck-deep in it, eyes closed, mind oblivious. No thoughts of Jonathan Webster, Alan Cooper, the Norrises, Dave Phillips, Edith Fitzroy, Ian Bailey, Danny Black, Kris Jordan – none of them. But it was only temporary, the delicious quiet disappearing as quickly as the water ran down the plughole and I stepped naked back out into the horrible uncertainty of my life.

After supper, Karen and I talked while Carter disappeared upstairs. She'd changed, opting for a heavily black-eyelined post-punk look. But she seemed to have softened in attitude since our last meeting when I had had a go at her father. It was curious: she seemed physically scary on the outside, yet calmer on the inside.

I still felt bad about throwing up on her father's carpet earlier, and maybe for want of something to say found myself telling her about it.

'Jesus, you're a dope, aren't you?' she said. 'Think that stomach of yours could cope with an orange juice or two down the pub?'

'Sure, I mean . . . I'd love to,' I flustered, before remembering my empty wallet. 'Only . . .'

She smiled. 'No money, no memory. Not much of a catch, are you?'

Twenty minutes later we sat before an open fire in the same hikers' pub, now heavily decorated with Christmas tinsel. As there was still six weeks to the big day, I felt the festive atmosphere was a touch premature, until Karen told me that the landlord was a 'Christmas freak', who even started dressing up as Santa as the twenty-fifth approached. 'It's just Edale,' she said. 'Most of us are a little nuts here.'

If it was meant as empathy, then I was glad. 'Listen,' I said. 'About the other morning . . .'

She waved a hand. 'It doesn't matter. I was probably out of order going off on one like that.' Her fingernails were painted black. She'd died a black streak into her brown hair, too, and had completed the ensemble with a black cardigan, long black skirt and Doc Martens. Carter hadn't said anything when first setting eyes on her, but from the occasional puzzled look he gave her over supper, I guessed he'd long since learnt to hold his tongue in the face of her fashion sense.

'Anyway, I'm sorry,' I reiterated, trying to work out if I found the Gothic look attractive or not.

'Done and dusted, then,' she said, taking a large pull at a double vodka and lemonade.

'How are you getting on staying with your friends? Are they, you know, into all this black punky stuff as well?'

'This?' she replied, shaking a wrist that I now saw was laden with thin silver bangles. 'Shit, no. This lot belongs to Carol, mate of mine. Used to be into the scene last year. Hates it now. No, I just fancied something different. Besides, I like to see Dad's face as I walk through the door.'

'He didn't seem that bothered.'

'He was, believe me.' She drained another inch from her glass. 'Thing is, he never says too much because I remind him of Mum. She was always dressing up, doing all sorts of crazy stuff.' She paused, looked lost for a second. Then said, 'Maybe that's why I do it. To get back at him. She hated it here.'

'The pub?'

'Edale, fool. Too boring for her. Christ, the pub was the only form of life she had. Mum was . . . well, Mum was kind of mental, really. There we were, living in London, Dad getting all this recognition and overseas trips, when suddenly he decides we're to come up here. Says he wants to opt out of the rat-race, play the country gentleman.'

It felt like prying, but the more I listened, the more I wanted to know about Carter's past. After all, he seemed to know just about everything about mine.

'Just like that, you moved here?' I asked.

'Out of the blue. One minute I'm thirteen, going to private school in North London, the world buzzing around me.

Next I'm up here.' She briefly flicked a bored hand over her shoulder. 'Welcome to Dullsville, Derbyshire.'

'Must have been hard.'

'Nightmare. OK, Mum and Dad put me in another private school, but you know what it's like. I go in the fourth year, a London kid amongst all these Wilmslow image queens whose fathers earn tons and half of whose older sisters are shagging Man. United Reserves at the weekend.' She finished her drink. 'Total bloody nightmare.'

She subbed me a tenner and I bought more drinks.

'Then your mum died?' I said as I sat back down.

She nodded. 'Three years ago.'

I said nothing in the silence, just waited it out, feeling a little embarrassed to find her frown so suddenly attractive.

'Mum used to do this sort of thing a lot,' she finally said. 'Dress up, come down to the pub, shock the locals. She once hired a wedding dress and told everyone that Dad was her brother, and she'd just married a Bolivian window-cleaner from Hull.'

'Quite the party animal.'

'Boredom, crossed with a sense of mischief. Wanting to be the centre of attention.'

'And to embarrass your dad, presumably?'

She thought about it. The smile returned. 'Maybe. Yeah, she sure embarrassed him.'

'How did she die?'

'Pointlessly. She used to drink. I mean, heavily. Again, the boredom thing. Missing her friends, the Hampstead circuit. And one day . . . one morning shortly before the accident, she told me something I thought was total crap. Until recently.'

I took a sip at my drink.

'She was badly hungover. Still in bed mid-afternoon. Dad was away somewhere, on another of his "trips". I started having a go at her, saying she was a crap mum for doing what she did; an embarrassment, you know, the standard petulant teenager stuff.'

'Which we've all done . . .'

'Oh, but it got bad, though. I said she didn't love Dad. Well, she turned to me and told me that the only way you ever really loved someone was to hate a part of them, too. The acid test. Love overcomes all, accepts imperfections. 'Course, I thought it was more drunken bullshit, and told her so.' She ran black fingernails slowly round the rim of her glass. 'It wasn't till after she'd died that I realized what she'd said.'

'How?'

'I realized how much I hated my dad. That it was my problem, not hers. Because, for all the psychology degrees in the world, he couldn't face dealing with my mum. Oh, sure, he'd go halfway round the globe to be at some lunatic's beck and call, but to sit down with my mum, help her through her depression – that was way too personal, too close to his own failings. And I hated him for that. For two long years after Mum died, I hated him every day for not dealing with her, making her well.'

'I'm sorry,' I said, making a mental note to hug my own mother really close the next time I saw her.

'Then I remembered what she'd said.'

'The love–hate thing?'

She nodded. 'Hating him was part of loving him. It proved that I loved him. You hate the person because you feel let down, and you only feel that because you love them. And I realized that he hurt just as badly as I did.' She took another swig at the double vodka. 'Yeah, it's been hard. I miss her every day. I miss him, too. Because he's changed as well.'

'And it doesn't exactly help when you get whingers like me taking up all his time, eh?'

'Perhaps. I don't know.' She looked at me, suddenly smiled. 'But, hey, I thought we were finished with apologies for the other morning?'

'We have now,' I said, taking her empty glass. 'Another? That is, provided you're not about to dip into your mother's party genes and leap up and perform a solo strip number to Barry Manilow on the juke-box.'

She strained to hear the big old machine in the corner. 'Is it "Copacabana"?'

'I think so.'

She winked. 'You never know your luck.'

At the bar, I asked them to turn the music up. Back at the table, Karen teasingly played up to it, throwing her arms out wide and shaking her shoulders in a way that did more for my mental well-being than any psychoanalyst ever had. We clinked glasses when the track ended.

She asked me about my day, and, relaxed in the comforting neutrality of the pub, I soon found myself telling her all about my efforts to track Danny Black.

'The thing that really bothers me,' I concluded, 'is how did Kris know about my past. I mean, is your dad likely to have told anyone at the poly?'

'No. He may be an infuriating arsehole at times, but his own style of professionalism is vital. He just wouldn't broadcast that sort of stuff. But . . .'

I hung on the pause.

'References,' she said, eyes widening.

'References?'

'For the house. The rental agreements.'

'I'm not with you.'

'OK,' she explained. 'Just a thought, but you never know. This is how it worked with a friend of mine. She was studying at Sheffield, right? At the end of her second year, one of the other housemates leaves. They're both working over the summer, so it's not a problem, but in September they approach a rental agency, who come up with about half a dozen names they've been handed by the university of first-year undergrads who are looking for accommodation.'

It became a little clearer. 'And the girls want to see references,' I said.

She nodded. 'You could end up sharing with anyone. So the company sends them references for them to make a shortlist from. Four lads, two girls. And it turned out that one of the lads had a criminal record, which the rental agency was forced to disclose. Well, my mates don't fancy sharing with a robber, so they drop him from the list, opt for one of the girls instead.'

I paused to think it all through. 'And you think Kris would have asked for references?'

'As a single girl looking for two more housemates? Yes, I do. Maybe there was some sensitive information on yours. Perhaps it's legal to declare if . . . you know . . . you'd had some sort of injury.'

References. Maybe, just maybe.

'Where are you going?' Karen asked as I stood.

'I've got some calls to make,' I replied.

She aped looking forlorn. 'So that's it then. You've got what you want, and the date's cut short?'

'Was it ever a date?'

'What do you think? That I make it a habit to invite my dad's clients out for a drink?'

'I rather hoped I was the exception.'

'Word of advice,' she said, finishing the double at triple speed and taking me by the arm. 'Next time, make sure it's you who does the asking.'

We parted outside the pub, Karen kissing me briefly on the cheek before walking briskly away under a clear, freezing sky. Just a peck between two friends, but nevertheless I felt quite marvellous as I watched her go. Then I turned my head to the night and found myself under the starriest sky I'd ever seen. Millions twinkled above me. I was nothing, less than a speck, standing on a minute planet revolving gently in ever-expanding space. And, in that moment, a happier speck you couldn't have met anywhere in the universe.

Back at Shallice House I quickly dug out my address book from my bagged belongings and rang my uncle Trevor in Kent from the quiet of the blue box room. As the one who'd managed to 'find' me the accommodation through his interests in the Mancunian property rental company, I hoped he could shed some light on Karen's reference theory.

He picked up after the third ring. 'Uncle Trevor?'

'William?'

'How are you?'

'Surprised. What can I do for you? Are you OK?'

'Fair to middling. Listen, I need to know about something.' I felt Carter's presence; he was standing by the doorway in the corner of my vision.

'Fire away. I'll help if I can.'

'How did you manage to get me the house in Fallowfield?'

A slight pause. 'Well . . . I guess it was luck, really. I knew some people who had a rental business and –'

'Did they need a reference?'

'Absolutely. William, is everything OK? You sound –'

'What did it say?' There was another pause, then a sigh, during which I pictured him slumping into the sofa in his lounge.

'Pretty much everything, really. I mean, it had to. You can't fudge these things.'

'What things?'

'Some of the problems you've had. Couldn't leave those off.'

'Such as?'

He took a breath. 'Your suicide attempt. The coma, subsequent treatment with various analysts, the lot.'

'Who wrote it?'

'I did. Said I thought that regardless of your troubles you were a trustworthy young lad who'd do your best to fit in.'

I rubbed at my eyes. 'You know, two weeks ago if you'd told me I was a potential suicide case, I'd have thought you were the one with the mental problem.'

'And that's why I couldn't tell you. Felt a bit sneaky, to be honest, going behind your back, but the only way was honesty. After a couple of weeks, the rental company told me they'd found a place for you, and that the girl who lived there wasn't too bothered about sharing with you. But she had some understandable concerns. She rang me.'

Pay-dirt.

'And you told her a whole lot more besides, I suppose?'

'William, don't have a go at me. I was the one prepared to put my reputation on the line for you.'

'Sorry.' It was petty, beneath both of us, and I shouldn't have said it. But at least I had some form of answer. Kris Jordan probably knew a hell of a lot more about me than I did myself when I first stepped into the house, and all under the perfectly legitimate guise of a reference.

'William,' he asked. 'What's wrong? Your mother's in quite a state. She's tried calling the house recently and no one answers. I even called the property company on her behalf, and they just said it was a police matter. And when I eventually called the Manchester police, they said the house was now part of an ongoing enquiry. We're worried witless. What on earth's going on?'

'There's been some problems.'

'Jesus,' he sighed, an uncle weary of his nephew's exploits. 'What now?'

'A guy in the house was killed.'

'What?'

I pictured him sitting suddenly bolt upright, face incredulous.

'Just that. The other lad I shared with got stabbed in the city.'

'And he's dead?'

'It's an unfortunate by-product of being killed.'

'William, don't get smart.'

'It's hysteria, I assure you.'

'Where are you now?'

'Somewhere else. Safe. Listen, the reason I haven't phoned Mum is that . . . you know, I know how she'll go off at the deep end. I really don't want to worry her till the whole thing's sorted out.'

'William, for Christ's sake,' he implored, 'just ring her, will you? Please.'

Which I knew in my heart I simply couldn't do. Not till I knew more, had something positive to feed her. 'When I'm ready, I promise. And thanks for the info.'

'William, don't . . .'

But I hung up.

Carter took a few steps into the room. 'Well,' he said, nodding towards the phone. 'You going to ring her, then?'

'Not yet.'

'Fine. William Dickson does it all at his own pace, regardless of anyone else's feelings.'

I really didn't have the heart or the energy for the argument I felt he was pushing for. 'I'm tired. I want to go to bed.'

'Fine. But just to let you know. Something's come up. I'm going to have to go away for a few days.'

'Go away?' I said, trying to keep an edge of panic out of my voice.

'Just until next Tuesday. Four nights. It's a conference, in the States. I've been booked to speak there for months, and what with one thing and another –'

'You're going to America? Just buggering off and leaving me in all this crap?'

He nodded.

'You can't.'

'Yes, William, I can.'

I shook my head, tried to connect with some kind of reason. 'Why? I mean, is this part of your approach? To build people up, then dump them?'

'William, it's ninety-six hours. Just keep the appointments at the police station and keep out of trouble. I don't know what you were up to this afternoon, but I know for a fact that you didn't meet up with your tutor till gone five this evening.'

'You've been checking up on me.'

'Just sit tight and keep your nose clean till I get back.'

'What did you do, hire a private eye to follow me?'

'What were you up to this afternoon?'

'Things.'

'Petulance will get you nowhere.'

Something rash and cruel stirred inside. I wanted to hurt him, make him feel a little of the pain I felt. 'Par for the course for you, isn't it?' I said coldly. 'Disappearing when people come to depend on you? Perhaps now I know how your wife felt when you flew off and left her alone with her problems.'

He didn't look in the least stung or concerned. 'Ah, we've been talking to Karen, haven't we?'

'She hated you for what you did to her mother.'

'Old ground, William. A predictable and – if I may say so – disappointing effort from you.' He stood in the doorway. 'You might have a visitor tomorrow morning. I suggest you drop the attitude and listen hard to what they say. It's going to be a tough few days for you, so you'd better get some sleep. If you'll excuse me, I've got packing to finish.'

He went out, leaving me alone in the small room listening to his receding footfalls on the stairs. And though I despised myself for it, I felt nine, not nineteen, scared and fearful.

'What about Bill?' I shouted after him.

The footsteps stopped. 'What about him?'

'What if he tries to kill me again? Throw me out of another window when you're away?'

Carter reappeared in the doorway, leant casually against it, arms folded. 'How do you see him, William?'

'See him?'

'What does he look like? In your mind?'

I fought to steady my breathing, regain control, analyse the panic. What the hell was wrong with me? Three weeks previously I'd had Carter pegged as just another useless shrink, now I was coming out in a cold sweat at the thought of not seeing him for a few days.

'What colour hair does he have, for instance?'

'Jesus, I don't know.'

'Think.'

I tried to picture the killer inside me. 'Black, I suppose.'

'Fine, we'll go with black.'

'Please. Don't go.'

'Eyes, William? What about Bill's eyes? Blue, hazel, grey, green, brown? Try, William. Really try and see Bill. Give him form.'

I searched for an image, then startled myself with the figure who appeared.

'Who is it? Who do you see?'

And he was there – Bill – a grinning ghost-face, hideous mouth stretched obscenely, black eyes staring at me, screaming. The same Screaming Man who had obsessed me as a child, my best friend, the features heavily lined and cut, abstract hands holding an alien head. But no longer my friend, this time laughing at me. Enjoying my distress.

'Describe him to me, William.'

'It's the figure from a picture at my grandmother's house. She had a reproduction of *The Scream*.'

'I think,' Carter said carefully, 'that maybe you're making too much of a monster out of Bill.'

'Yeah, well, forgive me, but hasn't he already tried to kill me twice?'

'Sure, but remember when I said he was scared?'

Of course I remembered.

'Try to picture him a little differently.'

'Such as?'

This'll be good! Can't tell you how much I'm enjoying this little charade! How's he going to describe me – as a cute little girl in a frilly pink dress?

'You say he's like the Munch figure – I say he's like a spider.'

'A spider?'

'We look at the spider,' Carter said, 'and recoil in horror. Can't begin to understand that we're thousands of times bigger than it, and the poor thing's probably close to dying of fright when we stick our ugly faces close to it. You with me?'

'In all honesty?'

He nodded.

'Right now, I'd probably say whatever you wanted to hear.'

'Precisely my point. Just like a frightened child, William. Just like Bill. That's all he is. A frightened child. Forget your Munch figure. He's you as a kid, that seven-year-old boy the police found stuck up a tree, too terrified to move.'

Something screamed inside.

'ICT,' Carter continued. 'Inner Child Therapy. It's big Stateside. And in the way of these things, it'll become just as big over here in the next twenty years. People will spend thousands with costly analysts trying to find their inner child – the moment they lost touch with themselves for any number of reasons. But with you, it's a little more complicated. Not everyone's inner child is hell-bent on killing them.'

'I just must be the lucky one, right?'

'Like I say, he's frightened. Think of disturbed kids, anxious kids, scared kids. Believe me, the first thing they do when they're cornered is lash out.'

'Like I did with Tremaine?'

He nodded. 'You want to see Bill? Just look at a photo of yourself as a boy, William. You want to keep yourself safe, try befriending him. Talk to him.'

'Talk to him?' This was too much.

'Sure. Just talk. Anything will do. My bet is that little Bill is still stuck up that tree in Tilbury, William. Still screaming somewhere in the back of your head, trying to blot the horror out. Maybe he feels guilty in some way, maybe he saw something that he can't forgive in himself. Whatever the reason, I think that with me out of the way for a while, now might be the best time to establish some sort of dialogue with him.'

'Sounds ridiculous.'

'Any more ridiculous than him trying to kill you, reinvent

your past, redefine your memories, change everything about you that you know to be true?'

'Maybe not.'

'Just give it a try. I have a feeling, much as Tremaine did, that if anyone's going to talk little Bill down from that tree then it's you, William. And only you. Goodnight.'

He turned and left a second time. This time, I didn't call him back.

Couldn't. Something held my throat.

Something very black and very angry.

28

When I finally slept that night, it was only to surrender to a series of terrifying nightmares. Nothing could have prepared me for the vivid intensity of them. Every breath felt real. Each sensation seemed cranked up to unbelievable heights. Previously, I'd managed to master the classic nightmare-escape technique, lucid dreaming, in which the dreamer recognizes certain images for the dreams they are, then sets about bending them into less threatening scenarios. But not that night. I was powerless. Such was the reality that I never even realized I was dreaming.

Images, freeze-frames from that night still recur to this day. Shrimp and Harris from Stockport CID were coming to arrest me, chasing me up the Tilbury tree, grabbing at my ankles, cursing me, laughing, gaining on me. On the way up I passed the butchered body of Alan Cooper. As I drew level the eyes opened and the face changed. Ian Bailey looked back at me accusingly, his bloodied hands reaching out to my face. Danny Black sat smoking a giant spliff on a higher branch, boots on my head, casually pushing me down to where the others waited. The harder I tried to grip the dried bark, the heavier his boots became. Then a chopping sound from down below, as I saw the broken-necked figure of Edith Fitzroy take a shining axe to the trunk, head rolling grotesquely with each swing.

Three times I woke, each time bathed in sweat, hearing just the one sound in the still of the night – the distant echo of a child's laughter. And realizing it came from inside my mind.

Twice Carter came to the room, sat with me, told me nightmares were to be expected, were all a part of the healing process. I didn't have the words to reply, simply clung to his hand, fighting a steadily losing battle as the sleep and the nightmares moved menacingly back to reclaim me.

I felt utterly powerless, which scared me most of all.

*   *   *

I woke to the sound of a car-horn and the front doorbell. There were voices, too, drifting up from outside. I checked my watch: it was just gone ten. Then I moaned. Although I was grateful to see daylight again, I realized that by sleeping in so late I'd missed Carter leaving. Worse, from the commotion outside, I guessed his 'surprise' guest had just arrived.

Cursing, I stumbled out of bed, threw on a jumper and jeans, then stumbled groggily downstairs in bare feet.

'Coming!'

I breathlessly opened the front door to find my mother standing on the step.

'Mum?' Was it really her?

'William.'

We hugged. After a moment she disengaged, took a look at me, smiled. 'Come on,' she said. 'You're letting all the cold air in.'

I watched bemused as the taxi-driver struggled with a suitcase, dumping it in the hallway and waiting for his money.

'Hungover, was you, son?' he said gruffly, annoyed at having to wait.

'Something like that.'

My mother paid him and he left. By the time I had shut the front door, she was already calling from the kitchen, 'Where do they keep the tea bags, then, love?' My mother was here, in Edale, rooting through Carter's cupboards for the PG Tips. Crazy! I rubbed at my clammy face, pinched the crusted sleep from my eyes and let out a small laugh.

'William, come on and make yourself useful,' she said. 'I haven't had a proper cup since five this morning. That rubbish they give you on the plane wouldn't wet a guard's whistle.'

I got slowly to my feet and somehow made it into the kitchen. 'Cupboard, top left. Second shelf down.'

She dropped two bags in two mugs, turned, then crossed the room and hugged me again. 'Hello, son,' she said into my neck. 'Oh, it's good to see you.'

'One question,' I said. 'How?'

She pulled away, took off her coat, sat at the table. 'I flew up first thing,' she said proudly.

'Flew?'

'Gatwick to Ringway. Oh, William, it was wonderful. Had to get up at dawn, mind you. That's the strange thing about flying. By the time you've booked in and all that, you might as well have saved yourself the money and caught the coach.'

My mother, the seasoned traveller. The nearest she'd ever got to a plane before was watching the Biggin Hill airshow on the television. I sat. 'I'm stunned,' I said. 'Completely bloody stunned.'

She looked around. 'Lord, it's a wonderful place he has here, isn't it?'

'Carter told me I had a surprise guest arriving,' I said, watching as she poured from the boiled kettle.

'He rang me earlier in the week,' she explained. 'Told me you were staying here for a few days as you had some "problems". Good job, as you obviously weren't going to tell me anything. And when I did find out, William, I was . . . well, I was hurt you didn't tell me.'

'I just didn't want to worry you.'

She ignored that, taking milk from the fridge and pouring it into both cups. 'Anyway, Dr Carter said you might welcome some company this weekend. Then he arranged the flight, everything.'

'He paid for it?'

'He's a good man, William, despite what you think.'

I frowned.

She wagged a finger. 'Oh yes,' she said. 'He's told me how suspicious you've been.'

I scratched my temple. 'You don't know the half of it.'

'No. But I've always taught you good manners, William. Now get upstairs, have a shower, take your pills, get dressed properly, while I see what I can fix us for breakfast.'

I stood, took the warm cup in both hands, shook my head in quiet disbelief. 'It really is you, isn't it?'

'Upstairs, shower. Now, William.'

Bacon, eggs, sausages, beans and fried bread awaited me when I got downstairs again. Mum sat opposite, watching me eat, a small pile of lightly buttered toast next to her half-drunk tea.

'Who's paying for all this?' I asked between mouthfuls.

'It's only a few bits I found around the place. Nothing I can't pick up from Tesco's –'

'Not breakfast. All of it. Carter's time, your flight? He's even got some high-powered solicitor called French working on it. It must be costing a fortune.'

'Uncle Trevor.'

I nodded, a private suspicion confirmed. Had to be him really, as the only relative with any big money left.

'Always has done, love. Right back to the old Chetwins days. Your private sessions with John Tremaine, all down to the goodness of Trevor and Suzanne.'

'Mum,' I said, 'I've had to listen to a lot of crazy stuff this last few days . . .'

'I know,' she said quietly.

'But we paid for Chetwins, didn't we? I mean, regardless of what kind of school it may or may not have been, we paid, didn't we? Out of the premium bonds win?'

'Premium bonds win?' She stared blankly back.

'Don't do this to me.'

I watched her struggle for a moment with her own memories, then saw a glimmer of recognition cross her confused face. 'Yes, you're right, love. We did win a few bob on the bonds.'

'A few bob – a hundred and fifty thousand pounds?'

'A hundred and fifty,' she said, taking my hand. 'Just pounds, not thousands.' She laughed, stroked the side of my face. 'It's still all muddled in there, isn't it, eh?'

'Understatement of the flipping year.'

'It takes time, that's what all the experts say.'

'Tell me Mum, tell me everything. I get so confused with it all.'

She sighed. 'It's not that simple, love.'

'Sure it is. You start from the beginning and take it from there. I'm ready for anything.'

She shook her head. 'I can't. Dr Carter made me swear not to.'

'Do you see how crazy this is for me? People know. People have vital knowledge about my life, yet keep the damn stuff to themselves.'

'But it has to be ordered, love,' she replied. 'Done properly. Staged. I mean, look at the damage I nearly did telling you about dear Dr Tremaine in the hospital.'

'Mum,' I insisted, 'it got me out of that fucking hospital.'

'No need for language.'

'You know what I mean.'

'Sorry, love. I can't do it. I'm not qualified. I could end up telling you something that could wipe out all Dr Carter's good work. You may not believe this, but it cuts through to my heart to see you so confused. But my hands are tied, and that's that.'

I tried to smile, a fairly hopeless effort.

'How are you feeling?' she asked, pouring more tea.

I paused for a second, trying to marshal some kind of explanation that she might be able to relate to. 'It's like someone coming in here right now and telling you you're not Theresa Dickson, never have been. You are in fact Terry Smith, a fifty-eight-year-old car mechanic from Luton. Then there's a million other people telling you the same thing, and more besides. Not only are you a man, Mum, but you've been married four times, sired twelve children, and were the first person to fly solo round the moon in a hot-air balloon.'

She looked up, fixed me with uncomprehending eyes. 'Not me,' she said. 'Never could stand heights of any kind.'

A while later we sat in the lounge. My mother cooed admiringly at the leather three-piece suite, the antique furniture and the large black iron wood-burner.

'How much did Carter tell you?' I asked when she'd eventually settled.

'I know you're in trouble, William. Your flatmate's been –'

'Murdered.'

'And that you gave the police a wrong address. They want you to report to them every day. That was such a stupid thing to do, William.'

'They think I did it, Mum.'

'Don't be so –'

'Ridiculous? See it from their point of view. That there just happens to be a loony living in the same house as the deceased; that he's already lied to them; and furthermore that he has a previous involvement in another murder enquiry.'

'The woods? But listen, love, you were a potential victim, not –'

'Mrs Fitzroy,' I cut in. 'Not the woods.'

She paused, frowned. As her brow creased I realized how much older she looked, frailer. The guilty thought crossed my mind that I'd somehow made her that way. My madness had aged her.

'But didn't they get some gypsy for that?' she said. 'A conman who'd been duping her with false cures for the cancer? I'm sure I read something about that in the paper. Or was it off the telly? Can't remember now. Funny, isn't it? The pair of us with bad memories.'

'Hilarious.'

She frowned. 'Mrs Fitzroy's death was dreadful, love, but it didn't have anything to do with you. You just did some work there, that's all. Made a good job of it too, from what I heard.'

'Try telling that to the police. According to them I was the last person to see her alive. When the case against the conman collapsed, it put me into the frame.'

'You?'

'And the only reason they never followed it up was because they were diverted with some high-profile railway rapist, or something.'

'Oh, I do remember that, yes. That I do remember. Awful business. We were all petrified to go on the trains. A terrible time.'

'Maybe not for me. Perhaps it got me off the hook.'

She shook her head dismissively.

'Mum, you're not listening to me.'

'I'm not listening to rubbish, William. Why on earth would you want to kill a dear old lady like Mrs Fitzroy? Doesn't make any sense.'

Why wouldn't she accept it, face it? 'Christ's sake, Mum, I can't remember what the hell I've done, or haven't done. Don't you understand that? Don't you get it?' Scenes from my nightmares flooded my mind, horror action-replays of Edith Fitzroy's broken neck as she chopped at the tree below, the lolling head blazing with pitch-black, accusing eyes.

'You're just confused, that's all. You'll get right, you'll see.'

The doorbell rang. Cursing under my breath, I left the room and walked through to the hall to answer it.

'Taxi for Mr Dickson,' the punky-looking girl said brightly.

'How much is a one-way fare to Disneyland?'

Karen pretended to think it over. 'More than a loser like you'll ever afford, I'm afraid.'

'Story of my life . . .'

I felt a figure at my shoulder. 'Mum,' I said, turning, 'this is Karen Carter. She takes me out to the pub at nights, then apparently drives me back down for opening time.'

'In your dreams,' Karen replied. 'We've got an appointment with the duty sergeant at Stockport police station to keep.' She offered a hand to my mother. 'Pleased to meet you, Mrs Dickson.'

'Likewise,' my mother replied, doing a slight double-take at the black fingernails and strange garb. 'Thinks he's a proper comedian, he does.'

'He's never made me laugh.'

'Most men don't, do they?'

And then they both laughed at some private joke that I suspected my sex would probably always deny me.

I sat in the back, silently making plans as my mother and Karen chatted in the front. It was raining again, gusting in a high wind, causing the car to lurch or sway gently as we rounded corners to the steady rhythm of the hard-working wipers. After reporting in at the police station I intended to use a little subterfuge to give Karen and my mother the slip so that I could continue my own investigation into Ian Bailey's death. I had to speak to Kris as soon as possible, simply didn't believe her version of events at all. I couldn't imagine Ian being the type to disappear down some seedy alley for a quick piss, no matter how badly he wanted to go.

Of course the possibility existed that I was just a poor judge of people, or that Ian was completely drunk and acting wildly out of character, or maybe that Danny Black had been bullshitting for his life when he'd spoken to me over the phone. I needed to speak to Kris, even though I was not sure how much of her version of events I could trust. In the front of my mind was the Monday we'd spent waiting for Danny to turn up at the house. Never, in all that time, had Kris mentioned seeing Ian and Danny at the club. Why not? And if she was so innocent, shouldn't she have been more worried about Ian not coming home rather than Danny missing his lunch? The last time she'd seen Ian he'd been heading off down a dark alley. Unless – and here's where the William Dickson paranoia kicked in with a cold sweating vengeance – unless she already realized she had the perfect fall-guy in me living under her roof.

However, my plans to lose Karen and my mother evaporated as I left the police station after checking in with the duty sergeant.

'Right,' my mother said purposefully. 'Leeds, please, Karen.'

Karen nodded, already looking at a map. They'd been planning this while I was inside the police station.

'Leeds?' I said.

My mother turned to me, offered me a boiled sweet. 'Have one,' she offered. 'It'll take us close on an hour.'

I resisted the temptation. 'Listen, I've got things to do. We can't just go traipsing off to –'

'We can, William. And we will. We're going to see your father.'

With that, Karen passed the map back to my mother and started the engine.

29

And then things slipped from barely tolerable to really strange.

Trying to place my thoughts in that speeding BMW, I realized I had very little idea what to expect of my father, or where he'd be when we met him. Trying to place him, I imagined a run-down flat somewhere, Dad having put weight on, now living with a hard-faced Yorkshire woman who chain-smoked and scowled. Sure, the image was more than a little clichéd, but where do you start when you have so little to go on? He had left Mum a few years ago, had loved the wretched television and a few beers – it was all I had of him. And my feelings towards him? Certainly I felt a measure of anger, but mostly it was an apathy, punctuated by a few memories, none outstandingly special. Dad was simply Dad, the man who'd suddenly left. Besides, I'd coped well enough without him in the last few years.

When the moment came, we weren't standing outside a terrace house, listening to his shuffling footsteps as he made his way to the door. My first sight of my father in five years was when he walked slowly in line through the cream steel doors of Armley Prison's visiting room.

Now there are plenty of places a confused murderer would rather not be, and prison ranks pretty high up on the list. Damn high up really, as high as Armley itself, standing as it does like some sort of forgotten castle over Leeds city centre. The place is as bleak and soul-destroying as it is imposing and oppressive. Yet here I was, sitting at a small table in a low-ceilinged room full of other visitors, crying babies and small children, watching as the grey-and-blue-overalled cons threaded their way to loved ones under the watchful eyes of a dozen or so warders.

'Hands above the table at all times!' one barked. 'Any infringement and the visit will be terminated, relevant authorities informed!'

Nothing prepares you for prison. To talk about another 'world' is a little optimistic. Worlds feature variety, changes of colour, landscape, environment. Prison has none of this, just an all-pervading atmosphere of fetid boredom, corporate paint, ridiculously highly polished floors and, most disturbing of all, a quiet, beaten, desperation. In all ignorance I'd imagined something dungeon-like, gloomier; in reality it was quite light – but nearly all of that is emitted from flickering electronic strips, maintaining a uniform and intense pale yellow, regardless of conditions outside.

As I looked at the crudely shaven faces of inmates making their way to waiting loved ones behind small chipped tables, I was struck with the real punishment of prison – the simple denial of variety. It was difficult to comprehend that children played in gardens just a few streets away, that shoppers trawled for bargains less than a stone's throw from this life-sapping environment. There was no outside on the inside. Even the bright coats and anoraks worn by visitors and their children seemed to have become duller the moment we'd entered the high walls.

My father sat opposite me, staring. My mind went blank, unable to face the enormity of what was happening. I had too many questions, and no place to start. If I could have walked straight out of there, I would have done.

To our left a woman struggled to control a squirming youngster and a crying child. My father still hadn't said a word. The striplights buzzed overhead and warders walked between rows of tables, scrutinizing everything. Two tables away, an elderly couple were swiftly separated when they tried to embrace. I turned briefly back to where my mother sat on the far side of the room, waiting her turn with my father. She nodded at me encouragingly, though I could see her eyes were glassy with tears.

And then, finally, his voice. 'Been a long time.'

'Five years,' I replied.

He shook his head. 'Ten months.'

'Dad, I haven't seen you in five years.'

Again: 'Ten months.'

'Whatever you say.'

His eyebrows lifted fractionally, and I saw how soft his face looked, the once strong ferryman's jaw now flabby and pallid. The eyes, too, were yellow and worn.

'February,' he went on. 'Norwich. Four months before I got transferred to this dump. You, your mother, Nicola, out from school on the half-term. Saturday afternoon. Spent the best part of two hours together.'

'Fine.'

His brow creased. 'No, son. It ain't fine. It was fine. It was going really fine until you went and tried to top yourself at Tremaine's place. What in God's name were you thinking of?'

'I've no idea.' I could have told him about 'Little Bill', his insatiable desire to end my life, the whole hideous mess it had become, but what was the point? I hardly believed it myself.

He leant back fractionally in his chair. A passing warder watched him carefully. 'Trouble with your memory, so I've been told.'

'That's the gist of it, yeah.'

'So where do we go with that then, eh?'

'How about we start with why you buggered off and left us in shit-street all those years ago?'

'Not got a lot of respect for your old man, have you?'

It was strange, in the car the thought of his abandonment of us hadn't bothered me. But now, sitting opposite him, it grated. It didn't matter how many prison visits he described where we had all supposedly played happy families, I felt angry. 'What are you doing here, then?' I asked.

'Twelve years for murder.'

I said nothing.

He cleared his throat. 'Category A, I am. There, don't that make you proud, eh? Your old man, Mr he'll-never-amount-to-fuck-all Dickson's a real category A hard-nut. What a turn up, eh? The old bastard comes good in the final reel. But of course now you're thinking, "Who did he kill?", right? Sound familiar, any of it?'

'No.'

'You knew the lot before you decided to try flying out of Tremaine's windows.'

'Maybe that was what finally tripped me off,' I said. 'Maybe I couldn't stand another day with a father like you.'

He clicked his tongue against the roof of his mouth. 'There's always that possibility. Can't deny it. Ain't been what you'd call a perfect father.'

If he wanted a compliment he was going to have to try far harder. So he'd killed someone. Big deal. The point was that he'd been stupid enough to get himself caught. OK, I'd been somewhat taken aback at the thought of him doing the deed, but the end result was as wearily predictable as the rest of his life. People like my father don't make for successful murderers. A lifetime of failings makes them too easily caught.

'Twelve years,' I said. 'Long time.'

'Could've been worse,' he continued coldly. 'I could've been given the full twenty-five. Except the judge reckoned there were special circumstances. Mitigating, he called them. Kind of legal jargon for the fact that the bastard deserved it.'

'OK, Dad, you win. Put me out of my misery. Who did you kill?'

'Dave Atkins. Three years ago.'

My mind struggled to trace the name. Then retrieved it, held it up for brief inspection, tried to file it into the few firm memories I had. Dave Atkins, yes, there he was. The grinning face from the newspaper that Carter had shown me. The shot that had been taken outside Chelmsford Crown Court in 1971 as he stood trial for the murder of Margot Norris and Alan Cooper. The same face I'd mistaken for an older version of the leering schoolboy tormentor, Jonathan Webster.

'What's so funny?' my father asked.

'Everything,' I replied, unable to stop smiling. 'And nothing.'

He frowned, then nodded over my shoulder at my mother. 'She tells me you won't remember what happened, and it's all got to come from me.'

'OK.' I tried my best to pull down the smile.

'Do you remember me coming to visit you in the hospital? You woke up, looked right at me. Well, me and the screw I was cuffed to, of course.'

A question answered. He had been there. 'Yeah, I remember that. Remember you sitting there. Stupid, really, I've been thinking it was another hallucination.'

'I was there, son. Worried to death about you. They tells

me you're a fifty-fifty case for never coming round at all. So I gets a permit to see you, you know, with all the tubes and stuff sticking out of you? Eight hours I sit there. Then you opens your eyes, clocks me for just a second. I go berserk, don't I? Call the doctors, but you're back under again. Next I know, I'm being taken back to Norwich, being told not to get my hopes up, that even if you do come round, chances are you'll be . . . you know . . . impaired in some way.'

Impaired, it sounded comical in the setting.

'Least you're not, you know . . . I mean, at least you can use all your limbs and that.'

'Oh, sure. Just watch me become the new Daley Thompson at the Impaired Olympics.'

His eyes narrowed. 'Don't get smart.'

'Dad, I'm having real trouble taking any of this in. It's been a hell of a few weeks, and –'

'I killed Dave Atkins,' he interrupted, as if suddenly aware of time being short. 'Had to, didn't I? Bastard had only served seven years for doing Margot. He got early parole for good behaviour. Model prisoner, he was. Should've strung him up.'

I nodded, without knowing why.

He shifted slightly. 'Living in the oast-house, we were. You remember that, don't you, son? Trevor and Suzanne's weekend place in Kent?'

'Sure.' But now it was a 'weekend place', not a house we'd financed with a massive premium bonds win.

'Good people, your auntie and uncle. Real bricks. Offered us the place when things became too stressful for your mother in Tilbury. And for a while, it was OK. Chetwins took you on, which was a relief. You seemed to be making progress, starting to come to terms with what had gone on back in those woods. Your behaviour improved. Tremaine had started taking a real interest. Trevor and Suzanne lent us a few grand to put Nicola through a private school, so's your mother and I could begin to start rebuilding our lives. But then, it started to get on top of me. I had no work. No prospects. I began hitting the sauce too hard, behaving like a right . . . well, I just lost the plot a bit, I guess.

'The years fly by, and suddenly I gets word from an old mate on the docks that Atkins is back outside, sniffing round for a job back there. It's just too much for me, you know, especially after what he done. So I went down there, sought him out. I just meant to scare him off. Smack him about. But when I sees him . . .' he tailed off, head tilted towards the flickering lights, '. . . I just flipped. Set about him with a monkey wrench in one of the sheds. Couldn't stop. Next I know, it's dark. The coppers come pouring into the shed, drag me off. I'd sat there for nearly six hours, but couldn't remember a damn thing that I'd done. Like you and your memory problems, son. Six hours sat next to a corpse, and I still can't remember a bloody minute of it. Nearly killed your poor mother, it did. But she knows why I did it, why I had to do it. Why I couldn't let him live.'

'Because he killed Margot?'

A squint this time. The eyes studied mine, and I sensed he was trying to fathom the true depths of my ignorance. 'Not just Margot.'

'Then who?'

'You know who.'

I nodded, felt suddenly colder. Alan Cooper.

'A lad called Cooper. Alan Cooper. Local boy. Lived in the next street to us when we was in Tilbury. Big mate of yours.'

My left leg jerked under the table. The dark crack in the centre of my world opened a fraction wider. It wasn't funny any more.

'You remember the woods, don't you, son? That Saturday afternoon? The three of you heading off for a lark?'

'Bits of it.'

'Ready for the rest?'

'Don't know.'

'The three of you headed off to the park, the little bit of woodland that ran between it and the railway line.' I saw him hesitate, a frown cross his face.

'And?'

He looked up, back with me. 'Something terrible happened. A couple of hours later, an old girl walking her mutt lets him off the leash. She heads into the woods. Finds Cooper's little body. Poor old dear's traumatized, barely makes it back to her daughter's place. Anyway, they call the Old Bill, who belt round and find another body, further in – your other mate,

Margot's kid, Fat Norris. Then one of them looks up, sees you way above their heads, mouth opening and closing, trying to scream but no sound coming. You'd lost your voice, screamed yourself hoarse. You must have been there for hours, but it still took the best part of an hour to coax you down.'

The young baby at the table to my left began to cry. But not a baby's cry, a boy's. When I looked, he was asleep, silent in his mother's arms. I began scratching at the side of my head.

''Course, your mum and I knew nothing about it until we gets the call from the police station.' His eyes lost focus, drifted back to a late Saturday afternoon another lifetime ago.

'You went to the police station?'

He nodded. 'Got told you were wrapped in a blanket in the back somewhere, in shock. Something had happened up at the park. Your mum was going ape, and there's all these coppers saying the doc's checking you over right now, that you was all right, but traumatized. So we sit, wait.'

I risked a look back at the sleeping tot. No screams. Laughter this time, giggling I couldn't crush.

'You OK, son?'

'Sure . . . just go on.'

'Soon after, we see Margot coming in, face white as a sheet. Then the Coopers. Then all these other police – uniforms, plainclothes – all milling around, telling us to be patient, then asking us a million different questions.

'After about an hour, they finally let us see you. You was quiet, lost. Bit bruised, scratched, no voice, but apart from that, looked unharmed. A CID bloke pulled me over while your mother was with you, told me about the other two kids.' He took a deep breath, held it, exhaled. 'Just . . . knocked me for six, son. Two or three days later, it was all over the papers – horror in the woods. We tried to screen you from it, did what the experts told us. The Old Bill was champing at the bit to interview you, but their shrinks kept telling them they had to wait. You were still too traumatized.'

'I can't remember Cooper going in there, no matter how hard I try.'

'He did. He died in those woods, son. The forensics people had been over the scene and found two sets of different adult footprints . . .'

Adult footprints? The giggling suddenly stopped. Nothing but silence in my head. I felt as if I'd just been winded.

'. . . a lot of broken branches, signs of a struggle. But it was quite a way into the woods. Chances were that no one would have bothered to go and look if they'd heard a few kids screaming; they'd probably think they were playing in the trees.'

He lies, William! He lies, he lies, he lies! Look at him, the disaster father, a useless heap of self-pity wallowing in his own inadequacies. How can we trust a word that sicks its way up from that putty-soft mouth? And he thinks he's a killer? Come on, William, engage! Listen to me. He's a broken-down shadow of a man who gave up on life years ago. He pollutes our mind with his pathetic fantasies. Him, a killer? Ha! Only if he bored his victims to death with his 'woe is me' life story. But we could show him what a killer is, couldn't we? We could really go to town on him, end his lies and prattling once and for all. Imagine his face, William, seconds from death, as he finally realizes who the real killer in the family is. Oh, give me that chance . . .

'Adult footprints?' I whispered, watching as my hands began to jump and twitch. I fought the urge to command them to fly up to his lying neck, squeeze with all my might, watch that hateful, useless, prison-swollen face turn purple and die . . .

'They reckoned that the three of you ran into a couple of sick perverts. The lad Cooper, well he'd been . . . interfered with before he died. They found, you know, evidence.'

How I hated his attempt at tact. How I hated this broken excuse of a father spouting his sick little fantasies to me. He'd never been much of a father to me, ever. And he was in danger of becoming less and less of one with each passing second.

'Round Christmas,' he continued, oblivious, 'Margot drops in on your mother. You're still not saying a dicky-bird about what went on. Police are calling once a week, but nothing. It's like you've erased the thing entirely. Anyway, she was hitched up to Atkins, the geezer I killed . . .'

Hit-and-run, William, hit-and-fucking-run! Christ's sake, let's get out of this place! He's mad, insane, brain's gone bad from all that porridge. No more of this, no more lies . . . We know the truth, not some pitiful jailbird of a father . . .

'. . . Christmas Eve, it was. Margot was in a terrible state. She'd found a couple of porno mags of his. Really sick stuff – kids and that. So she puts it all together and remembers how he left early on the Saturday afternoon, didn't come back till later. Then she told your mother she was going to confront the bastard that night when he got back from the pub. When I got back, she was still going on about it. But drunk, mind. Ranting. We told her to go straight to the police, but she weren't having none of it, just seem possessed. Wouldn't stay with us, nothing. So . . . so we let her go back, William. Next we hear, she's dead. Won't ever forgive ourselves for that. Should've kept her over at our place till after Christmas, let the cops sort it all out. But we never. We let her go. So Atkins did her, on Christmas night.'

'And that's why you killed him, is it?' I whispered, unable to disguise my contempt. 'Because you reckoned he was in the woods that day?'

'William, I ain't proud of what I done.' He was looking right at me. 'Sure you're all right, son? Only you don't look too good . . .'

I was having trouble with my breathing. Part of me wanted him dead. The rest of me needed to hear him finish. 'I'm fine. Just keep talking.'

'When the police found her body, we told them about the magazines, and what Margot had told us. 'Course, they couldn't find a thing. Atkins had obviously hid the lot and buggered off. But they caught the evil sod trying to make for Holland on the overnight ferry. Bought him back. Confronted him with our story. Several of the footprints in the woods matched a size eleven docker's boot – the type he wore.' He allowed himself a small smile. 'Guess the evil nonce must have shat himself when they told him that.'

'Fifteen minutes!' a warder suddenly barked from behind me.

My father went on, unfazed. 'Then the deal's struck.'

'What deal?'

'The police tell Atkins that they knew two people were in the woods with you kids that afternoon, and, what with the footprints, could probably place him at the scene. If he gave them the name of the other bastard, and pleaded guilty to the murder of Margot, they'd go easy on him. It was a kind of plea-bargain. They wanted to get the other nonce. Are you with me?'

I nodded, a fantastic effort of will.

'He took their bait. Initially, anyway. Reckoned he was most likely looking at twenty-five years for killing Margot anyway. Reckoned he could shave it down to fifteen if he co-operated.'

'And?'

Dad shrugged. 'He confessed to killing Margot, and to being in the woods that Saturday afternoon. Which bought you back into things.'

'Me?'

'You were the only living witness, son.'

I shot a look back to Mum, still waiting, intently watching the pair of us.

Dad's voice: 'It was vital you could remember. They needed you to ID Atkins as one of the men who'd been there, tell your side of things in court.' He looked away, and I had a brief sense of him trying not to cry. ''Course, you never could. Couldn't pick the bastard out of a line-up, couldn't remember a bloody thing. Police asked you over and over, at our house, in the station, they even took you back to the woods again. Each time, nothing. No mention of Atkins, or another man.

'By the time Atkins got to court, the Crown prosecutors had to drop all charges connected to the murders of Alan Cooper and Paul Norris. They managed to get a conviction for Margot Norris, but there was no evidence besides a matching shoe size to link him back into the woods. When his brief found out that you were in no fit state to testify, he quickly got Atkins to retract his original confession, the lot. Said it had been made under duress, police bullying.

'Sometimes I reckon it was all some part of Atkins's master plan. And his brief was well sharp. By the time he finished, he had the jury believing Atkins had been virtually tied to a chair and had the confession beaten out of him. The whole case tumbled. All the time, Atkins just sits in the dock, looking like some sad little victim. Made me want to tear his bloody heart out.'

'You were there? In court?'

'I had to testify against him, didn't I? And your mother. Tell the jury all about Margot's last night with us. How the man was a nutter, used to beat her up, how she had these terrible suspicions about him after she'd found the filthy pictures.' He closed his eyes. 'I looked at that bastard, son, and I vowed then, that if ever he walked the earth amongst children again, I'd kill him.'

'Ten minutes!'

My father, used to prison life, was impervious to the shouted instructions, while I nearly jumped right out of my sweating skin. But I needed to hear more, regardless of my feelings towards him. I had to know what he knew.

'So they sent him down for Margot's murder. But not your friend's. Charge was thrown out four days into the trial. Son, listen to me. Please. Look at me.'

'I'm trying. I just . . .'

'Those two lads weren't the only thing that died that afternoon. We died, too. Us, as a family. Atkins took that from us, an' all. He screwed up your mind, and did mine in as well. I couldn't cope, see? Couldn't hack the fact that all the time while I'd been sitting at home, him and another bastard had been –'

'This supposed other man,' I asked, shocked to hear my own voice so clearly. 'Who was he, then?'

'Atkins never said. When he learned he wasn't going to be done for the murder, he never breathed another word about it. I guess part of the reason I went down to the docks was to beat the name out of him.'

'So?'

A shake of the head. 'Like I say, when I sets eyes on him, I just lost it, big-time. Next I know, he's dead. Most stupid thing I ever did in my life. Didn't give him the chance to tell me, son. Just whack!, then nothing.'

'You're full of so much shit, Dad. And sick shit. Really weird. You should see someone about it.'

'You wouldn't have thought that before you tried to top yourself.'

'I would.'

Anger in his voice: 'You knew all of this!'

'Bollocks.'

'Tremaine was trying to reach that part of your memory that would –'

'I know! I've heard the bloody tapes!'

'And they're all crap, too?'

'I don't know. I just don't know anything any more.'

He briefly looked around, then made a furtive grab for my hand. Held it tightly as I struggled in his grip. 'Son, I love you. I've always loved you . . .'

'Get off me!'

'. . . But sooner or later, you've got to start believing what people tell you. Get back to where you was.' He let go of my hand.

'It's the least of my problems at the moment.'

'Your mother's told me. Gone and got yourself caught up in something bad, haven't you?'

'Like father, like son.'

'Just be a bloody sight smarter than me, William. That's all I ask.'

'Won't be difficult from where I'm sitting.'

'Only telling you what I know, son.'

With nothing else to say, I left the table, motioned to my mother, who walked quickly over and took my place. I went and sat in hers, trying not to be drawn back to the pair of them, my parents, once proud lovers, now forbidden by the consequences of a confused and corrupted past even to hold hands.

I felt confused, exhausted, angry, frustrated and strangely touched watching them. I would have wept, but didn't have the strength for a single tear.

30

'He wanted to go to Strangeways, you know,' Mum said as we walked slowly back towards the car. 'Put in for a transfer as soon as he knew you were headed up this way. Leeds was the nearest he could get. Wanted to be near you.'

'Right.' I had my head bowed against a biting chill that temporarily seemed refreshing after the fetid air inside. We took small steps, a drifting crowd of melancholy leaving the main prison entrance, denied various loved ones, left alone with private pain and fears.

'Really loves you, he does. Despite what you think.'

'Sure,' I said, fighting a bubble at the back of my throat. 'Tell me, have I seen him in prison before?'

'A few times. At the Scrubs, mostly, before they moved him to Norwich.'

'Just can't remember a thing about it.'

She looped her arm through mine. 'Regular little lost boy, aren't you?'

'Prodigal son?'

'You're not home yet, William. But hopefully you're on the way.'

Karen waited anxiously by the BMW, trying to look suitably scary as she guarded her father's pride and joy. Certainly, it stood out in a small car park dominated by beaten-up Fords and Vauxhalls, although most of the visitors seemed to be heading away down the hill towards a windswept bus stop. The thin young woman I recognized from the next table struggled with her baby in a buggy and a tired, reluctant toddler by her side. I watched the young boy's face from thirty yards away, red, creased, silently screaming, his voice drowned by traffic and the uncaring chaos of the city on all sides. I studied that innocent screaming face until I couldn't stand it any more, hypnotized by the pain of his lonely ferocity.

* * *

I slept when we finally got back to Shallice House. Soundly. Two hours of uninterrupted sleep, while my mother pottered about downstairs. Or so I thought. By the time I wandered down, she was sitting in the lounge, grim-faced.

'I feel better for that,' I said, taking a seat beside her on the sofa. She'd managed to light a fire in the grate behind us, but the small yellow flames failed to warm any aspect of the room.

My mother simply sat, tight-lipped in the oppressive silence.

Then I spotted them at her feet. A cassette player with headphones and the series of tapes made by Carter as I'd detailed my confession to him. I sighed, neck suddenly stiff with tension. 'How much have you heard?'

'Enough. More than enough to break my heart.'

'I'm sorry.' What else could I say? It wasn't as if I could deny them.

'It's going to take more than a simple "sorry", William.'

'I know.'

Her face creased in disgust. 'I mean, how could you even *think* those things? It's like . . . it's like I just don't know you any more, William.'

'Jesus, Mum. You know the score. I'm a bloody mess. And whatever you heard on those tapes –'

'He left them for me, you know. Dr Carter. Left them with a little note suggesting that I should listen to them.' She laughed, full of bitter sarcasm. 'He thought it would give me a better perspective.'

'Mum, listen to me. When we made those tapes, I just wasn't thinking straight. I –'

She reached across, gripped my arm. 'Look me in the eye, William Dickson, look me in the eye, and tell me I'm the kind of woman who'd steal about in the middle of the night splashing blood from a jam-jar over my friend's dead body.'

But I couldn't look her in the eye.

Her voice rose. 'Or that your father's the type to creep about with a body in a sack, for God's sake! I mean, good Lord, what are we, your dad and I – Tilbury's answer to Burke and Hare? It's ludicrous, William, absolute tosh!'

I stood, anxious to retain some distance. 'Mum, at the time, it was all the reality I had. Don't you see that? I had these fucking memories . . .'

'You watch your mouth!'

'. . . and they were *all* I had.'

She stood, came to me, wheeled me round with a strength that belied her fragile frame. 'No, William,' she said slowly, the beginnings of a tear in her eye. 'You had common sense, too. But you wouldn't bloody well use it. You just ran with these damn memories. They were all that mattered.' She poked herself hard in the chest. 'My love for you, your father's love – counted for nothing. And that's what hurts the most.'

'Mum, I . . .'

But she was way beyond listening to excuses. 'Do you really think I'm the type who would have calmly carried on peeling vegetables with a dead body in the kitchen? Do you?'

'I just –'

'No!' She shook me hard. 'Never. Ever. You should have damned well realized that when you started having these ridiculous fantasies.'

'Mum, they're memories! They were real for me! Try and understand. Please. Christ's sake, I'm sick in the head!'

She stepped back, took a deep breath to compose herself. 'There's being sick, William. Then there's being very, very wrong.' She turned, began walking for the door. 'Trouble is, I just don't know which one you are any more.'

I hung my head as she left the room, barely knowing the answer to her question myself.

At six that evening, I stole Carter's car.

As crimes go, it was laughably easy. My mother was taking a nap upstairs, Karen had returned to wherever she was staying locally, and the car keys were hanging on the hook in the hallway. All that was left to do was to quietly open the garage door, de-activate the alarm, slip into the driver's seat, adjust the mirrors and slip away. If I'd been truly heartless, I could have got a couple of grand for it inside the hour.

I suppose many a lad my age would have cherished every second driving such a flashy machine, appreciating the response, plush interior, overall sensation of power and luxury. But not me, not that night. I drove on autopilot, mind divorced from all immediacy. However much it begged to be properly assembled, I knew my past would have to wait. Right now, my immediate future was all I could come to grips with. The trip to Armley had been a brutal reminder that I could easily end up in a place like that. Whatever I'd done, not done, whether I'd killed or not killed, I had to concentrate on one thing at a time, and right now the murder of Ian Bailey in a Manchester alley was all I could reasonably cope with. I drove back to Fallowfield determined to speak to Kris Jordan.

Finding the house wasn't as easy as I thought. Whilst I could remember the road name she'd given to the police as her temporary address, the number eluded me. Undeterred, I parked in the next street, started from the top and began knocking on each door of every red-bricked terrace. After forty minutes, I'd done most of one side, had been told to 'bugger off', and worse, several times, twice been invited in for a smoke and – most bizarrely – mistaken for a plumber by a little old lady only too keen to give me forty pounds to sort her sink out.

I struck lucky just before the end of the street. A young girl answered in what I took to be a student nurse's uniform. Although I'd never met her, I remembered a conversation I'd had with Kris when she'd first seen my medication. Something about one of her mates being able to get me some 'cheap' tranquillizers, as she was doing a training stint up at the Royal Infirmary. Knock-off knockout drops, she'd called them.

'Yes?' the young Nightingale asked, dripping milky spoon in one hand, bowl of cereal in the other.

'Kris around?'

She hesitated. All I needed to know. 'DC Donelly,' I boldly announced. 'Stockport CID.'

'Oh. Right.' She never gave it a second thought, simply walking back into the house and calling up the stairs. Maybe she was tired, or used to dodgy-looking blokes posing as coppers with no form of ID turning up at all hours.

'Kris. For you!'

Kris's voice: 'Coming.'

The nurse wandered away, leaving me to watch as my former housemate came downstairs, pushing her short brown hair from her face in order to get a better view of me. And the look on that face was one to bank and treasure. A brief flicker of confusion, then fear, before she forced her expression to return to one of friendly surprise. She stopped on the second stair.

'William.'

'Kris.'

'I don't think you should be here, do you?'

I shrugged.

'DCI Shrimp would be rather interested to know.'

'Phone him. We could all pop down to Stockport nick and have a little chat.'

But she didn't race for the phone. 'I think you'd better go.'

'Why?'

'Come on, you know the rules. We're not supposed to see each other, or have any contact with each other. You, especially.'

'Especially?'

'Since you gave the false address.'

'So, we've been chatting to Shrimp and Harris, have we? What else have they told you?'

'That they think you probably killed Ian. Running like you did more or less proves it.'

'To you? Or them?'

The nurse returned, stood leaning against the wall a few feet away, still eating cereal. 'You OK, Kris?'

'Fine.'

She pointed a cheap spoon at me. 'My hunch is that he isn't a proper bobby at all.' A teasing smile accompanied the accusation.

'He isn't.'

She tutted, turned, and wandered off into another room.

'What do you want?' Kris asked.

'To speak to Danny.'

'Danny? He's not here.'

'Oh, but he will be in a minute.'

Confusion briefly flashed across her face. 'He's coming here?'

'Sure.'

'You've spoken to him?'

'Forty minutes ago.'

'How? I mean . . . ?'

'Let's sit down. I don't want to do this in the hallway.'

'Do what?'

I reached out, felt her flinch when I playfully grabbed her arm. 'Tell you what I've been up to, of course. What did you think, that I was going to lock you in a room and kill you?'

'No. I . . .'

'The lounge? Or your bedroom?'

She removed my arm. 'The lounge is through there,' she said, pointing behind me.

I stepped aside, followed her into a small front room with a 1940s sofa, shelves of LPs and dusty rubber plants placed on huge loudspeakers. There was a large poster of Bob Marley on the wall.

She sat. I stood.

'So?'

'I think Danny's trying to set me up,' I said.

'You've definitely spoken to him?'

I nodded.

'You know the police have been trying to trace him for days?'

'It's not difficult if you're convincing enough.'

'Shouldn't you have given the number to Shrimp?'

'Not until I've spoken to Danny first.'

'I think we should tell Shrimp,' she insisted. 'I mean, chances are he could have murdered Ian.'

'I thought I was supposed to be the killer.'

'I never said that. The police might think that, but I don't.'

'How kind. So tell me, why do you think Danny's the mad Manchester slasher?'

She blinked twice, stalling. Then said: 'You said so yourself. Just now. That he's trying to set you up.'

'And I do think that, Kris, I really do.'

'Why?'

'I think the bastard got me deliberately drunk that Sunday night in order that I wouldn't remember anything. He knows about my coma. Maybe I told him other stuff as well. Secret stuff.'

'What secret stuff?'

I sat down beside her. 'Kris, we've all got secrets.' She

didn't react. 'Anyway, I reckon Danny conspires in some way to meet up with Ian, kills him, then reckons if he's ever arrested for it, he can point his double-crossing finger at me.'

She nodded a little too enthusiastically. I could see her mind working frantically to process it all. The whole scenario was ludicrous, full of far too many ifs-and-buts, but she tried her best to look convinced.

I said, 'But then it all went wrong when the police discovered the key-ring near the body. The one you'd given him. So the set-up falls apart. And, Danny, not being the brightest of chaps, legs it to regroup, give himself time to think.'

'But why kill Ian?'

I shrugged. 'Probably just a scrap that went too far. I reckon Danny had the hump that Ian was coming on to you, decided to have it out with him.'

She tried a stab at disbelief, making a bold fist of playing devil's advocate. 'Not Danny. I just can't see it. He wasn't the type.'

'But can't appearances be deceptive?'

'And you told Danny all this on the phone?'

'Good God, no. He'd hardly have agreed to meet me here if he knew I suspected him of being the killer, would he?' I began counting in my head – one-elephant, two-elephant – wondering how long it would be before she asked the obvious question. I'd got to eight elephants before she spoke.

'What did you tell him, exactly?'

On went the reassuring smile. 'The amazing thing was, he more or less dropped himself right in it.'

'He did?'

'Sure. Came out with some cock-and-bull story that beggared belief. I mean, Kris, this was seriously screwed-up stuff.'

After six elephants this time: 'Like what?'

'He starts telling me that he saw you and Ian together in some dingy backstreet drinking den shortly before Ian died. I mean, how daft is that?'

'Ridiculous.'

'He said he was there with some other girl when the pair of you just walked in. Then there's some kind of row, and you and Ian walked out again. He swears it's all true. What a liar, eh?'

She cleared her throat, saying nothing, just nodding, staring at the far wall.

'But then comes the curious thing.'

Three elephants. 'What?'

'He told me that the only reason he's on the run is because he couldn't prove you two were ever in the club.'

She rallied at this. 'Of course he couldn't. Because it's not true, that's why. I spent the entire night at the house.'

'I know that, Kris. But Danny reckons he's got some kind of photograph.'

Her head turned. 'What?'

'He told me most of the blokes in the club were scallies like him, and would rather shoot their own mothers than turn out as witnesses on his behalf. However, one of them has sold him a photo.'

'A photo?'

'A Jamaican bloke was having some kind of a party down there. Someone shot a few Polaroids. Stuff Danny didn't even realize was being taken at the time. Anyway, in one of them, he reckons he can clearly see you and Ian in the background, red-eyed but recognizable. He says there's a clock on the wall behind, and that the police will match Ian's clothing to the stuff he was wearing when he was killed.' Two more elephants. 'Weird, eh?'

She stood, went to the window, drew the curtains on an already dark winter's night. 'And now he's coming here? With the picture?'

'What do you think?' I replied. 'It's got to be a bluff, hasn't it? I mean, how could you and Ian have been in that club? I tell you, Kris, the guy's messed up, done too much dope. His mind's gone, and he's coming out with anything that he thinks'll save his miserable bacon.'

She walked quickly to the door. 'You'd better go.'

'Why? We need to confront him.'

'I'm going to call the police. Get them here before he comes. You'll be in trouble if they find you here.'

'Kris, calm down, it's not a problem . . .'

'Yes, William, it fucking is a problem! A big problem, all right?'

I went for confused. 'Why?'

'Because you're not supposed to be here, you jerk! It could . . . it could . . . I don't know, jeopardize an arrest if it turned out you were here too.'

'I don't see how.'

'William, please. Go. For your own sake. Please.'

I shrugged, made a business out of getting up from the sofa. 'Only if you're sure . . .'

'I'm certain.'

'You'll be OK?'

'Yes, the police will be here with me. Now go. I've got to ring Stockport.'

'Fair enough.'

At the front door, she pecked me briefly on the cheek. It felt odd to be kissed by a murderer, maybe a little disloyal to Ian's memory, even. But the way I saw it, if there was such a thing as an afterlife, hopefully Ian would have a front-row seat as he watched Kris make frantic plans to wrestle a photo that never existed from a man who'd never turn up.

And in contrast to the journey down, on the drive back to Edale I savoured every luxurious moment in Carter's BMW.

31

I felt quite chipper on the next morning's drive into Stockport. Karen didn't seemed to notice that the fuel gauge was lower than when she had last driven the car, or that the rear-view mirror needed a slight readjustment as we climbed in. So far, the gods were with me, I thought.

It was a bright Sunday morning, frost gently thawing under a pale-blue sky. A few people ambled around the streets, but generally all was quiet. At the police station I was greeted by the cynical smiles of DCI Shrimp and DS Harris. I can't say I was terribly surprised.

'Morning, Mr Dickson,' Shrimp said. 'Couldn't spare us a few minutes, could you?'

'Certainly. Sorry to get you both back to work on a Sunday.'

'No problem, Mr Dickson. No problem at all.'

I guessed it wasn't. Their families were probably glad to see the back of them as well.

As I followed them past the desk into the bowels of the station, I glanced back in the direction of Karen and the car. As per instructions, she had already gone.

'So,' Shrimp began, as Harris closed the door to the interview room, 'Sergeant Harris and myself thought it was about time we had another little chat.'

'What with it being nearly the season of goodwill to all men and that,' Harris added, scraping a chair over the worn floor and joining us at the table. 'Looking forward to Christmas, are you, William?'

I didn't bother replying. I'd fully expected to be 'delayed' that morning. It didn't take a rocket scientist to deduce that Kris would eventually have contacted the police the night before. Perhaps waited a couple of frantic hours before realizing she'd been had. But dangerously had. Had by someone who knew too much about Ian's death. The very fact that Shrimp and his grinning monkey were waiting for me proved her guilt in my mind beyond all reasonable doubt. If she'd been innocent, Kris would have rung Stockport police the moment I'd left her friend's house. I'd have been picked up the moment I arrived back at Edale. Instead, she had obviously waited till much later, maybe even putting it off until morning, hoping that Danny would still show, that she'd somehow contrive a way to take the non-existent photo from him. And then what? Would he have met the same fate as Ian?

Harris was grinning now, noting my silence with glee. 'Think he's gone and lost his voice, guv'nor.'

Shrimp play-acted trying to remember. 'Now where have I heard something like that before? William Dickson, losing his voice? Any ideas, Sergeant?'

'Could it be,' Harris dutifully supplied, 'from that file we were reading just the other day?'

'Remind me, Sergeant.'

My eyes flitted from one to another, possibly the worst double-act in the northwest.

'You know the one, guv,' Harris said. 'The little lad in the tree. He was called Dickson as well, wasn't he?'

Shrimp flicked his fingers in recognition. 'Excellent, Sergeant! Of course, the little lad in the tree. Screamed himself hoarse he did, according to the case notes . . .'

'The unsolved case notes,' Harris added. 'Because they never found out who'd killed those other two lads, did they?'

'Sloppy police work, Sergeant?'

'Nothing of the kind. One of the largest regional investigations of its time. Turned up nothing but a few broken branches and some footprints.'

'But surely the boy would have been able to furnish the officers with a clue or two?'

'Bugger all. Kept as quiet as the dead.'

'Really? For how long?'

'Ever since, sir.'

I folded my arms, settled further back into the bucket seat.

Eye-contact from Shrimp. A theatrical frown. 'Forget a lot of things, don't you, William, eh? Like your temporary address.'

'That was a mistake,' I said. 'I've been over this with you already. I was confused –'

'Confused,' Shrimp cut in, turning to his stooge. 'Covers what we policemen might call a multitude of sins.'

'Am I being arrested?' I put in.

'Would you say you were "confused", William, when you caused the first of many recorded disturbances at Chetwins School for Young Crims – sorry, disturbed and misunderstood little cherubs? Were you "confused" when you threw yourself from Dr John Tremaine's window?'

Harris: 'Ambulancemen found heavy bruising on Tremaine's neck, William. Police reports state they thought the doctor was crazy not to press GBH charges against you.'

'Not confused,' I said. 'Hypnotized. Different thing entirely.'

'You have no idea, William,' Shrimp persisted, 'just what good reading you make.'

I held focus with my rights. 'I think I'm allowed a phone call.'

'Who're you going to call, then, William? Your old man? Daddy Dickson, doing twelve years in Armley for murder?'

'Enjoy yourself yesterday?' Harris asked. 'Little trip out to Leeds with Mummy to hold your hand?'

'Prison authorities passed us the application for the visitors' papers,' Shrimp explained.

'Runs in the family, I expect,' said Harris. 'Spot of unprovoked violence.'

Shrimp rose, leant over me, hands gripping the table-top, a large pulsing vein standing out on his shining forehead. 'And the man your demented old dad topped was none other than the killer of the mother of one of those little lads who were murdered in the woods. The lads you were with. And you say you have no idea how those lads died. Or who did it.'

'Very suspicious,' Shrimp said from behind.

'According to you.'

Suddenly Shrimp slammed his fist onto the table. 'Back to fucking square one, aren't we! Eh? Fucking square one! You don't remember this; you're confused about that! Let me tell you something, Dickson, we've got shitloads of strange stuff on you, lad. And a fraction of it would be enough to bury you. What were you doing at Kris Jordan's temporary address last night?'

'Testing a few theories.'

'You broke conditions agreed by you and your solicitor regarding your behaviour during this enquiry.'

'Kris Jordan killed Ian Bailey.'

'Of course she did. Who needs a police force at all when you have William-the-Amnesiac Dickson on the case, eh?'

'Ask her where she was on the night of the murder.'

Harris: 'You telling us how to –'

Shrimp: 'Strange, because Miss Jordan reckons it was either you, or that shiftless pot-pushing creep Danny Black who did for Mr Bailey.'

'Ask her where she was on the night of the murder.'

Harris: 'We already have, Dickson. She was back at home.'

'Any witnesses?'

'You've got to stop asking questions, and start answering them. Like this one. Who makes a better suspect: you, an untrustworthy, lying, suicide case; or Miss Jordan – model citizen, student, all around law-abiding member of the community?'

'Ask Danny Black. He'll give you all the answers you need.'

Shrimp sighed. 'Mr Black, in case you didn't know, has fucked off. A fact that makes us just as suspicious of his scabby little arse as we are of yours. He's got a record longer than a gorilla's arm, and isn't doing himself any favours by making us waste our time playing "hunt the fugitive".'

'If you know where he is, you tell us,' Harris added.

'I've spoken to him on the phone, that's all.'

Shrimp: 'How very convenient.'

'It's the truth.'

'It's lies, all lies! Bullshit from a messed-up –'

Through the puff of his hot, angry breath, I heard a commotion outside, a familiar voice arguing with other officers. Harris stood, went to the door, opened it. 'Well, well,' he said quietly. 'Guess it's the cavalry.'

The furious figure of Brian French strode into the room. 'Inspector,' he said, taking my arm and pulling me to my feet, 'if you're not arresting my client, then I'm escorting him out of this kangaroo court.'

'Not yet,' Shrimp hissed back.

'I beg your pardon?'

'I'm not arresting him yet. But soon, very soon.'

French moved me towards the door. 'I think you'll need a good deal besides prejudiced conjecture for that, Inspector. Evidence, perhaps, is a good place to start. You have any?'

'We've got ninety per cent of all the evidence we need, Mr French,' Shrimp replied. 'Kris Jordan's been telling us quite a lot about Mr Dickson.'

French shot me a what-the-hell's-she-got-on-you? look. I returned what I hoped passed for 'I'll tell you later'.

'His past links to other murder enquiries,' Shrimp added. 'And now his flatmate's been stabbed to death.' Shrimp fixed me with a glare. 'Guilty or innocent, what jury in the land's going to allow him to walk free after hearing that kind of evidence, eh?'

French paused for a moment, then grabbed my arm and led me towards the door. 'William, let's go,' he said emphatically.

'You got here quicker than I thought you would,' I said, buckling up in the passenger seat of French's hastily parked Mercedes.

He fired the engine. 'Not much I'd give up Sunday morning on the golf course for. But an emergency call from my niece is one of them.'

'Karen's your niece?'

We turned out onto the A6. He smiled. 'Spooky, isn't it? My sister married Dick, and in so doing swapped the honourable name of French for the highly disreputable one of Carter. To be expected really: she always was a mad one.'

'He told me you were one of the best, not his brother-in-law.'

He took one hand off the wheel, tapped his large nose. 'Serendipity in action, William. Though what in God's name has Karen done to herself? I thought the bride of bloody Frankenstein had come roaring into the clubhouse car park.'

'Don't ask me. I'm sort of done with unanswerable questions for one morning.'

'Shrimp and Harris getting to you?'

'Not listening to me, more like.'

'Why should they? They're policemen. They've got an unsolved murder riding high in the local press, and no real motive or suspects apart from a kid with suicide history, amnesia, and a dodgy past. It's all they need for a conviction if there's a good CPS brief on their side.'

'You really are a joy, you know that.'

He laughed, slapped my thigh. 'Listen, as far as I'm concerned it's a beaten-up attaché in a nine-storey tower block.'

'Sorry?'

He took out a half-smoked cigar from his jacket pocket and lit it from the dashboard lighter. 'A crap case,' he said, 'with no grounds.'

We found Karen sitting at a table in a discreet corner of the clubhouse lounge. 'Some poncey old bloke with a handlebar moustache made me wait here,' she moaned as French and I sat opposite.

'Mr Taylor-Oakenfold,' French confirmed. 'Club captain. Probably trying to be discreet.'

'Discreet? An old guy in a Pringle sweater ordering me about?'

'Karen, my precious,' French soothed, 'there's a list longer than the first fairway of Altrincham's richest stockbrokers desperate to join up and swing a nine-iron here. Can't be done to have an extra from a cheap Hammer horror film sitting in the main bar area.'

'Social elitism, is what it is. Fashion prejudice.'

'Listen, it's only because you're a relative of mine that you're allowed in here at all. Be grateful they didn't drum you out of the place entirely.'

'I'd have liked to have seen them try.'

'Me, too,' I said. 'Certainly a woman of surprises, aren't you?'

She looked a tiny bit guilty. 'The uncle thing?'

'Why didn't you tell me?' I asked.

'Does it matter?'

I thought about it for a moment. 'No. Not really.'

'Well stop going on about it, then.'

French held up both hands. 'Quiet, children. This is neither the time nor the place for a lovers' tiff.'

I seriously thought Karen might explode. 'Lovers' tiff?'

'We have bigger fish currently bubbling in the pan.' He turned to me. 'William, care to tell me what the hell you've been up to that made Shrimp and Harris so keen to talk to you this morning?'

So I did. Gave them both as much as I knew about the story so far. Afterwards, French took a while to order his thoughts. 'So your gut instinct tells you Kris Jordan killed Ian Bailey?'

I nodded.

'Gonna take more than that, William. A lot more. Precisely, a method, and a motive.'

The method seemed more than obvious. 'She stabbed him.'

'With what?'

'A knife, of course.'

'Which she just happened to be carrying in her back jeans pocket, right?'

'Perhaps she bought it off one of the dodgy characters in the club,' I suggested. 'Maybe she was already so pissed off with Ian that she knew she wanted to kill him.'

'Why?'

Here I had no answers.

'What I'm saying, William, is that while the key-ring left by the body, and your tales of Kris's rather contradictory behaviour both last night and on the morning after the killing could well point a finger of suspicion her way, all we really have to go on are your theories and instincts. Not enough, old chap, not enough by a long chalk.'

'But I know it was her.'

He smiled. 'William Dickson, up until the middle of last week you thought you knew you were a student serial-killer with four victims to his credit. You know less about yourself than you do about other people. The problem you have is two-fold . . .'

'Two more problems, great.'

'Firstly, for all its bold intentions, all your amateur sleuthing has achieved is to shift the police spotlight straight back onto you. Secondly, this case is now what's termed "cold".'

'What do you mean?'

He slipped off a shoe, began rubbing his toes through expensive-looking black monogrammed silk socks. 'There are two principal phases in all murder enquiries. Firstly comes the hot phase, where tremendous resources are marshalled, CID squads put together, house-to-house interviews conducted, criminal records laboriously researched, forensic evidence pored over, informers contacted. Generally lasts for about forty-eight hours for a homicide, ninety-six for a missing person.'

He swapped legs, took off the other shoe, began massaging the other foot. 'And in the majority of cases, the police generally get their man – or woman – during this first phase.'

'But not in this case.'

'No. Indeed not. Shrimp and Harris have entered that most reviled arena as far as all murder-squad detectives are concerned – a cold case. Resources will be being stripped away, sidelined to fresh cases. Ian Bailey's murder will be hanging over Shrimp like a swinging noose. We can presume, since no one has been arrested at this point, that he doesn't have sufficient evidence to press any charges. The forensics guys and the informant network must have come up with a big fat zero.'

'So surely they'll drop the case,' Karen said. 'List it as "unsolved", or whatever they do.'

French slipped his shoes back on. 'Not that simple, I'm afraid. In order to do that, Shrimp and Harris have to clear it with their superior officer. He's going to take one look at the crime file and see three potential suspects, each without an alibi. William says he was too drunk to remember getting home that night; Kris Jordan says she was at the Fallowfield address but has no witnesses to prove it; and Danny Black's lover apparently risks permanent disablement from her disgruntled husband if she admits she slept with Black that night.'

'So what's likely to happen?' I asked a little nervously, wondering if indulging in a bout of toe-rubbing myself might ease a little of the tension I felt.

'Barring the last proviso, they'll look at the previous form of the three of you, charge the most likely suspect, then give the lot to the CPS. Buck-passing really, but at least the police will have played their part. If the CPS decide not to prosecute, or if the case falls apart in court, then it'll be the vultures with the white curly wigs who'll have egg on their faces, not our old chums Shrimp and Harris.'

Karen leaned forward. 'And what exactly is "the last proviso", Uncle?'

'A confession,' he said simply. 'Kris Jordan breaks down and confesses.'

'Unlikely, somehow,' I said. 'She's played it pretty cool so far.'

'On the outside maybe,' French replied. 'But if she's any kind of a human being, inside she'll be going through seven shades of guilty hell. If she did this terrible thing, William, then believe me, there'll be a way in to her conscience. Find that way in, and she'll crack.'

'You telling me to break her down? I thought you said to steer away from the private-eye stuff?'

A waiter arrived, shooting a distasteful look at Karen and me as French pointedly ordered coffee for himself 'and my two charming companions'.

'Let me tell you a little of what I know about you, William,' he said after the waiter had left. 'I've read a lot about you, Carter's told me masses about you, and I've spent a fair deal of time talking to you myself.'

'Is this going to get personal?' Karen asked. 'Only I can leave if you want me to.'

'It's fine,' I said. 'Please, stay.'

French raised an eyebrow, then continued, 'You're a bright, affable young man with some sort of delusional short-circuit. Carter's got all the jargon for it, but basically I see a confused kid who's clinging on to some sort of unreality because he's too scared of his past to face it. Really, it doesn't take Hercule Poirot to work out that Edward Norris died after being murdered in the Tilbury Woods killings; his mother was killed by Dave Atkins; Jonathan Webster died in a freak school sporting accident; and David Phillips got barbecued in his Triumph because the damn thing was a liability from the off. Four deaths you had nothing to do with. Absolutely nothing.'

I waited for the screaming to start in my head. Nothing. Where was Little Bill, the objections, the incitements to attack French and shut him up? Strange, but the silence was more unnerving than his previous outbursts. As if Little Bill was allowing French to continue for reasons I really didn't want to know. Silence as an agenda.

'You're forgetting Edith Fitzroy,' I said. 'No one was prosecuted for her murder. As far as I know, I'm still the main contender for that one.'

French frowned. 'That's a difficult one. And strangely, all I have to go on with Mrs Fitzroy is my own instincts. I'm willing to bet my Merc you never killed the other four – ergo, you didn't kill her, either.'

I wished I could share the weight of his convictions. While I was almost prepared to concede that my other 'victims' mightn't actually have died the way I seemed to remember so clearly, Edith Fitzroy's shocked, terrified face falling away from mine refused to surrender to French's well-meant 'instincts'. Her face, I already knew, would haunt me for many years to come.

'But now you face a certain sort of irony,' French said. 'Here you sit, a non-killer, potentially facing a life sentence for a murder you didn't commit. A murder you never even fantasized about committing. And sure, I told you wandering around doing your Philip Marlowe impressions in Fallowfield and Hulme mightn't be the wisest thing, but I can understand that sometimes you look at a situation and say, "Sod it, it's my arse on the line, here, I'm going to do what I have to."'

The waiter arrived with our coffees.

'Sure, you do what you have to, William,' French added, stirring three spoonfuls of brown sugar crystals into his cup, 'but you'll do as well to remember that, if she has killed, there's no saying she won't try again.'

For the next few minutes I finished my coffee as French and Karen tried their best to small-talk.

And all the while, not a laugh, not an objection, not a single scream from 'Little Bill'.

32

I cried last night, William. Real tears. Bet you find that hard to believe, you and your psycho-cronies, eh? Oh, there I go again, presupposing things. Little Bill finally turns cynical. The crowd gasps. Sod off, I've got grounds! Christ's sake, I build us both a perfect world, carve us an impregnable reputation, and you never once thank me? I hope you'll never know how it feels, William, to wake up one day and feel that nothing you do or say will have the slightest impact on anyone. That regardless of all you've done, you're empty. Real tears, William. And then I got angry. I filled up on wrath. Because it just isn't fair, William. You can't leave me like this. But you want to, don't you? The more of their rubbish you swallow, the more of their tales you ingest, the more you just go their way, so fucking complicitly . . . But then I thought, if communication's the problem, how can I make myself heard? And when the anger subsided, I knew. I'll give you some leeway for a while – I want to see how this crazy thing's going to end. Don't forget, I've already seen the final reel. There're plenty of delicious moments still to enjoy. But, William, once it gets dull, it's over. You're going to have to finish this to my score. I'll make you. I can make you do all sorts of things. Don't believe me? OK, let's come clean. You've given me pause for thought – I'll give you this: I made you jump, William. That Tremaine and his stupid questions! And you selling us both out, then not having the backbone to finish the idiot off. Which made me mad, really mad at you. So I turned you, pointed you at the window, and pressed the accelerator . . . See, I can make you do all sorts of things, William. You may not be able to hear what I say, but you know what I'm capable of, don't you? A warning, to spice things up a little – don't make me cross again, or sad. Keep the laughs coming until the final curtain. Then we'll go backstage and tear the cast apart. And my guess is you'll be the only one who doesn't understand why the hell he's doing it.

Just like with the good Mrs Edith Fitzroy . . .

* * *

Karen dropped me back off at Shallice House shortly after two that same afternoon. Predictably Edale was heaving with Sunday afternoon hikers enjoying a few hours' break from the rain as the clouds parted to reveal a pale-blue winter's sky. I stood outside the house for a few moments, lost in the scene, watching ramblers head for various cuts into the hills, all thick socks, creaking leather walking boots, bright anoraks and hip-flasks. Strange, this human desire to climb, I thought, to escape the humdrum with a spot of altitude, to find a brief peace away from troubles played out below. Sooner or later, they all have to troop back down. Yet for a few precious moments they can stand on those barren windswept tops and gain sustenance from distance alone. Closer to the gods, further from the devils below.

And me? How far had I 'climbed' in the last few weeks? I knew a boy at Chetwins who had epilepsy (a real memory this time, not one of Little Bill's manipulations). I had witnessed him fitting several times, watched mesmerized as panicked staff tried to contain him, stop him swallowing his own tongue. One day I asked him how it felt to know that at any instant a fit could rise up and take that amount of sadistic control over him. He looked at me, said simply, 'You just get used to it, I suppose.' Which was my life at that moment: getting used to the idea that I could, at any moment, hurl myself under a passing bus, throw myself from an upstairs window, surrender to increasingly murderous urges, and have rock-solid memories explained as mere fantasy.

'Little Bill' was the puppet-master in my own head. But really, hadn't Carter said I pulled all the strings? That he was me, a part of me, a memory of me I couldn't accept? A boy born out of a tragedy, who'd lain low until a therapist called Tremaine gave him a birth that was almost murderous and suicidal at the same time? A boy who had lain low and screaming in my own head for the last twelve years?

And what of the 'real' William Dickson? The pre-coma teenager who'd agreed to the hypnotherapy in the first place. What kind of a person was he? A good character, according to my mother, an OK bloke. Perhaps one of the worst things was that I wasn't sure I had any real memories of him/me any more. I simply had to go on what others said, believe that he was a decent person.

Until I came to think about Edith Fitzroy. Here things became blurred, shadowed by a smothering black that manifested itself in just the one searing image – her mouth agape, eyes fearfully confused, her head tilting into the gloom of the cottage stairwell as she fell backwards into the gloom . . .

You crave the answer to this one so much, don't you, William? Tell me: why her, above all the rest? Why the Fitzroy hag? The old bat was an interfering crone – one of Tremaine's spies, doing her best to convince Mummy that the gardening job was supreme charity on her part. Edith Fitzroy, with her big doe-eyes and earnest expression. The woman made us puke, William. Made us puke at Chetwins, then again in the depressing intimacy of her shabby home. Little wonder we did what we did, eh? Like I said, I'll show you if you like. Run the memories. Grab some popcorn, Kia-ora, settle down in the front row of your own nightmare and see it as it happened . . . No. You couldn't cope. You'd be gone before the opening credits. Because Edith Fitzroy – she was different, wasn't she? The others you can dismiss as one of my inventions. But not her. Not the interfering cancer-ridden wreck that was Edith Fitzroy. Even now, you know that, don't you? Not one of Little Bill's capers, was it? It was one of yours.

Oh yes, William, she was all yours . . .

I knew that the moment to let myself back in to Shallice House couldn't be put off any longer. With it would come the inevitable conversation with my mother. She'd be waiting for me. We both knew that there had to be some kind of resolution of our misunderstandings. If the last few months (years? – I had no real idea) had been confusing for me, then I guessed they'd been just as difficult for her, too. Sighing slightly, I turned from the stone wall, took out Carter's spare keys and walked the short distance from the road to the small front porch to let myself in.

My mother opened the door while I still had the key in the lock. It hit me then – pure instinct, the real voice from inside – that this was all wrong. Terribly wrong.

'Where have you been?' she said. A normal enough

question, but already I was looking past her, trying to see who else was in the house.

'About.'

'You've been gone ages.' She stood aside, letting me through.

'It took longer than I thought.'

'Someone's here,' she whispered, trying to be so polite, oblivious to the danger I felt in every pore.

'I know.'

Kris Jordan appeared at the kitchen doorway. 'Hello, William.'

The hairs stood on the back of my neck. 'Kris.'

My mother went to her, stood by her side, relaxed, oblivious. It scared me to see her so close to a murderer, a real killer.

Kris smiled. 'Got this idea from you,' she said. 'The phoney CID thing.' She turned to my mother. 'Mrs Dickson's been very helpful with our enquiries so far this morning.'

My mother frowned, confused, four beats behind the conversation. 'You mean, you're not a real policewoman?'

'Sorry, Mrs D.'

I took a cautious step closer, watching as Kris quickly pulled my mother back into the kitchen. She gasped, tried struggling, was held tighter for her troubles.

'Let her go, Kris.'

'I'm afraid that's not possible, William.' A black-handled kitchen knife appeared in Kris's other hand. My mother let out a short cry as she felt the blade at her throat. 'Bet you're wondering how I found you, eh?'

'Just let her go.'

'Simple, really. I've known where you've been all along.'

I took another two steps, moving deliberately slowly, trying to force some saliva back into my mouth, watching as they retreated, maintaining the distance.

'Back off, William. Now!'

Another strangled cry from my mother, wide-eyed with fear.

'Tell me,' I said, eyes rooted on the steel blade pressed against her throat. 'Tell me how you found me. I'm interested, really.'

'Bollocks!'

'Honestly. You're obviously a lot smarter than I thought.'

'Oh, I am that.'

I took another half step, closing the gap to around six feet. Kris moved to her left, placing the large wooden kitchen table between us. If I wanted to do anything heroic, I'd either have to charge round or leap over. Both options looked unpromising. All I could think of was to keep her talking, buy some time.

'My lecturer, the Aussie woman,' I said. 'She knew, didn't she? You went and asked her.'

Kris nodded. 'Stupid woman's got the loosest mouth in the northern hemisphere.'

Another cautious step towards the table. 'What did you try, the undercover copper routine again?'

A small self-congratulatory smile. 'Told her I was pregnant. Gave her the full works, tears, everything.'

'And that I was the father.'

'Naturally.' She grabbed my mother's wrist, pulled it sharply round behind her back. 'Not that you're about to become a grandmother, Mrs Dickson,' she hissed. 'I doubt mental William here has it in him, frankly.'

'Please,' I said, trying to ignore my mother's low moans. 'Just let her go.'

The eyes narrowed. 'Don't patronize me, William. Imagine my surprise when I came here this morning to talk about the folly of your little phoney-photo stunt, and instead I find your dear and helpful mother all on her lonesome. Just think of the rush that gave me.' She whispered into her captive's ear. 'And we were having such a nice chat, weren't we, Mrs D, eh?'

'Just leave her be. You and I can work something out. You don't have to –'

'I know how to do it, you know,' she proudly announced.

I flinched as she moved the knife from the front to the side of my mother's throat.

'No good trying to slash away at the Adam's apple, William. It's far too tough. Like trying to cut through raw gristle. No, just here's the place.' My eyes widened as she made a light cut into the side of the neck. My mother screamed, struggled, but was quickly contained. 'The carotid artery. It's messier, but far quicker.'

'Which achieves what, precisely?' I said, watching a single drop of blood spill onto the shining steel blade. 'Living proof that you killed both Ian and my mother?'

'Dying proof would be rather more appropriate,' she said, looking down distastefully and taking a slight step backwards. 'Now Mrs Dickson, we've not gone and wet ourselves, have we?'

'She's got a heart condition,' I quickly lied. 'You won't need to slit her throat. Any more of this, and she'll die in your arms.'

Kris shrugged. 'Saves on the dry-cleaning, then, doesn't it?'

'What do you want?'

'Ah, we get to the nub of it.'

'Please. At least let her sit down.'

Kris ignored the plea, shuffled my mother back into her. She stood with her back against the sink-unit, my mother screening most of her front. I glanced down at the table, looking for some sort of missile, a knife of my own, salt or pepper, anything I could use to hurl at her. Nothing. Ironically, my mother, in all her house-proud boredom of the long morning, had tidied Carter's kitchen immaculately. The normally cluttered table was now just a flat, polished surface.

So I sat, instead. Pulled out a chair, and settled down opposite them. Kris watched suspiciously. 'Both hands on the table, please.'

I did as she asked, wondering if I could kick the heavy wooden kitchen chair opposite me into them both. Chances were it would wind my mother, but maybe the sudden commotion would give me my chance to dash in, effect some kind of rescue. Then again, perhaps Kris would simply end my mother's life right there and then.

'So why did you kill him?' I asked. 'What the hell had Ian Bailey ever done to you?'

'Getting a little cocky, aren't we? Or is this a new tactic: confront the assailant?'

'Just curious, that's all.'

'You're assuming, of course, that I did kill him.'

'I know you did. You lied to me. You and he were seen in the drinking club on the Sunday night. What happened, did he come back from his parents' house early, then get persuaded to appear in one of your "Let's get Danny jealous" games?'

'He was only too willing.'

'Then again, he thought of himself as a contender rather than bait, didn't he?'

'Why do you look at me like that? Why the hatred?'

'I have to explain it?'

'Real Mr Cool, aren't you?'

'Not really. Mr I'm-Getting-Pretty-Fed-Up-With-This is nearer the mark.' I began drumming my fingers lightly on the table-top, inching both feet forward under the table, desperately hoping they'd eventually connect with the chair legs opposite. And if I looked cool, then it was the biggest lie of my life.

'He was going to rape me, you know.'

I nodded. I'd already imagined the scene. Ian Bailey, infatuated, unsure, strung along by a housemate who'd all too readily bad-mouth her boyfriend, invite him into the bathroom for teasing 'chats', then openly kiss him in front of an indifferent Danny. Ian Bailey, his first time away from home, muddled, immature, a hormonal time-bomb exploding in his bedroom as he fantasized about the second-year mathematician in the next room.

'Did you see his library?' I asked.

She frowned.

'The Kris Jordan Library. His big autumn term project. He named it after you. All these plans on his drawing board. All those hours spent carefully inking in little people and bushes, glass atriums, reading rooms, reference –'

'Oh do shut up!'

'He did that because he was smitten with you, Kris. Because you let him think he had a chance.'

Her eyes blazed. 'OK,' she said indignantly. 'You want to know what happened that night?'

'You just told me. He tried to rape you.'

'He wouldn't take no for an answer.'

'Perhaps you weren't listening to his questions.' Contact.

My left foot nudged gently against what I prayed was a chair rather than a table leg. Gingerly, I began inching my right leg out and across, maintaining eye-contact as my mind frantically tried to work out the location of the other leg.

'You told him, didn't you?' I said. 'You told him as he tried to get amorous sometime after leaving the club. You told him he was just a stooge, and that you'd only been using him to get back at Danny.'

'Not in so many words. But I guess he figured it out.' My heart missed a beat as she glanced down. Something had changed. She was getting nervous. Maybe my calm had unsettled her. It was paramount to keep her feeling she was boss of the situation.

I went for empathy. 'And then he got angry, and started attacking you?'

'He was drunk. We both were. But he was stronger.'

'And then the bastard decided to take what he thought was his, right?'

Kris looked at me suspiciously for a moment, gauging this new change of tack, scanning my concerned face, searching for cracks in its integrity.

'Yes,' she slowly replied. 'He did.'

'And the knife?' I said. 'That was his, wasn't it?'

'A Stanley. Used it for his coursework. But he also carried it around to protect himself. Said he felt vulnerable without it.'

'But he pulled it on you, didn't he?'

'He tried.'

'You got it off him?'

'He dropped it. I got to it first.'

'Then you stabbed him.'

'He was pushing me down. Tearing at me.'

'Self-defence, Kris, anyone would have –'

'All the time there's such anger in his voice. "Bitch!", he kept yelling. And other really filthy things. And he's just not going away. It's late, we're too far from the road, no one's coming to help. I keep saying no – over and over. We fall down, right there in this shitty alley. He's trying to get on top of me. And I feel his hands, so cold, on my belly, trying to unbutton my jeans . . .'

My mother's tiny breaths punctuated the long silence. She looked right at me, utterly fearful. I tried my best to return some kind of comforting smile, still inching out my right leg towards its hidden target.

Kris came to, snapped out of the memories of that night. 'What choice did I have?'

'None.'

'I'd told him, hadn't I? Lots of times. I'd told him to leave me alone.'

'Of course you did.' Contact! My right foot now rested against the other chair leg. I began pulling both feet slightly back, hoping I still had enough strength and leverage to kick the chair straight at the pair of them.

My mother began to sob.

'Then I panicked,' Kris continued. 'You know, afterwards. Crazy, I should have gone straight to the police, told them everything, but –'

'You just wanted to get away.'

'Yes!' she said, eyes widening. 'Just run from that horrible place. I didn't even know if I'd killed him. I looked, checked. He didn't move.'

'You felt frightened.'

'And cold. Really, really cold.'

'So you left the key-ring to implicate Danny?' Both feet were now coiled, ready to strike.

'God, no. That really did drop from my coat. The stupid lump had given it back to me in the club.' She thought for a moment, frowning again. 'Well, not exactly "given". It was on his table. I just wandered over and took it while he was engrossed with that slut he claimed was his cousin. I mean, he didn't need it any more. There was no way he was going to think he could drop round and use me whenever the fuck he felt like it.'

I tried to take deep, even breaths, ignore the searing cramp beginning to set into both calves as I struggled to keep my feet still and pointed.

'Next morning,' I said, 'you simply pretended nothing had happened.'

'It was the only way. Part of me was desperate for some kind of a phone call from the hospital, news that Ian was

OK, laid up in some recovery ward somewhere. And I suppose if I'd been any kind of a friend, I'd have made an anonymous phone call to the ambulance people.'

'But by then, it was too late.'

'That Monday was the worst day in my life.'

'And when the police found the key-ring, you knew you were really in the shit.'

She smiled. 'Partly. Then again, I had two excellent suspects in you and Danny, didn't I?'

'Know what you are, Kris?' It was coming . . . now or never . . .

Another smile. 'A thoughtless, scheming bitch?'

'Worse. A mathematician. Think about it.'

I kicked out with all my might, jamming the heavy chair-back into my mother's midriff. Kris started to cry out, but I was already up, one leg on the table.

But to my dismay, she was quicker than me, stepping out from behind the clattering chair. 'I'll do it, William! I'll slit your bitch-mother's throat if you so much as take another step towards us!'

Taking a deep breath, I stood back down, began slowly walking round the table. 'You never told me what you wanted, Kris.' Passing Carter's heavily laden knife-block, I casually emptied it in full view of her, ignored the knives, opting for the block instead, feeling the weight of it in my hands. It felt like being reacquainted with an old friend.

'Stay back!'

'What do you want, Kris?'

She released my mother's arm, began fumbling in one of her jacket side-pockets, pulled out a folded piece of A4, then tossed it onto the table. 'Read it. Then sign it.'

I never gave it a second glance. 'It's a confession, I presume,' I said, still marvelling at the fantastic weight of the knife-block. So much heavier than I'd ever imagined. This thing, wielded correctly, could cause real damage. 'It's simply a crude piece of fiction portraying me as the killer of Ian Bailey for reasons I can only guess at.'

'Because you're a mental case, William Dickson. A fucking loony who can't remember jack-shit about anything! Does there have to be any other reason? Either you go down, or I do.'

'Won't be me.'

'Nor me!'

I took a step closer. Less than four feet separated the three of us. I watched her knife-hand, warm, slipping under the sweat trickling from my mother's bulging neck. Blood, too, oozing from the wound, added to the oily mix.

'Let me tell you what I can remember, Kris,' I said, feeling the adrenalin kick in big-time.

'Stay back!' So much fear in her eyes now. All it would take would be a slight glance away to get her bearings, and I'd strike. It's not easy to back up slowly with a knife and a reluctant hostage.

I lifted the knife-block. 'I've killed with one of these, Kris. Already done it. Years ago. Can't have been more than seven at the time. Imagine that . . .'

'I said back off, you freak!'

'. . . a little kid killing a full-grown woman with one of these.'

'Put it down!'

She was taking tiny steps backwards, slowly retreating to the far corner. I followed, just out of reach, dropped the block to my side, holding it in my right hand.

She stumbled slightly, quickly recovered, but nevertheless fresh blood trickled over the steel blade. Another fall, and she'd be through to my mother's artery.

'Last warning, William! Sign the paper, give it to me, and I'm gone.'

I laughed. 'You think I'd let you leave?'

'No choice,' she replied, voice cracking. 'You'll be busy tending to your dying mother. The one whose throat you slit in your anguish over killing Ian.'

She took a final backwards step. The last. She was cornered.

'I'm not signing anything, Kris.'

She frowned, looked away, a beaten confusion in her eyes. She slowly took the knife from my mother's throat. For a moment I thought she was about to surrender.

'Sorry, Mrs D.,' she whispered.

My mother let out a huge gasping breath, utterly relieved. Then tried to croak some kind of reply. 'Oh, that's oka—'

'We've all got to die sometime.'

I saw the knife flash back up, but although the block was heavier, this time I was the quicker, fuelled by rage tearing into every muscle, guiding my hand, calculating the swing, until Carter's block crashed into the side of Kris Jordan's head.

Searing pain shot through my wrist on impact.

Wood smashed against bone with a horrible 'clonk'.

Kris moaned.

My mother screamed.

They both fell to the floor.

33

Seventeen hours later, the cell door opened.

'Hello, William.'

I glanced up at the tall, familiar figure. 'Of all the police stations in all the world, you have to walk into mine.'

Carter smiled, came and sat next to me on the hard wooden bed. 'Seems I missed the fun.' He made as if to take off his overcoat, then thought twice about it. It was so cold you could see your breath in there.

'Don't tell me,' I said. 'French rang you in the States with the news, and you caught the red-eye straight over to gloat over the latest adventures of your favourite "enigma".'

'How are you?'

'Cold. Tired. Hungry. They've even taken my shoes.'

'Your mother's out of the hospital. Just given a statement to Shrimp. She's very shaken up, needed a couple of stitches in her neck, but apart from that, seems fine.'

I felt the relief flood over me. 'I did the right thing this time, didn't I, ringing the police?'

He put an arm around me. I didn't resist. 'Yeah. You did the right thing.'

'What about Kris?'

'Shrimp's been liaising with the hospital. They'll be keeping her in for a few days as a precaution. She's had a brain scan for the concussion, but he reckons they'll be able to interview her later today.'

'I did a Margot Norris job on her. You know, the old William Dickson knife-block number.'

'French told me all about it.'

'He's been good. A rock. Without him . . .'

'What?'

'I don't know.' I thought back to the previous afternoon, the overriding sense of nauseating panic as Kris and my mother had fallen to the floor. How Kris had started to twitch, red foam flying from her mouth, while I prised my mother free. Then dashing for the phone, punching nine-nine-nine, trying to stay calm as I talked to the operator. Just yesterday, but it could have been another me in a separate lifetime.

The police had arrived first, a full sirens-on job, screeching to a halt outside the house where I'd already opened the front door. Two uniformed officers jumped out, one staying with my mother and me, the other dashing inside. A minute later, a second unmarked car arrived, disgorging the wheezing figure of Shrimp, closely followed by Harris, barking orders into walkie-talkies and generally acting as if it was the most exciting thing that had happened to them for years. Maybe it was.

Lastly, the ambulance pulled up. Lots of doors slammed, a stretcher was quickly taken inside, followed by another serious-looking medic with two briefcases marked with red crosses. He came straight to where I stood with my mother on the front step, made her sit down, then began attending to her wounds.

So much activity. A rapidly swelling crowd of interested hikers stood watching on the road. And it occurred to me then just how easy it would be to slip away, head for the hills, unnoticed, free.

'You all right, son?' the medic with the cases suddenly asked.

'Yeah, fine. Just done my wrist a bit.'

'Give it over.' He had a look, turned it left and right. 'Nowt broken. Probably just a sprain. You want something for the shock?'

'Like what?'

But he didn't answer, went back to bandaging my mother's throat. She was shaking now, complaining of the cold. 'Mrs Dickson,' he said loudly, 'we're going to put you in the ambulance now, OK?' He nodded to me, and together we lifted her to her feet. 'Can you walk, my love?' he asked. Then turned to me. 'She'll be fine. Don't fret.'

Shrimp got to me just as my mother had been seated in the ambulance wrapped in a thick blanket. 'OK, William,' he said. 'Care to come to the station and try and talk your way out of this little lot?'

My mother's teeth were chattering. It gutted me to see her like that. I gave her a small nod, but couldn't tell if she returned it or not.

In the cell, Carter stood, went to the yellowed meshed window and peered out. 'Lousy view.'

I yawned. It had been a long night. Four further interviews with Shrimp and Harris, two of those with other officers I didn't recognize. Thankfully, French had been on hand throughout, coming more or less the moment I'd made my one phone call. 'As in, doesn't compare with the magnificent vista from the twelfth floor of the Dallas Hilton, or wherever the hell you were staying, I suppose?'

He turned, a glint of mischief in his eyes. 'Now what makes you think I was staying in America?'

'You told me.'

'I lied.'

But before I could ask the obvious question, the cell door opened. French strode in looking drawn, tie askew. 'Room service,' he said. 'Time for Mr Dickson to check out.'

'They're letting me go?' I could see Shrimp leaning against the tiled passageway beyond the door, rubbing at his face. He didn't look as if he'd had much sleep, either.

'That number you gave me last night?' French replied over a stifled yawn. 'It came in for you, big-time.'

'Remind me.' I felt like I could sleep for a week, too.

'Your pal Danny Black.'

Danny – of course. After the second (or was it the third?) small-hours interview, French had pulled me to one side and insisted we have back-up to my story that Kris and Ian Bailey had been seen in the drinking club on the Sunday evening of the murder. Even though I'd been reluctant, I had no other choice but to give him Danny's secret phone number. He was, after all, my last hope. And to have a long-haired dope-dealing pyromaniac as your last hope is a sobering thing indeed.

'The police have spoken to him?' I asked, picturing Danny being rudely awakened by a group of coppers shining torches in his sleepy face.

French nodded. 'And he came good for you. Gave a statement down here at five this morning.'

'He was in the building?'

'And cursing you, my friend.'

'Christ. But he backed it up, my story?'

'Once I'd managed to get the duty solicitor out of the way and tell him Kris Jordan had put herself so spectacularly in the frame, yes. Still cursed you, though. Right until he left the place at half-six.'

'That's twice,' I said.

'What?'

'That he's saved my bacon. The bloke seems like an absolute pot-head, but I wouldn't be alive without him.'

French gestured to Carter. 'Spot of breakfast would do us all nicely at this point.'

'I'm buying,' Carter offered.

'Too bloody right you are.'

As we stepped back out into the passageway, Shrimp held up a hand, looked me square in the eye. 'If your mother's story rings true, then I guess you're off the hook, Dickson.'

'She's got no reason to lie.'

'Call me pedantic, but I'll have a squad checking every damn word of it. I'll have forensics checking photos of that knife-wound on Ian Bailey's body, for starters. You'd better pray it matches a Stanley knife, son. One inconsistency in Ma Dickson's fairy-tale, and you'll be back in here faster than you can say "convenient memory loss".'

'Wouldn't expect anything else of you, Inspector.'

'Don't get too cocky, son,' he warned. 'Still plenty of skeletons left in your closet, aren't there, eh?'

I felt French's hand on my shoulder, pushing me gently towards the end of the passage.

In the front office, French and Carter stood to one side as the bearded duty sergeant made me sign a series of forms saying I'd been afforded all my legal rights during my time in custody. Next came an inventory of possessions confiscated the previous night, followed finally by a black bag containing my meagre belongings.

'The hippy left this for you this morning,' he said, handing me a folded piece of A4. On it, Danny had scrawled, 'I guess you've done me a favour, Billy-boy, but I'm fucked if I can work out how. You owe me a night's kip and several days on the ale. Stay lucky, Dan.'

'Is my mother still here?' I asked, stooping to put my shoes on. They'd taken the laces out.

'Left about forty minutes back,' the duty sergeant replied. 'Some young lass dressed as a vampire abducted her in a flash motor.'

Karen. My, people had been working while I'd been locked up. I felt quite choked.

'Between you and me,' the duty sergeant continued, lowering his voice, 'DCI Shrimp's not entirely a happy bunny at the moment. Try keeping a slightly lower profile from now on, eh, son?'

I stood, took the coat from the bag, began buttoning it up. 'I'll try,' I replied. 'Thing is, you never know what's around the corner, do you?'

I think he smiled, but I couldn't be sure.

34

Breakfast was a quiet but thoroughly greasy affair. French knew a place that apparently made 'the best bacon sarnies in Lancashire'. To be honest, I was past making comparisons, but they were big, smelt wonderful, and tasted delicious.

Afterwards, French offered to drive us back to Edale, but Carter declined, sensing the portly solicitor needed sleep as his first priority. I thanked him profusely for all his efforts.

'Odd, isn't it?' he said as we stood outside the café. 'A week ago you were desperate to be some sort of psycho-murderer, but when Kris Jordan gave you the chance to confess to actually being one, you fought it tooth, nail and wooden knife-block.'

'Because I knew I'd never killed Ian,' I said.

'I think it was something else,' he replied over a massive yawn. 'I think you knew you never had it in you to kill anyone.'

'I could have killed her, though, couldn't I?'

He gave me a weary smile. 'William, with a knife-block? Why not just use the flippin' knives, for Christ's sake?' He gave Carter a quick hug. 'Good luck with it all.'

Carter nodded as French broke away and headed back towards the police station.

'Good luck with what?' I asked.

'The next phase.'

I started to ask, but he raised a hand. 'Wait and see, William. Wait and see.' He kept his hand raised, and moments later a black cab pulled up beside us.

We'd barely got past Hazel Grove before I surrendered to the wonders of overdue sleep.

Seven o'clock that evening and, after sleeping for most of the afternoon, I wandered downstairs to find quite a crowd seated in Carter's kitchen. The police and scenes-of-crimes squad had left at midday. Now the room played host to a far more appealing bunch: Carter, Karen, my mother, Uncle Trevor and my aunt Suzanne, all chatting over soup, rolls and wine. Indeed, they were making such a din that I could watch unobserved from the hallway for several moments.

My mother still looked pale. The hospital had removed the bandages and replaced them with thick cotton pads over her neck-wounds. A shudder ran through me as I remembered the last time I'd been in this room. I wondered how she was coping with the knowledge that she could have died in here.

Karen, of course, was predictably loud and expansive, arms flying as she retold some tale to the appreciative audience. The problem I had with Karen Carter was this: the more I watched her in these candid moments, the more I realized how much I could fall for her.

I couldn't look at Trevor and Suzanne without remembering happier times. Christmases in their house in Kent, my father and Trevor getting drunk and silly, wearing paper hats, linking arms and doing Greek bottle dances while we all laughed. So, so long ago.

And lastly Carter, half listening to his daughter's story, but his mind elsewhere, leaving his soup untouched, elbow on the table, stroking his chin, nodding distractedly when he heard the others laugh.

It was Carter who spotted me. 'William. You're up.'

We were back to the Western scene again – all silence as Mad Bill Dickson strolls into the saloon bar.

'Evening folks,' I offered.

There was a further two-beat pause before my mother spread her arms and gestured me close. We accidentally bumped heads as I tried not to brush against her neck dressings.

'You OK?' I whispered.

She nodded, beamed me the biggest watery-eyed grin I'd seen.

'Can you talk?'

'Few days,' she croaked. 'Still sore.'

I hugged her again, then turned to the others. 'I just want to thank you all. God only knows what hell I've put you through, but thank you.'

Uncle Trevor offered me a hand from over the table. 'Good to see you, champ.'

'Come here and give us a hug,' my aunt added.

'Me as well,' Karen added. 'I've never been hugged by a real-life kitchen hero before.'

After the hugging, I sat down to eat, listening to the small-talk but drawn to Carter, wondering what was going through his mind. After supper, I followed as he went to the living room while the others washed up.

'Thanks for letting me sleep,' I said. 'I needed it.'

He sat down in a deep armchair. 'How are you feeling?'

'Relieved, I think. Any news from the hospital?'

'Kris Jordan? French rang me at five. Said he'd heard a whisper she'd more or less confessed. Once the doctors have given her the all-clear, Shrimp and Harris will go to work on her.'

I tried to feel sorry for the girl, but couldn't. Just over twenty-four hours previously she'd held a knife to my mother's throat. 'She said Ian tried to rape her in the alley.'

'Whatever. It's up to her legal team now.'

'That's a bit cold,' I said, 'from you. The man who tries to unravel the psychological mysteries behind life's great dramas.'

'I'm an analyst, William. Not a saint.'

I sat. 'Trevor and Suzanne are here to take my mother home, aren't they?'

'Does it bother you?'

'Maybe. She bothers me more. The state she's in, you know.'

'They seem like good people. They'll keep an eye on her.'

Silence for a while.

'I guess,' I said eventually, 'that I'm off the hook, then?'

'How's that?'

'Now that I'm no longer a suspect for Ian's death. I mean, I can go back to the house, college. Mind you, I'm going to have to get a couple of new tenants pretty sharpish.' A brief image of sharing a flat with Danny Black popped into my mind. Dan and I, out burning furniture on Sunday mornings, talking shit and getting wrecked . . . no, maybe not the wisest choice.

'You never asked me,' Carter said, interrupting my thoughts.

'Asked you what?'

'Where I've been these last few days.'

'Dr Carter, would you be so kind as to tell the court where you've been these last few days?'

'Tree hunting.' That pulled me up. 'Tree hunting in Tilbury.'

My good mood evaporated fast. 'Tilbury?'

'Looking for your tree, William. And Little Bill's. Your screaming tree. And you want to know something else?'

'Not really.'

'I found it.'

I preferred to think it was sleeping so much during the day, rather than Carter's announcement, that meant I stayed awake most of the night. After coming back from a trip to the pub with Karen, I showered and got straight back into my clothes. My mother had optimistically laid out some pyjamas by the sofa-bed in the lounge (Trevor and Susan were sleeping in the other spare room that night), but they remained untouched. Instead I sat in Carter's easy-chair, fighting a growing sense of unease that still hadn't abated come dawn.

He'd found my tree.

After breakfast, we all said our goodbyes. More hugging as I helped Trevor ease my mother into the back seat of his car and watched them set out for Maidstone. I'd miss her, I knew that. She knew it too, and had held me especially tight before we parted. I told her I'd ring her when it was over.

A short time after, it was Carter's and my turn to leave. Karen turned up to wave us off, sidling up to me as her father put our luggage in the boot.

'You nervous?' she asked. The punky look was less pronounced today, the eyes softer – more Cleopatra than Dawn of the Dead.

'You know what he wants to do?'

She nodded. 'He's told me bits. Spot of tree-climbing in Essex, isn't it?'

I took a deep breath, felt my ribs shudder slightly in the

cold. 'There's this great expression,' I said. 'I read it once, always remembered it: "I'm as nervous as a long-tailed cat in a room full of rocking-chairs".'

'Know what?' she said, giving me a quick peck on the cheek. 'I'm going to remember that for a while, too.'

'William, you ready?' Carter asked, standing by the driver's door.

'No,' I mumbled.

''Course he is!' Karen shouted for me. 'Off you go. Have fun.'

'Fun?'

'Why not?'

And for the life of me, looking into her smiling face that bright December morning, I couldn't think of a single reason.

The journey dragged. We stopped for fuel at a service station, ran the gastronomic gauntlet of a lunch that could possibly have bankrupted and poisoned the average family in one go. Then we soldiered on, moving south in heavy rain. With each passing mile I began to feel more agitated.

'You OK?' Carter asked.

'Fine,' I replied, irritated. 'And please, stop asking me. Every ten minutes you ask me if I'm OK. I feel like I'm being scrutinized.'

'So, obviously you're not OK, then.'

Touché. 'Not about being asked all the time, no.'

'Heard anything from Little Bill?'

'Like what? He's going to start whistling "There's no place like home" the moment we cross the Essex border?'

Carter briefly glanced across. 'Why the attitude?'

'Because this is stupid, that's why. A two-hundred-mile trip to climb up a sodding tree.'

'Why agree to come, then?'

'Can we just drop it, please? And if you intend asking me in the next twenty miles if I'm bloody OK, then let me save you the bother. I'm bored stupid of all this. That OK enough for you?'

Carter smiled, eyes focused on the wet road, fingers lightly drumming the wheel. 'OK, Little Bill,' he said. 'Loud and clear.'

'Fuck off.'

'Feisty little chap, aren't we?'

I didn't rise to it, didn't have the stamina or the energy.

'Tell me,' I said as we passed the Milton Keynes exit on the M1. 'If this Little Bill is so intent on killing me, why is he allowing all this to happen? Surely he wouldn't want us to be travelling back to Tilbury again? Why doesn't he simply make me grab the wheel and steer us straight into the central reservation?'

'How do you feel, William?'

'OK.' Through clenched teeth.

'Tired?'

'Very.'

Carter nodded. 'Because he's tired, William. Little Bill must be utterly shagged by now. Keeping up the pretence of a fantasy life for you has drained him. Making you believe the things you did was a massive psychological undertaking. Huge. He can't keep up that kind of thing indefinitely. Your subconscious is most probably shattered. Two weeks ago he had more of a handle on it. But then French and I began punching holes in it. Even better, you yourself began to question things. His first reaction was to try and end it for you both again.'

'By pushing me under a bus?'

'Absolutely. Then, when that didn't work, I suspect he took some kind of stock. Realized that perhaps you were the key to this after all. And whatever secret he's so carefully guarding up there in his tree, he now wonders if it's worth giving up, coming down for. William, he's letting you go, letting you find out for yourself. Mind you . . .' He tailed off, smiling.

'What?'

'It's fun seeing him come to life a little the nearer we get to Tilbury.'

Christ, the guy was presumptuous! 'What the fuck do you mean by that?'

'Precisely that, William. Precisely, that.'

'Arsehole!'

'You too, Little Bill.'

* * *

Forty minutes later: 'So, William. Care to tell me what you know about yourself to date?'

I sighed. 'The full story?'

'Starting from the Saturday afternoon, the day of the woods murders.'

'But surely you know it better than I do? That's the whole miserable point of this. Everyone else has a far better picture of me than I do myself.'

'Indulge me. I've worked hard for you.'

The rain had eased, but still the spray from heavy lorries made driving like trying to slice through a fine mist. My mind felt the same, as I tried marshalling my thoughts, realizing it was the first time I'd actually tried to piece together the fractured picture of my life as a complete whole.

'OK,' I said eventually. 'I left the house with Fat Norris sometime after four. Apparently, we met up with Alan Cooper somewhere along the way.'

'You remember where, how?'

'No.'

'Go on.'

We switched into the fast lane, Carter touching eighty as conditions improved a little. 'We went into the woods. Then something happened there. Fat and Alan were . . .' I found myself struggling to say the word, '. . . killed. Supposedly by Dave Atkins and someone else. And although Atkins may have initially admitted to being in the woods, the identity of the other guy was never known.'

'Good,' Carter encouraged. 'Now, why on earth would Atkins admit to such a thing?'

I struggled for a second to find the connection, finally recalling the conversation with my father in Armley's crowded visiting room. Jesus, that seemed like a very long time ago. 'Because . . . that's right, he was arrested for killing Fat's Mum . . .'

'Name?'

'Margot. Margot Norris. He got drunk, apparently, and killed her on Christmas Eve.'

'Why?'

'Shit, hang on.' The questions were coming too fast. I needed time to focus, override the old memories, apply the newer ones. 'Because she suspected him of being one of the killers in the woods. She was just as drunk as he was. Told my mum and dad about her suspicions. She'd found a porn mag with pictures of children. Anyway, despite my parents' protests, she went back to confront him later that night. He killed her.'

'Fair enough. So why did he offer police a snippet of what went on in the woods?'

It was getting easier, the replies coming virtually before he'd finished asking the questions. 'In order to shave time from a possible life sentence for the murder of Margot Norris. Mum and Dad had been to the police, told them about what she'd said, how Margot suspected he'd been in the woods that afternoon. The police applied some pressure –'

'They're good at that, aren't they?'

'Very.'

'Imagine how they would have leant on him if they thought he was caught up in child murders?'

'He breaks down,' I went on. 'Admits he was there, but says he wasn't the killer. The police already know there were two men there from the sets of footprints. Atkins sees his chance and says he's prepared to trade the name of the other man in order to reduce his own sentence by a few years.'

'And did he?'

'No. His solicitor stepped in when police discovered I was in no fit state to identify him. Atkins then quickly refuted all previous allegations and confessions and was only tried for the murder of Margot Norris.'

'I'm impressed, William.' We switched back into the middle lane. 'And after the trial?'

'I supposedly had trouble adjusting to normal school life. Still wouldn't say a word about what had happened in the woods. I was disruptive, eventually went to Chetwins in Kent when I was thirteen. Uncle Trevor and Auntie Suzanne stepped in, paid my fees, let Mum, Dad and Nicola live in the oast-house for free.'

'And there you met . . . ?' Carter prompted.

'John Tremaine, apparently. A psychologist assigned to the school. He took me under his wing. Wanted to help me remember what had happened.'

'Why?'

'Because the case was still under investigation?'

'Sort of,' Carter replied. 'It was listed as unsolved. What concerned Tremaine more were your behavioural problems. He knew your history, listened to your stubborn denial of events that afternoon, thought that by unlocking your traumatized memory it would cause a positive shift in your sociological problems.'

A question emerged. 'At that stage,' I asked, 'did I know Cooper was with us in the woods?'

'Sure. You knew he died, too. It was just how he died that you wouldn't divulge. You had memories of the three of you arriving, beginning to play, then nothing until the police finally managed to coax you back down from the tree. Classic traumatic amnesia – as if three hours of your life had simply disappeared.'

'What about Cooper's parents? How did they cope with all of this?'

'He lived with his aunt,' Carter replied. 'No parents. They'd died in a car-crash four years earlier.'

I felt a sudden pang of sadness for the friend I'd completely forgotten. 'What was he like?'

'Like?'

'What did he look like? There must have been pictures in the paper. You haven't showed me any of them.'

'Didn't think there was any need. Truth is, William, young Alan Cooper looked pretty much like the boy you described saving at Chetwins. Small, blond-haired, frail.'

'But he was a friend of Fat and mine?'

'Same class, same local school. The three of you hung out together. Inseparable, according to the testimonies of shocked teachers that appeared in the papers.'

I frowned, confused. 'Then how come I can remember so much about Fat Norris, yet so little about Alan?'

Carter shot me a brief look. 'When was the last time you went to the toilet?'

'Sorry?'

'The last time you used the loo?'

What did this have to do with anything? 'Before we left.'

'That was a piss, though, wasn't it?'

What the hell was he on about?

'What I'm asking, William, is when was the last time you had a proper bowel movement?'

'Jesus, I don't know.'

'Try to remember.'

'Yesterday,' I answered, thrown. 'Probably.'

'My guess is, you haven't had a bowel motion for days. Chances are, you're probably the most constipated person on the M1 right now.'

'Weren't we talking about Alan Cooper?' I asked, eyes fixed on the man at the wheel.

'In a way. We were talking about why you couldn't remember him as well as you did Edward Norris.'

'And that's relevant to the last time I had a shit, is it?'

'Sure,' Carter replied. 'The two are linked, William. Psychologists and doctors have known for years that psychological problems often have physical symptoms. Some holistic healing therapies base their whole philosophies on the notion.'

'Sounds like a load of old crap to me.'

A small smile from the good doctor. 'Your body withholds because your mind withholds, William.'

'And this is down to Bill again, I suppose?' I said, unable to quell the sarcasm.

'Bill – your subconscious. They're one and the same. We invented Bill in order to give it a platform to be heard. And you have heard him, haven't you, William?'

I didn't want to open that particular box again. Sure I'd heard something, but couldn't it as easily have been a real child giggling or screaming somewhere close by? Even at that moment, the eleventh hour of my madness, I found it easier, safer, to deny what possibly scared me the most. I asked another question instead. 'I'm withholding something about Alan Cooper?'

Carter nodded. 'Cooper's vital. He was there, yet even now you have no memory of it. Edward Norris you can recall, but not Alan Cooper. I think perhaps there's a part of you that blames yourself in some way. It fits the fantasy Bill created, the one where you save him from the junior Atkins figure.'

We sat in silence for another three miles.

'Six days ago,' I finally said.

'What?'

'The last time I had a crap.'

'You see? Progress.'

'Mummy was always on at me to use the toilet. You know, twenty minutes after meals and suchlike. I'd have to sit there reading a Jack and Jill book or something, just waiting to crap.'

'William?'

'What?'

'You just called her "Mummy".'

'I did?'

'You did.'

'Christ.'

'It's a good sign, William.' Carter eased back into the fast lane, gunned the throttle and shot us back up to eighty-five. 'I think that, after eleven years of screaming, little Bill Dickson's finally beginning to find his voice at last.'

35

Carter had booked us in to a large hotel just outside Southend, the type that sales reps tend to frequent. After a five-hour journey, all I wanted to do was go to my room, shower and sleep. Carter, however, had other plans.

'See you in the bar in about an hour,' he said as he let himself into the adjoining room.

'To be honest, I'd be pretty crap company tonight.' Hadn't we spent enough time together that day? We'd already eaten; all I wanted now was space and a bed.

'Someone will be joining us.'

Dr Richard Carter and his damn surprises.

An hour and a quarter later, I made my way back down to the hotel bar. A few suits sat around, reading papers or talking quietly; two bar-staff were giggling as they attempted to hang a few pitiful Christmas decorations around the overly large room. They'd have needed at least another three hundred metres of tinsel to make the slightest impact. I thought briefly of the hikers' pub in Edale, resplendent in all its Christmas finery, the eager-Santa landlord, the log fire, Christmas Greats playing on a loop-tape behind the bar. And, of course, Karen. I thought about her too, wondered if she'd be sitting at 'our' table. On her own, wondering about me? Or with a group of her mates, heaving a sigh of relief that finally the lad with the odd ideas, scars and overly attentive mother had finally gone?

Someone was waving to me from the far corner. Carter. No turning back. I walked over, trying to make out the other figure with his back to me. A few steps from the table, he turned, looked at me, a slight trace of fear in his eyes.

'William,' Carter said, introducing the mysterious guest. 'This is Dr John Tremaine.'

The older man smiled, nervously offered a hand, which I shook. 'Hello, William. I guess this is therapy for me, too. Meeting the client who tried to kill me.'

I tried hard to dig up a memory of the man, but could find nothing save the fleeting glimpse at a photo that Carter had shown me months earlier. A man and his wife, standing with my mother and me in a back garden. The same man I'd automatically assumed was Bob Squires, landlord of the local pub. Dead, I'd assumed, but now clearly not so. Here he was, risen, and placed in a proper context at last – Dr John Tremaine, early fifties, a little overweight, in a faded tweed suit. He had the kind of face that you couldn't help but take a liking to, as if you couldn't ever imagine the man getting angry over anything. And yet, if others were to be believed, the last time I'd met him, I'd nearly slain him.

'Please,' he said. 'Sit down.'

I sat. Took a sip of the squash Carter had already bought for me. 'It's all a bit of a shock for me,' I mumbled, looking across, hoping that either Carter or Tremaine would leap in and fill the awkward silence. They didn't.

'And . . . and I'm sorry about the . . . you know, the strangling thing.'

Tremaine nodded.

'And all the damage to your house – I mean, what with all the windows and mess when I jumped out.' I was babbling, knew it. Wanted to shut up, but somehow the mouth just kept on pumping out the gibberish. 'If there's any way I can repay you for the damage –'

Tremaine put his hand on mine. 'You're about to, William.'

'What?'

'You've haunted my nightmares for the last five months. I can't count the times I've woken up sweating and terrified, still feeling your hands around my throat . . .'

'Like I say, I'm really sorry about all that. I only found out about it when Dr Carter –'

'Do it now.'

'What?'

'Put your hands round my throat.' He leant towards me, slipped his jacket off his shoulders a fraction.

This was crazy. I shot a confused look at Carter, who merely raised his eyebrows and nodded.

'Please,' Tremaine whispered, eyes tightly shut. 'Just for a moment or two.'

'I'm not sure I . . .'

'Do as he says, William,' Carter instructed. 'Put your hands round his throat.'

'But –'

'Just do it.'

So I did, hating the feel of his shaking throat, the dry skin under my fingers. But for at least five seconds I put my hands around John Tremaine's throat.

After, he opened his eyes and eased his jacket back on.

'You OK?' I asked, hoping none of the customers or staff had seen.

'Perfectly,' Tremaine replied. 'Sometimes the only way to banish fears is to relive them.'

We talked until the bar closed, Tremaine more or less confirming everything that Carter had told me about my life and himself in the years before my coma. It was surreal to look at the man as he described intensely personal events, but still to have no memory of him whatsoever. Throughout, I kept expecting a flash of recognition – a Eureka! moment – when I would suddenly snap my fingers, and say 'Yes, I do recognize you now.' But it never happened. Tremaine left the hotel that night just as much a stranger as when I'd first spotted him. He had brought photos to show me of him and me together, but they could have featured look-alikes as far as I was concerned.

Just as peculiar was the change in Carter that night, the stillness in him. He hung on all of Tremaine's words, nodded, ingested, but rarely contributed. When he did say something, it was to question a theory, learn something from an older psychoanalyst whom he still clearly respected. Strange to see a man I'd come to regard as something of an unflappable mentor now morphing into attentive note-taking student.

I watched from the lifts as they said their goodbyes in the lobby. After, as we made our way back up to our rooms, I asked Carter what he most liked about Tremaine.

'He never took any unnecessary risks,' he replied. 'Apart from you.'

'But you take them all the time, surely?'

'And he's the only one who's never criticized me for doing it.'

The lift doors opened and we walked to our rooms.

'See you in the morning, then,' Carter said over a yawn. 'Sleep well. Big day ahead.'

'How can you be sure I won't run from here the moment you go inside?'

'I can't. Goodnight.'

With that, he was gone.

36

Well, here we are. This is where it ends, is it? A December Wednesday, back in Tilbury – could be the first line of the William Dickson Blues, couldn't it? Featuring Screamin' Lil'-Bill on sax and paranoid vocals. Know what? Yesterday, in Carter's car, I heard about the only thing the prick's got right so far – I am tired, William. Dead beat. Sure, I've fussed about with the old grey matter a tad but, as I explained, only to save you from the grislier stuff. It surprises me that you still haven't made the connection: the ease with which we walloped that Jordan creature – there's not many who could do that, William. Most folks would have given in, done whatever the daft bitch wanted, but not us. We fought back as only real killers can. See, all the proof you ever needed was staring you in the face as that fucking lunatic slumped to the floor. Sorry about the wrist, though. It'll get better. Just like us.

And now to today – this poxy little exercise. I'm going to let it happen because you seem so utterly in Carter's grip. Maybe the only way to teach you is to let you off the leash, see things for yourself, see him for the charlatan he is. I mean, come on, last night's little 'stunt'. The Tremaine surprise. How in God's name do we know it actually was the man, eh? I had a good look at him, and he didn't ring any bells with me. Just some fluffy old granddad from central casting. One nice moment, though. Sliding our hands round the old fool's neck. I hope Carter paid his stooge a good whack – chances are he never knew how close to death he really came. This memory thing comes with one or two drawbacks. Like, once it starts flooding back, once I set the reels rolling, there's very little I can do to stop it. Roll up! Roll up! Showing today at the Dickson Memory Cinema – The Tilbury Woods Murders. Please note that children were harmed during the making of this movie . . .

Wednesday 8 December. Midday.

Dr Richard Carter and I find ourselves standing outside the former Tilbury home of the Dickson family. It's a light, clear day, mild for the time of year. And quiet.

'Feels strange?' Carter asked.

I nodded, staring at the house. I said, 'It's a different colour. Someone's painted it.'

Carter glanced at the sky-blue semi. 'A lot can happen in twelve years.'

'Who lives there now?'

'No idea. Want to knock?'

'Not really.'

'Why not?'

'Because I don't.'

'You hear that?'

'What?'

'You, just now, your response.'

I sighed. 'What about it?'

'Kind of thing a seven-year-old would say.'

Shit, it was going to be a long day if he kept this up. If I felt annoyed, Carter cited it as proof that Little Bill powered me, which was guaranteed to annoy me and make me behave even more childishly.

'You feel anything?' he asked.

'Stupid. Embarrassed. Worried.' Pissed off, too.

'Worried about what?'

'That someone's going to come running out and ask what the hell we're doing loitering outside their house, for starters.'

'What would you do if they did?'

'You don't get it, do you? This is doing nothing for me.'

'Try tuning in.'

'To what?'

'You know exactly what I mean.'

I looked around the silent street, tried to imagine the same scene on a summer Saturday afternoon twelve years previously, listening for ghosts of children playing on bikes, fathers washing cars, mothers chatting. I tried to summon the neighbours of my memory, but there was nothing. 'Maybe it's too long ago,' I said. 'I feel blocked. Perhaps we should have tried this in August. The weather's not right, it doesn't feel the same. It's too quiet, the houses are different colours; none of it's like it should be.'

Carter nodded, sat on the low brick wall outside the front of my old home. He thrust both hands deep into his greatcoat pockets. 'William, we're never going to be able to re-create the exact same Saturday. And if we wait till August, then chances are the moment won't be right. We have to strike now, while you're winning.'

'I'm winning?'

'Sure. The logical side of your mind is getting back on top, questioning certain things and dismissing others. We've got to play the advantage. Please, just try and shut everything off, tune in at some basic level.'

He stood, briefly opened his coat and pulled out a slim black leather document-holder. Inside was a photocopied map marked in yellow highlighter. 'This, as far as I can tell, is the route you took to the park that day. You were eventually able to give most of these details to the police, but very little else.'

'And we're going to follow it, right? How unbelievably exciting.'

'Spot of irritation creeping in?'

'Boredom.'

'Ah.'

'Sometimes you're so bloody smug, you know that?'

'Yes, Bill, I do.'

'For fuck's sake, will you shut up with all the Little Bill crap?'

'Lot of language for a little boy. Mummy ever tell you she'd wash that filthy mouth of yours out with soap and water?'

'Christ's sakes, listen to you. Isn't it me who's supposed to be the mad one?'

'Or Daddy? Did he ever hold your head over the sink, ram that hard frothing soap bar into your mouth? Did he do that, Bill? Did he?'

'You get a kick out of this?'

'You haven't answered my question.'

'I'm going to walk back to the car if you go on like this.'

'Your choice.' He watched me waiting. 'Well, Bill, go back if you want to. Me, I'm going this way. Coming?'

How do you describe a moment that seems to last for an eternity?

*   *   *

Halfway down the third road on the route, Carter stopped. I wondered if he'd left the keys back in his car or something.

'What now?' I asked. 'Got the map the wrong way up?'

He pointed to the house on my left. 'Recognize it?'

I stared, bewildered. Just an ordinary semi, the same as hundreds of others nearby. 'Am I supposed to?'

Carter stood quite still. 'Shut your eyes for a minute. Think back.'

I went with it.

'You stopped here that afternoon. Chances are a woman would have answered the door.'

A flash of something . . .

'You and Edward Norris called for someone else at this house.'

A face. There! I saw the woman. The shock of it jolted me. I opened my eyes.

'Shut them!' Carter barked.

I closed them once more, wanting to sit, and feeling warm – suddenly far too hot in my coat. Was that sun on my face?

'You see him now, William?'

I gasped as from behind the smiling woman a smaller figure emerged. Frail, sandy-haired, looking nervously about him. He was wearing a small white vest and shorts, torn plimsolls.

Alan Cooper.

'This is too much!' I shrieked, opening my eyes. 'We've got to go now. My mind's fucked, I'm seeing things!'

'Remembering things,' Carter said.

It didn't matter that I had both eyes open, the landscape had changed. It was summer now, Carter fading away, trees shrinking, houses peeling back to their original brickwork.

'Take me back, now!' I yelled.

'Tell me what you see, William.'

To my utter horror, the little figure now walked warily towards me, holding out a hand.

'Jesus! He's going to touch me!' I said. 'Get him the fuck away from me!'

Carter's voice, hard in my ear. 'Then touch him, William. He can't hurt you, he *is* you – a memory, a part of you that you lost many years ago. He is Alan Cooper as you remember him.'

'No!' I moaned. 'Not Alan. Not him. He wasn't there that day.'

I screwed shut my eyes as tightly as possible, willing the horror away. I counted to five in my mind, then opened them – but he was still there, head cocked slightly to one side, amused at the shaking adult before him.

'Get away!' I screamed.

He withdrew his hand, face confused, changing, beginning to frown.

'Leave me alone! You're not me! I can't help you. I'm sorry, but I can't. I don't want you!'

The little face fell. For a moment I thought he was about to cry. Suddenly there was a commotion behind. A car passed by, the summer scene fell away, and was replaced in an instant by a winter Wednesday.

I let out a deep breath. Then another. 'This is seriously fucking weird,' I said, feeling myself begin to topple sideways.

Carter caught me, sat me on a low wall. 'Just rest.' I felt his hand gently rub my shoulders. 'Lower your head. Let the blood get to it.'

I slumped forward. 'This is . . .' But I couldn't find the words.

'Just rest.'

A few minutes later Carter helped me back to my feet, and we began slowly tracing the route again. I walked by his side in confused silence, unable to get the image of that little boy out of my head. The reality of him – solid – as if he would have bumped right into me if he'd kept on walking.

Alan Cooper, undeniably.

Half a mile later we'd reached the high street and were sitting on a bench outside a large carpet shop, its windows plastered with gaudy posters announcing buy-now pay-later Christmas deals. A few shoppers browsed round the small parade; women pushed well-wrapped babies in creaking buggies. It was windier now, colder.

Carter didn't say anything, simply waited for me to begin.

Eventually, I asked, 'How can it happen like that – be so real?'

'The hallucinations? Because they're still completely fresh in your memory.'

'I don't get it.'

'Try to understand that the memory you have of collecting Alan Cooper twelve years ago is still probably only four hours old, deactivated the moment you began screaming yourself hoarse in that tree. It's simply been lying dormant, like a cassette that hasn't been played. We stand outside the house, and suddenly it all comes back, pristine, immaculate, as fresh as when it happened.'

'There's more of these to come, aren't there?'

'Yes, William. I'm afraid there are.'

I watched a lad about my age come out of a newsagent's carrying a newspaper and some fags. Not a care in the bloody world. 'Why me?' I mumbled.

'What you have to try and understand is that your subconscious is one of the most remarkable I've ever encountered. Unbelievably powerful. Most clients I've had will only experience a partially suppressed memory – just a smell, perhaps, or a fragment of conversation. But with you . . . well, you get the whole thing.'

'Lucky me.'

'Thousands of people hallucinate every day. It's not always that you can't trust your eyes, rather that you can't rely on your brain to interpret the truth from them. It seems so real, because to all intents and purposes it is real. Hence your memories are real, too; fresh, bursting to be revealed.'

'So why is it winter now? Why can't I feel the sun on my face any more, see the kids, hear dogs barking?'

'Because you've never denied that you came this way to the park. But you've always denied stopping at Alan Cooper's house.'

'That simple, huh?'

'Trust me, William. I'm an expert.' He unzipped the leather folder, brought out the map again. 'Recognize this place?' he asked, pointing at the carpet shop.

I looked it over. 'No.'

'It went up about four years ago.'

'You've been doing your homework.'

'An afternoon with the town-planners, that's all.'

'And there was me thinking you were living it up in America.'

'Some chance,' Carter replied. 'Anyway, this place replaced a row of three small shops. A grocer's, baker's, and –'

'A sweet-shop,' I heard myself saying.

'Go on.'

'Godwin's. We used to stop for sweets there. Fat Norris always had some cash. We'd fill up with pop, crisps, chocolate, and then go on to the park.' I looked at the bleakly unimpressive glass-fronted carpet shop. 'Mr Godwin went out of business, did he?'

'Couldn't compete with the big chains,' Carter replied.

'Shame,' I replied. 'Nice old guy –'

The black! Rearing up out of nowhere – up, up, further towards me, extending its hand, feeling for a thrashing ankle as I scream, and scream, and scream . . .

'William, are you all right?' Carter's face, inches from mine. 'Are you OK?'

'I . . . just . . .'

'What?' he asked urgently.

'Just felt something.'

'Felt what, William?'

I looked into Carter's eyes, knew at some base instinctive level that I didn't have much time. 'You said you'd found the tree.'

'I did.'

'Take me there,' I urged. 'Now.'

37

We continued up the high street, moving quickly now, Carter hurrying to catch up with me, having stopped to consult his map once more. I didn't wait for him, already knowing – sensing – the way, every step confirming I was headed in the right direction, that in a matter of minutes I'd be back in the park with the dark woods at its border, the railway line running parallel beyond.

I recrossed the road, running now, and turning left into an avenue that I already knew led to a small alley between the houses, and into the wide open playing fields beyond. What greeted me there, however, was totally unexpected. No straight avenue, just a thin snaking road. No familiar small semis, instead a bizarre collection of brand-new detached homes, a nightmare testimony to some corporate architect's vision of the perfect housing development.

Everything I remembered had gone. In an instant I'd gone from feeling certain to feeling quite lost.

'Wait!' Carter shouted from behind.

'The park?' I asked as he drew level. 'Where's the alley to the park?'

'There is no park. Not any more.' He pointed to a large sign up ahead.

Welcome to Butterlands Village.
A magnificent development of over 600 brand-new
three-, four- and five-bedroom luxury homes.
Phase Four homes available shortly.
Visit our site sales office and luxury show-homes
for more information.

I read it through twice, trying to make some sense of it. 'The park's gone?'

'Not gone, as such. You're standing in it now.'

'What?'

'The council sold the land to the developer two years ago.'

'But the swings, slides . . . ?' I couldn't take it in.

'All developed,' Carter said. 'There're more than four hundred of these brick boxes that have been built so far. Eventually they'll reach almost to the railway line.'

'The woods?' I said. 'The tree? You said you'd found my tree?'

He nodded. 'Follow me,' he said. 'And for Christ's sake don't go running off again. This place is a maze of identical little avenues, alleys and cul-de-sacs. You get lost in here, and it could be the New Year before the search party finds you.'

'Show me,' I said. 'Quickly.'

He reached back into the leather folder and this time pulled out a larger map. 'Site plan,' he explained, looking round and taking his bearings, his finger tracing the highlighted path. 'It's this way.'

We walked briskly, side by side, past numerous new homes of shining yellow brick. Once or twice I caught sight of figures within, vacuuming or watching the television, oblivious to the two strangers striding purposefully by.

'When I first found this place I was devastated,' Carter quickly explained. 'I'd managed to speak to a Superintendent Shaw at Southend police station, who had access to the original unsolved crime file. When I told him why I wanted to find the tree, he eventually let me see photographs of the crime scene. I had one copied, then headed here, to find this,' he flung his arms out wide, 'a rabbit warren of architectural lethargy obliterating the park and the woods.'

'Somehow I don't think that's how the brochure would have put it.'

'I went to the site office, eventually got permission for a complete site plan.'

He turned left, and we headed down another identical-looking road. 'They must have figured me for a potential customer, because they also faxed their head office and had a copy of the original land-use plan sent over for me.'

We crossed the road, walked down a small alley with tall, freshly creosoted fences on either side, funnelling us into another cul-de-sac. Another alley followed, bringing us to yet another snaking road. Carter was right, losing yourself would have been all too easy. Each road appeared to be a replica of the last, with no shops, bus stops, or other distinguishing features.

'They gave me some time alone with the plans in one of the show-homes,' Carter continued at my shoulder. 'From the police photograph and the two maps, I was able to pinpoint the approximate position of the tree. Smack in the middle of the latest phase of building – Phase Four.'

I looked up from the pavement, suddenly aware that the landscape had changed. The road was running out, giving way to a deeply rutted muddy track leading to a locked metal fence beyond. Inside its meshed perimeter, I could see diggers and various construction vehicles. Surrounding them were the homes – two dozen or more, all in various stages of readiness. Some had roofs, others merely skeletal timber joists. A few were complete with window frames, while others boasted black empty holes like sockets on an ancient skull. The ground below was all shades of brown, an undulating sea of hard, cold mud.

On the fence, a further sign.

Butterlands Village – Phase Four.
A development of 130 four-bedroom homes,
to be completed in May 1982.
Visit our site sales office or show-home
to reserve your luxury home now!

'Welcome to the woods, William,' Carter said, reaching into the leather folder and pulling out a key. Tongue resting between his front teeth, he set about the large gate padlock.

'They gave you a key as well?'

'The developers? Good heavens, no.' Carter smiled, turning the lock, pulling the padlock to one side. 'A call from Superintendent Shaw at Southend to the building contractor got me this. He's as keen as everybody else to put an end to it, William.'

'Put an end to it?'

Carter swung open the rusting gate. 'To see if you can remember who the other attacker was,' he said, gesturing me by with an elaborate flourish. 'After you.'

'Where is everybody? Lunch-break?'

'The builders aren't working this week. That's one of the reasons why today had to be the day.'

I took a few hesitant steps into the site, ankles turning on the uneven ground. Carter closed the gate and walked briskly by. 'This way.'

A light pounding began in my head, a warning, a ripple along my scar. In minutes, I knew I would be in the grip of another blinding headache. I stopped, reached into my pocket, took out and dry-swallowed three Paracetamol before heading after Carter.

'This used to be the woods?' I said. The place looked raped, eaten by diggers.

'The railway line's about a hundred yards in front. By the time they finish this lot, the last houses will be less than forty feet from prying commuters.'

'What did they do with the trees?' I asked as we slipped into a windswept alley between two partially built houses.

He stopped midway along, turned to me. 'Here's the thing that lifted my spirits, William.' He had an unusual touch of excitement in his normally placid voice. 'The sales reps kept going on about their wonderful Phase Four, saying how different it was going to be from all the others. Landscaped, they kept telling me, with specially selected established trees.'

I stared breathlessly into his weathered face, tried to stop myself from pushing past. 'They kept some of them?'

'Only the most characterful, the ones they felt would appeal to the discerning new home-buyer.'

The pounding in my head grew. 'They kept mine.'

He reached back into the folder, quickly drew out a black-and-white photo, gave it to me. 'From the police at Southend.'

And there it was, flat, grey, diminished, two-dimensional, but unmistakably my tree. The shape as suddenly familiar as my own face, as if I'd spent a lifetime studying it, marvelling at the size, textures, weight; watching the impact of the seasons on its ageing bark. I knew this shape so well, so intimately – a lifelong déjà-vu.

'That's it,' I said quietly. 'That's my tree.'

Carter stepped back, took my arm, led me slowly out of the alley. 'No, William,' he said, pointing to the vast gnarled structure that awaited me there. It was the same shape as the photo in my shaking hands, but this one was alive, coloured, vivid in three terrifying dimensions. 'This is your tree.'

It stood on a roped-off island, surrounded by a sea of rutted, churned mud, bordered by a further cul-de-sac of a dozen half-completed houses.

Its bare branches seemed to reach out longingly, almost as if the old oak wanted desperately to be plucked from this strange place and set down in leafy woodlands once more. Strangely, my headache began to recede the longer I looked at it. A feeling of pity arose from somewhere, as if on some subconscious level I could understand its loneliness, and perhaps it could sense mine. Crazy thoughts flew in at all angles: how similar we were, two old friends reunited, both out of place, surrounded by half-built dreams and ideals, both victim to that same dreadful Saturday.

'I want to touch it,' I said.

Carter nodded, watching as I made my way over, stumbling in deep tyre-ruts, before crouching under the rope, then walking towards the vast trunk.

I stopped, looked down at the sprawling root system. 'This is where Fat fell,' I said.

'What do you feel now, William?' Carter asked behind me.

'Weird. Really weird. It's an oak. I've always loathed them.'

'It was the cedar avenue for you at Chetwins, eh?'

'Yeah,' I quietly replied. 'Always the cedars for me.' I stretched out a cautious hand towards the cold grey bark. My fingers began shaking as they inched towards the time-riven wood.

'William, you OK?'

'Sure I just need to . . . is it getting dark?'

'Just a passing cloud.'

'The breeze,' I said. 'It feels warmer.'

'Touch the tree, William.'

'It's hot.' I took off my coat, then took two deep breaths before finally touching the twisted surface of the huge trunk.

'Anything?' Carter asked.

'Nothing. Just an old tree, isn't it? Just me touching an old tree.'

'Try again. Both hands this time.'

I did as he asked, but still no memories came. I waited a while, searching for Cooper, an image of Fat Norris and myself, perhaps, anything to help me back into the woods. 'He's not here. Cooper's gone,' I said, opening my eyes and turning from the trunk.

So too had Carter. Together with the houses, diggers, the oceans of dried mud. All replaced by trees.

'Dick!' I cried out. 'Dr Carter!'

No answer.

Then to my left, they came.

Three young boys in shorts and vests, laughing, but not seeing me. Walking past, to wait by the tree.

And suddenly, I knew exactly who they waited for.

38

It had to be a secret. Had to.

I knew it was wrong, but that was half the fun of it. The thrill. Like stealing sweets from Godwin's shop. Wrong, but wild. Besides, Fat Norris had told me he'd done it before, even shown me the pound note as proof. A pound, just for doing that?

But it had to be a secret.

It was during school dinnertime when Fat had taken me to one side and whispered what he'd done that previous Saturday, how easily I could be involved the next time. At first, I'd said no. Straight off – no. But in the days after, alone, I began thinking about it, weighing it up in the gap between bed and sleep. All the time thinking of the money, the dare, the risk. Easy money, really. Money I'd have to hide from Mummy and Daddy, but money none the less.

Three days later, I spoke to Fat after school, asked a little more, tried not to appear too eager for details, when it must have been obvious I was already hooked.

'Not just you, though,' Fat had said, which took me back a little. 'He wants another one.'

'Someone else?'

'Besides us two.'

'Why?'

'Because he's a filthy fucker, stupid.' Said so simply, so finally. Words I didn't dare say aloud, yet slipped from Fat's lips as casually as he blinked and breathed. 'Any ideas?'

I pondered the problem, tried to imagine who else would do it. 'And we still get a quid each?'

Fat nodded.

'I don't know,' I said, thinking hard.

'What about Cooper?' he asked, in a way that made me momentarily suspect he'd weighed the whole situation beforehand. As if Alan Cooper and I had always been part of his plans. Which worried me a little, because surely Fat wasn't that calculating, was he? 'He's always following you round like a lost dog, ain't he?'

I forced a laugh. 'Sometimes, but . . .'

'He'd do it if you asked him. Do anything, he would.'

I thought of Alan Cooper – my best friend Alan. He was smaller than the rest of the class, paler, a boy who lived with his auntie and had to endure jibes about that. A boy who'd latched onto me, but in whose company I grew: leader to his slave. Yes, chances were he would agree to come, just to please me.

'What if he doesn't want to?' I asked.

'Lose your quid then, don't ya?'

And I didn't want that. Because it wasn't only about the money, it was about face, my standing with Fat. Fat Norris, Alan Cooper, William Dickson. We were an unlikely trio, but together we remained strong.

'Tell you what. Don't tell him nothing about it,' Fat instructed confidentially. 'Just say we'll knock for him about four-ish on Saturday. Say we'll go up the park for a game of pirates or something. You know how he loves all those shitty kiddy games.'

Just as much as I did, I thought. Not that I would ever admit it to Fat. Here was my chance to be more like him, more grown-up. He'd included me in his latest 'scheme'. A refusal could cause long-lasting offence.

'But what happens when we get there?' I asked, trying to appear casual.

'He'll do what we do and get a quid an' all. Honest, it ain't nothing, easy money. We play it right and we could have fifty quid for Christmas.'

'I don't know, Fat. I don't want to get done or nothing.'

'You going chicken on me, Dickson?'

I looked into the puffy face, saw the threat in his eyes.

'I'll try, OK?' I said.

'Don't let me down,' he said. 'Just get Cooper in on it and it's easy money for all of us.'

And now, in a clearing beside the oak tree, we waited; Fat chewing on spearmint gum; me anxiously listening for strangers' footfalls in the thick undergrowth nearby;

Alan Cooper simply confused, squinting in the thin afternoon sun.

'Are we going to play pirates then?' he asked, brandishing a crude wooden sword.

'Nah,' Fat Norris replied.

Cooper looked at me. 'What we going to do, then?'

A nervous laugh shot from the side of my mouth.

'We're waiting, idiot,' Fat informed him.

'What for?'

'Shut up and see.'

We stood in silence for another minute, listening as the dried summer leaves whispered their warning in the dense canopy over our heads. Forty yards away a train trundled by, echoing through the wood.

Then they came.

Instantly, I stiffened, as Fat's uncle Dave and Mr Godwin from the sweet-shop stepped into the clearing. I hadn't been expecting him. Surely he didn't . . .

'Hello boys,' Atkins quickly said. He appeared nervous, nodding briefly to Fat. 'Well done, Eddy-boy. Not such a useless blob, are you, eh?' He tousled Fat's greasy hair. 'Managed to find a couple of mates for Mr Godwin, did you?'

Alan Cooper shot me a confused look; I avoided his gaze.

Atkins strolled quickly over to me, while Godwin lurked behind. 'You're the Dickson kid, aren't you?'

'Yes,' I managed, the beginnings of fear coursing through me. I wanted to have a pee, go home, be with Mummy and Daddy again. Instinct told me this was all wrong. More than wrong. Dangerous.

'Know your dad. He works on the ferries, don't he?'

I gave a small nod.

'Well listen, son. Not a fucking word to him about this, right? One word and you're history, right?' He turned to Fat. 'Am I right, Eddy-boy, or what?'

'Sure,' Fat replied, almost bored. 'Has he brought the money, then?'

Atkins nodded, turned to me. 'You done anything like this before?'

'No.'

'Ain't nothing to it, son. Just get it out, you touch his, he touches yours. Easy quid. You want to go double-or-quits, give it a quick suck. Then not a word to anyone, right?'

'Right.' A cold sweat had broken out over my back. Godwin had taken a few steps towards us, eyes flicking over me, smiling. Why did it have to be him? Someone we knew. Who knew us. Fat hadn't mentioned anything about Mr Godwin. Maybe it was a joke, the whole thing a set-up at my expense. Any minute now, all four of them would burst out laughing and tell me I'd been had.

It seemed odd seeing Mr Godwin anywhere but behind the counter of his shop. I realized it was the first time I'd seen his lower half. He was fatter than I thought, with a pronounced belly. He had tracksuit bottoms on, an odd combination with the brown brogues, tie and shirt. A thin sheen of sweat covered his forehead as a plump hand slid beneath the elasticated waist of his trousers. Perhaps he wanted a wee, too.

Atkins turned to Cooper. 'What about you? Ain't seen you before. Speak up. What's the matter, you dumb, or something?'

I somehow managed to find my voice. 'He doesn't know why he's here.'

Atkins angrily turned to Fat. 'You what?'

'He'll be fine, don't worry,' Fat replied with a casual shrug. 'Look at him, he ain't going to tell no one. Gonna shit himself in a minute.'

I turned to my best friend. The betrayed, frightened eyes begged the silent question, What's happening, William? 'Do you want a pound, Alan?' I asked, voice cracking.

But his instincts, too, had already told him that whatever was about to happen was dangerously wrong. He shook his head, eyes brimming with fear. His legs begin to shake. He held the wooden sword close to his chest. 'I want to go an' play pirates,' he said softly. 'Somewhere else.'

'We can't,' I said.

'Why not?'

'Because . . . because we're here.'

'All right, listen,' Atkins commanded. 'You all be good boys, you'll get the money. And if you're very good boys, you'll get lots of money.'

I jumped, startled, as he suddenly made a grab for Alan, spinning him quickly round and pinning him face-first against the tree. I watched horrified as he placed a hand over my friend's mouth and began grinding his hips into Alan's backside. 'Like this,' Atkins said, turning to Godwin and laughing. 'You'll give 'em a fiver if they go all the way, won't you?'

'If they're willing,' Godwin replied, his voice detached, husky.

I stared into my friend's terrified, betrayed eyes. The image burnt itself into my subconscious.

Godwin was getting restless, openly fiddling with his crotch and edging closer. 'Jesus, Atkins, is this going to take all day, man?'

Atkins turned, whispered angrily. 'Will you shut the fuck up! Jesus Christ, the way your trap's rattling anyone could hear us!'

'I can't leave the shop for too long. Maud will be suspicious.'

'Look, sod Maud! I'm just checking these three will keep their gobs shut. Unless you want to do another stretch in the nonces' wing, that is!'

The outburst seemed to silence Godwin.

Atkins addressed us sharply. 'Just do what he says,' he ordered, before turning back to the shopkeeper. 'Right,' he said. 'Which one do you fancy first?'

I felt every hair on my body stand on end as Godwin moved slowly closer, the glassy eyes looking straight at me, then a hand coming out, gently stroking my shoulder. He put a finger to his lips, turned, then did the same to Alan, who was still standing rigid, his young white knuckles gripping the home-made sword . . .

'This one, I think,' Godwin whispered. 'Good-looking lad, aren't you? I've seen you in my shop, haven't I? It's little Alan Cooper, isn't it?'

Alan began to moan as I stood terrified by his side.

'There, there,' Godwin soothed, stroking Alan's fair hair. 'No need to be worried. I'm not going to hurt you.' He took hold of one of Alan's hands, began guiding it towards his fat groin. 'Just a little stroke, Alan. For Mr Godwin, eh? The nice man who gives you sweets?'

'Can't . . .' Alan cried, a single tear falling from his cheek onto Godwin's belly.

'Try, Alan,' Godwin encouraged, forcing the hand inside his waistband.

I glanced over at Atkins, now smoking, nervously scanning the nearby trees and shrubs for strangers. 'Hurry it up, for fuck's sake,' he said.

'Oh no,' Godwin replied, breath shortening. 'Can't hurry this, can we Alan, eh? Too nice to hurry, isn't it? No more tears now. See, nothing wrong with this, is there?'

Fat Norris giggled, made a gesture I didn't understand. 'Leave some for all of us, Cooper,' he said. 'I want my quid as well.'

After several dreadful moments, it was my turn. Godwin sighed, replaced Alan's hand, then took a short step sideways to stand in front of me. He was shorter than I thought, and the crazy thought struck me that he must have stood on some kind of a box behind the counter in the shop. Glancing to my left I noticed urine running down the inside of Alan's leg.

'Now,' Godwin said, his puffy breath foul on my face. 'What about you, eh?' He began lightly stroking my hair. 'The Dickson boy, aren't you? Little thief who thinks he can steal from my shop and never pay me back.'

'No,' I said, realizing the strange new sound was my teeth beginning to chatter.

'I wonder what your father would think if he knew just what you got up to?' He made a grab for my hand. 'Steady now. Relax.' He began to lean slowly against me, pinning me back to the tree. His weight felt enormous, suffocating. 'Perhaps we can take things a little further than with your friend, eh?'

'Please. Let me go. I'll never nick anything again, I swear.'

'But those are just words, aren't they?'

'It's true. I promise.'

Fat Norris had come to watch. 'Get on with it. Just let him have a feel.'

'I . . . I . . .'

Godwin smiled, pulled me slightly away from the tree and slid a hand inside my shorts. Another followed, until he gripped both buttocks. I felt like puking, began repeating 'Jesus Christ, Jesus Christ,' over and over.

Suddenly, Godwin yelped, screamed, then roared in outrage. He let me go and I fell to the floor. Alan Cooper stood behind, brandishing his wooden sword, pure anger in his young face. 'I'll stab you again, you fat git!' he said. 'Come on, William, let's go!'

'What the hell . . . ?' Atkins said, before ducking as Alan aimed a swipe at him, too.

'Come on, William,' Alan urged.

But although I badly wanted to run, my legs wouldn't move. Paralysed in shock and fear, I could only watch dumbstruck as Godwin recovered sufficiently to pick up a fist-sized stone and hurl it at my young rescuer's head.

The noise of that impact in the quiet woods was dull: just a thud followed by a great gasp of escaping air. I watched Alan take a half step backwards, wooden sword flailing, before he dropped, blood already pulsing from the wound.

'Jesus wept!' Atkins screamed. 'What the fuck have you done! You didn't have to hit him! Jesus fucking Christ, are you bloody mad?'

'He was going to blab,' Godwin said, turning to all of us. 'You heard him, the little prick-teaser was going to blab. You heard him, didn't you? All of you!'

Atkins knelt close to the twitching body.

'Is he dead?' Godwin asked.

'I don't fucking know!' Atkins said. 'He's all sort of fitting about.' I watched horrified as he moved Alan's head. A geyser of bright red blood spurted three feet into the air. 'Jesus Christ! We've got to get some kind of sodding help!'

Godwin frantically massaged his face. 'Can't do that,' he said. 'Can't. Can't. Can't.'

'He's going to die!'

Fat was crying now, his bottom lip jutting with each sob. I could only watch, a blank, as Godwin seemed to make up his mind about something, then walked quickly over to Atkins, throwing him away from the jerking body.

'What the hell are you going to – ?'

'Shut up!' Godwin hissed. 'Don't you see? He goes to a hospital, and I'm ruined! I lose everything.'

'But he'll die, for Christ's sake!'

'Then let him!' He pushed Atkins away a second time, and

stood over the body. The pumping blood was ebbing, and with it, I knew, my best friend's life. The one person who'd tried to help me was dying in front of me, when all I'd done for him was bring him to this foul place, these obscene people.

'He's dead,' Atkins said in a high-pitched wail. 'You've gone and let him die.'

I began to cry. Tiny, dry sobs tore at my throat.

Then came a stinging slap across my face. 'Shut it,' Godwin said. 'We're not done yet!'

'Eddy-boy!' Atkins suddenly yelled, backing further away. 'Run! Run, you stupid fat bastard! Get out of here!'

Fat managed to pick himself up, tried to scramble away, but slipped. Godwin was on him in a trice, hauling the blubbing boy up, throwing him back against the tree-trunk. 'We're all staying here!' He called to Atkins. 'No one leaves until we bury this kid!'

But Atkins had already gone, leaving Fat Norris and me alone with Godwin in the silence of the forest.

'He's gone to get the coppers,' Fat weakly tried, tears streaming over plump, grimy cheeks.

Godwin thought for a moment. His whole face had changed, the panic had disappeared, the breathing was now menacingly level. 'I don't think so, fatty,' he sneered. 'You think your "uncle" Dave wants to be implicated in all this? With his form? I've known him for a long time and, believe me, the police would love to nail that bastard.' He looked at the body at his feet and tutted. 'Killing a poor wee laddie. Now that's very serious, isn't it?'

Fat shot a look to me, begging for back-up. 'We'll tell them it was you,' he tried. 'You killed him, not my uncle Dave!'

A strong hand shot out and grabbed him by the throat. 'But no one knows I'm here, do they, eh?' he snarled, turning to look at me. 'No one knows Atkins was here.' He started to laugh. 'You're just going to be three little lads who got into some trouble in the woods one day.'

Fat began to choke, trying to sob through a constricted throat. Still I remained frozen, rooted as firmly as the tree behind me.

'I . . . promise . . . I . . . won't . . . say . . . anything,' I whispered, lips shaking violently. 'Nothing . . . to . . . anyone . . .'

Godwin seemed to revel in my distress, bask in my fear. He

closed his eyes, lifted his head, took a deep breath of the woodland air. When he spoke his voice was flat, devoid of normal emotion, as if something completely evil had flown down from the darkening canopy and swept straight into his perverted soul.

'It has to be this way, you see?' he said. 'No other option. Little Alan lies dead. An accident. He hurt me. You saw that, didn't you? He hurt me first. And you wouldn't want me to go to prison for that, would you, boys?'

His awful face came closer to mine. 'And you?' he said quite softly. 'Here you stand, Dickson, shaking like a little girl. So scared. I bet they call you a scaredy-cat at school, don't they, eh? And shall I tell you something?'

I nodded, petrified, my breath coming in tiny spasms.

'I know your mother, too. How upset is she going to be, I wonder, when she learns her boy secretly gets his prick out for a pound?'

'. . . don't . . . know,' I mumbled.

'Now, we three are going to sort this mess out.' He looked towards Alan Cooper's body. 'There's just been a terrible accident, that's all. Now we need to make it all better. Make it so the police don't catch us. Hide the evidence. Bury him. Then work out what we're going to say.'

I felt myself begin to collapse against the cool trunk of the tree behind.

The tree! A hope, a distant hope! My only hope . . .

From somewhere I finally found the strength to scream, pure fear and adrenalin powering me round to the back of the large trunk. Still hollering, I flung up both hands, jumped, found a branch and, ignoring the pain from a badly grazed leg, began hauling myself frantically upwards.

Godwin was onto me in an instant, grabbing my loose ankle. I shook it violently, never looking down, still screaming like a maniac, my arms trying to pull me up, away from his grasp.

Roaring indignantly, he finally let go, and I continued up to the next branch, kicking madly. Then, the shock of my life! I found myself staring into Fat's equally terrified face. He was climbing too, but on the other side of the trunk.

I made it up onto the next slimmer branch, but knew Fat would beat me to the top. Despite his weight, he was stronger, a better climber.

Godwin's curses grew louder, closer. He was after us, heaving his protesting bulk up through the aged branches, puffing heavily, getting closer.

Another scream, as I felt the powerful grip of his hand on my trailing foot. Fat was coming round to my side, checking the way ahead above, realizing that mine was the easier path. If he beat me, Godwin would have me. I'd never get past him, he was too big, the trunk was too thin . . .

I looked down, stared into Godwin's massively bulging eyes, screamed again. My foot came free, and I pulled it up towards my chest, managed to roll onto the next branch, heaving myself upright by pulling on Fat's waist.

'Fuck off me!' he panicked. 'Just fuck off me!'

But I was out for myself now, slave to my own survival, simply had to pass him, escape Godwin's clutches at any cost. And I would beat Fat Norris . . . I would survive . . . I would get past him . . . I would live . . .

We stood level on the same dangerously creaking branch, Fat trying to reach for the next, me working my way further out, using the spring to reach up, grab, and –

'Come down, both of you!' Godwin spluttered. 'You get down here, now! We're not finished yet!'

Standing one branch above Fat, I made my way back to the trunk, lungs burning with the effort. I stood, looked up, realized I'd never make the next branch: the distance was too high, the gap too great. Fat began making strange guttural noises as Godwin climbed a little higher.

'I'm coming for you! Both of you!'

There was only one way, one human stepping-stone to salvation. I screwed shut my eyes and screamed loudly as I stepped onto Fat's shoulders.

Next came the effort of the push onto the branch above, having to kick out to straddle my stomach onto its thin, life-saving wooden finger. Then the recoil as I kicked away, finally transferring the weight from one branch to another.

Finally – inevitably – a sudden gasp. Fat, uttering his shocked and terrified last as he plunged to his death through breaking branches below.

* * *

Moaning, I opened my eyes. Looked down. All was quiet. I was alone. Nothing stirred except for rustling leaves close by, and the pounding of my heart in my chest. I finally puked, heaved a thick yellow rope of warm vomit, watched it splash and fall through the branches, splatter on the dry ground thirty feet below.

For there lay Fat Norris, twisted and broken. But there was no sign of Godwin. No sign of Alan's body, either.

I began to shake violently, hugging the trunk close.

Next, a voice from below. Godwin, slowly walking back into the clearing.

'Well, well, well, Dickson,' he said through cupped hands, craning his neck to see me. 'What a naughty boy you are.'

I watched transfixed as he rolled Fat over with his foot. The face was pulped, having taken the full force of the impact from a protruding root. 'Another dead friend. Dear, dear, what will the police say? What will you tell them, eh? How about the truth, that you pushed him out of the tree? Quite deliberate, William. Quite blatant. And you know what that means, don't you? You'll be going to prison for ever and ever, William. Because you're a murderer, lad!' He stopped, looked around. I heard his heavy breaths, saw him wipe the sweat from his brow. 'I've gone and dumped little Alan in the bushes. But I wouldn't tell the police that if I were you. After all, he wouldn't even have been here if it wasn't for you, eh? Your fault again, William. What a wicked boy you are.'

'Go away!' I sobbed, face pressed against the bark.

'Oh, I'm going to, William, don't you worry. But if I were you,' he picked up the bloodstained stone, then hurled it into the far undergrowth, 'I'd spend a bit of time thinking about what you're going to tell the police. And if you so much as mention me, or Atkins, then I'll tell them exactly what you did to your fat friend here.' He waited a few seconds. 'You understand me, lad?'

I said nothing, wanting nothing but to die. The adrenalin was beginning to ebb, leaving me shivering, cold, expended. I shut my eyes, painful cries racking my body, still feeling the horrendous weight of Fat's twisting body leaving my foot as he'd fallen.

Then I began to scream, eyes wide open now, staring straight ahead over the tree-tops. And scream . . .

'William?'

. . . and scream, watching as the green slipped slowly away . . .

'William!'

. . . to be replaced by grey skies . . .

'William!'

. . . the tops of unfinished houses . . . still screaming all the while . . .

'Come down, William!'

I slowly opened my eyes, felt the fire in my throat, screamed one final time as I looked down and saw Carter gesturing to me. I blinked three times, felt the cold wind rush around me. I was thirty feet off the ground, with no idea how I'd got there.

'William,' Carter called. 'It's time to come down. And I want you to do it very carefully.'

'He says I'm a murderer,' I sobbed. 'And he's going to tell Mummy about it! About everything!'

'Bill? Listen to me. It's time to come down.'

'Can't!'

'You must be cold up there.'

'Don't matter. I'll be sent to prison for ever!'

'Listen to me, Bill. I'm here to help . . .'

'No!' I shouted down. 'You're going to get me into trouble!'

'You have to trust me.'

'Leave me alone!'

I watched warily as he took a step closer to the base of the tree. 'William wants you to come down now, Bill.'

'He's not here! He's never here!'

'He wants you to come down.'

'Where is he? Where's William! I want him!'

'Bill,' Carter slowly said, 'you know how William always protected you? You know how you got him to hurt all those people who were trying to hurt you, get you down from this tree?'

'They all deserved it.'

'Bill, there's no one left to hurt you any more.'

'Everyone wants to hurt me.'

'Not any more. Mummy wants to see you, Bill.'

'No,' I heard myself wail. 'I'll be in trouble. Godwin will tell her about the money. About what we were going to do for it. About what happened. That I killed Fat. And Cooper.'

He shook his head. 'She loves you, Bill. She just wants to see you again. You're not in trouble. Whatever happened all those years ago is done, forgotten. I promise. Now please, come down.'

Next, I felt tears well from deep inside as I surrendered to years of suppressed, shaming guilt.

Some time later, under Carter's careful guidance, I began to take the tentative first few steps back down from the tree.

Finally, after twelve years, I was down.

39

Twelve months and two weeks after what Carter and I had come simply to refer to as 'Tilbury'. Standing alone on the windswept peak of Kinder Scout, some way off the main hiking path, I mulled over the events of the previous year, now known as 'Year One' – another of Carter's suggestions.

Frightening, that was the word for it; almost as terrifying as what I now knew to have happened to me as a petrified youngster in the woods. Nothing would eradicate the fears, the nightmares, the anger of that Saturday afternoon. Time, Carter kept telling me, would eventually smooth away some of the crueller edges, but the greater part of that horror would stay. It was up to me how I lived with it, how much of an impact it would have on my life.

And what was my life, I wondered, standing on that ravaged mountain top? How far had I actually come? Again, there was no gauge, no handy crisis-measurement system by which Carter and I could plot my progress against other memory-damaged patients. On the outside I'm sure I appeared to be recovering well. Being accepted back into the poly helped, and it was easy to convince people that I had settled back into a normal routine after my ordeal. But inside I remained unsure of who I was, what I'd been, and how much of myself I'd lost along the way.

Even today, nearly twenty years on, I still struggle to find the hardest part of that first year. Getting to know me, I suppose, a twenty-year-old searching for some kind of self-forgiveness in the aftermath. Or perhaps it was something else – trying to live without the psychotic comfort of believing myself to be a killer – a William Dickson to be feared, not abused. For once Carter had unblocked the dam of truth, so came the tidal wave of shame. Believing myself to be a killer had been an indescribable rush. And for those few months, I had revelled in the power it gave me. Twenty years on, and the same tidal wave still crashes over me.

I spent a lot of time in that first year wishing I'd been the one to kill Godwin. Mother Nature beat me to it. Cancer ate his insides before the police could question him further about the afternoon in the woods. I simply hoped that he had suffered.

I used to ask Carter why it was that Godwin had been passed over in my murderous fantasies in favour of easier targets. Whereupon the good doctor would sink into one of his customary pauses before answering – 'Give it time, William, give it time . . .'

Twenty years on and I'm still waiting.

Standing in the buffeting wind that Christmas afternoon, my thoughts strayed to those below: Carter, Karen, my mother and sister, replete after lunch in Shallice House. All good people, who'd invested so much in me, and maybe – it pained me even to think it – deserved the whole of me back, rather than the shell I was. But how could I give them so much when one face refused to leave my mind, one secret refused to be dislodged?

One terrified, screaming face, hands up to the side of her cheeks, howling in fear as she fell backwards down her own cottage stairs. Edith Fitzroy, I knew, would haunt me for many years to come. Edith Fitzroy was the one, you see, the death that made it all possible, gave my mind the raw material for its worst inventions. Without her, none of it would have been possible. My mind would have rejected the role of murderer as too ludicrous to accept.

But little Bill knew another side of me. Just as Edith Fitzroy knew.

Perhaps she had been well intentioned, simply badly trained. After all, when Tremaine had veered too close, I'd lashed out, too. Who's to say that her interest in me – her concern – hadn't also stretched to trying to unravel the same mental mess as Tremaine was attempting to probe? But whereas the old professional survived, perhaps the amateur didn't get so lucky.

I've tried not to think about it too much in the intervening years. Some things are simply too painful to bear. But no one can run for ever. And I know full well that the memories of that time, the knowledge of Edith Fitzroy's interest, will come back one day, and I'll stand victim to the revelation. At present it's simply an instinct, a sense that I killed her.

She lives in my dreams. One night, the nightmare will run to its logical dread conclusion: the beast who follows me through those tugging, dark woods will catch me before I reach the haunted boy holding the button. The same hand will wheel me round to face my pursuer. And it will be her, eyes blazing vengeance, devoid of forgiveness or hope.

I'm not sure that I'll wake. Or that I'll ever tell Carter the root cause of my need for the red button and his tapes. All that I'm certain of is that she'll never stop chasing, and I'll die with the scream on her face seared into the blackest part of my soul.

It could even be tonight.